ACCEPTANCE
STORIES AT THE CENTRE OF US

ACCEPTANCE
STORIES AT THE CENTRE OF US

Published in Canada by Engen Books, St. John's, NL.

Library and Archives Canada Cataloguing in Publication

Title: Acceptance : stories at the centre of us / edited by Ailsa Craig, Sulaimon Giwa, AJ Ryan,
  Sarah Thompson.
Other titles: Acceptance (2021)
Names: Craig, Ailsa, editor. | Giwa, Sulaimon, editor. | Ryan, A. J., editor. | Thompson, Sarah,
  1982- editor.
Description: Short stories.
Identifiers: Canadiana 20210369272 | ISBN 9781774780640 (softcover)
Subjects: LCSH: Sexual minorities—Fiction. | LCSH: Canadian fiction—21st century. | LCSH: Sexual
  minorities' writings, Canadian. | CSH: Canadian fiction (English)—21st century.
Classification: LCC PS8235 G38 A73 2021 | DDC C813/.608066—dc23

Distributed by:
Engen Books
www.engenbooks.com
submissions@engenbooks.com

First mass market paperback printing: November 2021
Cover Design: Ellen Curtis

CONTENTS

INTRODUCTION

Stories are part of how we connect with each other both across our differences, and through finding and recognizing what we have in common. We are thankful that Engen Books has asked us to partner with them on this anthology, and grateful for their generosity in donating the profits from the sale of this book to Quadrangle NL's work. When Engen Books approached Quadrangle NL about creating this book, we were excited to participate as editors for this collection of fiction by, for, and about 2SLGBTQAI+ folks. Helping to compile this book is parallel to the mission and vision of Quadrangle NL. A charitable organization, Quadrangle NL is working to build a 2SLGBTQAI+ community centre for Newfoundland and Labrador. Our central aim is creating and holding space for 2SLGBTQAI+ people and organizations from across the province—both through the programming we offer, and with the physical bricks-and-mortar centre we are working toward. The social space Quadrangle NL creates, while it acknowledges the range of challenges that our community faces, is also a space for sharing and building the strengths we bring to each other, and to the larger community. Stories too, can be a communal space that helps us to live a bit bigger, a bit longer, and a little bit differently. With our stories, real and imagined, we make space for each other to breathe ourselves into. This is similar to how shared places and events can be central to recognizing and reinforcing the contributions of our community to each other and to this province, contributions with impact and importance and strength, even as (and because) we reach out to support each other in times of vulnerability or hardship.

Representation is important. It's important because being invisible or going unrecognized, can be a weight that contributes to some of the challenges faced by 2SLGBTQAI+ people and communities. And representation and recognition can bring moments of connection and of joy that help lighten the weight of marginalization. Representation can also help support greater acceptance of lives that are different from what (and who) we know in our own experiences. While it is important that 2SLGBTQAI+ lives, experiences, and creativity are communicated with those who are outside of our communities, the stories we have access to and the representations we can find are also central to how we come to know ourselves, and the broad range of experiences and identities that make up our community. But representation is not just about seeing who we are. Representation is also about seeing what we make, what alternative realities we can imagine, and how we build planes of existence that have 2SLGBTQAI+ folks at the centre of their own lives, living their own stories, whether in representations of our world as we know it now, in imagined futures or pasts, or in other realms of existence and reality.

Stories can also be a powerful catalyst for change and transformation. They invite us to find aspects of ourselves in others, whose stories have often not been told, toward building bridges of understanding and mutual respect, where differences are valued, respected, and supported. As glue for building empathy, stories remind and thrust us into the realm of infinite possibilities, where our imaginations give way to transformative change in everyday interactions, across cultural and social institutions. Stories awake us to the web of narratives and systemic power of myths that organizes and govern our lives, so that we can author new narratives about our selves. Such reframing of cultural narratives can bring about change in the social environment and support collective storytelling for a good life. For 2SLGBTQIA+ people, moving toward overall transformation of society can enable their way out of the shadows and into the light. Their contributions, once overlooked, can now be recognized and celebrated. The rich tapestry of collective experience they embody can meaningfully serve as a bridge for opportunities previously unseen or unthinkable. The manifestation of a desire for doing things differently connects to a legacy of struggle and triumph, where complete liberation is the only acceptable path forward. In a way, stories are about the kind of world we want in the present and future; they animate a collective consciousness, which unites us in our obligation to each other, as human beings worthy of dignity and respect. It is in these moments of togetherness, of shared alacrity, that we sow the seeds for a better and more inclusive world.

The stories in this book are fun, suspenseful, affirming, heart wrenching, creepy, joyful and important. Having 2SLGBTQAI+ lives and characters represented in a range of stories and genres is part of what makes it important, but inclusion is not just about being represented. Inclusion is also about 2SLGBTQAI+ authors having access to publishing our creative work, to write the stories we want to explore for an audience that wants to explore them with us, and being paid for those stories. And inclusion is also about being addressed as the intended audience. By, about and for us—just like Quadrangle, with our programs, events, and eventually our shared public space, this collection puts 2SLGBTQAI+ people in the centre of our own stories, as we dream into what comes next, remember what's come before, and reach out to hold space for all of us, here. To read more about Quadrangle NL, go to www.thequadnl.com.

Ailsa Craig and Sulaimon Giwa,
board members for Quadrangle NL Community Centre.

ACCEPTANCE
SHERI SINGLETON

In Blair's mind the important days of her adult life were always tied to rain with heavy skies and damp oppressive days that didn't match the joy in her heart. Sure, there were happy memories of jumping through sprinklers on her childhood lawn, or long summer nights spent lying on a blanket searching for shooting stars. But all the great days, the truly big ones, those were grey.

The day she met the woman who would become her wife, the forecaster had reminded everyone to take an umbrella. She hadn't listened. When the skies opened up and found her caught in the middle of an open-air market, Karen had jogged over and thrust her umbrella over both their heads. They ran, giggling, into the nearest coffee shop and sat all afternoon chatting, drying off, and falling head over heels in love.

The day they'd gotten married had started off sunny and blue. Then, as was common in the midwest, an afternoon storm had blown in. Rain had splashed in huge drops against the vaulted roof and the air had taken on the unmistakable smell of suppressed electricity. In the twenty or so minutes the storm had lingered above them, they'd stood in front of family and friends in a turn-of-the-century barn and vowed their undying love and companionship to the music of a lone harp and the howling wind.

Last October, at the tail end of Hurricane Louie, the call had finally come. After years of interviews, social worker visits, and home studies, their baby had entered the world—all seven pounds and four screaming ounces of him! While they hurried to the hospital, the wipers fought bravely to clear away the rain just as Karen's sleeve had reached across and dried her happy eyes.

That's what made this morning all the more strange. The rain pelted the window so heavily she could feel the glass tremble beneath her fingers. There were little flecks of ice mixed in with the drops. They cascaded down the pane and gathered on the sill forming a miniature mountain range. But, instead of happiness or hope, she felt hollow.

The streetlights lining their small lane were flickering out one by one and with the diminishing glow she felt a growing sense of dread. The sun would come up, Karen would stir and rise, padding to the window in her bare feet to press a kiss to her neck. Like every other morning for the last four months, they'd go downstairs to the empty high chair and flash forced smiles at one another over a quiet breakfast. Karen would suggest, gently, that maybe they should move the highchair to the spare room today and she would refuse. She just couldn't understand how Karen could take that step so quickly. Deep down, in her heart of hearts, she resented Karen for her ability to endure in the face of such inconceivable sorrow.

The day of the funeral had been sunny and clear, one of the first real summery days of June. The black sunglasses she'd chosen to hide her bloodshot eyes had let her blend in with the other mourners, everyone wearing black on black, vividly invisible. It should have been a day for them to stroll through the park, or give Louie his first taste of ice cream. Instead, they'd placed their infant son in the warm, fresh earth.

Back in university psychology, the professor had droned on about the various stages of grief. She'd laughed then at how a group of supposedly intelligent people believed that all human grief could be summed up in one simple pattern. Now she knew it to be true. Denial—check. Anger—check. Bargaining—check. Depression—check. Acceptance... That one seemed to be a long time coming. She wasn't sure she ever wanted it to.

The grief she had welcomed. It felt almost comfortable. When her first serious relationship ended, she had grieved. When her father died during her first year of university she'd grieved. When her mother had remarried not one year later, she'd grieved again. Yes, grief she understood. The panic attacks though, those had been an unpleasant surprise. The bubbling fear that brought the sharp tang of blood to her throat and stole her breath away had stopped her in her tracks and, quite literally, brought her to her knees. Still, even they would be preferable to the emptiness she felt on this rainy October morning; the day that would have marked Louie's first birthday.

The bed rustled behind her as Karen rolled and stretched, the normal sounds of normal things. It grated on her nerves. She knew it was irrational, but that meant little when it came to grief. As she predicted, she heard Karen's feet making little suction sounds on the hardwood. Her toes cracked as she walked, something Blair had always found adorable, and she felt herself softening, just a little. After all, she reminded herself, I don't hold the monopoly on sorrow.

Karen wrapped her arms around her from behind and nuzzled into her neck. "You shouldn't be standing here in the dark. Your arms are frozen."

"I thought I heard freezing rain," she whispered, knowing that her wife could see through the flimsy excuse. She loved her all the more for not calling her out on it.

In unspoken agreement, neither of them acknowledged the significance of the date. They went through the motions of showering and dressing, each treading carefully around the other. She couldn't face the highchair discussion, not this day, not this morning, so she lingered in the walk-in closet, absentmindedly fingering through her shirts, until she heard Karen head for the stairs.

Standing there in just her jeans and bra, Blair was suddenly overcome with the foreign desire to look nice, to be a good wife, to put on a strong face as Karen did for her every single day. She reached up to the top shelf to retrieve the bag of Christmas gifts they'd picked up while vacationing in Toronto last May. She remembered a blue sweater made from the softest cashmere. She'd fallen in love with it but couldn't justify spending all that money on herself. Instead, she'd casually placed it in the cart and informed Karen that she was the best wife in the world to buy her such a beautiful present. Karen had simply rolled her eyes and smiled.

She rummaged in the bag now feeling for the soft material. Instead, her hand closed upon a small box. A tingle ran down her spine. In one fluid movement she dropped the bag, extracted the box, and slumped to the floor. It was as cold sitting in her bra and jeans on the chilly hardwood as it was outside the window in the icy rain. She knew she should stand up, get dressed, go down to breakfast. Instead, with shivering fingers, she pried the top off the box and looked down at the tiny pair of winter boots inside.

Hot tears fell around her like rain. They melted through the ice in her heart. She could see his big blue eyes, his curly brown hair, the chubby little feet she'd intended to toddle around in these very boots. She cried for him, for the life he would not lead. She cried for Karen and herself, for knowing so briefly the joy of being a Mommy. She cried until there were no tears left and, for the first time, didn't want to throw herself into the ground after him. The world didn't end.

She carefully put the lid back on the box and placed it on the shelf. The blue sweater forgotten, she hauled on an old favourite shirt and headed down for breakfast with her wife at a table she found set only for two. She didn't yell, she didn't scream, she simply sat and took the cup of coffee handed to her with a tentative smile. It would be a long road, one without end, but at least it was a start.

So this, she thought, is acceptance.

Sheri Singleton is an author from Newfoundland and Labrador.

TIME OF THE MONTH
K.A. MIELKE

If there is a worse place, in the entire world, for surprise hormonal changes than gym class, don't tell me. I'm going through enough here without imagining greater horrors.

I notice the bushy fur on my hands first, tickling my cheek when I narrowly save my face from being pulverized by a speeding dodgeball. I fumble the ball before catching it between palms that look like every Catholic kid's worst nightmare, causing Lip Morris to groan loudly and shuffle to the sidelines. A chill floods through my veins and I look around for a mirror before remembering I'm in a gymnasium, holding a dodgeball, expected by overbearing teammates to do literally anything other than stand still and panic.

Tough to stop when I'm turning into a werewolf in the middle of the day.

"Jesus, Barker, just throw the ball!"

I swallow, but my throat's gone dry. Stepping forward, I cock my arm back and lock eyes on the slowest moving target. If they catch the ball, I'm out and I can go to the locker room. Perfect plan.

A red blur shoots toward me—

The dodgeball smacks me in the face. I collapse, my nose a blossoming flower of pain, blood trickling onto my upper lip. I hear Mr. Clipper shout, "Great shot, Hutcherson!"

I really thought being a werewolf would make me cooler.

Clipper blows his whistle, hauls me to my feet, and drags me off the court with arms only marginally less hairy than mine are about to be. I'm just dazed enough not to care how embarrassing this is, but not so dazed I don't hide my Sasquatch hands in the pockets of my gym shorts.

"Maybe if you got a haircut, Barker, you could see the ball coming. How many fingers am I holding up?"

I focus, forcing the double vision back together. "Five."

"Wrong. A thumb isn't a finger." He pats me on the back, or maybe shoves me toward the locker room, it's unclear. "Go get cleaned up. You don't look so hot."

Mr. Clipper's whistle chirps as the door closes behind me and I'm embraced by the silence and safety of the empty locker room. If there's a silver lining, it's that I can't smell the years worth of post-gym stank my heightened senses couldn't ignore at the start of the period. I go to the sink to check the damage.

My face is red with blood, both under the skin and leaking from my nostrils, and my nosebleed drips onto the grey fabric of my gym shirt and the howling, open jaw of the North Park Timberwolves logo. Despite the pain, I don't think it's broken. I pinch the bridge of my nose and tilt my head back, tasting iron in the back of my throat.

The door opens and every muscle in my body tightens until Ezra says, "Declan? You all right?"

His reflection in the mirror waves at me. Sweat glistens on Ezra's warm ochre skin, flattening some stray hairs against his forehead and plastering his gym shirt to his chest. He pinches his round, wire-rimmed glasses between the hem of his shirt, cleaning the lenses. For a scrawny, clumsy nerd, he never gives less than his all in gym.

"You're supposed to lean forward," he says, fitting his glasses back on his face, "so you don't choke."

His hand hovers over my shoulder, not quite touching me. I bet he thinks I haven't noticed the way he started acting differently around me once I was turned. Or sired. Or whatever the word for "transformed into a werewolf" is. Like I'm contagious.

I mean, I technically am, but it's in my saliva. It has to enter the bloodstream, or something. I didn't exactly get a handbook.

I relax, leaning over the sink. "How'd you break free from the torture?"

"Told Clipper I had to go to the washroom."

"Clipper never lets anyone pee in the middle of dodgeball."

"Yeah, well, I had to embarrass myself more than number one for you, didn't I?" Ezra's gaze lingers first on my bleeding face, then on my furry appendages, before he cups the back of his neck and turns away. "How is it?"

I release my nostrils with a nasty squish. "Stopping, I think."

"Not the nosebleed."

"Oh, right. Manageable. Nowhere as bad as last time."

This is my second full moon. The first, I got lucky because Ezra and I were walking to the nearby pizza place when I suddenly threw my head back and howled at the moon poised high in the blue sky. I went home early, locked myself in my room, and woke up with my pillows torn to shreds and my room trashed. Thankfully, my mom was at her boyfriend's house overnight. I immediately called Ezra and panicked into his ear.

"Are you going home?" Ezra asks. "Do you want me to come with?"

He's asked me before why don't I just stay home when it's my, for lack of a better term, 'time of the month?' Take a self-care day, play some video games, then have him tie me to my bed for the night? (The last part he said with a noticeable flush of his cheeks, because innocence is his brand. You know the game where you shout "penis" as loud as you can in a crowded place? Ezra would spontaneously combust from embarrassment if he played.)

My answer was that I don't have the grades to skip, which is true. But it's not why I keep coming to school on the full moon.

I go to the sink and splash my face with icy water. Diluted pink blood streams from my nose and lips and the bangs of my shaggy hair unsticking from my face.

In the reflection, Ezra's finger twitches against the side of his thigh, each digit reaching out to me like he's about to hold my hand. My chest seizes, like my heart's reaching back.

I force the thought out of my head. He made it plenty clear he doesn't think of me like that when I made the mistake of kissing him on New Year's. Which is fine. We're still best bros. I've moved on, anyway.

Grabbing several hundred paper towels to dry my face, I straighten and turn to face him. "I've got the coat and the gloves with me, I should be good for the rest of the day."

"What if today's different? The transformation has been in bits and pieces so far, but—"

The bell rings.

"It'll be fine," I say, heading to my locker before the other guys rush in. Skipping the shower today, but that's nothing new for my socially anxious ass. "This isn't my first rodeo."

"I don't think rodeo clowns are proficient by their second, though?"

"I figured I was the cowboy in this analogy, but I see how you think of me."

"Impaled on the end of a bull horn," he mutters.

***

When I was a kid, I thought the moon was chasing me. In the car driving home from Grandma's, in bed as it shone its light through my window, even during the day at school. The sight of the moon gripped my heart with terror. I don't know if it's funny, or a self-fulfilling prophecy.

Probably didn't help that my last name is literally Barker. Either the universe has a sense of humour, or *she* does.

Now I walk the halls in a trench coat and leather gloves, not because the warm, mid-April weather calls for it, or because I'm a closeted Goth, but because I need to hide the monthly hair and claw growth.

Sometimes the Goth life chooses you.

Everyone looks at me like a school shooter in waiting, even though Goth kids were a patsy and really it's entitled incels, meninists and racists who engage in mass murder—but the mainstream doesn't care about rehabilitating the image of a subculture that adores Satanic imagery. I'm starting to think I'd be stared at less if I just wolfed out in the middle of math.

"I'm just saying," Ezra huffs behind me, struggling to match my stride. "What if there's, like, a secret werewolf hunter hiding amongst our student body?"

"Amongst?" I repeat.

"Shut up, this is serious. You're being careful about silver, right?"

"Sure I am," I say, only half listening as I scan the class transition crowd, brushing shoulders in a packed hallway with my eager eyes on the lookout for a pink undercut, gleaming piercings, black makeup.

"Because I looked up household objects with silver in them, and you might wanna steer clear of refrigerators, mirrors, forks..." Ezra trails off, counting *Beauty and the Beast* characters on his fingers, or whatever.

My heart skips a beat when I see her, leaning against her locker door in an oversize pink sweater, phone in hand. Ezra drops out of my periphery.

Skylar grins when she looks up from her screen. "That's certainly a look, Dec."

"Hey," I say, my throat dry. I stop a good foot or two away because, again, I made the mistake of skipping a shower and I probably smell like wet dog. But maybe she can smell me either way, on account of wolf nose. "I was hoping I'd see you today."

Her lips tug upward, which in turn tugs on my butterfly-brimming stomach. "Good to know you're thinking of me." Before I protest too much, she pushes herself off the locker and takes a folded piece of lined paper from the back pocket of her black jeans. "We're hanging out tonight. It's time you meet the rest of the pack."

"The pack?" Apparently I'm unable to form any words worth saying. Maybe I can blame it on wolf brain, if that's a thing.

"Instructions are right here," she says, pressing the paper into my hand and her other hand to my thundering chest. "It's time to stop fighting your urges, Dec. We'll be waiting for you."

Her hand trails down my torso, black fingernails tapping the buttons of my coat, and drops to her side. I turn to watch her until she's out of sight and instead of Skylar's butt, there's just Ezra's frown, moping at me like I skipped his hamster's funeral.

"What?" I ask.

"What?" he counters.

"You're giving me that look."

"What look?"

"The 'you're so down bad you're gonna get yourself hurt' look."

"I would never—"

"You literally said that to me last week."

Ezra shrugs, adjusting the strap of his bag. "I can't help but be cursed to see the truth."

"What's your problem with her?"

"She?" he squeaks, looking around the crowded hallway like he's suddenly been transported to some upside down world where only he makes sense. Lowering his voice and leaning closer, he says, "Turned you into a werewolf?"

"But it's fine?" I say, matching his inflection. "It was..."

I stop myself from saying "consensual" because that implies I knew I was getting turned before it happened, and Ezra already knows that's not strictly true. One second, we were making out in the back of my mom's sedan, and Skylar was saying stuff like, "Do you want to live forever?" and, "Have you ever wanted to be a wolf?" and I'm not about to kink-shame in the middle of a date with a possible furry, so I said something cringe but affirmative like, "Yeah, baby." The next second, Skylar had sunk her teeth into my neck. But like, in a painful but sexy way. And then we kept making out in between explanations of what came next, and attempts at stopping the bleeding.

And it is fine. Honest.

"Please tell me you're not going. What if it's a trap?"

"Why would she go to all the trouble of trapping me when I've proven over and over I'll go willingly?" I ask. At least I'm a little self-aware.

"I don't know! What if she's just using you for—for something nefarious?"

"SAT words do a lot of the heavy lifting to make things sound spooky."

"Spooky? Do I really need to keep reminding you what she did? A literal monster literally turned you—"

He stops himself, because when he talks about me it's

different. My condition, my affliction, my issue. She's a monster to him, while I'm his friend "going through a hard time."

"Even if she's using me, even if I didn't like her, this is what I am now," I say. "And she's the only one who can teach me about it."

"At least let me come with you."

"No," I say, a little firmer than I mean to. The crowd around us dwindles as everyone heads to class. "The fewer opportunities werewolves—including me—have to eat my best friend, the better."

"You never listen to me."

"Your parents will be pissed if you skip the first night of Passover," I say. "And I told my mom I was joining you, so I need you home."

Ezra frowns and crosses his arms. "You'd rather I cover for you than be with you."

He says it with such venom, my skin itches with shame. My heart hammers in my ears, and there's that constant desire to reach out and hold him close, like his touch is the antidote. "Not, like, as a rule," I say. "In this one specific case."

"Fine. Don't come crying to me when you're being eaten alive!"

"Ezra, don't—"

But he storms off, and I'm left alone in the empty corridor. A hairy loser in a trench coat.

***

I walk the forest trail as the sun sets, splashing the sky with one final bucket of colour before giving the world over to the blues and greys of night. My left hand holds a flashlight, my right the note. I left my car on the side of the road about ten, maybe twenty minutes back. My heart pounds against my breastbone like a feral animal throwing itself against a cage.

The rest of the pack. That's a little like meeting Skylar's family, right? A big step in a relationship, not that we're putting labels on it.

I was hoping to run into her by now. She could give me the basic rundown, I could ask her why she's been ignoring my texts and only coming to school to give me cryptic messages on the full moon...

My proxy for her, the curly, multicoloured gel pen instructions, has me on the lookout for an arrow carved in a red oak, as if I know the differences between a red oak and a... another type of oak. Brown oak? Whatever. I keep alert, squinting at trees on either side of the trail until I catch it.

An arrow leading off the path.

I'm not an off-the-path kind of guy. Paths exist for a reason, and usually stories of leaving them involve being eaten by hungry witches, or detained by power-hungry cops. I might be a slacker, but I'm not typically a rule breaker. Just a guy cursed to be attracted to rule breakers.

I check my phone. Ezra isn't replying to my texts, even though 50% of them are variations of apology. If I turn around right now, I bet I could show up at his place, no questions asked. If I continue on, there's no going back.

Closing my eyes, I'm met with the memory of New Year's Eve, of leaning in and kissing my best friend and the look on his face when I noticed he wasn't kissing me back. My heart aches all over again.

I suck in a lungful of air and step into the underbrush. My coat drags on stray twigs, and plants I hope aren't poison ivy.

Another handful of minutes, another degree of light lost. I hunch over in my swaying coat, actually grateful for the extra warmth. The deeper I go into the forest, the less I can see of the sky.

But my body will know when the sun sets.

The ground slopes steeply downward and the trees ahead are all towering, skinny white trees blocking the sky from view. Birch, or maybe aspen, I dunno, Skylar's got me thinking about tree species. The earth vanishes into the dark, only visible in a small, circular clearing bathed in moonlight a little ways on.

I click on the flashlight.

Between the trees stand a dozen people looking right at me. Waiting for me. An East Asian woman with a Mohawk lights a cigarette. An older white guy in a bomber jacket snaps a hardcover book shut—two half-naked and overly attractive models embrace on the cover. A Black girl with curly pigtails, my age or a little younger, smiles at me, her orange braces glinting in the light.

"Um, hi there," I say, giving them the dorkiest wave of my life.

"Thought you got lost," Skylar says, stepping forward from the group.

"Only a little. I'll just, uh, come down..." The ground slides loose beneath my shoes as I ease down the hill. I hop the last bit of the hill with no grace whatsoever. "So, how's everyone's lurking in the forest going?"

"Has he been prepped?" the man with the romance novel asks in a British accent.

"Where's the mystery in that?" Skylar says.

The man grunts. "I thought we talked about this. He has to want to be here. We can't afford another close call."

"I said I was sorry!" says the girl with the pigtails and braces. "I wasn't really gonna go to the police. But I maintain that it was one hundred percent Sky's fault. Girl's addicted to the drama..."

"I want to be here," I say. "What do I need to do?"

"It's easy, Dec." Skylar takes my hand and leads me closer to the pack, into the moon-soaked clearing.

The moon shines full in the sky, round as a coin and brighter than my flashlight, ringed in rainbow. There's a tug in my chest, like the pull of the tide, and maybe it's weird to feel a connection between me and a giant floating space rock, but I do. Stepping into the clearing is like stepping into a hot shower, moonlight washing away grime and toil. I drop to my knees, sliding my coat from my shoulders.

"Let go," she whispers into my ear. Maybe the voice belongs to Skylar, or maybe the moon. Maybe there's no difference until the morning. "Embrace your new self."

I'm ready.

"Get away from him!"

Half-dazed, my head turns on reflex, and I look over my shoulder to find Ezra stumbling downhill, grasping for the trees to steady himself and finding nothing. He falls backward and slides down the hill on his butt.

"Who is this?" the British man asks, not sounding particularly bothered.

"Dude, you can't be here," I say. "Go home."

"I'm not going anywhere."

"It's too late," Skylar says, looking at me with her blue eyes wide, her words and expression more intense than I've ever seen her. She steps back out of the light. "It's begun."

I look down at my hands.

No, not hands.

Claws.

My limbs seize and I double over, a tidal wave of agony crashing into my prone body. My hands clench into fists, claws digging into cold earth. The hair of my arms stands straight up and thickens into coarse fur that covers my skin. Sharp teeth push through gums and overfill my mouth. My bones make like Rice Krispies and snap, crackle, pop into new shapes—they shatter and reform, and my knees bend backward. There's a distant cry, someone screaming from deep in the woods, and too late I feel the vibration of my throat and the taut corners of my wide open mouth, stretched until the skin tears.

Ezra steps in front of me. I smell him, the savoury meat beneath his skin, the blood rushing to and from his heart. I hear the speedy *thud, thud, thud*, from his breast as he pockets his glasses and marches closer.

Saliva gathers in my mouth. My muscles tighten like compacted springs. I snarl, a growl starting low in my throat. A final warning to go back home and eat his matzah and pretend he never saw us.

Ezra winces, but he doesn't do the smart thing and back off. His expression tightens, his brows drawing together. There's fear in his eyes, but there's something more, too.

He takes my face in his hands.

I'm letting go of myself.

But Ezra's not.

I lunge.

Our bodies crash together in a tangle of elbows and teeth and hands, warm hands that pull me in and soft lips that lock on mine. I hesitate, tasting iron on his mouth — but then I give in to the rush of humanity, to the butterflies in my stomach and the longing, yearning part of me that's waited for this moment with every brush of our fingers over popcorn and our legs on the bus. I can feel my claws recede as my fingers reach under his shirt, hold tight to his back. Fangs retreat back into gums as his tongue glides over them. His hands rake through my hair, over twitching, angular ears losing their fur and their shape.

When he pulls away, tears track down his cheeks, and blood stains his mouth. My stomach lurches like a chew toy whipped around in an eager dog's jaws.

"I infected you," I say, hardly able to get the words out.

"I infected myself," he says. "I bit my own tongue. On purpose."

"And you kissed me."

"Yup." He turns away from me. "I kissed you."

"I... didn't know you liked me like that."

Ezra's perfect lips break into a smile. But then he winds up and smacks my still residually furry chest. "How is that possible? Why else would I put up with a werewolf love triangle?"

"Because you're my best bro?" I ask, and he smacks me again. "How did you even find me?"

"Your phone."

"You tracked my location?"

"You were walking into the woods to find werewolves, obviously I tracked your location!"

"Damn, Ezra," Skylar says, reminding me that we're not the only two people in this patch of moonlight and that we are, in fact, surrounded by eleven strangers and the girl I'm kinda sorta dating. "I would have shared him if you'd asked."

The werewolves in the darkness chuckle. My cheeks flush. "What happens now?"

As I ask it, I squeeze Ezra's hand, ready to take off into the dark with a pack of wolves on our heels.

Skylar grins. Maybe she can smell my fear. I'm pretty sure *I* can smell my fear, a distinct funk rising from my pores. She glances back at the British guy, who gives her a flat, indecipherable glare.

She turns back to me and Ezra, tangled up in one another.

"Looks like we're welcoming two members to the pack tonight." Skylar's smile widens, her teeth elongating, sharpening. Behind her, the others step into the moonlight, mid-transformation. A howl echoes throughout the forest. "Are you ready to run with the wolves?"

K.A. Mielke in an Ontario native who has a gift for melding the strange with literary sensibilities. He is best known for his short fiction, which has appeared in nearly a dozen short fiction anthologies throughout the country since 2010.

MELODY OF A MERROW
VERA NUGENT

They say when you hear a melody whispering up from the depths of the ocean, it is best to turn away your ear. To listen to the song is to doom yourself to the whims of a dark creature who will lure you away to the bottom of the sea, they say. Well, that's what my grandfather always said anyway, and I assume someone told him, but I don't actually know if I give much weight to the idea.

As a kid, sometimes I'd think I heard something like a voice amid the crashing waves and the wind on a particularly harsh day. Hearing it filled me with such a sense of dread that I didn't quite know how to name, always hearing Pop's words echoing in the back of my mind. "Don't let the sea maid lure you, son, you'll never surface again," he'd say.

It doesn't happen so much anymore, but even if it did, I now know better than to think it was anything more than the whistling wind playing tricks. Besides, their sweet song is meant to lure naive and unsuspecting men into the depths, and *that* I most certainly am not.

So, going down to the wharf doesn't really scare me

like it once did. I find it the best place to go sit and clear my head. Sometimes I just sit with my thoughts, but sometimes—most times, these days—I bring my fiddle with me, and play a song to nobody but myself. Lucky thing, I suppose, that there aren't many fishing boats out on these waters anymore, or else they might blame *me* for the siren's song.

It's a crisp morning, the wind biting at the fingers wrapped around my fiddle's case as I make my way down to the wharf. I like to come down early these days, as it gives me a chance to take things in before the world is really alive for the day. I especially prefer to do so on days like today, when Nan is gone to Sunday service. She understands why I don't want to go, but it's still easier to avoid the disappointment in her eyes.

Settling on the edge of the creaky old wooden wharf, I take a moment for myself before snapping open the clasps on my case and flipping the top back. Pop gave me this fiddle for my birthday just before he passed, so every time I lift it out of the case, I can almost feel his rough, gnarled old hand patting my cheek.

I know many songs by now, but there's always a few I find myself drawn back to; and so it's one of those I start with. I don't even have to think about the motions of it all by now. I just let myself listen to the notes as they echo out over the waves.

As I dragged the bow over the middle of the song, I could swear I heard a voice singing along. I stopped the song short to listen and see if I was just hearing things, and as the whine of the fiddle stopped, so did the imaginary voice. I shook the thought from my head and picked up the bow again. It must just be playing on my mind, thinking of Pop and all.

There it was again, a few phrases further into the song. I continued playing, this time with more of an ear out for the sound. Even if the wind was just playing tricks on my mind, it sounded really pretty all the same.

The song came to a close as I pulled across the last few notes, and again my imaginary accompaniment ended. I sat for a moment, wondering which song I'd play next, and how long I'd—

"Why'd you stop?" A voice cut through the silence, pulling me from my thoughts.

I looked around for the source, because surely *that* was real. A faint voice coming from the water was one thing, but this was someone actually speaking to me.

"It was a really nice song, why'd you stop?" The voice asked again.

"Who are you?" I asked, searching a little more frantically now. "And more importantly, *where* are you?"

"Down here, silly."

I laid my fiddle back in the case and leaned forward until I could see into the water directly in front of the wharf. As I looked into it, a set of eyes blinked up at me.

"Hi there," the voice said, this time coming from the head that was breaking the surface of the water beneath me.

"You- you're- I-" I stammered as I scrambled back a few feet. Two hands slapped wetly onto the wood, and next thing she had pulled herself up to be leaning on the edge of the wharf, resting her head in her hands. I swear I saw something flick up in the water behind her, but I couldn't be sure.

She blinked at me with a kind of curiosity you normally only see from kids. "What do you call that song you were playing?" She asked. "And what is that stringed article you play it upon?"

"M-my fiddle?"

"Fascinating," she said, eyeing the fiddle, before shifting her gaze upon me. "Will you play another? I shall sing along. I quite enjoyed it last time."

"I- um-" I swallowed. "I'm not sure I…"

"How exactly does one make this sing?" She asked, now reaching for the fiddle in its case, though it was not quite within her reach. However, extending her hand let me see the thin, translucent webbing between her fingers. The shadow of doubt in my mind was slipping away by the minute.

I leaned forward and picked the instrument up in my hands, which lifted her gaze to mine expectantly, as if to say "well, what are you waiting for?"

"Any requests?" I asked, trying to steady both my hands and my voice as I spoke.

She shook her head as I brought the fiddle to my shoulder and settled it in position. Well, no time like the present, I suppose. I lifted the bow and began to play once more. She seemed content with this, as a soft smile spread across her face and her eyes fell closed as she took a breath and began to sing along. Her voice was as lovely as before, but I could appreciate it far more now that it was ringing out clearly over the waves rather than from below them.

Without her intense and curious gaze fixed upon me for the moment, I took the chance to take her in as I played.

Her hair fell below where I could see and was a deep, radiant green—not unlike the dyed kind I sometimes saw on people my age, but hers was less washed out and lacking any dark roots to convince you it was anything but natural. That smile spread across her face lit it up with a warmth that was, admittedly, rather beautiful. I began to see why they say it's so easy to become entranced with her sort.

My admiration was cut short as our song once more came to a close, and her eyes slowly opened and flicked up to meet mine.

"That was delightful!" she said, clapping cheerfully. "You possess great skill at this 'fiddle,' human lady."

"Oh, um, thank you," I replied, my gaze falling to my lap as I felt my cheeks flush. "You have a very lovely voice. And um, my name is Saoirse."

She giggled at that. "Thank you kindly, Saoirse, I was starting to have concern that my voice was scaring humans away, which is very counterproductive, you must agree."

"I guess so," I laughed. "Do you have a name too?"

"I am known as Mera," she replied, smiling at me a little wider this time. From behind her parting lips, I could see her teeth were sharper than I had noticed before. It reminded me a little of a shark.

"Nice to, uh, meet you, Mera," I said. I dropped my gaze as I continued, not quite sure how you would politely ask such a question. "So, you are, um, a siren then? You know, the whole lure sailors to their drowning death and all?"

She snorted at that. "Is that what they call us now?

And no. Not just sailors, necessarily. Merely men with selfish hearts who care not for the sea nor land they live amongst. Not so many of them are out on the waters these days as there once was though, so it makes my days rather fruitless."

"I see," I replied, not really sure what else you say when someone admits to hunting people.

My concern must have been written all over my face because she laughed and waved her hand at me. "Worry not, Saoirse, for my song has no effect on the hearts of enchanting women such as yourself," she winked.

"I- uh, thanks for the heads up," I smiled shakily, my face pretty well on fire now. I'd never been called 'enchanting' before.

"Besides, you do not seem as though you wish harm upon the ocean as you sit here and play for it a lovely melody."

"No," I chuckled. "I like the sea."

"I as well," Mera laughed too. "But that much may be obvious."

I smiled. Although when she spoke her words sounded as though from another world, Mera had a good sense of humour about her.

"Do you reside nearby, Saoirse?" Mera asked, the echoes of her laughter still ringing in my ear.

"I- yes," I replied. "I live with my Nan just down the road. Why do you ask?"

"Fantastic! Then you are familiar with these lands!" She exclaimed. "I have not been on land before and this would be a wondrous opportunity."

"What do you—"

Before I could finish that sentence, Mera reached down below the wharf and from who knows where whisked out a small red hat. It reminded me of the ones Pop used to wear when I was a kid, like Nan knit for him. She tugged it on over her long green waves, and I swear her hair began to glimmer.

And then, when I thought I was done being surprised by Mera at that point, with one huff of breath she swung her tail—her *tail*—up on the wharf. However, it wasn't just that she swung her tail up, but as it hit the creaky old wood and flicked drops of salty water in every direction, it shifted and somehow before my eyes became a pair of legs. That is, Mera was now sitting across from me on the wharf wearing nothing more than a red knit hat.

My eyes were probably wide as saucers, and she looked at me with confusion. I averted my eyes for risk of making her uncomfortable, but I noticed out of the corner of my eye that she glanced down, then snorted at me, as if I was foolish and some kind of prude.

Since she clearly intended to be shown around town so to speak, I had to do something about the state of her, even if she was perfectly comfortable the way she was. I unzipped my own oversized jacket and held it out to her, arm outstretched blindly as my eyes were still in my lap. I felt her take it, and I finally let myself meet her gaze again. She had slid the jacket on and was fumbling with the zipper. I was about to reach out to help when she got it and pulled it up tight to her chin. Her hair was caught under the jacket, and that looked rather uncomfortable, so I leaned over and slid my hand underneath, gently tugging her hair out from under the collar. As I did, I realized just how much of her hair there was, and wow, it was really soft for hair that spent most of its time under the saltwater.

I pushed myself up onto my feet and held my hand out to Mera. She looked at it curiously for a moment before grasping it tightly with hers and let me hoist her up. She wobbled a little bit, and as I grabbed her arm to steady her, I was beginning to see the truth in the fact she'd never been ashore before. I suppose you could say she has some sea legs on her.

Not wanting to make her wait when she was clearly excited to explore this so *terribly* thrilling little community, I quickly packed up my fiddle and motioned for her to follow me. I watched her stumble through a few steps but become a little sturdier as she met where I stood. She smiled at me, and to my surprise, looped her arm through mine as we began to walk up the wharf.

The walk back to Nan's was a short one, yet Mera spent the entire time taking in every little detail with an awe that reminded me of the first summer I came up here to visit, when everything was still so new to me and the small-town charm had yet to fade. Every time Mera saw something that particularly excited her, she'd squeeze my arm and let out a little gasp. I'd look around for what prompted it, and each time I'd see something I hadn't even noticed was there or hadn't noticed in a while. I guess it takes a fresh set of eyes to help you appreciate the little things.

As we came up on the house, I felt a pang of anxiety wash over me about the chipped paint on the old boards of siding, the rusted banisters on the step, and the other little signs of age that most people would find far beyond quaint. Then I reminded myself that Mera wasn't most people and would probably take in the weathering and wear with the same sense of awe as everything else. This was all new to her, so what reason would she have to judge? Honestly, I shouldn't even be ashamed at all, because this is a house that my family was raised in, and which raised my family.

The few steps leading up to the old screen door creaked as I led Mera up them and pulled the door open. She brushed past me into the porch and as I closed the door behind me and joined her, her gaze met mine with expectation in it once more.

"Well," I said rather plainly, gesturing vaguely at the room around us, "this is where I live."

"How curious! I adore it," Mera exclaimed, passing under the doorway into the living room. She began to look around at all the little knick knacks Nan had the place littered with.

"I'm glad to hear it," I chuckled. "I can, uh, lend you some actual clothes—well, more than a jacket that is. My room is just down the hall."

She eagerly followed as I headed into my bedroom and stood patiently by the bed while I began to dig through my closet. As I shuffled through the pieces, I realized that most of my clothing probably wouldn't be the best fit for Mera—we had entirely different body types. I started to have a bit of a panic, but then an idea hit me.

"Stay here, I'll be right back," I told her, then dashed out of the room and further down the hall to Nan's room. I quickly scanned her closet, and the drawers of the chest nearest to it. I helped her with her laundry sometimes, so I knew where most of her things were, and was able to find what I was looking for in no time.

I came back into my room, arms full, to find Mera sitting on the bed. I noticed that she was holding the picture frame from my nightstand in her lap, looking fondly at the photo. I cleared my throat and she glanced up at me.

"I borrowed some of my Nan's clothes, it should probably be okay on you."

I handed her the outfit I had chosen, and she laid down the photo to take the pile of clothes from my hands. I reached over to pick up the frame off the blanket and put it back in its place on the nightstand.

"Is that you in that… image?" Mera asked as she unfolded the clothes and held each piece out to examine it.

"Yeah, it's me and my Pop- er, my grandfather, when I was a kid," I said quietly, averting my gaze. Though I cherished it, I didn't usually like people seeing pictures of me at that age.

"Your… Pop, he is a nice man then? You look happy in the image," Mera asked genuinely.

"He was," I smiled kind of sadly.

"I see," Mera replied, nodding to herself thoughtfully.

"I'll, uh, step out and give you a chance to put those on," I said, after a moment of tense silence. I stepped out into the hall and pulled the door closed behind me, but not all the way, just enough to still hear her, should she need help.

After a very long couple of minutes, Mera emerged from the bedroom, this time my jacket pulled on over the outfit I gave her. Nan's clothes fit her well, and she looked like the image of a hipster trying to be from around the bay. It was cute.

Now that she was properly dressed, I had to figure out exactly what sights I was to show Mera. This tiny place wasn't exactly a lively hub of activity or landmarks, but I was sure for someone who'd never been on land before even the smallest, everyday things would fascinate her. In the meantime, I could hear the voice of my Nan in the back of my head telling me to be a good host and put on the kettle, so I almost instinctively made my way to the kitchen to do just that. Mera followed close on my heels. As I busied my hands at the counter, she sat at the tiny kitchen table, the chair creaking as she eased into it.

"I'm not really sure what you would want to see around here, Mera," I said, as the kettle rattled on the stove. "If you wanted the grand tour it might take about ten minutes," I chuckled softly.

"Anything would be splendid," she replied. I glanced over my shoulder at her, to find her grinning warmly at me. "What are you doing there now, Saoirse?"

I looked down at the cups in my hand as I brought them over and set them on the table between us. "Making you tea," I said, popping a tea bag into each cup.

"Tea?"

I returned to the counter to grab a plate of toutons Nan made yesterday morning, a knife, and the tub of margarine beside them. "Yes, tea. It's a drink. And I'm going to feed you," I said, lifting the plate of toutons as confirmation.

As I laid the plate on the table, she picked one up and

sniffed it, then squished the bread between her fingers.

I laughed. "They're good, trust me."

She looked skeptical but tore a piece off and popped it in her mouth. After a moment she grinned and licked her lips.

"See? But they're even better with a bit of butter," I waved the knife to point at the margarine. She held out the touton and I took it, spread a slice of margarine across, and handed it back. She took a full bite into it and her face lit up.

"Oh, I do enjoy this 'butter!'" She said, taking another bite. The kettle began to whine so I pushed myself up from the table.

"Some people, like my Nan, would say they're better yet with molasses, but I couldn't be bothered," I said, bringing the kettle over to the table and filling our cups with the steaming hot water.

"Let that sit for a minute," I warned, as she went to lift the drink to her lips. Her eyes went wide, and she laid the cup back down. "I don't want you to burn yourself."

Mera touched her lips curiously, then reached out and placed her hand upon mine.

"Your compassion is admirable," she said, squeezing my hand gently. My face flushed at the comment and I couldn't even blame the heat on the tea.

Before I could say much of anything in response, I heard the door click open and then smack shut again a moment later.

"Saoirse, are you home, doll?" Nan's voice bellowed in from the porch.

"In the kitchen," I replied. Mera looked at me with

confusion written all over her face, but before I could respond, Nan sauntered into the kitchen.

"Oh my, we've got a friend over, have we?" Nan asked as she took in the sight of Mera and me at the table, raising an eyebrow cheekily.

"Yes, Nan, this is Mera," I replied, perhaps a little too quickly. Nan chuckled to herself.

"Mera, hm?" she looked Mera up and down, eyes lingering briefly on her red knit cap. "Well, dear, it's a pleasure to meet you. I see my girl has treated you to some of my fine baking and best box of Tetley."

Mera looked down at the cup of tea and plate of toutons then smiled up at Nan. "Yes, she has been most hospitable," she replied.

"Glad to hear I raised her well," Nan laughed, patting me on the shoulder.

"Do you want some tea, Nan?" I asked. Nan shook her head.

"No, my love, that's quite alright," she replied. She picked up the kettle from where I had set it and shuffled over to the sink to refill it. "Did I mention that Frances is having a little bit of a crowd over to hers this evening?"

"No, Nan." It was likely that it was just brought up this morning after church. Nan forgets who's with her and when all the time.

"Yes, she said to us she couldn't be bothered steaming her house up with a scoff of Jiggs on a fine summer day, so she'd be making a cold plate instead, and since you knows now the girl can't cook for less than an army, she insisted we all come over for a spell," Nan explained, turning to face us once more. "I tell you I'm not complaining over her hospitality saving these weary old bones from having to cook this evening, no sir."

"That sounds like fun," I agreed. "Do you suppose I should bring the fiddle? It always turns into a time up to Frances's like that."

Nan's face lit up. "Oh yes, that sounds like a great idea. Get a real kitchen party on the go, everyone loves when you break out that trusty ol' thing." She glanced at Mera with a little smirk. "You'll have to bring your friend here too, I'm sure she'd have a time too."

I looked at Mera, she looked a little bewildered but nodded at the suggestion. "It will be a good time, and far better than anything else I could've shown you around here," I said, lowering my voice a little.

"Then I would be delighted to attend," she smiled brightly at me, then up at Nan.

"That's settled then," Nan nodded firmly. "I'm going to watch my Coronation Street tapes now, don't you girls have too much fun out here now," she winked at me.

As she began to make her way out of the room, she paused in front of Mera. "My, that sweater looks some familiar," she noted, eyes squinting at the pattern. "You've got good taste, my dear."

Mera and I burst out in a fit of laughter a moment after she shuffled out of the room and we heard the TV click on and the buzz of British voices whir in from the other room.

When Nan's programs had run their course, we got suited up and set off. Frances only lived down the road, so Nan insisted we walk and not waste the time and the gas of getting the car on the go. It wasn't a long walk, but

I once again got to watch Mera take in all the little sights along the way, from all the little coloured stones in the gravel beneath our feet, to the butterflies hopping from blade to blade in the grass. She was filled with such a fascination over the things I took for granted every day, it made my heart feel light to watch.

The path up to Frances' house was lined with these big flat stones, but they were uneven underfoot in the shifting mud, weathered and worn over time as well. When I was younger, I used to play with Frances' grandson, but he didn't come up this way much anymore.

Mera wove her arm through mine and situated her hand in the crook of my elbow as we came up to the steps. Two older men I didn't quite recognize were just off to the side having a smoke. One of them took a long draw on his cigarette and nodded to Nan as she began to climb the steps.

"Evening, Annie," he said in a low, scruffy, smoke-laden voice. "How's she gettin' on?"

"Oh, best kind, Ed," Nan replied with a soft chuckle, giving his arm a light squeeze. She turned back to Mera and I and waved us in as she pulled the heavy door open with a grunt. "Come on girls, let's get in for a plate before it's all gone."

Frances' kitchen was as alive as I've seen it in a while, a crowd like this would almost make you think someone died or had a baby, if you didn't know better. Seats were filled all around the kitchen table and then some, and even more crowded was every corner with someone toting a bottle of beer or a heaping paper plate that nearly drooped right out of their hands.

"Saoirse, my girl. Good to see you!" Frances said as she came to greet us. She squeezed my arm and smiled. She then raised an eyebrow in Mera's direction. "And who's this here?"

"That's her little *friend*, Mera," Nan chimed in, winking at Frances before she brushed past her towards the food. She put her own offering—a loaf of bread fresh from yesterday morning—on the counter with everything else.

"A *friend*, huh?" Frances smirked. I felt my face heat and chuckled nervously. Mera merely smiled at her. "Well, any friend of Saoirse's is welcome here! Help yourself, girls."

After assembling two plates of salads, meat and all the fixings, I gestured for Mera to follow me to the nearest empty nook of the room. We ate in silence, and I spent those few moments watching Mera watch everyone else as they gabbed the night away. I can't imagine the gossip from the old busy bodies across the room or the fellas talking about their latest hunting trip were particularly interesting to listen to, but I suppose if you'd never experienced it before, everything has a bit of charm to it. Besides, I wasn't going to complain about anything that lit her face up with such a pretty smile again.

It didn't take long for somebody to pull out a guitar and get the music ringing through the entire house. Nobody would be surprised, but this was always my favourite part of these parties, and it made everything else that was entirely overwhelming worth it. An older man standing in the corner that I vaguely remember as one of Pop's friends came over to me and thumped his gnarled old hand on my shoulder, telling me that "he knew I had

Jim's old fiddle with me, and I should bring the ol' girl out," and who was I to argue with that? I pulled the case out from behind my seat, taking it out and settling it under my chin, waiting for the right moment to join in with the guitar, and now also accordion. At this rate all we needed was a bodhrán and we'd have a full band on the go.

We dove right into some lively jigs, and soon enough there were people up dancing in what space there was left on the linoleum tile between us all. Every now and then I took a glance out of the corner of my eye to see Mera laughing and clapping along to the music as everyone else was swaying back and forth in front of us. She seemed to be enjoying herself, and I was glad to see it.

A few more songs in and my arms were thoroughly worn out. I bowed out of playing and tucked the fiddle and its case back in the corner as I sagged a little in my seat.

"You continue to amaze me, Saoirse, with your skill in the fiddle," Mera said in a low voice, leaning in close. Or perhaps a normal voice, just under the bustle of the room.

I smiled at her, making the decision to reach out and squeeze the hand she had resting on her knee. "Thanks."

I continued to watch Mera watch the crowd for another while, and as songs changed and the light in her face never dimmed, inspiration washed over me. I pushed myself up on my feet and offered her my hand.

"Would you like to dance?" I asked, as she put her hand in mine. It was warmer than I expected.

Though I thought it impossible, her face seemed to light up even more. "Yes! However, you may have to lead us in this endeavour."

I laughed and led her out a few steps onto the lino-leum as the song changed and picked up anew. It defi-nitely wasn't without hiccups, but she only managed to step on my toes a few times, and in between that it was a lot of fun. I hadn't danced with anyone other than my Nan since I was little and a girl from down the road used to chase me down and make me dance with her on occa-sions like these. Needless to say, this was far better, if only because it made my heart feel light to see how much Mera was enjoying herself.

We stumbled our way through another song, and then when the old fellas decided to have a rest, I led her out-side for some fresh air. We were practically panting from it all as I pushed the door open and the crisp evening air hit us.

We stood in silence for a few moments, just taking in the view of the yard dimly lit by the half-burnt-out light over the door. I motioned for Mera to sit on the step with me, and as she did, I snuck a glance at her, only to see a very calm smile spread across her face. I couldn't help but smile myself at the sight of it.

"This has been a most delightful day, Saoirse," Mera said, breaking the silence at last. "Humans are utterly fas-cinating."

I chuckled. "I'm glad you think so," I said. "Showing you around here today really made me stop and appreci-ate all the little things I haven't noticed in a long time, so thanks for that."

"I had not considered that this adventure would be good for both of us, but I am pleased that it is so," she said. She took a deep breath and let it out very slowly, then finally looked my way. "I wish to stay."

I'm sure I looked rather comical as my head whipped around to meet her gaze. "I'm not sure I—Stay?"

Mera laughed gently. "Yes, stay. The human world is filled with so many wonders, I know I cannot have possibly experienced them all in one day. I wish to see more," she explained. "And besides, I have much enjoyed our time together, and I hope that will continue as well, should I choose to."

My face went hot against the evening chill. "I... enjoyed it too," I replied. "Is it even possible though?"

Mera was uncharacteristically pensive, and her focus made a chill run down my spine. After a moment, she reached up and pulled the red hat from her head. My breath caught, as I was sure she was going to be a lot more like a fish out of water on these steps, but nothing really happened as she took my hand and placed the hat atop my palm. It was soft.

I opened my mouth to ask her what was happening here, but she spoke before I could. "I am offering you this to show you that I am serious, Saoirse. Without my hat, I am unable to return home, and I am offering it to you to show you that I truly wish to stay here by your side."

Immediately a pit formed in my stomach. "No."

Mera jumped back in surprise, likely equally from the answer and the unintended force with which I said it. I took a deep breath and gently tugged the hat back over her emerald waves, and she quietly reached up to touch the hem of it as I spoke again.

"If you're going to stay, I want it to be because you

want to be here, not because you feel trapped here… by me or anything else. It's sweet of you to put so much trust in me, but I don't want to hold you back from feeling free," I continued.

Mera considered this for a minute, then took a deep breath. "You have a beautiful heart, Saoirse. I hope that you are aware of this."

I shrugged nonchalantly. I guess I still wasn't used to how honest Mera could be.

"If you still want to stay, I'd be happy to have you," I said softly, forcing myself not to look away as my face heated further.

Mera reached out and gently touched my cheek. "I would like that."

We began to gravitate towards each other, and in the next moment I felt her soft lips pressed against mine. The kiss was feather-light, but it still made my heart skip a beat. I pulled back and couldn't hold back the biggest smile. At the sight of my smile, Mera's face lit up with her own. I held out my hand to her, and she gently wove her fingers between mine.

That night didn't last forever, nor did the time Mera spent on land with me, but they were both something I would cherish and hold near to my heart forever. Eventually, Mera did leave for the sea again, as I suspected she would, but not without a parting kiss and a promise to return. She did return, and left again, and returned, and I never knew when I would see her for certain, but every moment we spent together was precious. Every time she came ashore, I tried to show her something new, but most times it turned out to be her shining a new light on something old for me.

They say that when you hear a melody whispering up from the depths of the ocean, it is best to turn away your ear. To listen to the song is to doom yourself to the whims of a dark creature who will lure you away to the bottom of the sea, they say. Well, I don't know about the doom and darkness, but most days I still find myself wandering down by the water, listening for a song, and just hoping it brings back that ray of light from the depths, and maybe let me lay eyes on her beautiful green hair and sharp smile once more.

Vera Nugent is an Ontario-born author who calls Newfoundland and Labrador home. This is her first published work.

CRIMSON PURPOSE
STACEY OAKLEY

"Would it really be so bad, lass?" Owen asked as Elizabeth tugged the fabric across his shoulders to get a better fit. She had been a seamstress since her days as a human, and a long life made her a master at it, especially when it came to historical outfits. "It'd make her happy, and probably you, though I know it'd be easier to pull your fangs out than to get you to admit it."

"Even ignoring my nocturnal schedule, furry creatures and fabrics aren't a great mix." Elizabeth knew she was just searching for excuses, but that was something else she wasn't willing to admit. "If I wanted to spend the next two decades dealing with that, I would have stayed with you," she added as she pinned the fabric and gave it a critical look, ignoring the return of her English accent with her tension.

"Low blow, leech," he said without anger. Elizabeth smirked in the mirror so he would see it and tugged at another bit of fabric. "And not a good distraction. What's this really about?" They really had known each other for too long.

Elizabeth sighed. "Tessa will be almost fifty. And not just in age. She'll actually be *fifty*, slowly becoming an old woman." Which would never happen to Elizabeth.

Owen turned his head to look at her. "Fifty isn't so old anymore."

Elizabeth stepped away and wrapped her arms around herself. "I know, but it's getting old. One day she's going to die and I'll still be here, like nothing ever happened."

Owen carefully pulled the pinned shirt off and laid it aside. "My offer stands, just so you know."

"I know," Elizabeth started pacing. "I know, but she doesn't want it. She's happy the way she is, as a human sorceress, and if she changed... I mean, you and I both know that becoming something else changes you. It's not just becoming a vampire or werewolf. It changes you on a fundamental level. I'm not who I was as a human." She took a breath, trying to calm down.

"Yeah, I remember," he said.

"And I don't want to pressure her into a fate she doesn't want. I didn't get to pick this life; I won't force it on anyone else." She couldn't deny that part of her wished Tessa wanted to become a vampire or werewolf.

"Yeah." Owen ran a hand through his hair. "What about a deal with somethin'? Powerful witches can live for centuries. Just look at Amethyst." Owen's fiancée was older than both of them.

"Yes, look at me, but why this time?" The witch asked, wandering into the room.

"Long life and youth through magic," Elizabeth replied. "But her power comes from within, and Tessa's comes from bargains with demons and other beings."

"And not many of them are keen on offering something resembling immortality for a reasonable price," Amethyst said. "Or if they do, there's a trick."

"Exactly." Elizabeth sighed and sat on the couch. "I can't ask her to do any of that just because I don't want to deal with grief. It's not right."

"What about reincarnation? It's working out so far for my younger sister in this lifetime. Though, I suppose, now she's distant cousin. Or niece?" Amethyst shrugged after a moment.

"Didn't that involve an ancient spell, a prophecy, and a few centuries as a ghost?" Elizabeth asked.

"Well, when you put it like that it sounds unpleasant," Amethyst replied. "And we're still figuring out the prophecy part. Never get involved in a prophecy."

"I know that, but I don't know what to do about now," Elizabeth pointed out.

"Get a dog, enjoy your time together. I hate to be the one to point it out, but she's a demon specialist. Her work is dangerous as it is and if you get stabbed in the heart or spend more than two minutes in the sun, you're a goner."

Elizabeth glared at him. "I'm using silver pins for your next fitting."

"Aye, go ahead. I'll change my shirt colour to olive green and hot pink stripes."

Amethyst scowled at both of them. "No. Normally this is entertaining, but you're messing with the wedding, which means you're messing with *me*. Now play nice or I'll turn you both into frogs."

Elizabeth picked up the shirt and handed it to Owen to

put back on. He did have a point, as much as she hated to admit it. "I need to check the length of the sleeves since I pinned the shoulders," she said, then looked at Amethyst. "I have a mock-up of your dress done; we can do your fitting at my place."

"Thank you," she said, smiling.

***

It was nearly dawn when she got home, and she was happy to see the lights on and Tessa's car in the driveway. She usually worked later in the day unless something urgent came up, the better to match Elizabeth's nocturnal schedule.

"Honey, I'm home," she called out with perfect sitcom cheeriness as she shut the door.

"Hey," Tessa called back, and there was something in her voice that immediately drew concern. Elizabeth hurried to get her things put away and headed into the living room. Tessa was there, on the couch.

But she wasn't alone.

A huge black wolf was sprawled over the couch and her lap. It lifted its large head and looked at Elizabeth with deep, burning red eyes that were filled with an alien intelligence. She stood frozen as it got up and walked around her, sniffing at her clothes before licking her hand and pushing at it with his cold nose.

"He wants you to pet him," Tessa said helpfully.

Elizabeth did so, patting the hellhound's back with tentative movements. "Love, why is there a *hellhound* in our living room?"

"We talked about getting a dog," Tessa replied.

"Yes, a *dog*. Like a lab or a bloody chihuahua. Not a

hellhound!" As if the massive beast could understand her perfectly, and really, it probably could, the hellhound looked up at her as it shrank, turning into something akin to a black lab, though its eyes remained red. "Seriously?" She asked the hound. It dropped its jaw and wagged its tail in response.

"See? He can be cute," Tessa replied. "And he'll be able to help me with my work, and he'll be fine with a more nocturnal schedule."

"But can he really stay like that for a long time? Because otherwise, this whole place will be carpeted with hellhound fur." The hound actually looked offended at that. She scowled at him. "Am I wrong?" He made a grumbling sound and looked away.

"There's magic and robot vacuums," Tessa pointed out.

"What is he getting out of this, anyway? Belly rubs and a few games of fetch?"

"And the occasional prime rib," Tessa replied.

"I hate that I'm sure you're serious," Elizabeth said, and headed into the kitchen. She was hungry, and that wasn't helping matters. She pulled a bag of blood out of the fridge and stuck a metal straw in it instead of pouring it in a wine glass. She preferred it warm and fresh and especially from Tessa, but this would have to do for now. When she looked over, the hound had followed her, looking up at her with big, red, weirdly sad eyes as it slowly wagged its tail. She walked back to the living room and joined Tessa on the couch. "I'm guessing you already made the deal."

"Yup."

"And it can't be unmade."

"Correct."

She sighed. "I'm not happy about this."

"I know, I should have talked to you, but there wasn't really any time. I was hunting down a demon earlier and when it cornered me Arcana showed up and brought it down long enough that I could kill it."

"Please tell me that was already its name and you didn't name a hellhound after tarot cards."

Tessa looked over at her. "I'm not *that* bad."

"Sure, go on."

Tessa rolled her eyes. "Anyway, Arcana offered the deal and it was good, so I took it."

"So, you get a pet and a working partner and he gets to be a pampered pet?"

"He's ten thousand years old and wanted a vacation."

Elizabeth nearly spit blood at that. "Seriously?"

Tessa shrugged and wrapped an arm around her shoulders. "There is a little more to it than that, but please, trust me. Things will work out. Just give it a month to see how it works out."

Elizabeth sighed and looked over at the hellhound, who was trying to look forlorn. "Fine." Arcana wagged his tail enthusiastically and joined them on the couch, sprawling over both their laps. "He's not sleeping on our bed," she declared, trying to put her foot down on at least one thing.

"Fine," Tessa said, petting him like he really was just a normal dog. "I'll pick up a dog bed tomorrow."

"Okay." She still wasn't happy with the situation, but there didn't seem to be much point in arguing about it further. Maybe it wouldn't turn out to be the worst idea.

***

Two weeks later, Elizabeth was hand-sewing delicate embellishments onto a bodice with a hellhound relaxing at her feet. For the most part Arcana seemed happy to stay a black lab with red eyes and pulled off the act fairly well, with a few exceptions. They had discovered that he enjoyed chasing pixies through the woods the day before, and that it was very difficult for even Elizabeth to hold him back with vampiric strength when he really tried to go for it. She was very thankful that Tessa's fae co-worker had been able to smooth things over so they didn't end up cursed. Pixies were particularly creative and vindictive. It was bad enough they'd had to just toss their muddy, forest debris-covered clothes into the wash as soon as they stepped through the door, plus, getting all of that out of her hair. As though Arcana could read her mind as well as Tessa's, he looked up at her with those big eyes and wagged his tail a little.

"Yeah, that whole cute and innocent thing won't work on me. I found another leaf in my hair this morning," she grumbled, going back to her sewing. Tessa was out on an emergency call, something involving a child who was afraid of dogs, so Arcana was left with Elizabeth for the night. She'd be lying if she said she was upset about it, as much as she was annoyed about yesterday. Arcana put his head back down on his paws and yawned as he went back to watching television. Oddly enough, he seemed to like cartoons best. Maybe it wouldn't be so bad if he stuck around longer than the end of the month… it would make Tessa happy. Elizabeth didn't hate having him around.

And she would enjoy the time they had together. Better a few decades with Tessa than never having met her at all. She felt she was almost at the point where she could truly accept that. Tessa wanted to be with her. That meant more than anything else.

She'd just put in the first few stitches on the next part of the embellishment when Arcana suddenly stood, his eyes glowing.

"What's wrong?" She asked. He made a low whining sound that turned into a menacing growl. As she stared, he grew back to his full size and wolfish appearance before a glowing red circle of runes and symbols appeared beneath him and he vanished in a flash of light. The only sign that he'd been there was the scent of Tessa's blood.

Elizabeth sat frozen in shock for several seconds before she was finally able to act, tossing aside her sewing with little regard. She considered calling Tessa, but if she was working Elizabeth didn't want to distract her. Instead, she called Blackfyre's headquarters. Maybe it was nothing, but the way Arcana acted…

"You've reached Blackfyre Incorporated." She recognized Amethyst's voice.

"Is Tessa okay? It's Elizabeth."

"I don't know much right now. She sent a distress signal a few minutes ago. Doctor Everett is with her." That was something of a relief, Jasper Everett was a vampire like her, and a clinical psychologist. "They were investigating a possible case of a child being cursed by a demon. Owen is about to head out as backup."

"Where are they?" She might not have been a warrior like Owen, but she was hardly powerless, and she had assisted on a number of Blackfyre's cases over the years. It was how she and Tessa had met.

"I'll send the coordinates to you. Bring anything you have to ward off demon possession." As Amethyst spoke Elizabeth's phone vibrated as she received the information.

She checked. They weren't too far away.

"Want me to tell Owen to meet you?"

"Yeah. There's a soccer field nearby. Tell him to meet me there."

"Will do. Want to start up the company app?"

Elizabeth did as asked, the flame symbol appearing at the top of her phone, allowing the witch to track her. "Am I good to go?"

"Yes," she said, and hung up.

Elizabeth ran upstairs and pulled on dark clothes appropriate for running around and possibly fighting. She also grabbed an amulet Tessa had made for her a few years ago that would protect her from demons, hoping it wouldn't be necessary.

After ignoring a few speed limits, Elizabeth pulled into the soccer field parking lot at the same time as Owen. They exchanged a look before she turned away as he stripped and shifted into a large grey and white wolf. She could just barely make out his own amulet, likely made by Amethyst. Together, they ran across the field into the wooded area behind it with supernatural speed, which was really just typical of something monstrous, along with wind that whipped around the normally sheltered area. Initially, she let Owen lead as werewolves had a far better sense of smell than vampires, but once she caught the scent of Tessa's blood, she raced forward, heart in her throat. Tessa was human, for all her magic. Human and fragile and mortal.

They were in a clearing. Tessa, the doctor, and a young girl knelt together in a glowing circle, braced against the wind that threatened to move them. A few paces ahead stood Arcana, growling with his sharp teeth bared and eyes glowing with a baleful light. The demon, not far away, was an almost human figure that flickered between a corporeal form and black smoke.

She and Owen were closest to the demon.

Quick as lightning the demon flew at her, passing through her body as it tried to possess her. Elizabeth gasped as it felt like her whole body was encased in ice so cold it burned. It gave an inhuman, ear-splitting shriek as it failed, the amulet glowing with crimson light, then passed through Owen, who snarled and howled at it. Arcana howled as well, a terrifying sound as he watched the demon.

Elizabeth fell to her knees as she caught her breath, not quite certain of what to do now. She looked over at Tessa, who looked about to faint, her arm pressed over her bleeding abdomen. But if she went to her, that would disrupt the circle, which was likely the only thing protecting the child, as both Tessa and Dr. Everett had protective amulets. The wind whipped higher around them as demon turned its attention back on the child. Arcana lunged at it, but the smoke figure moved too quickly. Elizabeth and Owen struggled against the wind to make their way closer to the trio, careful not to get too close to the circle and risk breaking it.

"What can we do?" She had to shout to be heard.

Tessa looked at her, pale and tired. "I only have one idea, and it's bad."

"Bad is better than nothing," Dr. Everett said as Arcana missed the demon again.

"We need to give the demon a host."

Elizabeth resisted the urge to agree out loud that it was a bad idea. She looked at Owen. If she took off her amulet, the demon could take possession. If Arcana failed, Owen would be able to take her down without killing her long enough for Tessa to figure something out.

But the doctor was faster. Before anyone could say anything, he put his amulet around the neck of the sobbing child and stepped out of the circle. The wind stilled with a shocking suddenness, leaves swirling in the air as if they hadn't quite noticed there was nothing tossing them around. The doctor's eyes glowed with red light before even the whites turned black. Elizabeth moved closer, to the edge of the circle, and Tessa pushed the child behind her.

Arcana leaped at the demon. Elizabeth expected the doctor to go down, expected blood and carnage. But just before he made contact, the hellhound took on an odd, translucent look, similar to how the demon had appeared before. He went through the doctor, the demon falling and getting pinned under Arcana's claws. The hellhound ripped at its throat, and the demon shrieked in agony. Elizabeth stared, transfixed as the two vanished in a flash of red. Owen went to the doctor, shifting before checking his pulse. Elizabeth went over to Tessa and the girl, throwing her arms around her lover, who hugged her back with one arm, and it was impossible to ignore that blood was soaking through both of their shirts. She moved back.

"Where are you hurt?"

Tessa moved her arm, revealing deep slashes across

her stomach. "The girl ran, and we followed. The demon got me when I tried to cast it back to the Hell it came from."

Elizabeth pulled out her phone and started to call an ambulance, but Tessa stopped her by taking the phone. "What the hell? You need an ambulance! This isn't something the first aid kit in the car will handle."

"Wait."

"Tessa…"

"Wait, please." She gave Elizabeth a wry grin. "Trust me, okay? I know what I'm doing."

"If you pass out I'm calling the ambulance," Elizabeth replied. She didn't like this at all.

"I know."

"Everett's out cold, but alive," Owen said.

"He'll feel like he has one hell of a hangover in the morning," Tessa said. "But he should be fine in a few days."

Arcana reappeared, and the girl screamed, but didn't run. He looked at her and shrank down until he regained his black lab look. Then he trotted over to Tessa and bumped his nose against the arm covering her wounds. She moved it and he leaned in close, almost resting his head against her stomach. There was more red glowing, and when he moved back, the only sign the wounds had existed were the rips in Tessa's shirt and the blood on both of them. Elizabeth looked from her to the hellhound.

"You're going to have to explain this."

"I know," she said. "I was going to at the end of the month. Let's get the kid home first and get Everett out of here." Elizabeth nodded and stood, pulling Tessa to her feet. She knew there were other things to take care of, but she couldn't resist pulling her lover close and kissing her. She was safe. They were all safe. Everything was okay.

***

With the girl returned to her very grateful parents and Everett in the tender care of Blackfyre's healer, Elizabeth and Tessa headed home.

"So, what do you think of Arcana?" Tessa asked as they settled on the couch. The hellhound in question looked over at her, apparently just as interested in the answer.

"I think I'd rather the explanation first," Elizabeth replied.

Tessa sighed. "Okay. Arcana is more than just a pet and work companion. I want to spend more than a lifetime with you, Elizabeth."

"But I thought you wanted to stay human."

"I'm still human. But part of the deal with Arcana is that I live longer. In exchange for living it up with us, which he considers far more interesting than any Hell, I won't age or get sick, and you saw that he can heal my wounds."

It was everything Elizabeth had wished for, and yet… "Are you sure? Is this just for me?"

Tessa smiled and wrapped her arms around her. "I love you, but this is something I want for myself, too. I want to see more and do more. I've been surrounded by people with insanely long lifespans for most of my life. It's hard not to want that too. I don't want to live forever, but there's a lot that I want to see and do, and I know it's going to still change me, but I feel like this way I have more control over myself."

Elizabeth hid her face against Tessa's shoulder for a

moment before lifting her head. "Why were you going to wait a month to tell me this?"

"There wasn't a lot of time to decide when Arcana offered the deal. But he agreed to do a month trial, basically. I wasn't going to make him a permanent part of our lives if you really didn't want him. And I thought that if I told you the whole thing you would feel obligated to say yes."

She chuckled. "You make it sound like a streaming service."

Tessa rolled her eyes. "What do you think?"

Elizabeth looked at Arcana, who was trying to do the big puppy eyes thing again. "Okay, he can stay."

Tessa pulled her in close and kissed her deeply. "Thank you."

Elizabeth smiled. "I love you." She reached down to pet Arcana, who was wagging his tail so hard it was a black blur. "And you're not so bad either." He jumped up with them on the couch, making himself comfortable. Elizabeth leaned her head against Tessa's shoulder.

"You know another benefit of this?" Tessa asked.

"What?"

"I can donate blood more than once every two months."

"I'll remember that later," Elizabeth promised, grinning as she kissed her neck.

Stacey Oakley is an award-winning author originally from Moncton, New Brunswick who became a vibrant part of the local Newfoundland writing scene. She has since gone on to independently self publish her own novels Hunter's Soul *and* The Necromancer.

GHOST PAGE
THOMAS WILLS

The wind on the water that day was, for the first time in months, biting through Will's clothes. He shuffled on the deck of his boat as another gust made its way through his jacket. "Jesus, it's a cold one."

His companion grunted. "Season's almost over. What'd you expect?"

"Just one more nice day is all. The winter hates my bones. Have I told you that, Charlie?"

"Ah, shuddup about yer bones this year, will ye? Winter's fine and dandy, its yer yapping about it that gets me going."

Will grumbled, but didn't bother answering. He turned to a small box and pulled down on a rusty, slime covered lever. "Anyhow, let's get going before I freeze my arse off."

"Sure."

The two men hauled in the mostly empty net as it was dragged up by the boat's winch. Will signaled to a third man that sat in the boat's cockpit and they sped off towards the nearby coast, the cliffs quickly rising above them as they drew near. Will was packing the net away when Charlie slapped him on the back. "Hey!"

Will was about to get angry, but Charlie's curious expression made him stop and follow his gaze. "You see that, b'y?"

"I do."

Will squinted. The afternoon light wasn't helping him make out the figure that was standing on the top of the cliff. "Is that a person?"

"I can't tell. Hey, Jones! Get me the binoculars!"

There was a shout from the cockpit. "Get em yerself! I'm drivin."

Charlie grumbled and went to rummage in the cockpit. Will stood as still as he could manage on the rocking boat. As they approached the cliff, he could see something was wrong. The shape didn't look entirely human to him. Though he could barely see, the figure's torso was much wider than it should have been. He realized with a start that the person was probably holding something, or standing in front of a sign. Charlie returned, pressing a grimy pair of binoculars to his face. "Thundering Jesus, I can't see a thing!"

"They're backwards, you oaf! Gimmie those."

They were nearly passing under the figure. Below it was nothing but frothy sea. With the binoculars, Will could see that it was indeed a person. A man, looking out over the waves. "It's a person, Charlie. Looks to be holding… a tackle box? An' a rope?"

"A what? No way ye can fish from up there."

"There isn't a rod, b'y."

Will lowered his arms and squinted again. "He was

grinning or something."

"Lemme look."

Charlie was able to get the orientation of the binoculars correct, and with a single look he declared: "Aha! It's a kid! Probably having a party or something, and we just can't see past the cliff."

They passed under the figure. Charlie tossed the binoculars onto a barrel as Will looked at him skeptically. "A party? We'd hear something."

They both listened for a minute. Charlie raised his arm to gesture dismissively when both heard a loud splash.

***

Isaac was one of the toughest looking men ever to live. He stood a towering six feet six inches, forcing him to look down on most people, with his bore-like gray eyes. Passing him on the street, people who were not familiar with the man would probably guess he worked under hard conditions, in some construction site or, as imagined by some of the youth of St. John's, as a bouncer, or even a hitman. Those who knew him were just as curious as to how he came to possess such an imposing body. He worked at a brewery as a foreman, attended church regularly and cared for his only son Nathan. When pressed on his imposing features at church functions or birthday parties, he would only laugh and attribute them to his "fine Irish breeding."

That day Isaac was not at work. No one called, or came around his house to ask where he was. The apartment he lived in was spotless. He had been cleaning it nonstop since that morning, and still he found small spots of grime or a misplaced crumb of last night's dinner on the kitchen floor. Earlier in the day, in his whirlwind of cleaning, he had entered Nathan's room to see what tidying could be done.

Apparently, before Nathan left, he had cleaned his room without being told to for the first time in his life. He had done an incredible job. All his sock drawers and bookshelves were organized, dusted, and fixed. As Isaac searched for something in the room to clean, he found himself becoming furious. The last straw came when he noticed that the fan on Nathan's computer had been cleaned out with a Q-tip. Isaac tossed his broom to the ground with a yell, cleaned it back up, and slammed the door. After a few more hours of cleaning, he was interrupted by a knock. He drew a deep breath and hurried to answer.

Two RNC officers were outside. One he recognized right away from church. Miles was his name, and his son was good friends with Nathan. "Mr. O'Sullivan?"

"Of course, Miles."

Miles averted his eyes slightly as he fumbled around in his pocket. "Yes, sorry. We're here to return your truck."

He held out an old pair of keys. The second officer spoke as Isaac took them. "You'd usually have to pick it up yourself... Miles thought it would be a nice gesture to return it to you directly..."

Miles smiled half-heartedly. "It's the least I can do, Isaac."

"Thank you. Excuse me."

He shut the door on the two and hung the keys up on a hook. The burst of energy from a few minutes ago gone, he sought the couch and slumped on it. He turned the T.V to something distracting. He heard Miles talking outside and turned up the volume.

***

The next day was a Sunday. Pushing through the dark cloud of sleep that insisted on clinging to him that morning, Isaac put on his coat and hat and walked through the streets. As usual, fog covered most of the city. Isaac was used to navigating through the fog, and never got lost. Still, he arrived late, pushing through a side door and slipping into a pew silently. He drew a few glances and even the pastor himself skipped a beat in the morning sermon upon noticing who had arrived. He continued, looking a little surprised.

After, Isaac joined a majority of the congregation for some refreshments in the church basement. He munched on a Timbit and nodded to another person giving condolences as he walked through the crowd, looking for the pastor, John. He saw the stunted man talking with a small group of elderly gentlemen in one corner.

As Isaac drew near, John excused himself from the conversation and took Isaac by the arm to a quieter part of the room. "Isaac! I'm glad to see you here. Are you well?"

"I... I'm alright. I enjoyed your sermon today."

John's face lit up. "Glad to hear it! I was struck by sudden inspiration a few days ago, but had trouble putting my ideas into words until last night."

Isaac nodded. "Indeed..."

"Hmm... I can tell that's not why you came to talk to me. What's on your mind?"

Isaac stared down at John, shifting from foot to foot,

making the much shorter man increasingly unnerved. "I have a question."

"Yes?"

"Is... Where is my son right now?"

All semblance of a smile was now gone from John's face. He still tried to add a positive note to his voice. "His soul is with our Lord." The pastor spoke as though he was trying to choose his words carefully.

Isaac nodded. "I'm just... trying to understand why. I took him to church, and to Bible study with the youth group... So why?"

Isaac's voice did not betray the fact that he was on the verge of tears. John swallowed. "Perhaps he felt like he had no choice?"

"Perhaps? My son committed a mortal sin!"

"I—I'm just being delicate."

Isaac balled his fists, but John took his arm again before he could speak. "I know you're in a bad place right now, but losing your temper won't solve anything. Come talk to me in confession once you've calmed down."

Isaac drew a deep breath and put his fists in his pockets. "I'm sorry. Good day, John."

He muscled through the crowd. John watched him until he disappeared through a doorway.

Outside, Isaac sat on the curb with his head in his hands. He held it there for a long time, trying to stop himself from slipping into a fit of rage. His hands couldn't hold it back, and he raised a fist. "Damn!"

He punched the concrete. Standing, he looked up at the crucifix that hung over the front doors. Turning his back, he crossed the street away from the church.

***

Returning home, Isaac stormed directly into Nathan's room. He began systematically undoing the cleanliness of the room, searching for something. Since no note was found in or around the truck Nathan took, Isaac assumed there had been one left in the boy's room. After ripping apart his bookshelves, books, binders, schoolwork and sketchbooks, Isaac sat down with a few of the notebooks and flipped through them. His rage drifted away as he read some of the poetry that had been scrawled on some of the pages. A couple were sappy love poems that made Isaac smile a little. One, written hastily in the final page, caught Isaac's attention.

Was that you?
I can't tell, they've put something over my eyes.
I swear I could feel your body heat nearby
But it was just my screen.
Dream.

Although cryptic, the poem instilled a sense of melancholy in Isaac. He pocketed the notebook and continued his search. Finding nothing more of importance, Isaac turned to Nathan's computer. He sat at the desk, sinking into the comfortable chair. He turned the PC on, only to be met with a lock screen. He tried a few things, like Nathan's birth date and the name of his favorite cat, but nothing worked. He kicked the machine and left the room. He spent the rest of the evening reading the notebook cover to cover. Although Isaac was not one to read poetry that often, he could tell the work was amateurish, but not without passion. The more he read, the less he recognized the words as Nathan's. If he didn't recognize the handwriting, he would have guessed that the notebook belonged to someone else.

Once he reached the final page, he re-read the poem scrawled there. He tore it out, tucked it into his wallet, and flipped to the beginning of the book once again.

***

Isaac awoke to a timid knock on the door. He almost missed it, and sat in his armchair for a minute waiting to find out if the sound was imagined. A second, louder knock had him up. He rubbed his eyes and lumbered to the door. A short, stocky boy was there. "Um, hello Mr. O'Sullivan."

"Aaron… What time is it?"

"It's like… 11:00…"

Isaac squinted against the hall light at Miles' son, Aaron. Ever since junior high, Aaron and Nathan had been inseparable. There wasn't a week that went by without Isaac coming home to the sounds of the two boy's laughter and loud video games coming from Nathan's room. Isaac yawned and rubbed his eye again. "Nathan's at school, go—"

He bit his tongue with how fast he shut his mouth. He resisted the urge to punch himself in the head. "Shouldn't you be in school?"

"I skipped."

There was a long pause between them. "You should go back."

"I don't want to. Everyone's staring at me there… I wanna see Nathan's room."

Finally finding the energy to focus on Aaron, Isaac noticed that he was almost entirely red-faced. He looked like he hadn't slept at all in two days. "Come on."

They walked silently through the house. Aaron gasped when he saw the state Nathan's room was in. "What happened?!"

"I don't know." Isaac said, turning to leave.

He listened to the sounds of Aaron digging through the mess as he picked up his phone. "Miles."

"Oh, Isaac! What can I do for you? I hope you're... doing well."

"I'm fine. Your son is here."

"My—What? Aaron? He's in school—"

"He's here. Come get him, please."

"Oh, of course... Be right there. Don't let him leave!"

The line clicked. Isaac returned to Nathan's room. Aaron was crouching beside Nathan's computer. "I called your father."

Aaron wheeled around. "Um... Yeah, that's alright..."

"What are you looking for?"

Aaron looked back at a small pile of paper that lay next to the computer. "I..."

He began to shake. "Anything."

Isaac crossed the room. "Here."

He held out the notebook. Aaron's face lit up a little. "Oh that's... it."

He held it for a moment, then slipped it into his pocket. He stood. "I'm gonna wait for my dad."

He scurried out. Isaac followed. He went into the kitchen and brought out some Oreos, putting them on the coffee table. Aaron munched on one as he perched on the couch. Isaac sat in his chair and clasped his hands together. Aaron spoke first. "I'm really sorry."

Isaac nodded. "Thank you."

Aaron shook his head. "N-no… I'm sorry f-for…"

He bit his lip and shut his eyes. Isaac furrowed his brow. "This wasn't your fault."

Aaron took a deep breath. "I should have done something different."

"This wasn't your fault, Aaron."

"Then who's was it?"

Aaron tried to meet Isaac's steely gaze, but couldn't for long. "I'm sorry."

"Aaron… do you know why Nathan did this?"

Aaron shook his head, but Isaac pressed. "You were his best friend, you must have seen something."

"I don't know."

"Please. I need to know."

"Okay, Mr. O'Sullivan… I really don't know why he would, uh… b-but he hasn't been himself lately. He told me not to tell you anything, but there's a way you can see… Uh, his password is dc_lord. Here, I'll write it down…"

Aaron quickly scrawled the password in the notebook, tore it off and handed it over. "I made a promise to him, Mr. O'Sullivan. I don't want to break it, but you deserve to know."

"Thank you…"

There was a knock on the door. Aaron sighed and stood. "Okay. Thanks for the notebook… Bye."

Aaron went to the door, and shortly after the sounds of a fierce scolding could be heard. Moments after, Miles came in, clutching his hat. "I'm sorry, Isaac, it'll—"

"Don't blame him, Miles. Just take him home and let him rest."

Miles was taken aback. He opened his mouth, but finding nothing to say he simply turned and left the apartment. Isaac looked at the paper and returned to Nathan's room. He logged onto the computer and stared at Nathan's desktop. There were some games, a couple homework folders, and some programs Isaac didn't recognize.

Isaac's own computer was scarcely used. He usually browsed a few sites, and then not that often, but it seemed like Nathan had been on a few different things.

First Isaac looked through the folders. He found some art projects and an English paper or two, but nothing out of the ordinary. Returning to the desktop, Isaac noticed a blue and white icon that was set aside from the rest of the items. He clicked it. It loaded, and took Isaac to a rather confusing screen. There were a few circles on the left-hand side that had semi-recognizable logos and symbols in them. He clicked on the top one, which had the logo for Nathan's favorite game on it. "Oh…"

It was a chat room. He watched for a moment as a few people discussed game strategies Isaac could barely understand. He was never good at deciphering text shorthand, and it didn't help that the people there seemed to be using game jargon as well. A sound made him jump. A red icon had appeared over one of the other logos. This one was simply a rainbow. Isaac clicked it. A message was highlighted in the chat room.

gigabowser said:
hey @solidus. where did you go? You missed cah night
Dreamcast Lord said:

Yoooo! Missed you!

Neon_bible said:

What's happening

oh

More messages from other users streamed in, welcoming Nathan back. They didn't know. Isaac raised his hands to his face. What should he tell them?

Dreamcast Lord said:

Hey, I was kinda worried, man.

gigabowser said:

worried XD look at Romeo over here

bottlefairy said:

he probably got mono from dream lol

Isaac frowned. The pit in his stomach decided to grow as more teasing messages streamed in. Whatever the case, this 'Dreamcast Lord' seemed to know Nathan. After watching the messages for a moment more, another sound blared over the speakers. This time, a new icon appeared on the left side of the screen. He clicked it, recognizing the icon from the messages Dreamcast Lord typed in the chat room. However, this time the message bore the username 'dc_lord'.

dc_lord said:

Hey

What's up? You were dark for two whole days lol

Isaac ignored it. What caught his eye was a message dated two days ago that sat above the new messages.

Dc_lord said:

Goodnight. Love you.

Isaac left the room. He paced his kitchen, listening to more notification sounds coming from Nathan's comput-

Acceptance

er. Isaac sat down, his head swimming with self-doubt. What had he done wrong? Were there signs? The sounds stopped, but after a good half hour of contemplation, Isaac returned to the computer. He sat back down, intent on explaining to the people of this chat room what had happened. Before doing so, Isaac noticed the banner. The title of the chat room was displayed proudly in bold white letters.

NewfieLGBT

Isaac sighed. He crouched down and ripped the computer's plug from its socket then walked out, donning his hat and jacket. He locked up and hurried out of the apartment.

Isaac strolled through the streets. He didn't usually get out much in the middle of the day, since he was usually at work. There was something unfamiliar with the way the noon sun made the world look. Isaac ignored this and hurried along his normal Sunday route. He arrived at his church, glanced momentarily at the cross above the door and pushed inside. After wandering the empty halls for a few minutes, he nearly bumped into a woman who was pulling a cart out of one of the multipurpose rooms. "Oh! Excuse me… Isaac?"

"Good afternoon."

Isaac stepped back as she pulled the cart full of plates out of the room. She shoved it down the hall a little before answering. "What can I do for you?"

"I'm looking for Pastor John. Is he still here?"

"Hmm… I'm not sure. I saw him in his office an hour ago, but he may have slipped by me. I'd check there first."

"Thank you." Isaac nodded, then turned.

"One more thing!"

"Hm?"

"My condolences."

"Thank you."

John was scribbling on a sheet of paper when Isaac arrived. "John?"

"Ah! Oh, it's you. H-hello, Isaac! What brings you here today?"

John sat up and motioned for Isaac to sit. Isaac folded himself into the small chair and crossed his legs. John waited for Isaac to speak, but it didn't seem like he had any words. "Isaac, is something the matter?"

"I've… come across something of my son's."

"Yes?"

Isaac took a long breath and explained. As he told the story, John's expression became harder and harder. Once Isaac finished, John looked almost as though he had taken a rather large shot of lemon juice. "So your son was…"

"A sodomite, yes."

John nearly sputtered. "Erm… I believe the term is 'homosexual.'"

Isaac frowned, but did not respond. John folded his hands together. "Well… If you've come here to ask me why…"

"I have come to let you know. I've solved my son's death. He was a sinner, and was already damned from the start."

"Isaac!"

"Am I wrong?!"

John sighed, standing up and peering out the window.

The sky had darkened. "It's not that simple. I've always... I believe in forgiveness."

"Sometimes you are too forgiving."

John shrugged. "Yes, many would say that. Nathan was given a test of faith. A very difficult one. One where his own body may have betrayed him. But... He is with our Lord now, and I don't think you or I could say that God will not understand why Nathan did what he did."

Isaac nodded. "... Maybe God can find it in Him to forgive Nathan and understand him, but..."

He trailed off. John sat again. "I believe you have been given a test as well. If you want answers... seek them directly."

Isaac gazed at the floor. He nodded, stood, and walked out without a word. "You're welcome." John said, his eyes falling to his desk.

When Isaac got home, he grabbed his laptop and went online. He found and downloaded the chatting service Nathan used and created an account for himself. He had some trouble finding the specific chat room from Nathan's account, but eventually he was able to join. The whole chat was notified of his arrival.

Issac has joined!
Bottlefairy:
and no, I didn't
Oh hey newblood
Gigabowser:
Yo, what's up?
Isaac gulped.
Issac:

hello

Keis:

Hi!

gigabowser:

if ya need any help or maybe 18+ verification just ping @ Dreamcast Lord he's the mod

Isaac scratched his head.

Issac:

thanks

bottlefairy:

anyway then he just tossed the whole thing in the trash. I couldn't believe it smh

Isaac placed the computer on the coffee table. He sat back and watched conversations come and go until his eyelids closed on him.

***

Isaac had decided to go back to work. His manager all but ordered him to take more time off, but Isaac wasn't liking all the freedom he had. Good, honest work was Isaac's refuge, and he took it. Even so, during the quiet hours at the brewery, Isaac's thoughts wandered. Once, on a break, Isaac spent the hour in the bathroom, watching water run from a sink. One of his coworkers came in after he was late checking back, and the sink was nearly overflowing.

At home, Isaac watched the chat room. He was learning some slang, but still most of the language eluded him. Even so, from his lurking position, he learned quite a few details about the lives of those in the server. Most of them were simply lonely and confused, looking for a lighthouse in the storm of their lives. Once in a while, Isaac even found himself pitying them. He paid particular attention to Dreamcast Lord, who ran the chat room. He was a jovial kind of guy, and always had something to say to lighten the mood. Still, he seemed distracted, Isaac could tell as much (even through text). One night, Isaac was sipping coffee and watching his screen. There was some chatting going on, and although Isaac sometimes joined in, today he was just watching. He sat up as a new message came through.

Dreamcast Lord said:

Hey guys. I gotta vent, I'm sorry.

gigabowser said:

what's up dream?

Dreamcast Lord said:

I still haven't heard from solidus. I'm getting worried.

bottlefairy said:

He's not answering his dms?

gigabowser said:

of course he isn't

Dreamcast Lord said:

No, he isn't.

I even tried calling him. He's not been online for a week…

Issac said:

hi dream. who is solidus? maybe he just left

Neon _bible said:

he wouldn't leave, not Solidus.

Dreamcast Lord said:

Yeah. @Issac, me and solidus have been dating for a couple months, so you can understand why I'm worried.

gigabowser said:

yeah, check the pins. Theyre the cutest couple on the inter-

net lol

Isaac had no idea how to "check the pins," but he probably would have gone out of his way to avoid doing so if he did.

Dreamcast Lord said:

Yeah. I miss him.

Keis said:

Don't worry, D. he'll come back. Maybe his dad took took away his phone lol

Dreamcast Lord said:

Haha, maybe. Anyone wanna vc?

gigabowser said:

nah. mic's fucked

Keis said:

maybe later

Issac said:

vc?

Keis said:

voice chat lol.

Issac said:

oh. thank you

Dreamcast Lord said:

I'll be sitting in vc1

An icon on the lower left corner of the screen changed, and Dreamcast Lord's profile picture was added under the first voice chat tab. Out of curiosity, Isaac clicked it, then "Connect to voice."

"Yo."

Isaac jumped. "…Hello."

"Wow! Hey, man, I gotta say that's the deepest voice I've heard in the server."

Dreamcast Lord's voice was rather soft, with a distinct lilt to it. He sounded young, but did not have a Newfoundland accent. "Thank you."

"So, what's up?"

"Hm? O-oh, I'm just drinking my afternoon coffee."

He took a sip. There was a soft laugh from the laptop. "I can hear that! So, you're pretty new, huh?"

"Hm?"

"To the server!"

"Oh, well yes."

"Well, welcome."

"Thank you."

There was a pause, then a sigh. "Sorry. I'm not much of a conversationalist. Especially since my boyfriend is missing."

Isaac clenched his fist. "I'm sorry to hear that."

"We met through the server, you know."

"Really." Isaac said, flatly.

Dreamcast Lord's voice was gradually becoming more wistful. "Yeah. Every server's got that couple, y'know?"

"I hadn't noticed."

The guy laughed, but before he could answer, Isaac spoke again. "And you didn't know him off the internet?"

"I do! We met five times! He's on the other side of the city, and I just recently got my license…"

"Hm. Congratulations."

He hummed. "I don't mean to pry, but you sound a lot… older than everyone else."

Isaac grumbled. "I'm not old."

"I said older! Not old. The oldest I know here is twenty-five."

"Not anymore."

"Ha! I won't ask your age, and you don't have to tell. Between us, I think it's cool."

"Hm? Why is that?"

"Y'know, you don't get many older gay guys in these servers."

Isaac's arm began to cramp, and he realized he was clenching his fist painfully hard. "I'm not—"

"...You're not what?"

Isaac sighed. "I'm not old."

"Okay, sorry. Anyway, how'd you find this server? It's not actually public anymore."

The conversation was happening rather fast, but Isaac saw an opportunity. "I found it through Nathan, actually."

There was a heavy silence on the other side. Dreamcast Lord's voice was now urgent. "You know Nate? In real life?! W-why didn't you mention this earlier?!"

"U-um, nothing like that, I... He invited me here from another chat room."

"Oh. Then, how do you know his name?"

Isaac bit his lip. "He told me."

"He never tells anyone his name..."

"He must have let it slip."

There was an awkward silence, then a sigh of frustration from Dreamcast Lord. "Sorry. I guess you don't know where he is, then."

"No, I don't."

"I-I'm just jumpy... I guess."

Isaac closed his eyes. Although he couldn't see the kid's face, he was clearly distraught. "I understand how you feel, son."

"Uh… really?"

"Yes. My wife, uh…"

"Your wife? I thought you were—"

Isaac choked up. "I can't."

"Hey, I'm sor—"

"How do you turn this damn thing off!?"

"J-just hit the red—"

Isaac clicked the red button until all sound was abruptly cut. He shut the laptop and sat back, willing the oncoming tears to recede before they eventually started rolling down his face. He pressed his hands against his eyes and wiped them away. It was the first time Isaac had cried in fifteen years.

***

Isaac found himself in bed the next morning without knowing how he got there. He was exhausted, but pure force of habit dragged him out of bed and into the shower. He skipped breakfast and went straight to work. While there, his thoughts were ugly. He muttered to God, cursing his own curiosity for bringing him to that den of sapphists and queers. After cursing for a while, he realized that his son was a part of that same group, and bottled the curses for the rest of the day.

That evening, he went straight to his laptop, intent on deleting the chat program and never returning. However, it was still open, and left for him sometime late last night was a long private message from Dreamcast Lord.

dc_lord:

Hey man. Listen, I know it's kinda late but I felt like shit after you left earlier. Like, I didn't mean to imply anything or, like, offend you I just didn't think before I spoke. I appreciate what you were trying to say… I don't know how well you knew Nathan, but he really means a lot to me and him being gone for so long is making me insensitive? Maybe? Idk. He's been in kinda a shitty place lately so I can't help thinking he just abandoned me or something. So I guess that's why I said what I said. I don't even know what I'm saying anymore. Sorry. Rant over.

Isaac clasped his hands in front of his face as he read it again. He resisted the urge to get angry, cracked his knuckles and altered his plan a little.

Issac:

i accept you apology. i have to write my own apology. i am not who you think. i knew nathen well.

Ten minutes passed before the message was seen.

dc_lord:

What do you mean?

Isaac typed and retyped a number of responses. For some reason, he couldn't put his thoughts into text. He sat back and gave the problem some pause, and realized he could better explain himself if he were looking this Dreamcast Lord fellow in the eye.

Issac:

i would rather explain it to you in person.

dc_lord:

Uh, that's a bit weird out of the blue.

Issac:

i need to tell you where nathan is. i am old, as you said, so i am not very good at using technology. i don't think i would be tactful enough in text.

dc_lord:

Who are you?

Issac:

i am nathan's father.

It took a few minutes before a response came through.

dc_lord said:

I kinda suspected. Yeah, we can meet.

A few short messages later, and a time and date was set. They were to meet at a coffee shop in the Avalon mall, during the busy hours. Isaac bid Dreamcast Lord good night, exited the program, then deleted it.

***

Isaac carefully pushed through a crowd of chattering tourists and grabbed onto a handrail before he could be pushed. He looked down at the lower floor, which was relatively empty. There were a few rides for kids along one wall, and an information kiosk in the center of the court. Lining most of the walls were a number of coffee shops, ice cream parlors and cafes. Sitting alone at one of the coffee shops, with a coffee cup on the table in front of him, was a kid. Isaac navigated to the escalator and rode it down.

As he approached, the kid looked up. He sighed. "Isaac?"

"Dreamcast Lord?"

The kid waved his hand and chuckled dryly as Isaac sat across from him. "You don't have to call me that. My name's David."

David was skinny. He wore a small leather jacket and a t-shirt with a flashy head-shot of some sort of neon animal. He perched on the chair, exuding the same nervous energy that a skittish rabbit might. "It's… Nice to meet you, David."

Isaac extended a hand hesitantly, and they shook.

David's shake was surprisingly strong. "So… you didn't bring him along…?"

Isaac shook his head. "I, uh… no."

David's hands shrank from the table. Isaac wasn't sure David was still breathing he was so still. "Is he… at home, or…"

"He passed away, David. He's dead."

David turned pure white. "…Suicide?"

"How did you… know?"

David broke down in the middle of Isaac's sentence. Going from white to red in a shockingly short time, David seemed to curl up like a leaf in a bonfire. He gave one, sharp sob, then stumbled to his feet. "'Scuse me…"

He walked away, turning a corner under a sign that pointed to that floor's bathrooms. Isaac stared at the sign, the image of David's face stuck in his mind. It bothered him. It bothered him how genuine it was.

Isaac was once at a funeral. A friend of his had died, one he had known since high school, but hadn't been in touch with for fifteen years. The guy's funeral was held a mere week after his death. His widow insisted on an open casket, and she conducted herself with the grace of a 19th century aristocrat throughout the entire service. However, when she thought no one was looking, she stood next to the casket and looked into her dead husband's face. Before Isaac came to the mall, the saddest thing he had ever seen was the face that overtook the widow in that moment. Now, though, he had the rare and not-enviable privilege of witnessing a human soul being crushed. He imagined that widow the day her husband died, and now knew how it felt to be the police officer that broke her the news.

Whatever doubts Isaac had about David were now gone, and it made him want to punch the kid in the face. He pushed that all to the back of his head when, after a good forty-five minutes, David reemerged. He took a seat, his face still red. "Sorry. I-I needed a minute."

Isaac nodded. David sniffed. "So, uh. H-how did he die?"

"Does it matter?"

"No... Not really."

Isaac folded his hands together on the table. "You didn't answer my question. How did you know?"

"Oh I didn't, uh, really know anything. I-I had a feeling."

"Was it my fault?"

The question hung over the table. David sipped his coffee before answering. "No."

The answer fared no better. David waved his hands vaguely as he sought the right words. "...It's true that, uh... He felt attacked. By the church. But I don't think that's why. Like, he knew that you don't, er, wouldn't hate him for what he is... was. D-does that make sense?"

Isaac didn't respond, so David continued. "I'm Anglican, actually... I felt hated by my religion but I talked to some people and I... don't anymore. I did the same for Nathan. T-that's why we fell in love..."

He wiped away a stray tear. "I know you don't approve..."

"I don't know if I would have approved or not."

"I really did love him, Mr. O'Sullivan."

"I believe you."

"Thank you."

Isaac leaned over the table. "If it isn't my fault, who's

is it?"

"It's... It's mine."

Isaac furrowed his brow. "What."

David began to lose whatever composure he had found in the bathroom. "T-the last time I spoke with him, he was really depressed. I-I don't know how I didn't notice it. I tried to comfort him, b-but he just blew up, he... He kept y-yelling at me to stop. I told him I was there for him and he just kept saying stop, stop, stop... 'Stop worrying. I don't want that, I never wanted that. I just wish everything was back to normal.' That was the last thing he said to me. I-I know I shouldn't have, b-but I went on this long rant about how I'd never stop and that it was my duty to help him through whatever he was going through. He just... L-left the call. I told him I loved him, and wished him a good night. Then he was gone."

He sobbed, striking the table. "I should have listened! I did exactly what he said I shouldn't, a-and now he's... I'm so sorry."

"I get it, son. We both fucked up."

David sniffed, meeting Isaac's gaze. "And...?"

"And nothing. That's the fact of it. This wasn't your fault alone. I mean, Christ almighty my own son is a complete stranger!"

David looked away, cowering slightly as Isaac's voice grew louder. "Whatever I did wrong made my own son feel so uncomfortable around me he couldn't even tell me he was in love! Or that he wrote poetry! Or that he was depressed or... Oh, hell! You just happened to be there at the worst of it!"

David tried to intervene, but once the seal was broken, nothing was able to quell Isaac's rage. "And look here, seems like we were both idiots! You didn't even know him until he was one foot in the goddamn grave! And you have the gall to say you feel guilty for something you had no control over. If you hadn't come along it would'a been some other twinky shit Nathan talked to on the internet!"

Isaac jammed a finger at himself. "I ate dinner with him every night. I helped him with his homework. I fed him and clothed him and played the role of mother and father and what?! Nathan was just dangling a puppet in front of me!"

Isaac grabbed his own face and yelled. "AARRG!"

By then David was almost afraid for his own safety. But as Isaac began sobbing as well, David sat up straight and wrapped his hands around the warm coffee cup. "I take your point…"

Isaac pulled out a handkerchief and tried wiping everything off his face. "Forgive me. I-I just snapped."

David stood and fumbled with his backpack, which was stuck on his chair. "I need to go."

He rounded the table.

"Wait!" Isaac grabbed his arm before he could run off. "Don't think… Don't think he didn't love you."

David was frozen for a moment before giving a quick nod. "You too."

"I think this is yours."

Isaac let go and took out his wallet. He handed the poem over, and David read it slowly. "Oh… T-thank you."

He turned and walked away, riding the escalator up. Isaac watched him until he was out of sight, then turned back, once again folding his hands on the table. David had left his coffee behind.

***

John was tending to the votive candles after mass. Someone had bumped them while the congregation left, and John was meticulously re-positioning each candle. He jumped when someone tapped him on the shoulder. "AH! Oh, Isaac!"

Isaac smiled apologetically as John clutched his chest. "You startled me! No, don't apologize! I'm glad to see you!"

Isaac scratched his head. "It is good to see you, too. I'm sorry I was gone so long."

John waved his hand. "Oh, you were only gone two months. I'm glad to see you back, though."

"Right…" Isaac bit his lip.

"Erm… you are back, right?"

"No. I came here to say goodbye."

"Oh? Whatever for?"

"I'm moving. Away from here."

"Oh. I see."

John nodded slowly. "I understand, Isaac. But if you've come here for permission, you don't need—"

"No! I just wanted one last favor."

"Okay. Name it."

Isaac looked to the votive candles and sighed. "Could you lead me in prayer? I'd like to say a few words. For my son."

John smiled. "Of course. Come, let us pray."

Thomas Wills is a new author from Corner Brook, Newfoundland, having been published previously in ZAUM Magazine #24.

THE PSYCHOPOMP
ANDAR WÄRJE

My terrier has psychic powers.

Laugh if you like, but I've seen it for myself. She's a West Highland terrier, all white and fluffy with pointed ears, and her name is Misty Morning; Misty for short. If you think that's dumb, well, I named her when I was twelve, so cut me a break.

I knew when she was a puppy there was something special about her. Not just because she'd sense when my mom was coming home and perch by the door of our double-wide waiting for her. A lot of dogs do that. Not even because she saved my baby brother's life, howling the house awake after he slipped his crib and wandered into a snowstorm. That could have been dumb luck and good hearing.

No, it was little things, like how she'd growl an hour before strangers came knocking, or climb into my lap to comfort me before I knew I had something to cry about. When my first boyfriend called to dump me, Misty barked at the ringing phone, fending off bad news like her fierce heart could protect mine. As my grandpa lay dying in the cabin he'd once built, Misty curled for hours in the crook of his wasted arm. I knew it was time to say goodbye when she wandered out past all my cousins and sat at my feet.

Misty never was an ordinary dog. She proved it one cold October night in the mid-90s when we encountered true evil on the back roads of our town. That was the night my childhood ended, when the border between ordinary life and the big truth beyond it grew thin, then burned away.

It was 4pm on Oct 31st, 1995, and I was fifteen years old. School was out, and I was careening down Fir Street perspiring in my parka and praying it wouldn't snow. Wind whistled up the highway chasing eddies of dead leaves, and the air smelled like ice. All I needed was one more night without the white stuff so my friend, Adi, and I could walk to Ben Neufeld's Halloween party later without freezing our asses off.

It didn't always snow on Halloween around here, but it usually did. Kids swarming the roadside bumming candy off the neighbours seemed to incite bad weather—the gods having their little laugh. We were studying Greek mythology that semester and it sounded about right to me: deities throwing punches like drunk hooligans, plunging human lives into chaos. "You think it's hot here?" read the billboard by the Baptist Church up the highway, although summer was long over, and no one did. Around here, we knew Hell was brisk, not balmy. Loneliness, fear, isolation: these were the real devils that plagued our town.

We observed many religions, all of them Christian. God was the word, and everybody said it. My single mom waitressed at the local bar and we slept in on Sundays.

Teenage missionaries threw Coke cans at me on the school bus shouting, "Get saved, dyke!" But the truth was, I believed in an invisible world as much as they did. I just wasn't as sure what it looked like.

Now, as I puffed uphill toward Adi's house, I hedged my bets by pleading with whatever gods might be listening: *Please no snow until tomorrow.* November 1st was a fine time for snow. On October 31st, it was a disaster.

Adi Forde had been my best friend since we'd met in detention in the fifth grade. I was there for reading in class (which, strangely, my teacher discouraged); Adi was there for being "mouthy" and "talking back." "Mouthy" was a thing Adi got called a lot, although I never heard her talk more than anyone else. Once we became friends, I asked her why she thought she was always getting in trouble. She shrugged, looking jaded in a way I'd never seen someone our age look before. "Racism?" she suggested.

I was shocked. Of course I'd noticed Adi wasn't white. Hers was one of two Black families in our area, so it was hard to miss them in the grocery store. I just hadn't realized adults could get mad at her for that. Adi's dad was a lawyer with an office above the laundromat, her mom sold jewelry at the Farmer's Market and her brother smoked pot and played guitar in the basement. I'd figured the Fordes were like any other family.

Now that I was older, I saw things more clearly. Most of our town was made up of two types of people: racists, and people who were so *not* racist the mere mention of a Black person could make them start apologizing. These saints would never let their children hiss the n-word at Adi during math class (like some ill-bred hicks), but they also didn't invite the Fordes over for dinner. Scared to do anything that might make someone uncomfortable, they did nothing at all, which was the same as doing something. I wasn't sure what, but I could feel it there in the air—the way Misty knew my grandpa was dying, and my boyfriend wasn't calling to ask me to the school dance.

Adi answered my knock, wearing her bathrobe and a plastic cap with flowers on it.

"Were you sleeping?" I asked as she let me inside.

"Showering." Adi pulled off the cap, letting her curls bounce free. "I want to look hot tonight."

I followed her to the kitchen where her mom was stirring something that smelled good.

"Hey Casey," said Patrice. "You girls hungry?"

We always were, so we perched at the counter while Patrice fed us chicken stew and fresh buns from the breadmaker.

"At least you'll have something in your stomachs," she said. "I doubt there'll be any real food at that party. You know I don't want you drinking, Adeline."

"*Mom*," groaned Adi.

"Yeah, spare me the song and dance. I just want to see your head move. No. Drinking."

We nodded, waiting until she turned to roll our eyes at each other.

After that, we went to Adi's room to get ready. She headed for her closet while I flopped on her bed, staring up at her Green Day poster instead of watching her get undressed.

"I have nothing to wear," she said, flicking hangers so fast they sounded like wind-chimes in a hurricane. "Look at this shit. They won't let me buy *anything* until I get my grades up."

"That sucks," I said, not looking.

From the corner of my eye, I caught a flash of bare, brown skin as Adi shed her robe. I knew she didn't care if I saw her naked (we'd been changing together forever), but I was scared of the little flips my tummy had begun doing. It had started last summer when I'd seen her in a two-piece—white with green clovers, its wet cups clinging to her newly rounded chest. I had no boobs to speak of and was mesmerized by the sudden appearance of hers. When I looked, a hollow ache bloomed in my own chest like hunger. So instead, I focused on the fried tips of Billie Joe Armstrong's hair—a shape I was getting to know so well, I saw it on my eyelids at night.

"*Hello*, Casey? Are you gonna help or what?"

Peeking sideways, I saw Adi upside down, half-buried in the laundry hamper. She'd put on her favourite gray Calvin Klein underwear set, which was better than nothing. In the spirit of teamwork, I went over to help.

Together we soon came up with a plan. Adi would look hot (as required) in ripped jeans and an only slightly stained Nirvana tee. I'd be invisible in loose overalls with a plaid flannel shirt thrown over-top. We'd need snow-boots for the walk, but stashed our Converse in our backpacks: hers sunshine yellow, mine classic black high-tops.

Then, I sat on the floor flipping through our shoebox of mix-tapes while Adi did her make-up. We had all the latest hits—minus the first few seconds it took to press record on the radio. We didn't really get the lyrics to "Zombie" by the Cranberries, but screaming along with Dolores

O'Riordan sure got us in the mood for the party.

We set out around 7pm. The sun had gone down at 4:30, so it was well and truly dark. Faint orange street-lights strained through the murk, illuminating nothing. Most kids were done trick-or-treating; we watched the stragglers get hauled indoors as the sky turned starless, thick with clouds that would probably break open soon, assailing us with snow.

The Neufeld farm was out on Old Marshall Hill. To reach it, we'd have to walk a mile up the highway, then turn north onto a rutted gravel track with no road sign. We'd follow this awhile, past ranchland dotted with cows and fallen-down fences. Then, we'd cut west across an overgrown field toward the forest. When we came to a deep ravine, we'd cross an old logging bridge over a creek that sank low in the summer and churned high and wild all winter. Everything the far side of that bridge was Neufeld land.

Both our moms had offered to drive us. We wanted to go alone. These hills and hidden shortcuts belonged to us. We'd grown up here, racing our bikes against the wind, carving our names on the landscape. Darkness didn't de-ter us, or the weather. We were fifteen and braver than we'd ever be again in our lives.

My mom's one rule was that we bring Misty, so we stopped by my house to get her. She bounced ahead up the highway, her big satellite ears tuned to sounds we couldn't catch.

"Stay close!" I said, over the *whoosh* of trucks passing.

"You think Dave's going to be there?" Adi scrunched her hair self-consciously. She'd ditched her hat the second we were out of Patrice's sight.

"Who cares," I muttered, soft enough that my words disappeared under a passing Chevy.

We reached our turn-off, stepping from the busy highway onto a deserted dirt road that stretched forever into the darkness. Misty led the way across the cattle-guard.

"Hey," said Adi when we got to the other side.

I turned to see her fumbling in her backpack. Grinning, she produced a mickey of Baileys and waved it at me. Her brother was nineteen and would sometimes bootleg for her when he bought a six-pack.

"Cool," I said, and held out my hand.

Adi took the first sip, smacking her lips and making a loud *ahhhh* sound before passing it to me. The taste made my eyes water.

Misty was a streak of white in the roadside. We switched on our flashlights, casting wide arcs of light into the gloom.

"I'm freezing," said Adi.

"Put your hat on," I suggested, tugging mine down.

Adi gave me the finger.

We paused for more Baileys; its burning sweetness warmed my insides, making me brave.

"Why do you like Dave, anyway?" I asked, kicking a rock from my path.

Adi looked at me sideways. "What's wrong with him?"

"I don't know. He's an idiot?"

She snorted. "Not everyone gets straight A's, Casey."

"I'm not talking about *school*," I started, and then froze in my tracks.

Misty had stopped by the side of the road and was staring into the darkness. She sent a sharp bark ringing over the silent fields—a warning to whatever else might be out there.

"It can't be a bear, right?" whispered Adi. "Could she fight a cougar?"

"No," I snapped. "Shut up and let me listen."

We stood silent for a minute, hearing the wind sigh in the grass. Then, Misty sniffed and started walking again.

"Probably a coyote," I said. "She talks to them sometimes."

Releasing our breath, we followed her, gladly moving past the awkward topics of Dave and our potential dismemberment by wild animals. The level in our bottle kept dropping, and we were hooting and holding onto each other by the time we reached the broken snake-fence at the edge of McMasterson's field. The sight of the rotten logs leaning on the ground sobered us up.

"Oh shit," said Adi. "I forgot we had to cross his land."

"Who cares?" I said. "It's just an old farm. It's not like it's haunted."

Adi's eyes shone big in the dark. "Don't we have to pass his house? How do you know that shit isn't haunted?"

I looked at Misty who was sitting on my boot. "She'd tell us. You know she's psychic."

"Duh," said Adi. "That's how I know it's haunted! She hated that old creep."

It was true. Roy McMasterson had been a local celebrity—a rich rancher who'd glad-handed everyone from the Mayor to the Ladies Auxiliary. For years he'd been a fixture at every church picnic, graduation, and barn dance, cutting the ribbon on every little ceremony we had. That's because his money usually paid for it. He'd swagger around, denim shirt straining over his belly, cowboy boots clacking. Everyone had loved him. Well, mostly.

Years ago, Adi and I had been helping Patrice sell jewelry at the Farmer's Market when McMasterson had slouched over to us like John Wayne, whistling through his teeth.

"Hey there girls," he said, grinning in the shadow of his big Cattleman hat. "Bit young to be working for a living, ain't you?"

"This is my mom's table," explained Adi. "She had to run to the bank."

McMasterson gnashed the wad of tobacco in his cheek. "Ain't she lucky to have a hard worker like you, then?" He said, staring at Adi. "I wish I had ten of *you* on my ranch."

Adi's smile disappeared. She started trembling, like a tuning fork struck at an old familiar pitch. I frowned, trying to figure out what McMasterson had just said.

"Can we help you with something, *sir*?" is what I was working up the nerve to say when Misty trotted out from behind the table.

"Now, who's this?" said McMasterson, hooking his thumbs in his belt and squatting down to her level.

"Misty," I said automatically.

Hearing her name, my dog pricked up her ears a little higher.

"Cute dog," he said, and reached out his hand.

Misty lunged, snarling viciously as she snapped her teeth at his approaching fingers.

"Misty!" I cried, and seized her collar.

Luckily, McMasterson was nimbler than he looked. He danced out of her reach, cursing. Then he dusted himself off, snorting to show he hadn't really been scared.

"*Whoa* there," he said, like Misty was a mare he was bringing to heel. "Got a temper on her, don't she?"

"I'm so sorry," I said. "She's usually friendly."

"Keep that thing on a leash," he said, eyeing Misty like she was a sewer-rat instead of a soft, mystical being. "I see strays on my land, I shoot 'em."

He hawked a spurt of tobacco juice at our feet, hitched his pants and sidled away, whistling while his boots kept time on the sidewalk.

"What the hell?" said Adi.

I shook my head, staring at McMasterson's broad, retreating back.

"He gives me the creeps," Adi shuddered.

She wasn't the only one. Perfectly calm now that McMasterson was gone, Misty let me scoop her up and sniff her fur for comfort.

"I know, that was so weird."

Weird was the only word we had for it back then. Now, I wondered.

"Do you think she sensed something about him?" I let my gaze drift past the ruined fence into the darkness.

"If she's psychic, she's psychic," Adi pointed out.

"But we have to go this way. If we stay on the road, it'll take hours."

"I know."

"He's dead," I said. "He can't do shit. Hey, there's no such thing as ghosts, right?"

Adi winced. Neither of us officially believed in ghosts, but we didn't do stupid shit like play with Ouija boards or say Bloody Mary in the mirror, either. If that crap happened at sleepovers, me and Adi took a walk.

"I guess," she said, hoisting her backpack. "Yeah, fuck it. Let's get this over with."

She swung one foot over the fallen snake fence, then the other. I followed with Misty behind me. Together we forded the overgrown field, flattening a brief path that vanished as the tall grass sprang up behind us.

"It's so creepy being here on Halloween," said Adi, edging closer to me. The beams of our flashlights swung and merged.

"They should charge for this shit." I forced a laugh that died beneath the vast, black vault of the sky. "Two bucks to see the closet where old man McMasterson hung himself."

"I thought he used a rifle," Adi said.

"Whatever. It all got hushed up because he was richer than God."

"Totally," said Adi.

"This town is so messed up. Shit always goes away if it's the *right kind of people*."

"I know. I can't wait until we're old enough to leave this fucking place."

"Remember that guy who disappeared last fall?" I asked. "It was like...*who*? People just forgot he ever existed."

"Oh *yeah*," said Adi. "That crazy dance teacher. Didn't

he just, like, vanish?"

"Supposedly. He left class one night and *boom*—never seen again!"

"That sucks," said Adi. "I liked him. He dressed like Prince."

"He did a dance to Purple Rain!" I cried, waving the Baileys. "He was cool as shit! That's the problem. Cool people can't survive here. It's like…an oxymoron."

"So's your face," said Adi. "Give me that before you finish it."

A vast shape grew on the horizon as we neared the McMasterson house. Its details emerged slowly from the gloom—all sharp gables and blank, staring windows.

"How about that guy who shot his wife?" I went on. "Or she shot herself, according to the cops?"

"Ew, that gross motorcycle dude?" said Adi.

"Yes! He dated my mom! He'd show up on his gross motorcycle looking for her. I'd hide behind the couch so he couldn't see me through the window."

"Are you kidding me?" cried Adi. "That's disgusting!"

"I know! He wouldn't stop coming around. He banged like half the women in this town. Then he shot his wife— or his ex-wife."

"Why didn't Misty bite *his* ass?"

"We didn't have her back then, or she *would* have! She'd have smelled his creepy ass a mile away and bit his dick off!"

We dissolved into giggles, leaning on each other while Misty watched us patiently.

All the time, the abandoned house crept closer,

crouching on the skyline like it couldn't wait for a couple of dumb kids to stagger up to it. At first, we didn't hear Misty growling because we were laughing so loud. Also, we were drunk.

"Hey," Adi said suddenly, seizing my arm.

I looked down and saw Misty poised in front of us again, hackles bristling. This time, she was staring straight at McMasterson's house.

"What is it, girl?"

I tried to bring her into focus, but she stayed a pale smudge in my wandering flashlight beam. I heard the sound she was making, though—a low, whining growl that made the hairs on my neck stiffen.

"Let's go," said Adi. "I don't want to be here."

I nodded. We needed to cut into the trees now, anyway. With a shaking hand, I snapped my fingers for Misty. She ignored me.

"Misty!" I hissed. If there was something in that house, I didn't want it hearing us.

No response.

"Fuck, fuck, fuck," chanted Adi softly.

"Misty, come!" I said as sternly as I could.

But Misty had other ideas. She shot into the darkness, disappearing among the tall grass before I could even try to stop her.

"What the fuck?" I said, staring after her.

"Oh my god!" said Adi. "Where did she go?"

I clenched my fists, fighting tears. "I don't know."

"I want to *go*," said Adi.

But I hardly heard her. I had already taken off running.

"Casey, come back!"

"I can't just leave her!"

"Shit!" Adi swore, but stumbled after me. "Let's find her and get the hell out of here."

But we couldn't find her. We thrashed around in the grass calling her name, but no wet nose popped out to meet us. The closer we got to the house, the tighter the night crowded in on us. Thick clouds lowered, releasing the first frenzied snowflakes onto our heads.

Suddenly, a sharp bark rang out. We swung our heads, trying to figure out where it had come from.

"Misty!" I yelled, not caring who heard me. I wanted my dog back.

Adi grabbed me again. *"Casey!"* she moaned, with the same shrill terror as when she saw a spider in the bathtub.

I turned to see her staring up at the house. Following her gaze, I saw nothing but the shadows under the eaves, where the roof's ornate angles created wells of darkness deeper than the night. I was about to ask Adi what her problem was when I saw it: something in the darkness moved. No, the darkness *itself* moved, sliding like an eel from its cave of jagged gables. One of the shadows was creeping along the wall toward us.

"Oh fuck," I breathed.

An unearthly howl split the night. I still couldn't tell where it came from, the sound muffled by the swirling sleet.

"What *is* that?" cried Adi, trying to pull me backward.

I twisted free. "I have to find Misty!"

The shadow thing—whatever it was—prowled the side of the house as deftly as any spider in Adi's tub. It had a quick, furtive way of moving, slipping between shadows so I almost lost it in the dark. At the sound of our voices, it stopped moving; even squinting, I could hardly make it out. Then a huge, misshapen head peeled itself from the wall and probed into the night like it was listening for us.

"Misty!" I screamed as loud as I could.

A white blur shot past me.

"There she is!" shouted Adi.

She took off, trailing my dog around the side of the house toward the back pasture. It was out of our way, not to mention farther onto McMasterson's property. But it was Misty. I sprinted after Adi, not even looking back over my shoulder.

The house was so big it took a couple minutes to get around. Out back, past the sagging porch and tractor corpses, we found Misty digging in a patch of frozen dirt.

"Misty!" we both yelled, rushing over to her.

She ignored us, sniffing the ground so hard she sprayed dust into her whiskers. I aimed my flashlight between her paws, trying to see what the big deal was.

"Casey!" said Adi.

I squinted at the ground. Something pale winked back at me from a fissure in the hard-packed earth. "What the hell…"

"*Casey!*" said Adi, even louder this time.

She spun me to face the house, where I saw what she was screaming about. The shadow thing had slid up onto the roof to meet us.

It was visible nothing. Darkness hunched like a gargoyle against the snow-pocked sky. It teetered on thick, crooked haunches, tossing its shapeless head like it was sniffing the wind for us. With a piercing tea-kettle shriek, it caught our scent and came careening down the roof toward us.

"Run!" I screamed.

We pelted toward the forest. Misty sent big, resounding barks back at whatever was chasing us.

"To the bridge!" shouted Adi.

"We're too far past it! We'll get trapped in the ravine!"

"No, we won't! Remember that tree across the creek? We can use it!"

"But it's snowing," I said. "It'll be too slippery!"

"We have no choice!"

She was right. I couldn't see the shadow thing, but I could feel it lurching along behind us in the dark. At the edge of the pasture, a barbed-wire fence rose up in our path, blocking the forest. Luckily this wasn't our first shortcut; we had a system. First we threw our backpacks over; then I bent and grabbed the bottom rung between its gnarled barbs, hauling upward until there was a gap big enough for Adi to crawl under. From the other side of the fence, she held the wire for me. Misty came last, slithering on her belly so she wouldn't snag her fur.

Ten steps into the trees, the forest sheered off into a steep ravine. Far below, we heard the rushing creek. There was no time for caution. We hurled ourselves over the edge.

For a minute, we were in free-fall, then we hit the hillside on our butts. Filthy snow sprayed up around us as we skidded down, flailing like salmon in a waterfall. We hit the bottom hard, our boots scrambling on the loose soil of the bank. I snagged Misty's collar a second before she disappeared into the churning water.

"Do you we think we lost it?" I gasped, peering into the forest above our heads.

"*Lost* it?" said Adi. "What *is* it?"

I shook my head, still squinting upward. Snow surged into my eyes.

"Let's go," urged Adi.

It took us ages to reach the fallen tree, hacking through bracken and skinning our knees on ice-slicked boulders. The big ponderosa pine had once clung to the creek's western slope; seared by lightning, it had let go and tumbled into the ravine. It lay now with its head in the water, the frills of its needle skirt dancing in the current like lakeweed. Just past it was the old logging bridge. Its pilings, dark with rot, almost touched the tree's lower branches.

From here we couldn't scale the rocky slope to the bridge. But, if we used the fallen tree to crawl out ten feet over the water, we might be able to grab one of the trestles and pull ourselves up. Last summer, fueled by boredom and Big Gulp Slurpies, we'd leaned down from the bridge and thought the climb looked easy enough. It didn't look half as easy from this angle, and it wasn't August anymore. Everything was icy. Everything was wet.

A loud *snap* in the underbrush made us jump.

"Go!" said Adi. "We have to risk it!"

I turned off my flashlight and threw it into my backpack. Without it, the snowy landscape looked stark and as ghost-lit as a dream. Gripping the rough, slimy tree trunk with both hands, I heaved my leg over it. The only way I could see surviving this was to straddle the thing like a horse and scoot my butt along it. Slivers and wet undies weren't fatal. Falling into the creek easily might be.

Misty had her paws up on the tree, trying to follow me.

"Give her to me," I said.

Adi boosted her into my arms. Undoing my coat, I stuffed her down the front of it; her little face peeked out under my chin as I zipped her up inside.

Traversing the fallen pine took all my concentration. With the heels of my hands, I boosted myself along its long, bare trunk until I was suspended out over the water. The creek crashed below me, slapping my ankles and streaming into my boots. The tree's coarse bark tore into my clothes, then my skin. I barely felt it. By the time I'd gone five feet, my whole body was numb. I was shivering so hard it felt like convulsions. I clenched my teeth, pressed my nose into Misty's wet fur, and kept going.

The tree bounced as Adi climbed on behind me. Frigid water surged over my knees. The further I went along the tree, the more unsteady it felt. The narrowing trunk sagged beneath me, my legs getting caught in the lower branches. Just when I thought the tree would snap, plunging us all into the heaving current, I looked up and saw it.

Right there in front of me was the bridge's first trestle. I was close enough to touch it.

I heard a faint sound; my ears strained to catch it over the thundering of water. It was music—hollow and strange—like the wind was singing, or the waves were, luring travelers to wreck against the shore.

Don't listen.

I reached out and grasped the trestle, giving it a shake to test its soundness. It was damp and half-rotted, but still solid enough.

I cranked my head around to see Adi scooting along the tree. Nothing was behind her. Still, that faint, faraway music swelled louder, like a tide. Whatever was chasing us, we hadn't lost it. It was rising all around us.

"Do you hear that?" I shouted, but the wind snatched my voice.

I'd had dreams like this before; fleeing something I could sense but couldn't see. My alarm always blared before it caught me. Now the only noise in my head was water and that weird, whistling melody. That's what it was, I realized; whistling. Like old man McMasterson keeping time with his boots on the sidewalk. But old man McMasterson was dead.

Forget ghosts and zombies. The problem facing me was real. Somehow, I had to lean out from this tree and swing myself up onto that trestle without plunging into the creek. If I waited much longer, I'd be too weak with cold to haul myself up there.

"Hold on tight," I whispered against Misty's cheek.

I threw myself toward the horizontal beam of the trestle, flinging my arms wide to catch it in an awkward bear-hug. I heaved myself sideways off the tree. My legs pitched into frigid water, trailing out behind me as I clung to the bridge. Adi shouted something I didn't hear. It took everything I had to wrench my right leg free from the current and throw it over the beam. Twice I missed, shredding my knee on the vertical piling as my foot crashed back down into the water. My shoulders screamed as I twisted away from the piling, trying not to crush Misty. Finally, I managed to hoist my leg over the beam. Arms shaking, I dragged myself up out of the water, collecting a trail of ragged splinters down each leg as I went.

"Fuuuuuuck!" I screamed at the sky. Inside my jacket, Misty licked my neck.

"Fuck *yes*!" yelled Adi, who was right behind me.

I hugged the piling, not wanting to let it go. "I can't do this. It's too cold."

"Keep m-moving," said Adi. She was shivering worse than I was, and her legs were still in the creek. "Misty f-first."

I looked upward. The main platform of the bridge was within reach, but I saw what she meant. If I pulled myself up by both arms, I could muscle my chest onto the deck and flop the rest of the way on my belly—but not without squashing Misty beneath me. Tightening my legs around the beam, I put a hand inside my coat and stroked Misty's ears. I had to be brave for her sake. Bracing my shoulder against the piling, I reached both hands inside my jacket and pulled Misty free. I held her warm, wriggling body against me.

"I love you," I whispered fiercely into her fur.

Before I could think about it, I lifted her high and lobbed her as hard as I could at the bridge like a football.

She yelped, and for a second I was sure I'd thrown her right over the bridge and off the other side. The momentum of the toss had sent me slamming into the piling in front of me with rib-cracking force. Wheezing, I craned backward to peer up at the bridge.

"There she is!" cried Adi, and my heart started beating again.

Misty's wet muzzle had popped over the side; she frowned down as if wondering what was keeping us.

I followed her as fast as I could. Stretching up, I gripped the lip of the bridge deck with one hand, then the other. I wasn't the best in gym class, but I wasn't the worst; I could do three pull-ups, and I only needed one. It was awful, hanging there by my hands with my legs suspended over the creek. But then my head was level with the bridge deck. I could see Misty's paws on the boards.

"You can do it!" cried Adi from below me.

Inch by inch, I slid my hand forward along the deck until I found a gap between the worn wooden boards. Digging my fingers in, I dragged one sore rib at a time up over the lip of the platform. My coat caught on the railing above me, then tore free. I sobbed when I realized I was actually on the bridge, lying flat on my face on the foul, creosote-smelling wood. I could have kissed it.

"Go Casey!" screamed Adi, like we really were in gym class and I'd just scored the winning touchdown.

Misty jumped around me as I hobbled to my feet. I leaned gingerly over the rotten guard rail, watching Adi fight her way up onto the trestle. I turned my head and looked along the bridge in both directions. The overgrown road trailed off into weeds and darkness on either side. I couldn't tell if the shadows moved, or just the sleet.

Getting Adi onto the bridge was easier with both of us. Lying flat on my belly, I grabbed the railing and hung my other arm down for her to hold onto. When she was safely up, we lay panting on the bridge deck for a bit. The snow sifted onto our faces.

"I can't believe we just did that," said Adi. "I thought we were gonna die."

"It was your idea!" I said, whacking her.

We both laughed weakly. It made my ribs hurt, but my heart lighten. I was still smiling when Misty stiffened, the hair on her back prickling under my fingers. With her eyes fixed on the far end of the bridge, she bared her teeth and let out a savage growl. Then somehow we were on our feet.

With a *thud* that shook the old bridge to its foundations, the shadow thing came crashing down in front of us. We screamed, clutching each other and backing against the railing. The creek roared. Sleet streaked into our faces. Misty lunged in front of us, barking her head off. The horrible thing had appeared from nowhere, blocking our path onto Neufeld land.

Close up, it was worse than ever. It towered above us, sniffing the air. Two ragged craters gaped where its eyes should be. Its crooked jaw hung wide, displaying rows of cracked teeth. Its hulking limbs bled claws of smoke into the darkness.

Tearing off my backpack, I fumbled through it until I felt my flashlight. I switched it on and aimed it directly at the thing. The light died in my hand like a snuffed candle. That's when the music started up again, weirdly cheerful in the face of our naked terror. The shadow thing was whistling, sending its strange shadow song into the night.

"It's McMasterson," said Adi.

"Fuck that," I said. "He's dead."

"Yeah, and this is what he looks like under all that

cowboy shit."

Adi's eyes gleamed with moonlight. I looked up and saw the clouds had parted above our heads. Stars shone beyond the swirling snow, seeming a world away.

"What does it want?" I cried, clinging to Adi.

"I don't know. Keep us here? Eat us?"

The shadow thing lurched forward, trembling the boards under our feet. It was maybe ten steps from us now, whistling and licking its slavering jaws. The shrill, wet sounds made my ears ache.

"Leave us alone!" screamed Adi.

"Don't make it madder!" I sobbed, pulling at her.

She rounded on me. "Why not? That's not a person anymore. *We* are!"

I stared at the terrible thing before us. Could this be what was left after a person was gone? Had there ever really been a person there to begin with?

"Now *I'm* mad!" shouted Adi. Her black hair whipped across her face. "I've got frostbite and bruises and slivers in my ass! We're missing the party. For this bullshit! You're picking on a couple of *children*, man! Does that make you feel big?"

The shadow thing roiled like a storm, growing bigger in all directions. Its massive claws raked the air. It gnashed its jaws like it could already taste us.

"What if it's not real?" I said. "We were drinking. Maybe we're seeing things."

We staggered as it took another step toward us.

"It feels pretty real," said Adi grimly.

"Misty sees things we can't. Maybe she's showing us a vision!"

"Or she's showing us what's really there. Why don't

you fuck off!" Adi yelled, showing the thing her middle finger. "Go die for real in that haunted old house of yours!"

Again the shadow thing shuddered, growing outward. I could see through it now in some places. One bright star winked in its mouth; the old logging road ran away through its belly.

That's what will be here when it's gone, I thought. *Stars. Water. Summer lightning that brings trees down from the hill.*

A strange calm started coming over me. I remembered the world past this night, past my numb feet and torn knees and the horror of what was happening. I remembered the shape of Billie Joe Armstrong's hair, and the green clovers of Adi's swimsuit.

Misty charged forward. I screamed her name, but she didn't stop. She ran straight at the thing, shooting between its haunches and circling back around. Then she charged at it again.

The shadow thing snapped and wheeled, swiping its huge claws at my brave little dog. Dark mist spilled from it, pouring over the sides of the bridge. I stared on in horror, sure I was about to see Misty's tiny body being flung into the icy inferno below.

That's when I noticed she was leading the thing away from us. Every time she darted forward, she drove it back a little farther. It flinched and shrieked, its shrill howls harmonizing strangely with Misty's.

"Holy shit," said Adi. "She's chasing it off!"

The shadow thing kept lashing out, but its limbs were losing substance. Its heavy blows dissolved before landing on Misty's fur. Still, I could see my dog was tiring. Her pink tongue lolled; her flanks were heaving.

It was a weird time to think about school, but I did. We'd been reading that week about Hercules—the strongest man alive. Yet even he'd needed help to defeat the nine-headed Hydra. Every time he cut off one head, another grew back. Evil regenerated, spreading and multiplying until even the strongest man couldn't defeat it. Our town was plagued by many-headed demons: silence, hatred, fear of the unknown. Each one of us could only do so much to fight back. Adi and Misty were doing their part. I was just standing there, watching.

"I like girls!" I shouted toward the worst nightmare I'd ever known. "I think I might be gay, and I'm scared about it!"

Adi turned to look at me. She reached and took my wet, gloved hand in hers.

"It's okay," she said.

And it was. Between the spreading tendrils of the shadow thing, snow flurries burst through. The road opened before us.

Misty pelted ahead, right down the centre of the scattering shadows. She made for the far end of the bridge, and the shadow thing followed. Turning from us, it trailed after her down the platform, leaking mist. When Misty reached the road, she turned once and looked back in our direction. Then she leapt off the bridge onto Neufeld land and disappeared into the darkness.

"Misty!" I screamed.

But she was gone.

The shadow thing hovered at the end of the bridge for a minute, and then dwindled into the night. Tendrils of dark mist dispersed among the trees along the logging road. Soon there was nothing but the slanting snow.

"Misty!" I cried again.

Nothing came back but the sound of water. We stood there in silence, holding tightly to one another's hands. Tears seared the back of my throat.

At long last, a pale shape appeared in the distance. It shot toward us, a furry missile on a collision course. We raced to meet it, our boots skidding on the icy bridge deck. We met at the edge of the trees. My dog hit me so hard, she knocked me backward into the snow. I lay there and let her lick my face while Adi collapsed beside us.

Fat flakes careened toward us, silhouetted black in the moonlight.

"Should we skip the party?" I said.

Adi laughed. "Well I don't know. How's my hair at this point?"

Ten minutes later, we were in the front hall of Ben Neufeld's house letting his sister make us tea while we used the phone to call my mother. The house was bright and warm, smelling of spilled beer and pizza. Any kids still left at the party had gone down to shoot off fireworks on the frozen lake; their shouts floated up to us where we sat wrapped in blankets by the door.

Finally, my mom's van rattled up the driveway. We told her and anyone else who asked, that we took a short-cut and fell in the creek. We caught shit for trying to cross a fallen log in the icy weather, but mostly our parents were relieved. We did a dumb thing, but we were home.

Adi slept over that night. We lay in my bed with Misty between us, still damp from her bath.

"I saw something behind that house," I whispered. "Where Misty was digging."

"What?" asked Adi.

"I don't know… Bones, maybe?"

Our eyes met in the dark.

"Should we tell your mom?" said Adi.

"She'd never believe it. Besides…it was probably just a cow."

We lay still for awhile, until I wondered if Adi was asleep.

"What you said back there," she whispered, stroking Misty's fur. Our fingers grazed a little as we both petted her. "About…liking girls or whatever."

"Uh-huh." I held my breath.

"I…already knew that," said Adi. "I guess I was just waiting for you to say something."

"Oh," I said. "Okay."

"Yeah," said Adi.

"Cool," I said.

In the comfortable dark of my room, the sounds of our breathing mixed, getting slower and slower. Soon, we were all asleep. Misty snored, but I didn't mind. The sounds reminded me of rolling thunder, or a rushing creek.

As it turned out, I was wrong about the bones. They didn't belong to a cow; they belonged to the missing dance teacher. When spring came, coyotes finished the digging Misty had started and soon the story was spreading like wildfire. Everyone knew someone who knew firsthand what happened. No one said "gay men" or "murder-suicide" but they said other, crueler words that meant that. Folks claimed they'd always known there was something wrong with that old rancher; if they'd only guessed how queer he was, they'd never have let him around their children.

Only Adi and I never spoke about it. We finished high

school and moved to different cities, saving pennies from our first jobs to call each other long distance once a week. Misty lived with me in my tiny apartment, snoozing on my lap while I wrote papers into the small hours. She loved watching the dogs on the street below our window, and always warned me when the mailman was due to arrive.

When I met my first girlfriend, Liz, Adi was the one I phoned to scream about it. I pictured her in her dorm room all the way across the country, doing her happy dance. She was studying hard to get into med school. Soon, she couldn't manage a phone call every week. We talked every second week instead, then every month or so. At Christmas, we'd hang out in the Fordes' basement drinking wine and singing old hits until we laughed like teenagers again.

Sometimes, when I couldn't sleep, I thought about that night on the bridge. Lying in bed with Misty under one arm and Liz under the other, I would remember the shrill whistling, the roaring creek, and the hulking shadow against the sky.

In school that year, we'd learned about Psychopomps—mystic creatures who guide lost souls between the worlds of the living and the dead. It made sense to me. Some barriers are too hard to get through on your own.

You can get lost, crossing bridges. I had been lucky. I never had to go alone.

Andar Wärje is an author living on stolen Coast Salish territory. He was previously published in "Hopeful Materials: A Nordic Trans Man's Response to Ibsen," The Malahat Review, Spring 2021.

ABANDONED LAND-CHILD
DAZE JEFFERIES

There are many names for my queer kind. Ocean keep-
ers, fathom fairies, and the broken blue-skinned whore-
fish. Together we come and go apart for centuries on these
haunted shores, holding the breath of black water in our
gills. Will you listen for a moment, old friend?

When I was born, there were fishy forms all around,
filling the void of St. John's Harbour. Merchant maids and
working girlies plied their trade as the heavens rained
down. Mid-September and the seawater warmed my
cold new flesh for a day or more. Then, when the glittering blue light filled my lifeblood I was ready to swim.
Through centuries of loss and a curse undone, I inched
my way closer to all other kin. Turning face first into the
forgotten. I didn't have toes or a tongue to suck on, hardly
a tiny stump of skin. Monstrous only in your eyes. So I
grew my own, darkling brown and buried like the bottom
I belong to. Here there are no words for gender. But layers of scum and sexless beings—breathless blowholes and
boney hooks and body-holding belly-humps. I can grow
another feeler just like a sunken star. I can show you how
to linger. Hidden with the octolovers.

Birth looks different from the drop-off. Blood and

brine fold into each other, honouring our mothers and feeding the ancients. Oceanic plastics wrapped around their hearts and my placenta dear. When I was born, another fathom fairy made her passage to the age-old surface. Each of us are given 88 years to survive the ecology of human violence. Lowly tone of her exhale, slow sea crossing over and airless. Torso bending back toward me, soul eternal floating in the fog. Hard to imagine just how grey. The world above becomes an archive. Bubbles whispered in the night that I would move to land like her. But of course, a cost remains. No returning, only distance. Held by ghosts of men at sea who had no right to eat our offspring. Mother took the fish from the goddamned water and put them somewhere safe and sound. Another kind of gaping place for dregs of time to start anew. Cod moratorium or get the hell out. The only way to keep your lost attention.

88 years of history escape as I take my turn to find the discarded. Loveform melancholic, settled in the coastal flow. Boy-girl suffering a youth of silence where the gentle shadows go. Blonde hair sun-bleaching as the rush of whiteness comes in waves, with unrelenting force to break against her secret beach. Never to be wrecked by the presence of bullies. Each evening she waits at the border, eroding earth and ocean, heavenly immortal, longing to be swept offshore. Dreaming of a moonwards witness in the flesh. I am what is left of a young imagination. Water angel promising to keep her safe. Abandoned land-child needing a friend, a true love, a language lost to tideways. Body betraying and island-bound.

What she needs is to learn some gibberish, first uttered in the early twentieth century. Find some hope among the beach stones. Hold a beating heart on the tip of her tongue, as paper epochs soak and tear into shards I couldn't save in linear time. All she cannot read or know. At home in the Bay of Loneliness. The shrill of dial-up digital connections in one earhole and out the hurting other. Portal won't translate postmodern plaintext, downloading slower than a salted slug. Feet in the sea foam, shriveled and smelly, she throws her daddy's desktop into the cove. Shockwaves sting like an electronic tentacle. Now all photos from her past have been expunged. Merciless and wishy-washy. Weight of absence on her heart. From gillnet to interweb, everything in ruins. Lacking the millennium on her side. 2 + 2 + 2 more ages. Waters widen with the mourning. Secrets spill from my soft fish lips, standing at a cliff's edge, praying for the pain to end.

This is where I find her fragile. Mermaid maternal and a pubescent phantom. Share with her a tenderness that lives in the Atlantic churning. When I was born, I encountered a current washing me wayward toward my purpose. Deep figuration of a child's desire. Mommy, please undo the devastation. Peach fuzz growing coarse, the lengthening of vocal cords. She says that she would rather be covered in scales. Let the water unevolve her. Fin over finger, dorsal displacement. Baby, it is better still to be your own creation. By and by a deep sea spirit she becomes, who drifts with me on the back of a tranimal. I tickle her until she learns to laugh again, give her my word that I will stay right here in the infinity symbol. Sheltered together. Fishy and ephemeral. Outmigrations under the blue.

Daze Jefferies is an author and vocal talent living on the Bay of Exploits. Her work appears in Land of Many Shores: Stories from a Diverse Newfoundland and Labrador, *as well as poetry and hybrid text which has been published in many journals, magazines, and anthologies.*

PAINT THE SEA WITH STARS
BRONWYNN ERSKINE

The dirt road swayed under Glenna's boots. She leaned into it the way she was accustomed to do with the roll of the deck, and stumbled when the ground failed to move. Scrambling a few steps, she managed to catch herself against a drying shed near the shore.

"You're drunk," she muttered aloud.

The dark, empty night did not disagree. She leaned her forehead against the rough wood and breathed deep, trying to ground herself. Sobering up now would be better than doing it while trying to manage the boat and navigate the reefs in the chancy light of early morning.

When her head felt a bit clearer, she released her death grip on the support post and straightened up. The ground stayed (more or less) steady this time, at least. She continued following the beaten dirt as it narrowed from a road to little more than a track.

The farthest pier from the village was in no better repair than the track that led to it. Its planks groaned wearily under Glenna's weight, and she could feel the give in them quite distinctly.

"Hello, Sparrow's Wings," she murmured fondly as she came up even with the stern of the boat. Her fingers trailed over the familiar shapes of weathered wood and coiled rope, and she swung herself deftly up to the deck.

"Hello, Hellspawn," she added a little louder, though the half feral dock cat that had added itself to her crew the last time she'd put in at Coal Harbour hadn't deigned to wake up and greet her. That was just as well. In her current state, she'd probably have tripped over it.

She opened the door to the boat's tiny cabin and stopped, blinking in the unexpected light. The cat dashed in in that instant; apparently, not asleep as Glenna had thought. The hurricane lantern beside the door was burning cheerfully, and the cat now purred placidly in the lap of the woman who sat waiting on Glenna's narrow bunk. Possibly the most beautiful woman she'd ever seen, with eyes as dark as the void between the stars, and skin like the honeyed light of a golden dawn.

"Hello Glenna," the most beautiful woman she'd ever seen said. Her voice, at least, hadn't changed as she'd grown from the pretty friend of Glenna's girlhood to a woman she scarcely knew. Her hair was braided and pinned at the nape of her neck like a proper lady now, but it was as dark and silky looking as ever.

"Mairi," Glenna blurted, still staring. And then, because the alcohol hazing her mind made it seem a good idea, she added "I heard you're getting married tomorrow."

Mairi's lovely face twisted up as if she'd bitten into something rotten. Her dark eyes held a familiar stubborn anger as she growled "I'm not."

"I didn't." Glenna fell silent when the cat raised its golden eyes to glare at her as well. She didn't know what to say in the face of that twin glare.

Mairi's softened a little at her obvious confusion. "I know what you heard," she said a touch less fiercely. "Uncle Peter's promised me to Caul MacOwen, to be his wife, in exchange for that bit of land they've been quarrelling over. So he can build a bigger barn, if you please. As if I'm no more than livestock myself, and less valuable than his precious cows, at that."

Bile rose in the back of Glenna's throat, and she didn't think it was because she was drunk this time. "He can't make you wed," she said, but she could hear the uncertainty in her own voice. Technically he couldn't, but...

"But no one'll argue with him," Mairi finished the thought that had been growing in Glenna's mind. "With my papa gone—gone to be with Mama, Peter's the only family I have left. And they'll all see it as him making a good match for me, so I'll be taken care of."

Glenna nodded slowly. "Caul's well off, least as folks go in the isles," she said just as slowly. She'd spent most of the night drinking on Caul MacOwen's tab after all, she and half the men in town. He'd been feeling generous, the night before he married a girl half his age.

"I don't give a fig about his money," Mairi snapped back hotly.

Glenna held up her hands defensively. "Alright. Alright, well if there's a lad you'd fancy in his place, Father Adam's not the sort to turn a deaf ear."

Far from being comforted, Mairi's eyes flashed sharper than ever. She sprang up off the bed, causing the cat to leap aside with a startled hiss, and stalk across the tiny space. Glenna backed up a step at the look on her face, barking her hip painfully against the corner of a shelf and narrowly avoiding treading on the cat as it dashed between her boots and out the door. By the time her footing was sure again, Mairi had her pinned against the doorframe with a steely glare and two fingers on her breastbone. In spite of being a hand and a half taller and a good deal heavier, Glenna couldn't make herself move.

"Glenna Aird, you are being intentionally hard-headed," Mairi growled.

"Not intentionally," Glenna whispered. Her mouth was dry and her heart beat so hard against her ribs that she was amazed Mairi couldn't feel its struggles. She swallowed with difficulty and added "I don't know what you want me to say, Mai."

The old nickname, unused in the years since they'd played together as children, seemed to bank some of Mairi's anger. "Say you understand," she said.

"I don't, but I want to."

"Then say you'll help me, at least. For old time's sake?" Mairi's voice was almost pleading.

Glenna's breath caught in her lungs again. "I'd do almost anything to help you," she admitted. "I just don't know what you want me to do."

Mairi threw up her hands in frustration and turned away. Her skirts flared out and smacked against Glenna's legs. "You are *too* being intentionally dense. You have a boat."

"I do, yes. We're on it." Glenna glanced quickly around to confirm this fact. The familiar cabin offered no clue to what she was missing.

"It's the middle of the night," Mairi went on. She'd turned her head just enough to watch Glenna from the corner of her eye.

"Closer to dawn than midnight," Glenna corrected with a frown.

"Well, there's no one else in town awake in any case. And you always leave harbour earlier than any of the other boats, especially on moon dark nights when you go out past the fishing grounds to meet whoever it is you get the Oormish brandy and the dreamweed from."

Glenna's mouth fell open and she sputtered like a wet cat.

"You think everyone on the island doesn't know you took over the smuggling trade after your father drowned?" Mairi demanded. "Why did you think Papa stopped letting me spend time with you?"

"I never knew he did," Glenna muttered, turning away and ducking back out the cabin door in hopes the night breeze would cool the sudden heat in her face. She should have known there was something to her friend's sudden absence. She should have questioned it. She had been too caught up in her grief and in the sudden need to provide for her mother and sisters to do much thinking at the time.

A small hand settled on her upper arm, as warm as a brand, even through her worn wool jacket.

"I'm sorry." Mairi's voice was surprisingly close, even with her hand as a warning.

Glenna jumped and turned sharply, putting her back to the rail. She immediately felt as foolish as she was sure she looked. She forced her shoulders to relax and cleared her throat, but could find no words.

Mairi had no such difficulty. "I don't mean to be crass about your father. Or to snap at you."

"It's fine," Glenna replied automatically.

"It's unkind of me," Mairi countered. "And I've never meant to be unkind to you. This isn't what I meant to say when I came down here."

"You shouldn't have come down here at all." Glenna regretted the words as soon as she heard herself say them and hurried to soften them. "You shouldn't be out alone so late, I mean. Hatcher's Point isn't as safe as you might think."

Mairi pressed her lips down into a thin line and folded her arms. "You were out alone, later than I was. And drunk to boot."

Glenna managed to bite back the first words that leapt to her tongue this time. Even as drunk as she still was, she had an idea that telling Mairi she was both beautiful and relatively helpless would not end well. Instead she said "No one much bothers me since I broke Matty Dobbin's jaw for him. I'll walk you home."

"Haven't you been listening? I'm not going back to my uncle's house. Nor to Caul MacOwen's, either, before you suggest that."

The puzzle pieces belatedly came together in Glenna's head. "You don't mean to say," she began carefully.

"Of course that's what I mean," Mairi interrupted. "You have a boat and you're leaving harbour before anyone will be awake to know I'm gone. It's the most obvious thing in the world for you to take me across to the mainland."

Glenna could only stare at her, heart racing and head reeling like she'd been struck with a shovel.

Mairi's expression lost some of its determination the longer Glenna remained silent. "I thought you'd understand," she whispered as the silence stretched. "I can pay you, if you want?"

Suddenly, she sounded so much younger. So much like the girl she'd been the day a cousin of hers had brought Glenna's father home wrapped in sail cloth. The memory tied Glenna's insides up in knots. It was still vivid after six long years, the weight of the body. Her mother's look of grim, terrified determination and the grief-stricken wails of her little sisters. The warmth of Mairi's body, holding her as the grief shook her to pieces. The single stolen kiss and the way Mairi's eyes had gone wide and startled as they parted. And then, of course, the empty distance between them in the days and months that followed, while Glenna was consumed with the growing pains of taking over her father's place in the village.

Mairi's eyes were just as wide now. Glenna forced the comparison out of her mind, forced herself to focus on the here and now. She'd turned away from that confused gaze once before, but she wasn't about to make the same mistake again.

"If that's what you want, I'll take you."

"It is!" Mairi cried swiftly. Her smile was bright as sun dazzle on the water, and she flung her arms around Glenna with an exuberance more in line with the girl she'd been than the woman Glenna had watched her grow into from a distance.

Glenna patted her back awkwardly, no longer sure what she was supposed to do with Mairi's embraces. No longer sure what she was permitted to do. "We'd best be underway, if we're going," she said eventually.

The work of getting the boat ready to sail was a welcome relief. Her body went through the motions of checking provision and rigging almost of its own accord, giving her time for her mind to try and sort things through. Mairi took a position in the bow where she was out of the way, tucked her skirts in around her feet, and watched Glenna work with an unreadable expression on her lovely face.

With one hand on the bow rope, Glenna glanced down. "Last chance to change your mind," she said.

"I'm not going to," Mairi replied with a familiar, stubborn jut of her chin.

Glenna nodded. "Just checking." She cast a final glance around the deck and the wharf, then raised her voice a bit to call "Hellspawn, I'm leaving now. You'd best be aboard if you're coming."

As she began unwinding the mooring line from its cleat, the surprisingly loud thump of galloping paws hurried up the dock. The cat leapt across the slowly widening gap of water, scrabbled up the cabin wall, and leaned down over the edge of the roof to yowl heatedly at Glenna.

"Same to you," she told it with a smirk as she coiled and stowed the rope.

"Why did you name her that?" Mairi asked a few minutes later over the creak of the rigging.

Glenna gave a final heave at the line she was working. "Hm? What?" she asked without looking away from her study of the way the sail had bellied out in the early morning wind.

"The cat. Why did you name her Hellspawn?"

She glanced over at Mairi, then up at the cat, who had climbed the mast to perch on a spar. "It's not a name. It's a description," she said with a shrug.

"But she's such a sweet little thing."

Glenna raised both eyebrows at that. "I have scars on my calves and throat that beg to differ."

"I'm sure she didn't mean it," Mairi said. She held up her hands towards the mast and made kissing noises at the little monster. "Did you, puss? I'm sure you didn't."

Glenna's skin grew hot and she looked quickly away. "Sailors don't name cats," she muttered aloud.

"Well, I'm not a sailor and I think she ought to have a name. How about Sorrel?"

"As long as you aren't going to ask me to eat it," Glenna replied.

"Is that another sailor's superstition?" Mairi asked.

Glenna shrugged again. "Not one I've heard, but I'll take no chances on it."

Mairi's laughter was spring sunlight after a long cold winter and shorebirds calling a sailor's heart home. "No one's going to eat you, sweet puss," she cooed. "You're much too cute to eat. You're just a bright little Sorrel adding spice to Glenna's life."

As she continued on in this vein, Glenna glanced over to see that the cat had come down to sit in her friend's lap again. Mairi was playing with its six-toed forepaws as if it were a baby, while the cat sprawled tolerantly, belly up, across her knees. Its smug expression suggested it was probably even purring.

"Traitor," Glenna muttered under her breath. "I'm the one who catches fish for you."

The cat blinked lazily up at her, and she would have sworn its smile widened.

The wind stayed calm and steady through the waning hours of the night. Glenna found herself with less to do than usual, and altogether too much time to think. When she realised she was adjusting the same rope for the fifth time, she brought out the one good velum map she'd inherited from her father and studied possible courses on that instead.

Always, she found her gaze straying back to Mairi, who'd fallen asleep in her spot at the bow. Sea wind had teased some strands loose from her burnished bronze braids and coaxed roses from her golden cheeks. It ruffled the collar of her blouse and the hems of her skirts. In the thin morning light, Glenna could see the curve of one dainty, stockinged ankle and just the slightest edge of one high collarbone.

"Have you slept at all?" Mairi asked, voice hoarse and only half awake.

Glenna jumped and looked quickly out to sea, hoping Mairi wasn't yet alert enough to realise she'd been staring. "No," she muttered. "The sea's tricky east of the islands. I don't usually sleep until I'm out past the reef, where I can drop anchor and nap while I wait for my contacts."

Mairi rose and stretched, and a burst of sea spray made the air sparkle around her with a thousand fractured rainbows. She didn't seem to notice, just smiled cheerfully. "Well, I'm happy to keep an eye out for them.

It's the least I can do, since you've let me sleep instead of helping you."

"You were always a terrible sailor," Glenna replied. "I let you sleep because at least that way you and the cat are both out from under my feet."

Mairi planted her tiny fists on her hips. "I was not. You taught me all the knots you'd learned from your father."

Glenna's lips curled upward of their own accord at the memory. "I taught them to you," she agreed. "That doesn't mean you were good at them."

"Almost as bad as your embroidery skills, then?" Mairi asked with an impish grin.

"Oh, even worse."

Laughing like the first fragrant blossoms of summer, Mairi aimed a smack at her head that Glenna deftly sidestepped. The deck chose that moment to roll under their feet. Unaccustomed to it, Mairi staggered. Glenna caught her about the waist before she could fall and they both froze for an instant, gazing into each other's eyes from a hand's breadth apart.

Remembering herself quickly, Glenna stepped away and busied her hands with one of the lines at random. "Have you given thought to what you'll do or where you'll go?" she asked, hoping to distract Mairi from the awkward moment and her flaming cheeks.

"There's a school of sorts, in Redfort," Mairi replied slowly. "I thought I'd go there."

Glenna's mouth dropped open. "I didn't think you liked the thought of teaching. And there's schools all over the place. You needn't go all the way to Redfort if that's what you want."

"No, as a student," Mairi corrected her.

"Of what? You can read and write, and you've been better at figures than the schoolmaster since you were still in pinafores. What more is there to be learned in school?" Glenna glanced over quickly as she spoke.

Far from being offended, Mairi's eyes gleamed bright with excitement. "There's so many things, Glenna. My papa went there when he was young. He used to tell me stories of the classes they teach."

"Like what, then?" Glenna asked.

"Practically anything," Mairi assured her. "How to write poetry and music, and speeches that really make people sit up and listen to you. And there's sciences too. You could learn everything there is to know about fish."

Glenna gave an unladylike snort. "Reckon I know more than I care to about them already."

"Alright, not fish then. But there's people at the university who study everything, and they'll teach you about it. Papa studied plants. That's what brought him here the first time, you know. He was looking for a particular kind of pine tree that only grows here in the islands."

"Pine trees?" Glenna repeated with an incredulously raised brow.

Mairi's face was flushed with excitement, her smile positively radiant. "Anything. They've got people who study rocks. Or weather. Or the stars."

"Plenty of people study the stars right here," Glenna said. "They don't need a school for it."

"Not like sailors do. I mean they try to measure their movements and determine what they're made of."

Glenna tilted her head upwards to where the last few

stars still held out against the dawn. "What they're made of," she mused aloud.

"I don't know, but you could come with me and ask," Mairi suggested. When Glenna glanced her way, she was looking studiously out to sea with a dark flush on her brown cheeks.

The breath caught in Glenna's throat. Mairi couldn't possibly mean that. Desperate to shift the conversation back from the brink, she asked "How will you convince them to let you in? I remember the gods awful fit the schoolmaster threw when you asked about reading the more complicated books he kept back for the boys."

"I do too," Mairi replied, pretty face scrunched up in a frown. "But the university's different. They'll let girls study right alongside the boys. As long as you're willing to work, they'll have you."

It made Glenna smile. "You really do have a plan for everything, don't you?"

"I try. I've thought about this for years," Mairi admitted. She cast a quick sidelong glance in Glenna's direction, then away again just as quickly.

Glenna's brows rose another fraction. "Years? You always were the one with the plan, but that's a while, even for you."

"It's—well, it's been in my mind for a while that I might need to do something like this."

"Like what? Running away in the night?" Glenna prompted when Mairi trailed off.

"Maybe, yes." Mairi wrapped her arms around herself and shivered a little. "It was alright while Papa was alive. He wouldn't have forced me to marry someone just to be married. But when he fell ill, I had to start making plans for the future."

Glenna shrugged off her jacket and wrapped it around Mairi's trembling shoulders. She was alarmed to see the glitter of tears on Mairi's long lashes, and brushed one aside with a calloused thumb as it slid down her cheek.

Mairi leaned into the touch and closed her eyes with a sigh. "I can't marry Caul," she whispered as she tugged the jacket in around herself.

"Alright," Glenna muttered.

"Nor any other man, before you suggest it," she added fiercely. That she was clutching Glenna's hand close somewhat ruined the effect of the glare.

Glenna didn't plan to tell her. She only nodded dutifully.

Mairi paused and visibly swallowed, like she'd expected an argument and wasn't sure what to do now. At length she added "I've thought *that* through for even longer."

"That doesn't surprise me, somehow."

Mairi's glare sharpened again at Glenna's smile. "I have. From every angle, 'round and 'round in circles 'til I made myself dizzy. I just can't do it."

"I don't doubt you," Glenna replied.

Mairi huffed and looked away, cheeks pink again then pale by turns. "I—I know something of what goes on. Between husband and wife. My mother thought I ought to know."

"She was a smart woman," Glenna said approvingly.

"You don't think it's scandalous?" Mairi asked shyly.

"Have you ever known me to be scandalised? By anything?"

Mairi's frown turned thoughtful and at length she shook her head. "No, I suppose I haven't. I've known you angry and hurt and far more amused than was ladylike. But never scandalised that I recall."

"I've never been ladylike either," Glenna replied cheerfully. "Your mother said as much, more than once, and I agree with her there as well. There's not a ladylike bone in my body, and anyone who's likely to marry ought to know what marrying means in a practical sense."

Mairi still looked unwontedly pale and peaky, but she managed to smile a little. "When you say it like that, it seems ever so sensible."

"I'm not sure I've ever been called that before."

Her exaggerated grimace startled a laugh from Mairi. "I'll try not to accuse you of it again, I promise." The merriment wilted again though, and Glenna felt her begin to tremble in earnest.

"Mai? What is it? You can tell me."

"I can't marry," Mairi repeated in a low voice. "When my mother told me those things... That I'd have to..."

She broke off and pushed away from Glenna to rush to the railing. When she'd emptied her stomach over it, she straightened up again and wiped her mouth with the back of a shaky hand.

Wide eyed, Glenna moved close again and wrapped a protective arm around her. "Here, come inside. The wind's cold and you should try to eat something. Seasickness is worse on an empty stomach."

"It's not that," Mairi said weakly, though she leaned into Glenna's arms and allowed herself to be guided across the deck back to the edge of the narrow bunk.

"Not seasickness? You're stomach sick over…" Glenna broke off and thought the words over carefully before finishing "Over the things that a husband would expect?"

Mairi nodded miserably. She accepted the wooden cup Glenna offered and rinsed her mouth out, grimacing at the taste. "Is this gin?"

"Watered about half and half," Glenna said with a shrug. "I got the mixture a bit wrong this time, but a bit of alcohol keeps the water from going stale or growing scuzz. Didn't bother to fix it because I wasn't planning to be out that long."

"Gin, though?"

Glenna shrugged again. "It's cheap."

"Yes, because it's poisonous half the time," Mairi replied.

"It's watered enough it's not going to do me much harm."

"You're impossible." Mairi managed to choke down another grudging mouthful, before handing the cup back.

"That, you're not the first to call me."

The joke got a wan smile from Mairi, but it didn't last. "I truly don't think I can marry any man, Glenna. The thought of them touching me like that. Of having to. I can't even say it."

Glenna knelt at her feet and took her trembling hands, marveling at how large and rough and pale her own were in comparison. In spite of working in sun and sea, her skin was island pale in contrast to Mairi's brown. "You don't need to say it. If this school of yours will take an unwed woman as a student, I don't see any reason you should ever need to think on it again."

"They will. I know they will. I just. I want you to understand, before you drop me off in Coal Harbour and head home. I want you to know." Mairi broke off indignantly when Glenna gave a snort of laughter. "What?" she demanded.

"Sorry," Glenna murmured. "Sorry, I didn't mean to interrupt."

"What's so funny?"

Glenna shook her head. "Nothing, really. Just thought of the welcome I'd get if I went back to Hatcher's Point."

"*If* you went back? What do you mean?" Mairi asked, scowling.

"You don't think they'll figure it out pretty quickly, who helped you slip away? Your uncle will have my hide if I go back, Mairi. Even get the constables involved, like as not."

Mairi could only stare, mouth open and complexion alarmingly pale again. "You never said," she whispered, "You just agreed to my plan and never said it'd have such dire consequences for you."

"Ah, it's not so bad," Glenna said, waving the concern aside. "My sisters are married to good men who'll have no qualms with supporting my mother, and I recon I can find something to work at in most any port."

"But you just threw away your whole life, just like that." Mairi tipped her chin up, lips pressed into a thin line that Glenna wasn't sure how to read. "Why would you do that?"

"You asked," Glenna replied with a shrug.

"I didn't ask you to throw away everything."

"You asked for my help," Glenna said, squeezing Mairi's hands. She thought about kissing them as well, but stamped that urge ruthlessly down. "I told you I'd help, and I will. Now, I've got to get back to the sails, but you ought to have a bit of a lie down until you're feeling less shaky."

Before she could do something she'd surely regret, Glenna rose and slipped out the door. She heard it creak open again on her heels, but she busied herself with adjusting the sails and refused to turn.

"You can't run away from a conversation when we're on a boat," Mairi observed in a dry tone. "Unless you plan to swim, I suppose."

Glenna shuddered and sketched a brief warding sign in the air. "Don't even joke about that," she grumbled.

"Then don't try to put me off like that," Mairi replied primly.

"I wasn't putting you off. The boat needs seeing to unless you want to fetch up on the reefs. I'm sure there'd be plenty of time for a conversation then."

Mairi's hand on her arm stopped Glenna short, and she felt herself flush with embarrassment. At least that was what she told herself it was.

"You're getting defensive because you know I'm right," Mairi said gently. "Please don't shut me out Glenna. You can talk while you tend the lines, can't you?"

Glenna nodded, but she couldn't seem to find any words. She was hyperaware of her body, of the coarse rope in her hands, the sun on her face, and the breeze that teased her nose with the scent of Mairi's hair.

"I just want to understand why you'd make that choice so easily. And why you didn't tell me." Mairi didn't move her hand, and the weight of her fingers kept Glenna pinned on the spot.

Glenna shrugged helplessly. She had to clear her throat before anything would come out, and even then her voice sounded unsteady in her own ears as she admitted "I didn't really think about it."

"What?"

"It's true, I swear. You asked for help and it was just, like, of course I'll help you. Of course I'll do whatever you ask me to. You're you."

Mairi was silent for the span of several minutes after that. Glenna remained frozen under her touch, a knot half tied in her hands.

"I don't know why you'd do that," Mairi said at length. "Not when I've been such a poor friend to you."

"You've been a good friend."

Mairi rolled her eyes. "I have not, and you know it. Even when we were little girls together I wasn't as good a friend as you deserved, and I certainly haven't been these last six years. And still, you'd just do that, just because I asked? Why?"

"I just. I don't know how to explain it." Glenna looked away, hoping to hide the rush of heat to her cheeks as she added "You were always the one to make things into words."

"Then show me," Mairi suggested.

The flush that flooded through Glenna made her feel sunburned and dizzy. Her voice cracked awkwardly as she squeaked out "What?"

Mairi's expression was solemn, with a frankness in her eyes that made Glenna shiver. "Show me," she repeated, folding her arms and tipping her pointed chin upwards.

Everything about it was a challenge, from words to posture to the wide, dark depths of her eyes, and Glenna had never been any good at resisting a challenge. Even when she knew she ought to. The rope slid through her distracted fingers as she turned away from it. She barely felt the rope burn.

All she could feel was the blood pounding in her ears. She raised a hand, slowly, wonderingly, and let her fingers ghost across Mairi's cheek. A tiny voice in the back of her head shouted for her to stop before she ruined everything, but she could scarcely hear it over the sigh of Mairi's breath. She leaned close, moving as if in a dream, feeling as if she was floating on a cloud. Her lips brushed Mairi's. She tasted the small gasp her actions drew, tasted the memory of watered gin, tasted the tender sweetness of Mairi's lips.

She drew back just as slowly, filled with a glow of wonderment that went to her head quicker than any liquor, and stared down into Mairi's wide eyes. The world seemed to spin about them with a roar like abused canvas.

A sudden crash made them both jump and shattered the moment. Glenna's hand went automatically to the knife at her belt and she pushed Mairi behind her as she spun to face the source of the noise. Only to find the sail sprawled untidily across most of the forward deck. The rope she'd carelessly released flopped down to pool around the block it should have secured to the top of the mast.

Mairi put a hand on Glenna's back to steady herself as she peeked over Glenna's shoulder, and promptly began to laugh. "I'm sorry," she said between giggles. "I'm sorry, but the look on your face."

Glenna's cheeks grew hot again and she started to step away.

Mairi caught her elbow before she could go far, and tugged her back around. "It was very brave of you to defend me like that," she whispered.

"From my own stupidity," Glenna muttered.

"Even so," Mairi replied with a shrug. She curled her fingers into the short hair at the nape of Glenna's neck and stretched upwards so her breath caressed Glenna's lips as she murmured "I thought you might feel the same as I do, but I had to be sure."

Glenna felt the cat wind itself around her ankles, purring loudly, as she leaned down to kiss Mairi again. Just to be sure.

An Ontario native currently residing in Newfoundland, Bronwynn Erskine is an avid steampunk enthusiast and acrylic landscape painter.

Erskine made her publishing debut in 2018's Chillers from the Rock *with her chilling tale: 'Scarlett Ribbons' and returned in 2019's* Flights from the Rock *with: 'Feather and Bone.' She returned with 'The Lindwyrm's Bride' in 2021's* Mythology from the Rock.

ALL CROCODILES GO TO HEAVEN
BRONWYNN ERSKINE

The line hadn't moved in at least ten minutes. Emily stretched up on her toes, hoping to catch a glimpse over the shoulders of those ahead of her, but all she saw was more shoulders. Straining her eyes made her head pound. She'd had one too many at the Christmas party last night. She'd known it at the time and had it anyway. She'd had several more afterwards. Why not? It was Christmas after all.

It wasn't as if she was the only one with a hangover this morning. Josh from accounting stood ahead of her in line with dark sunglasses that clashed with the faint grayish tinge to his skin. He'd already thrown up twice in the time they'd been waiting—thankfully into conveniently placed garbage cans.

What were they waiting for, anyway? She rubbed her aching temples and tried to make her brain function, but it felt as if she was thinking through several thick layers of gauze.

"Hey Josh," she murmured, wincing at the volume in spite of speaking hardly above a whisper.

He glanced back at her and grunted quietly, as if he couldn't quite manage speech yet.

"What are we waiting for?"

He continued to stare at her blankly for a long moment, before beginning to frown. "We're just waiting," he finally said, quietly, but he didn't look all that satisfied with the answer.

"We can't all just be waiting in line for no reason though." Everything was sort of foggy and disjointed, and thinking about it made her head pound harder than ever. If it hadn't been for the pain, she would have been tempted to think it was a particularly boring dream, or a nightmare. She mused aloud "D'you suppose this is what hell is like? Just endless, pointless waiting for nothing?"

"Nah. Purgatory maybe, but hell is a meeting that's already gone over into your lunch break, with that one guy who just won't shut up about something that's not even related."

The voice came from behind Emily, and she looked back to find a woman she recognised but had never spoken to before. She was a new hire, an engineer maybe. "You've met Mark?" Emily asked, scouring her mind for the woman's name.

She laughed like crocuses blooming in the spring, and Emily fell in love a little. "I haven't, but every office has that guy. I'm Pavrati Devaraj, by the way."

"Emily Kline." She shook the offered hand. Pavrati was too young for her to look at seriously, but there was no harm in being friendly. No harm in looking. She found herself smiling in spite of her headache. "Do you know what's going on? My mind's still back in bed I think, trying to sleep off last night."

Pavrati opened her mouth to answer, then shut it again as she too began to frown. "It's, something important," she finally said slowly. "But it's like my mind won't quite latch onto what it is. Isn't that the strangest thing?"

"It really is. I'm starting to wonder just what exactly was in that punch."

This brought a giggle from the younger woman that warmed Emily's chest and convinced her to put the subject aside in favour of one that might earn her more of that charming laughter. "So, how are you finding it so far?" she asked instead.

Another brilliant smile, teeth flashing white against the deep plum of Pavrati's lipstick. "It's great. Way better environment than either of the places I did work terms, and I know I'm really lucky to get in with such a prestigious firm right out of school. You're in IT, right?"

"I am, yeah. Nothing glamorous, but it's a decent gig."

Emily was pretty sure she hadn't smiled this much in years. Certainly, never at a co-worker. Not that she didn't like the rest of her department, but they were, overall, a surly and sarcastic lot who didn't give her much to smile about. She was pretty sure she could continue smiling for Pavrati as long as the other woman continued talking.

She didn't even notice as the line finally began to move ahead. Pavrati had to point it out to her, and grinned at Emily's chagrined expression. It was completely impossible for Emily not to return that cheeky grin. She could already feel her heart making plans. Young or not, she was a thoroughly delightful woman.

"Emily Kline."

Emily glanced up sharply at the sound of her name being called. She'd once again lost herself in Pavrati's conversation, and now found herself abruptly at the front of the line.

There were three screening stations, set up like airport security. Was she going somewhere? She felt sure she'd have remembered that.

"Guess I'll see you in a little while," she said over her shoulder to the still smiling Pavrati. Then, before she could lose her nerve or think better of it, added "We should get coffee."

"For sure." Emily was pretty sure she hadn't imagined something more than ordinary warmth in the other woman's eager reply.

Feeling as giddy as a teenager with a new crush, she turned away and stepped up to the empty screening station on the left. At the next one over, she could see Josh speaking quietly with a pretty blonde woman. She spared a moment to wish him luck in not throwing up on her.

Her own station was staffed by a portly, middle-aged man with a friendly but non-committal customer service smile. In spite of being not at all her type, Emily couldn't help noticing a kind of beauty to him that she couldn't quite put into words. It was in his eyes, maybe. They were a bland sort of dishwater grey, but there was something about them. A sort of light, almost.

"If you've got anything in your pockets I'll need you to place it in the tray, along with your purse," he told her. His voice was very pleasant as well. Oddly so. It wasn't a remarkable voice, just somehow pleasant.

Flustered, Emily realised she couldn't remember what might be in her pockets. When she checked them there was a bit of change from her morning coffee and, incongruously, some chipped bits of concrete. With a puzzled frown, she laid all of it in the plastic tray and stepped up to the metal detector.

"These things always make me paranoid," she admitted sheepishly, looking up at the plain metal frame with trepidation. "Like I'll step through and it'll go off and you'll discover I've got a knife I don't know about."

He chuckled. "I've only ever seen that happen once, so you're probably safe."

"Wait, you've seen that happen?" Emily squeaked.

"Just the once. Buddy was having a weird day. Come on through now, Ducky. We've got to keep the line moving."

She couldn't decide if he was joking or not, but either way it didn't do her pounding heart any favours. Holding her breath, she stepped through. When no alarm went off, she cracked one eye open and looked up.

The guard was grinning. "See, nothing to worry about. Now we just need to validate your documents and you're all set."

A second surge of panic raced through Emily. "My documents?" she whispered. Her hands were beginning to shake. "I think maybe they're in my purse? Oh god, I hope they are."

"Don't you worry about it, my love," he cut in quickly. "I've got everything you should need here already. It's hardly more than a formality anyway."

His fingers tapped away at the keyboard in front of him

for a moment. Emily could see data moving on his screen, though she couldn't read it at this angle. He seemed to be reading it, eyes flicking quickly from place to place.

"Ouch, that was a nasty breakup with Melanie Clearwater back in your twenties," he muttered briefly, shaking his head and frowning at the screen. "Very nasty stuff. Don't often see them that bad."

"Excuse me?" Emily asked. She didn't think she'd misheard him, but if she hadn't then she had no idea what it was he was reviewing.

His gaze flicked up to her briefly. "Not to worry," he repeated. "It's standard procedure, just a quick review. Weigh your heart against the feather of truth and all that. Ooh, hiking the Andes. That's a great trip. Great mountains."

Emily couldn't help staring. Was he really reading some sort of review of her entire life? How could he have gotten such a thing? And why?

"Parents' funeral. Those are always bad." He grimaced and moved on quickly.

"I'm sorry, but what exactly is going on here?" Emily finally got up the nerve to ask. "I think I've missed something."

He typed something on his keyboard that made the reams of data stop scrolling and looked her in the eyes with a sad smile. "Yes, I think you have. If it's any comfort, that's usually for the best. Over quick so you can have a nice clean break. Definitely how I'd want to go."

Her chest had gone tight and she realised she was shaking all over. As if some part of her did know, and knew it was bad. "I'm sorry," she began.

"No, don't be sorry," he told her gently. "There's no sense in that, and none of this is your fault anyway. But you're dead, love. Yes, I'm sure."

The words froze in her throat as he answered her question before she could voice it. She looked around for something familiar, trying to get her bearings. The line between its velvet ropes snaked back out of sight, fading into a sort of bland nothing. They weren't in a building at all. How had she not noticed it before? Everything seemed to be wrapped in a sort of pearlescent mist.

"No one ever notices where they are while they're waiting. Makes it easier, you see."

She turned to look back at him. He looked the same as before, like a suburban Dad going grey at the temples. The glow in his eyes had the same gentle, pearly tone as the fog behind her. He didn't have wings.

"How?" she whispered. She couldn't get any more than that out, but he knew what she was asking all the same.

"There was an earthquake," he told her, turning his screen a little so she could see a few final pictures in what she supposed must be the file of her life. "Right as you were getting to your desk, it hit, and down goes the whole building."

She recognised the potted spider plant from her desk amidst the rubble in one picture, the building's front steps in another. There didn't seem to be much left. She glanced back over her shoulder at the line, and the number of familiar faces she could make out made her stomach heave.

The angel held out a little trash can to her as she vomited up everything in her stomach. When the heaving finally subsided, she offered it back to him with a weak smile of gratitude.

"If I'm dead, how can I still throw up?" she whispered shakily.

His lips quirked upwards. "Because you believe you can. You'll still get hungry and tired as well, for a while, but eventually you'll forget things like that," he told her. "So, ready to head inside?"

"Inside?"

He cast an expansive hand over his shoulder, where the fog thickened to form a sort of wall. A small, plain door was set into it. As she watched, the blonde angel from the next desk opened this and ushered Josh inside through a swirl of glowing fog that blocked whatever was beyond the door from sight.

"What's inside?" Emily asked. She was still whispering, but it was more awe than fear that hushed her voice now. "Is that heaven?"

"If that's the way you're comfortable thinking of it, sure. It's got lots of names. And lots of different variations depending on who's looking, so don't bother asking me what it's like either."

She bit her lip and looked across towards the far desk, which was half swallowed in fog. "Will everyone else be there too?" she asked.

His chuckle was deep and knowing. "Will she be there, you mean?" he asked with a broad wink. "I think it's quite likely the two of you will find each other there."

Her cheeks flushed a painful red, she looked away quickly, then shyly back. "Even though I'm… we're."

"Lesbians? Please. As if we've got the time to try and

tell everyone who they're allowed to love." He smiled broadly and held out a hand to gesture her towards the little door. "There's a lovely coffee shop not far inside, where you can wait for her. And don't worry about the crocodiles."

Emily had her hand on the doorknob, already turning it, but she paused at that last comment. "The crocodiles?" she repeated warily. "At the coffee shop?"

"At the coffee shop, in the streets, digging in your back garden. They're everywhere, but they aren't dangerous here. You'll get used to it."

She couldn't think what to say to that. It sounded like a joke, except he looked so serious.

Seeing her expression, he shook his head with a sigh. "I know, it sounds a bit absurd. Look, you've heard that thing about 'all dogs go to heaven,' right?"

"You mean the movie?"

He nodded. "Yeah. Well, that's not true. There's a lot of dogs in purgatory, actually. They prefer to wait and see where their masters end up. Crocodiles though, they're a different story. There's no one they're inclined to wait on, and they just go right on through. They're quite a wide-spread and populous creature. So, there's a lot of them here."

As Emily stared at him, mouth hanging open slightly and completely unable to think of anything to say in response, he laid a hand lightly on her shoulder and guided her through the door.

"Don't worry, you'll get used to it," she heard him say as the door shut quietly but firmly behind her.

DOUBT THOU THE STARS ARE FIRE
BRONWYNN ERSKINE

The laws of spatial relation reasserted themselves as the *Delilah Rose* burst back into realspace on a wave of the superheated plasma that had accompanied its passage through jumpspace. The small plasma storm its arrival created crackled across the outer surface of the hull, audible all the way through to the crew compartments within.

Sunk deep in the cushioned depths of the pilot's couch, Ainsley gritted their teeth. The sound vibrated in their bones, and they fought down nausea while going through the motions of shutting down the jumpdrive and engaging the realspace engines. The nausea would pass. It always did, as did the wave of dizzying heat that set their blood blazing like molten glass in their veins. They focused on the familiar rituals while they waited, breathing slowly around the nozzle of the straw that was still tucked under their tongue.

"Status, Mauser?" Jill asked from her own acceleration couch at the center of the bridge.

Ainsley groaned and spit out the straw, allowing it to

swing back behind their left shoulder on its sling. "I don't think I'm going to throw up, but I haven't entirely ruled it out," they replied. "On the plus side holographic controls, being completely intangible, are easy to clean."

"I was referring to the ship, A," she said mildly.

"You always are ma'am." They flicked their fingers through half a dozen layers of holographic displays, checking numbers and gauges and colours, before adding "Ship's fine. Hull's a little hot, but still well within acceptable parameters."

They swiped the holographic cocoon down to 30% opacity, and the rest of the bridge came back into view. Jill had a navigational chart on the main display and was adjusting the ship's long-range scanners to compile a more detailed view of the nearest star system, though they were still almost a light minute from its outer rim. Her gaze flicked briefly in Ainsley's direction as they became visible to her.

On her far side, where the communications and science station formed a starboard mirror of the pilot's station, Indigo caught their eye and smirked. "The irony of a pilot who gets jumpsick never ceases to amuse me," she drawled. Her brown cheeks dimpled and her white teeth gleamed in the dancing light of holographic displays.

Ainsley freed one hand from their controls long enough to cast a rude gesture in her direction.

"Do I have to separate you, children?" Jill asked, her put-on 'captain voice' somewhat undermined by the hint of a smile she hadn't quite managed to hide. "Dr. Jones, have you got a fix on that transmission for us?"

"Sure, sure, yeah." Indigo gestured through her own

controls and a sector of the navchart lit up.

A small, rocky planet expanded to dominate the displays.

"It looks like there's three, maybe four planets within the Goldilocks zone," she said. "Second gas giant's a bit iffy, right on the borderline. Hard to say if it's warm enough. Anyway. Fifth planet from the star and well within the warm edge of the habitable zone, this bad boy is the only thing in the system besides us that's showing any sign of advanced tech."

A slight twitch of her fingers expanded the image again. A mountain range near the equator came into view, seen from space and just large enough to make out a series of concentric half rings jutting out onto a wide plateau.

"It's consistent with known examples of alien architecture, though nothing else I've seen has been this sparse. I'm thinking this is probably a border system or a new settlement."

"Are they still transmitting?" Jill asked.

Indigo nodded. "Yeah. Same message. I think it's a looped recording."

"How sure are we that this is a good idea?" Ainsley asked, looking away from the half dozen possible courses they'd plotted on their displays to study the image. "I mean, they've never seemed very welcoming when human ships have crossed paths with their settlements and vessels."

"They're not welcoming, but they're not hostile either. And it's a distress signal." Jill shrugged, the movement quick and spare like a heron, then squared up her boney shoulders as if she expected an argument. "If we're not going to answer a distress signal, I don't think we're a species that deserves to be made welcome."

Ainsley tugged at one of the snakebite piercings in their lower lip with their teeth and continued to stare at the image on the main screen. After a moment they nodded slowly. "Yeah, I suppose that's fair."

"Good. Bring us in."

"Yes ma'am," Ainsley murmured, attention returning to their controls.

Their stomach was still roiling. The jumpsickness was getting worse over time, not better the way their childhood seasickness had improved as they grew used to the roll of a boat under their feet. They would have to say something if it continued, but they knew what that would bring. The thought of being stuck planetside, of never handling the controls of anything more challenging than subsonic aircraft, made their skin crawl.

They focused on the small adjustments to thrusters and manifolds. They could stand it a while longer before it was worth risking that fate.

"You're awfully quiet A," Jill interrupted their thoughts some time later.

They didn't look away from their displays. "Just thinking. First contact. It's pretty huge, y'know. The kind of thing you expect to see in the news, not actually be part of. I always figured I was destined for a pretty boring life."

"You don't think advance scouting uncharted systems is exciting?" Indigo asked.

Ainsley calibrated a minor course correction to reroute the ship around the debris from an asteroid collision just beyond the orbital path cleared by a supergiant with a pair of huge red eye-storms that put them in mind of Jupiter back in the Sol system.

As the ship eased around the thickest patch of debris, they thought back to Indigo's question. "Exciting, sure. Just not really noteworthy. The task force as a whole will be remembered, but I doubt any of us will be more than a footnote in history if it weren't for today."

"Speak for yourself," Indigo retorted. "I've got a xeno-linguistics algorithm named after me."

Ainsley shrugged and made another slight course correction. "Sure, whatever. My point is no one's going down in history for system scouting. The only explorers history remembers are the ones who get major firsts. First successful jumpspace transit, first landing on an exoplanet, first encounter with the aliens. Those are the history makers. The rest of us will be lumped together under the heading of the task force and forgotten as individuals."

"How long until we make orbit?" Jill interrupted before the cousins could get too deeply involved in their argument.

"One hour, 13 minutes, and roughly 30 seconds," Ainsley replied without hesitation.

Jill nodded and stared at the settlement on the display. "Indigo, see if you can raise a channel and give that xeno-linguistics algorithm a real test."

***

"Commencing atmospheric entry in T-minus 10 seconds," Ainsley announced to the bridge at large. Their fingers and eyes never stopped moving, monitoring the displays that hovered around them and making minute corrections.

The *Delilah Rose* shuddered as its forward hull began encountering non-negligible atmospheric resistance. Ainsley adjusted the angle of descent a fraction of a degree, and the flight stabilised.

On the main display, Jill brought up a visual of their surroundings. Wisps of purplish cloud parted ahead of the ship's bow wave to reveal rolling hills covered in purplish vegetation. Directly ahead the alien settlement was visible, three opalescent rings surrounding a faceted dome.

"Every time we make planetfall, I remember again why I took this job," Jill sighed. "It's so beautiful."

"Orbital telemetry never does justice to the colours," Indigo remarked from behind her matrix of holographic displays. She had scanners and comms in front of her, with weapons systems relegated far back in her peripheral vision on either side. As an afterthought, she added "I still haven't been able to get any kind of response."

"But they're still broadcasting the distress signal?" Jill asked.

Indigo nodded, her dreadlocks flopping forward into her face for a second before she shook them back. "Yeah. It's possible they've taken their receiving capabilities offline in order to focus more power to the transmission array. That would explain why I can't get through."

"Or they just don't want to talk to us," Ainsley added without looking over. "They haven't exactly welcomed us with open, er, tentacle things, after all."

They heard Indigo huff loudly. "They haven't been hostile towards our scout ships that have crossed paths with them either," she pointed out testily.

Ainsley hummed and keyed another slight adjustment to their trajectory before replying. "I didn't say they had. I'm just saying, 'not overtly hostile' isn't quite the same thing as wanting to have us over for tea. I, for one, regularly refrain from punching people I would much rather never interact with."

"Not as often as I'd like, and if you could also refrain from taunting it would be much appreciated. I'm not above putting you both in time out if you're going to act like children," Jill interjected firmly. A smile curled her lips when the comment drew near-identical pouts from her pilot and her science officer, visible to her in the small windows in her holo display which she kept dedicated to real time images of her two crewmembers.

Indigo was frowning over a display that reflected blue-green light across her copper tinged skin. Ainsley was chewing lightly at one of their lip piercings again, and their fair complexion was still waxen with the lingering effects of jumpsickness. Jill frowned at that. All irony aside, she thought the effects were getting worse over time. She wondered if she ought to bring it up, since it didn't seem like they were going to.

"I'm picking up life signs," Indigo said, cutting across her captain's thoughts. "Whatever they build their habitats out of, it messes with our scanner penetration almost as much as their ships' hulls. It looks like about 50 individuals."

"That's a lot for a base this size, isn't it?" Ainsley asked.

"Remember they're smaller than us though. The latest estimates put them barely over half a metre in height." Indigo dipped her fingers through several layers of display matrix and with a deft flick sent a file to hover amongst Ainsley's displays.

A still image of a human silhouette standing beside a toddler sized being shaped something like a jellyfish appeared in its own small window amongst their navigational displays. "Really, that small?" they asked. "I thought they were supposed to be more like four and a half."

"Nope. There's an article about it in an issue of National Geographic I downloaded last time we stopped at a supply buoy. A scout ship in quadrant 143 got some better scans, and the xenobiologists who've been analysing them think we've been underestimating the aliens' physical density by a significant margin."

"Nerd," Ainsley muttered, just loudly enough to be sure Indigo would hear without making it seem like they'd meant her to.

"Jock," she muttered back.

Jill squeezed the bridge of her nose. She really hadn't appreciated how lucky she was to come from a very small family.

The ship slowed further under Ainsley's commands and settled in for a vertical landing. They checked the weight distribution across the seven points of the landing gear and adjusted the rear sets until the ship was evenly balanced.

"How ready do you want us to be to make a quick exit, ma'am?" they asked, looking fully away from their controls for the first time in hours.

Jill thought about the question. Thought also about the

lines of exhaustion beginning to show around Ainsley's eyes and the barely restrained twitching of Indigo's knee now that the prospect of open space was within reach.

"I expect we'll be here for several days, Mx. Mauser," she replied evenly. "Unless they decide to change their minds and get hostile, of course."

Ainsley tugged one of the orange metal rings in their lower lip between their teeth briefly before nodding. "Dropping anchor then," they said.

At a brief gesture, each landing foot unfolded four long, curved claws and drove them downward to grab a handful of earth and stone. The legs retracted slowly until the ship crouched only a quarter of a metre off the ground.

Ainsley sank back into the depths of their acceleration couch with a sigh and gestured their display matrix into its standby mode.

Indigo sprang up before her restraint harness had finished retracting. Stretching to her full height, she could lay her palms flat on the ceiling with ease. "I can't wait to get out of this box," she announced.

"I'm pretty sure there's a lesbian joke in there, but I'm too tired to figure out what it is," Ainsley murmured without opening their eyes.

Jill smothered her laugh into a faint huff but couldn't entirely suppress it. "Go back and get some shut-eye. You get cranky when you're tired."

The look Ainsley turned on her was surprisingly open, another symptom of just how close they were to the edge. "Wake me before you go?" they asked in a small voice.

Jill gave in to a moment of weakness and brushed

her fingers across Ainsley's messy blond hair. "We won't leave without you. Get some sleep."

They leaned into the touch for just a second before withdrawing to a more professional distance with a murmured "Yes ma'am."

Ainsley padded into the cramped living space that was only nominally separated from the bridge and ducked down to roll into their bunk. The space was narrow, coffin-like in Indigo's words, but they'd never minded small spaces. They pulled the hatch down behind themself, making sure the latch caught to seal the soundproofing.

"Idiot," they whispered, tears prickling at the corners of their eyes. They dashed them away with the cuff of a sleeve and stared up at the faint blue-grey glow of the canopy above them, completely unnecessary since they would never be in here when the ship was in motion. "Get your act together, before you do something even more moronic."

They pulled the blankets around themself, set an alarm for half an hour, Earth standard, and squeezed their eyes shut.

***

"You should say something," Indigo said out of the blue, breaking the silence in which she and Jill had worked for the last hour.

When Jill glanced over, her science officer wasn't looking at her. "Say something about what?" she asked.

Indigo finished her check of the third rebreather and met the captain's eyes. "You know."

"I really don't," Jill replied evenly.

Indigo jerked her chin to starboard and arched her

eyebrows.

Jill followed the glance, though she knew every inch of the ship by heart after so long onboard. The wall of bunks, two closed but dark and one with blue indicators illuminated. On the indicators, she could see that Ainsley was coming out of REM sleep, and that their temperature was still higher than it should be. "I have no idea what you're talking about," she told Indigo.

"Have it your way then," she replied, returning her attention to the equipment spread before her. "But they're not going to make the first move."

"No one is making any moves," Jill snapped back. "Obviously."

"There are no moves to be made."

Indigo lifted only her eyes, expression inscrutable.

"Seriously, there's nothing going on," Jill said, managing to keep her tone almost neutral this time.

"Of course there isn't. They're too shy and you're too chickenshit."

Jill was about to retort when the indicators on Ainsley's bunk went out and the hatch clicked open. Their head and shoulders appeared, hair more than usually tousled and jacket rumpled from being slept in, and they looked back and forth between their crewmates with a frown.

"Don't let me interrupt you talking about me," they said shortly, pushing up to their feet and disappearing with quick strides into the head.

Jill felt herself blushing for no discernible reason and looked quickly away before Indigo could comment. "We'll be leaving shortly," was all she said.

"Yes ma'am."

There was something in Indigo's tone, some comment that Jill knew she was supposed to infer, but she chose not to go hunting for it. Now was not the time to be distracted.

Ainsley reappeared, crisply presentable and expression arranged into a neutrality that was a near perfect mirror of their cousin's. "So, what's the plan?" they asked.

"We'll be leaving shortly," Jill repeated. "I've got the ship's systems tied to your mobile already. You can review them to be sure I didn't miss anything while Indigo finishes getting her biome sensors configured, and then we'll gear up."

"It wouldn't be like you to miss something," they replied, though they were already slipping on the glasses that would allow them to view their mobile system in the form of a heads-up display. Then, hesitating, they pushed the glasses back up onto their forehead and stared at her. "Wait, does that mean I'm going with you?"

Jill frowned. "I'm a little offended you think I might be enough of a jerk to make you wait with the ship during humanity's historic first contact with an alien species. But putting that aside, you're also my technical officer. There's a good chance whatever the aliens are in distress about is likely to be of a technical nature. So, I want you along for that too."

A startled flush washed across Ainsley's fair cheeks, obscuring the scattering of freckles there. They started to open their mouth, then seemed to think better of it and shook their head. "Yes, ma'am," they mumbled as their eyes disappeared behind dark lenses and the HUD came online. The blush remained quite clearly visible.

Indigo was pointedly not looking at her.

***

Half an hour later, the outer hatch hissed its way through decompression and the three crewmates stepped out into lush purple vegetation that came up almost to their knees. Indigo and Ainsley walked in a slow circle around the ship, trailing cable behind them as they laid out the biome scanners.

While they worked, Jill checked her HUD to confirm that everyone's equipment was online and operational. The planet's atmosphere wasn't high enough in carbon dioxide to be immediately dangerous if the bulky rebreather masks malfunctioned somehow, but she still wanted to know immediately if anything went wrong.

When the other two came back around the far side of the ship, she asked "Everyone ready to go?"

"Sure, why not," Indigo replied with a cheeky grin that was visible only by the way it scrunched up her cheeks above the mask. "Let's go introduce ourselves."

Ainsley only nodded. Their cheeks shifted briefly in what was probably a smile but could also have been a grimace. In her HUD, Jill could see that their temperature was still a bit elevated. If it had been any other mission, she probably would have had them stay with the ship and rest. But it would break their heart to miss this, and she couldn't bear that.

She tucked her concerns aside and shouldered her pack to take the lead. They weren't far from the base, or settlement, or whatever it was, but Ainsley had given the aliens a polite distance by bringing the ship down at the edge of the plateau that surrounded it. She picked her way through the not-quite-grass that crunched under the steel polymer soles of her boots and the low, dense shrubs whose needles rasped against her Kevlar coated pants.

Above these sounds, she could hear the movements of her crewmates behind her. Indigo kept up a low running commentary, recording her observations for the survey report she would prepare later, but Ainsley was uncharacteristically quiet. All she could hear of them was their footsteps, and she found herself glancing back frequently to reassure herself of their continued presence. The planet was too quiet without their cheerful voice.

As they neared the pearlescent walls, Indigo's voice fell away as well. The group crossed the last half-dozen metres in silence.

"Do we knock?" Jill mused aloud as they stood before the wide airlock entrance.

Indigo shrugged. "Either that or we stand around and wait indefinitely, until they get tired of us lurking outside."

"Shag that," Ainsley quipped. They raised a fist and thumped it heavily against the metal. The sound echoed back from within.

Indigo smacked the back of their head, though she was careful to avoid the straps of the rebreather. "Chain of command," she muttered under her breath.

Jill was too pleased with this show of her pilot's usual impetuousness to be particularly angry.

Another handful of minutes ticked by before a response came in the form of a drawn-out metallic groan, combined with the grinding of gears. Then, with a whisper of air pressure equalising, the hatch began making its slow way upward.

"Alright, this is it then," Jill said, tugging anxiously at the cuffs of her gloves. "I want you both on whatever passes for your best behaviour. Everybody ready to make history?"

"One way or another. First humans to be eaten by an alien species does have a certain ring to it," Ainsley replied.

Jill smothered a completely inappropriate giggle, which she chose to blame on nerves. She straightened up self-consciously and forced herself to take a couple of slow, deep breaths. "Everything is going to be fine," she said firmly, as much for her own benefit as her crew's.

The door rumbled upward ponderously to reveal a single being waiting on the other side. Its main body was a spongy looking mass around the size of a beach ball, supported by a metal frame with long, spindly legs curving outwards to meet the wheeled ring at the base. A filigree of thread-fine, whitish tendrils spread out and spilled down around its circumference. Some of the tendrils were raised to rest on what looked to be the controls of the cart, but most just waved and fluttered in a random sort of manner.

The crew and the alien stared at each other. At least, the crew assumed the alien was staring back. Without discernible eyes it was hard to be sure.

Jill cleared her throat and glanced quickly at Indigo. "Is everything ready to go?" she asked.

"Yup, whenever you're ready." Indigo gave her a thumbs up and held her tablet aloft as proof, as if its mere presence was answer enough.

"You'll do great," Ainsley whispered from behind her.

Trying to ignore the nerves that threatened to choke her, Jill took a deep breath and addressed the alien. "Hello. I'm Captain Jill Faulkner of the United Earth Space Exploration Taskforce. We picked up your distress signal and came to offer our help."

The translation the tablet produced was an eerie percussive wailing a little like drumming.

The alien went absolutely still, every tendril rigid. It didn't even seem to be breathing, though that was hard to be sure of. At length it opened a mouth that had been all but invisible in the texture of its body when closed. A trio of long, flat tongues uncurled and beat against the stretched membrane of its throat to produce its own drum call.

All three humans leaned close to the tablet to hear what it could make of the sounds. "It is unexpected of you to offer, but the [unknown sequence] are grateful for your mercy."

"Am I being slow, or did that not make much sense?" Ainsley asked. "No offence, Indy."

Indigo's face was scrunched up in concentration. She didn't even react to the nickname. "I think it means they would appreciate our help?" she suggested eventually.

"We're happy to help. Can you tell us the nature of the problem?" Jill asked the translator.

The alien's pause was shorter this time before it drummed out an answer. "I have catastrophic atmospheric controls failure in command module."

"Ooh, that one's much better," Ainsley said, clapping

Indigo on the shoulder. "Ask if they can show it to us, and maybe I can get things going for them."

Indigo nudged their shoulder and muttered "I'm sure the captain would never have thought of that."

"Sorry ma'am," Ainsley mumbled, a flush visible in the narrow gap between their high collar and the base of the rebreather.

Jill merely rolled her eyes and repeated the question for the translator.

"It is being this way, if you will accompany me," the translator relayed the alien's response. They waved a swath of tendrils in a 'follow me' sort of gesture and directed their cart away from the door. They didn't seem concerned about turning around to 'face' in the direction they were going, but since they lacked a discernible face it might simply not have been a consideration.

Jill took the lead again. The area they entered appeared to be meant for storage, with a few crates still stacked to one side. They passed quickly on, into a hall where she nearly bumped her head on the ceiling.

"I bet you're missing the comfortably roomy ship now, huh Indigo," Ainsley whispered as they watched their cousin hunch her shoulders and duck into the hall.

"Just because we're engaged in a historic human first, doesn't mean I won't smack you," Indigo replied without looking back. The ceiling would have been even with her biceps were she standing straight, making it even more awkward than it was for her crewmates. She thought several uncharitable things in Ainsley's direction during the walk, when she noticed that they could stand up almost straight when the group passed from service corridors to nicer looking rooms. Even with the slightly higher ceilings, she still had to hunch uncomfortably.

After about 20 minutes, the group reached another wide, sealed hatch much like the one they'd entered by. A second alien waited beside it, tendrils mostly tucked in close against the denser, stem like section of their body that hung down through what must have been a hole in the cart's seat.

The two beings exchanged reverberations for a moment, then their guide gestured with a swath of tendrils towards the new alien. Without waiting any further, they retreated quickly back down the hallway.

"I guess we aren't very popular?" Ainsley suggested.

The new alien raised a swath of tendrils and formed the end into a clump roughly the size and shape of a fist with a sort of lumpy protrusion on top.

"Any clue what that means?" Jill asked with a glance at her science officer.

Indigo could only shrug, but Ainsley cocked their head to one side thoughtfully. "What if they're imitating us," they suggested. "It could be a thumbs up. You did that earlier to show that the translator was ready. Maybe they want to be sure we know they're going to start talking?"

"Sometimes you're not entirely dumb," Indigo said. She held up the tablet and returned the gesture with a thumbs up of her own.

Apparently satisfied, the alien opened their mouth wide to drum out their message. "Stellar descent [unknown sequence] foliage informs me you have offered assist with atmospheric controls failure. I warn you of high nitrogen and helium concentrations. Must access controls in inundated sections."

"What about foliage?" Ainsley wondered aloud.

"Maybe it's a greeting that doesn't translate well," Indigo suggested. "Like how 'goodbye' is an archaic contraction of 'god be with you' but no one says that anymore."

Jill ignored Ainsley mouthing 'nerd' and asked instead "What about the nitrogen and helium concentrations thing? The rebreathers aren't designed for completely unbreathable atmosphere, but there's a lot of nitrogen in regular air. And is helium all that harmful? Biochem was never my strongest subject."

"Depends how high we're talking about," Indigo replied. "They can dilute with oxygen for a while if the levels aren't completely ridiculous. That's essentially what they're doing anyway. And obviously we'll monitor Ainsley's vitals while they're in there, so we'll know long before it becomes a problem."

Jill continued to frown. "If you're sure you can keep them safe Indigo, then we'll give it a go. Otherwise, I'm going to pull rank and insist on a full suit."

Indigo's nod was crisp and businesslike. "I can. Besides, A. hates wearing a tie."

"Great Mother give me strength," Jill muttered. To the translator she added "My technical officer, Mx. Ainsley Mauser, will attempt the repairs. We believe the atmospheric composition will be tolerable for a limited period."

The alien's pebbled surface faded alarmingly as they listened to the translation, from a pinkish orange shade to almost cream coloured.

"Did we know they could change colour?" Ainsley whispered, leaning close to Indigo.

She shook her head. "No one's ever seen them before in person. No one human, anyway."

"So we have no idea what that means?" they persisted.

"None."

"If it's so dangerous to them that they can't carry out the repairs themselves, they're probably just surprised that we aren't more worried," Jill suggested reasonably. "The same sort of thing it would mean for a human to go pale. Just, a more extreme change."

When the alien had recovered some of their former colour, they spoke at length in a long series of complicated reverberations. "The [unknown sequence] of exploration sector taste blossoming precipitation are grateful for your intervention. I will provide whatever assistance I can over comms, as my systems may vary from frightening tree. [Unknown sequence] is well chosen as defect space fire soon."

"Did they just refer to us as 'frightening trees?'" Ainsley asked into the silence as the human crew attempted to piece together the meaning of the translation.

"I mean, we are a lot taller than them?" Indigo replied with a shrug. "I'm personally a lot more concerned about 'defect space fire soon.' Is there a solar flare or something coming that they've detected?"

Jill nodded. "Could be. We haven't done a proper scan of the system, since we were in a hurry. The ship'll be alright, but maybe there's preparations they can't make without accessing this part of the habitat." To the translator, she added "Can you tell us how long before this 'defect space fire' arrives?"

Reluctantly, or so it seemed to the human crew, the alien said "I am not certain, but less than two planetary days."

"Planetary day is just over 18 standard hours," Indigo supplied.

"Alright, so we've got some time but not a whole lot. Let's get a move on things then." Jill glanced over at Ainsley to ask "You've got tools?"

They nodded, tapping the strap of the pack they carried.

The alien opened the first sealed hatch and showed Ainsley how to open the second once the first was resealed behind them, then quickly retreated back into the corridor to wait with Jill and Indigo.

***

Less than ten minutes later Ainsley was lying on their stomach, head and arms inside a control panel that came up almost to their knees.

"It's all just fried wiring," they reported to the comm unit integrated with their rebreather. "Won't take me more than an hour to sort out. Probably less."

From just behind their ear, Indigo's voice replied "Our friend out here seems convinced it's a major thing. Are you sure it's just wiring?"

"That's all I can see. I'll let you know if I find anything else," they said.

A text-only window popped up on the periphery of Ainsley's heads-up display, with a still of Indigo's face in the corner to identify the sender. "You noticed that's twice she's referred to you as 'hers,' right?" it read with a winky face emoji at the end.

They rolled their eyes, but obliged her by tabbing over to a private voice line before saying "You're grasping at straws. Her technical officer means about as much as her ship and her crew. I'm under her in the chain of command, that's all."

"I bet she'd like you under her in other ways too," Indigo's text box replied.

Ainsley felt an unwelcome rush of heat suffuse their body, almost as strong as the one that accompanied the jumpsickness. They swiped the text box away and blocked the comm line with her for good measure. "Stop distracting me," they muttered to the empty air, stomach roiling again and skin gone itchy-tight like a sunburn.

***

The aliens were suffused a deep red-orange with pleasure as they examined the repaired consoles. Ainsley sat cross legged on the floor with a small self-satisfied smile on their uncovered face, but Jill noticed that their skin had gone pale again. She wanted to mention it to Indigo, but the science officer was engaged with their alien guide in a slow but obviously intense conversation through the translator.

She sat down beside Ainsley instead. "You're not eating much," she observed. A safe enough topic to open with.

Ainsley blinked a little owlishly at her and raised their cup of the thick, pulpy liquid the aliens had offered as refreshment to their lips as if they'd forgotten they held it.

"Wouldn't want them to think we're ungracious guests," they murmured.

"I didn't mean that," Jill hurried to reassure them. "I just meant. How are you feeling? You're not still suffering the jumpsickness, are you? I know it's been getting worse, lasting longer."

Their head came around sharply, colour flushing high on their too-pale cheeks. "You know?"

"You're not very good at keeping secrets." Oddly, this made them flush darker. Jill frowned. The colour made them look feverish.

Before Ainsley could answer, a commotion among the gathered aliens distracted them both.

The aliens had all gone that alarmed cream colour and backed away from their human guests so quickly that their carts bumped and rattled together.

"What is it?" Jill demanded. "Indigo, what did you say?"

The science officer shook her head in bewilderment. "I don't know. We were talking about the planet." Turning back to the translator and the alien she'd been speaking with, she asked "Please tell us what's wrong. I hope we haven't offended you."

The aliens drew back farther, many wringing their tendrils in distress or curling in upon themselves. The alien science officer who had met them at the control center hatch waved a swath of tendrils in Ainsley's direction and drummed out "Defect space fire, as I warned you."

Indigo's frown deepened and she shook her head quickly. "They're not feeling well, that's all. It will pass."

Several of the other aliens lurched back farther and

began making distressed sounds.

"I can go back to the ship if that'll make them feel better," Ainsley offered in a small voice. "Maybe they're afraid they could catch something from me? Like in War of the Worlds."

Indigo repeated for the translator, but the alien science officer only seemed to grow more distressed at the suggestion.

They drummed out something very slowly and carefully. "Between space without shields. Genetic damage. Fire."

"Genetic damage?" Ainsley repeated. The fishy soup-paste in their stomach felt like it might make a precipitous reappearance, and it hadn't looked all that appealing the first time around.

"Are you saying what we call jumpsickness is more serious?" Indigo asked. "That it's done some kind of damage to our crewmate?"

The alien repeated the thumbs up gesture they'd picked up earlier. "Yes. Understanding. Very dangerous. Many killed."

Ainsley's whole face was white, except for the patches of high colour on their cheeks. "I think I'm going to throw up," they whispered.

"Can try to mitigate damage," the alien went on. "Maybe trees can survive."

"Yes," Jill said immediately, springing to her feet and pulling Ainsley up with her. They lurched and staggered against her side, and their whole body felt hot enough to burn her.

The crowd of aliens flinched back from her sudden

movement, but their science officer trundled forward resolutely. "Come. I will do what I can."

***

Ainsley's legs trailed over the edge of the medical table designed to hold one of the aliens, but they'd been assured this would be alright as long as their entire brain was within range of the scanner now humming away overhead. The situation was dire enough that Indigo hadn't even cracked a joke about that. In its way, that scared them more than anything else. They wanted desperately to turn their head and look for some kind of comfort in human contact, even if it was just Indigo's strained smile. Or Jill's grim frown. They hated to be the cause of her frown, but it would still be something.

The machine stopped humming and the alien said something, but Ainsley missed the translation. They almost didn't want to know the prognosis.

But Jill leaned in close and squeezed their shoulder. There were tears gathering in the corners of her eyes, making the soft hazel of them swim like honey on a summer day. Ainsley raised a hand without thinking to brush their thumb over the corner of her cheek. It was far too familiar a gesture, they knew, but they couldn't seem to stop themself.

"It's alright if there's nothing they can do," they whispered. "Do they know if it'll hurt?"

Jill made a strangled sound in the back of her throat. She leaned close and a tear dripped onto Ainsley's cheek a moment before her lips pressed warmly onto theirs. "There's a chance they can fix it, but the cure might also kill you," she whispered as she withdrew. "Indigo's not sure either. Or they can make it quick and painless. It's your choice."

Ainsley stared up at her, for once completely without words. After a long moment they managed to stammer "You kissed me."

Jill lifted a hand from their cheek to cast a rude gesture over her shoulder in the direction of Indigo's cackling. "It seemed like the thing to do," she said hoarsely, feeling her cheeks heat with embarrassment. "It doesn't have to mean anything, if you don't want it to. I just thought..."

"What if I do want it to?" Ainsley asked when she trailed off.

Her eyes gleamed brighter than they'd ever seen, in spite of the tears still leaking down her cheeks. "I'd like that," she whispered.

"Fucking finally!" Indigo crowed. "If you'd told me a near death experience was all it would take, I could have arranged that months ago."

For once, Ainsley was too distracted to rise to the bait. "I think I'd like them to try and fix me," they said quietly.

"I was hoping you would," Jill replied. She thought about kissing them again, but decided she probably wouldn't be able to stop if she did, and there were more urgent concerns right now. She squeezed their shoulder instead and stood back. "They would like you to proceed with the attempt," she told the alien scientist.

Evidently they'd finished the preparations while she spoke with Ainsley, because they responded by brushing their tendrils briefly across the controls.

The bank of machinery above Ainsley began to hum again.

***

Ainsley woke with the disconcerting impression that there was something different, but couldn't immediately place what it was. They were curled up on a soft pallet in a warm, dimly lit room that was much more spacious than the bunk they'd grown accustomed to. Distantly, they could make out the sound of voices as of a hushed conversation in the next room.

Their nose hurt and their head didn't, and both sensations seemed novel. As if they'd never experienced either one before. That thought made them frown. They'd had headaches after spending long periods in the pilot's couch, but everyone did. It wasn't as if they were constant, or even all that bad. So why did it feel strange?

"I believe your crewmember is regaining consciousness," one of the distant voices remarked. It had a faint but distinctive accent that Ainsley couldn't quite place.

A moment later a second voice repeated the words. This time it drew a reaction, the sound of clothing rustling and boots on a hard floor, then the rattle of something sliding aside. Brighter light washed over Ainsley from somewhere behind them.

The footsteps reached them before they'd gathered their wits enough to roll over, and a small, warm hand settled lightly on their shoulder.

"A?" Jill's voice asked, unusually quiet even for her.

They had to clear their throat a couple of times before they could get their voice to work. "Hi," they croaked.

"Hi yourself," she murmured, helping them over onto their back. "How do you feel?"

Ainsley felt themself blush, remembering Indigo's earlier comment. They pulled their focus back to Jill's worried face above them. "Not bad, I guess. Sort of weird."

"Weird how?" Jill asked.

"My head is. I don't know how to describe it. It feels different somehow."

Jill was frowning. Behind her indigo's voice said "They say their head feels strange. Do you think that's a side effect of the treatment?"

Another voice repeated the question, though it changed "head" to "brain."

The first voice, the one with the accent, replied "In a way it is." And the second voice repeated it again.

This time, Ainsley recognised the repeating voice as Indigo's translation algorithm. But that meant—! They jerked upright, almost smacking their face into Jill's in the urgency of their need to see past her. Indigo stood just inside the doorway, and the alien scientist sat in their cart just outside.

"What the hell did you do to me?" they demanded hoarsely.

The alien opened their mouth wide and drummed their throat, but the sound was drowned out by the voice that seemed to come from Ainsley's own mind. "I did what I promised your captain I would attempt, to repair the damage caused to your brain by extensive, unshielded jumpship travel. I warned her it would require the use of nanobots, and that I did not know if your immune system would fight their attempts to repair your tissues."

They fell silent and the translator in Indigo's hand produced a rather garbled version of the same explanation.

"What's going on?" Indigo demanded.

At the same time, Jill asked "Did they just understand what A. said? Without the translator?"

Ainsley ignored both their crewmates for the moment and continued to glare at the alien. "You did more than just repair my tissues."

Their tendrils fluttered anxiously and there was a great deal of reluctance in their voice as they drummed out "I apologise for the deception. It is not customary to proceed without consent and I am prepared to face appropriate consequences for my actions, but please understand that I alone am guilty of them. My comrades knew nothing of my plans."

The algorithm's translation of this statement was even more garbled than the last, and Ainsley had to clarify several [unknown sequences] in order for Jill and Indigo to understand. Indigo looked torn between fascination and concern.

Jill just looked angry. "I think you'd better explain exactly what you did to my pilot," she said in a tone at once quieter and more wrathful than anything Ainsley could recall hearing from her before.

The alien didn't wait for the translator to finish relaying her words before speaking. "Once the genetic damage had been repaired, I had the nanobots produce and assemble a universal translator array that integrated with your crewmate's neuro-linguistic processing centres. This external device you've built, while impressive, lacks the sophistication necessary for true inter-species cooperation."

"You put that into their brain? How could you know it wouldn't hurt them?" Jill demanded in that same dreadful tone of cold anger. Her hand rested possessively on Ainsley's shoulder, though they didn't think she noticed that she'd done it.

"I did not know with certainty," the alien replied just as quietly. "The translator array is highly adaptable and has been integrated successfully with the minds of many species, but without extensive study it was a risk. As I said, I am prepared to accept whatever justice your laws deem appropriate. But my people have lived in terror of yours for tens of cycles. It was my hope that, in doing this thing, I could give our two peoples the chance to know each other. To put fear behind us. Perhaps even to welcome you into the greater interstellar community. It is my hope still that, on the day your people accept a seat upon the Council of Peopled Worlds, perhaps you can forgive me for what I've done today."

"Maybe, maybe not," Ainsley said, putting a hand on top of Jill's on their shoulder and squeezing lightly. "I guess if nothing else I can thank you that I'll definitely make it into the history books now. First human xenolinguistic translator."

FRUIT OF ANOTHER'S TREE
CHANTAL BOUDREAU

Poma heard her mother moving in the room next to hers as she awoke. The room had remained empty until now, but her mother had been watching for signs that Poma might be ready to seek out her tree. As soon as the older woman had detected any of those suggestions, she had taken this as a cue to begin renovations.

Poma had been reminded of those signs year after year, so she had been able to recognize them as well when they had finally arrived. Her hips had grown fuller, her face and breasts had plumped up and she felt a near constant itch at the nape of her neck. Her mother had called that the travelling itch. It would remain until Poma sought out her tree.

Listening to her mother's bustling as she lay in bed, Poma wished she could be that excited. While her body might suggest otherwise, she didn't feel ready to become a mother herself. She wanted to cling to her youth, to that lack of obligation to anyone other than her. If she had had the choice, she believed she would have ignored the call from her tree completely.

As it was, Poma had probably put it off as long as she could. The instinctual yearning at her core had become so incessant that it existed as a persistent distraction. She had actually felt it before her mother had noticed, hiding the truth for as long as she could. She knew she would not be able to resist the call for much longer though. She had awoken twice already to find herself out of bed and headed for the door. If she waited much longer, her nocturnal travels could prove dangerous.

Getting to her swollen feet, Poma shuffled over to the closet. Her joints ached as she pulled on her robes and would continue to do so until she had done the only thing that would bring her relief. She was tired, tired enough, perhaps, to finally concede to making that long trek to the orchard.

Poma moaned and rubbed her back as she stepped into the hallway. Hunger had already set upon her innards like some noisy, rabid animal. It growled and quivered, demanding food without apology. Her mother made brief eye contact as she sailed past.

"You know what to do if you want to be rid of your troubles. It's in our nature, Poma. You can't deny that. Fighting it will just lead to further discomfort."

"Ridding me of these troubles but introducing new ones. I like my sleep. I liked my body the way it was."

"And if I had thought that way, where would you be?"

Poma followed her mother down the hallway. Instead of answering, she eyed the older woman up and down. Her mother still had a hint of youth to her form and face, her fading skin still more green than yellowish-brown, but would be considered past her prime. She would have difficulty finding a life partner now.

With that thought in mind, Poma considered her own fate. She had not found a partner yet either, and soon it would be too late. She no longer had the energy to visit the village mixers, plus those who were called rarely got the attention of anyone still fresh. She often wondered if she had failed to find someone because her mother had never set a proper example for her. She didn't want to end up raising her daughter alone.

Of course, she wouldn't be entirely alone. Others Poma's mother's age had a tendency to travel to warmer parts to retire, leaving the next generation to handle the child-rearing by themselves—but that was when they had someone with whom to travel. Poma's mother intended to stay.

"You would have had more time to find a partner? Instead, you were burdened with me to deal with by yourself. I don't want that. I want a full life."

Her mother shook her head and tsked.

"I never considered you a burden, and I have had a full life. If I was meant to find a partner, I would have found one. Who says we all have a match out there? You're a lot like me in spirit. We're not as flexible in our ways. That doesn't benefit us when we're trying to find someone out there in search of a co-operative partnership. We seem less likely to compromise."

And we are, Poma thought. Arguments with her mother often lasted for days, neither willing to concede. It frustrated her to no end, but at the same time, knowing her mother was so steadfast was a boon. They had always been able to rely on one another, that much about their relationship Poma appreciated.

"I have breakfast ready," the older woman said, heading to the kitchen. Poma joined her, but the moment she sat at the table in front of her plate of food, a wave of nausea swept over her. She felt even greener than she normally was.

"You're not eating," her mother remarked.

Poma shook her head. Nausea and hunger clashed within her, and a battle ensued. She gritted her teeth until the unpleasant feeling passed. She realized if she ever wanted to sit down and enjoy a meal again someday, without the inner turmoil, there was only one thing she could do.

It was time to concede to her fate.

"I'll pack my things after breakfast," she said with a sigh. "It's time for me to go."

Her mother clapped and laughed gleefully. "I've had one packed and ready for you for some time now. Did you want me to go with you?"

That wasn't the way things were normally done. If Poma had had a partner, they would make the trip together. It would seem weird—almost incestuous—taking her mother along. At the same time, Poma didn't want to offend her.

"Did your mother go with you?"

"No, no—of course not. I'm sure you'll be fine on your own. I just can't wait for this to happen, but I'll give you your space."

Poma hadn't expected it to be that easy. She was grateful her mother hadn't put up a fight.

An hour later, after making sure what her mother had packed was acceptable and throwing on her travelling clothes, Poma set out. She endured her mother's fervent hugs and tearful goodbye before starting up the hill towards the orchard. The trip would take her the better part of the day, but she would be able to reach her tree before dark.

She had made the practice trip on her tenth birthday, just as all girls did, so she knew the way, but it had been a far easier trip in that young spry body. Struggling up the hill with less limber limbs and the occasional bout of dizziness meant the trek was slower going. To Poma's delight though, her symptoms started to fade as she climbed. She assumed this was in response to her finally heeding her tree's call and enjoyed the sense of relief.

The journey gave her the chance to come to terms with what she was doing and realize that it was fear that had been the real cause of her reluctance. She had liked the rut she had slipped into, avoiding change for a reason. That was why she had never put her heart into finding a partner, why she had resisted the calling for so long.

When the orchard, and then her own tree finally came into view, she expected a sudden resurgence of the travelling itch and that pull drawing her to its fruit, but it didn't happen. Her symptoms still felt as though they were waning slightly, still persistent, but not as strong. And instead of that full, swollen feeling she had tolerated for weeks, Poma noted a distinct hollowness at her core.

Something was wrong.

She sprinted the remainder of the way to her tree and came to a screeching halt as she almost trampled the fruit lying on the ground below its branches. This wasn't the way it was supposed to be. She was supposed to arrive at the foot of the tree, pluck the ripe fruit from the lowermost branch, and devour it, up to and including the core.

Poma's anxiety increased when she bent down to pick up the fallen fruit and a foul smell assaulted her senses. She flinched away as a result, afraid to make contact. Despite her reluctance to touch it, she tapped the fruit gently with her foot. The side of the fruit fell away at even that slight a touch, revealing the rot below the surface.

She had lost her chance. Her fruit was beyond the point of consumption.

Poma didn't know how to react to this, at first. She had fought the compulsion to eat the fruit for so long that it had aged past ripeness, but she had always wanted to have the choice to eat it when she chose to. Trees rarely yielded two fruits, and if they did, they tended to ripen at the same time, giving that tree's surrogate the option to birth one daughter or two. It was highly unlikely her tree would ever yield another fruit. She would be the end of her family line. Her tree would be the last in their section of the orchard.

At first, Poma encountered a sense of denial. She seized a fallen branch from her tree and poked through her fruit's remains hoping to find even some small piece to salvage. Out of desperation, she would have eaten it if she had found anything not yet rotten.

When it became clear that the spoilage was complete, she fell to her knees beside the mess, ignoring the stench. She was angry at the world—angry at herself. Why hadn't she been willing to heed her mother's advice? Why had she been so stubborn?

And yet, a part of her bit back bitterly in her defence. Why should her tree and the calling get to dictate the timing of things? All she had wanted was a choice. She had felt robbed of that when her body had started changing and she felt robbed of that again now that her fruit was beyond her reach. A part of her wanted to fight, spitting mad. Another part of her just wanted the ground to swallow her up, the way she would have her fruit, and choke out the fires burning inside her.

She realized anger wasn't the only thing assailing her at that moment either. Even if she hadn't been sure about her trek, by the end of it she had been anticipating something she could no longer have, so grief lived inside her too. She had lost something. Her mother had lost something. And it wasn't just a chance at another generation. It was the seed of hope.

That was when Poma's tears started. She hadn't been prepared for it, her sudden urgent need for release. Believing that she was alone in the orchard, she wept loudly, rolling in the dirt, pounding and clawing at her chest, and kicking at the earth. Imagine her surprise when her meltdown was interrupted by the voice of another.

"What happened?"

Startled, Poma twisted herself around and out of a prone position, launching herself to her knees as quickly as she could manage. A strange girl stood amongst the trees in front of her. She did not have the kind of appearance that would have drawn Poma's attention in a crowd. Her green-brown hair had been cropped short. She was of an average height, and stout but athletic, with disproportionately broad shoulders and flat yet pendulant breasts. Poma noted genuine concern in the girl's tone, and she had kind, moss-green eyes. Her body might look hard, but her smile offered softness and warmth.

Poma tried to explain, but little came out.

"I was...and then it...and now...and I don't know what to do."

In the end, she resorted to gesturing at the decimated fruit. The other girl could not restrain a look of pity combined with disgust.

"Oh," the stranger said quietly.

After a moment's pause, she walked over to Poma and offered her a hand up from the ground.

"My name is Sitra, and it would appear we both have our own predicaments."

Poma took the offered hand and allowed herself to be pulled to her feet as she wiped tears away.

"Why? What's wrong?"

"Let me show you."

Sitra led Poma through the spaces between the trunks of many a mature tree, until they arrived at the base of one bearing ripe fruit. The low branch it dangled from bowed over due to its healthy weight. The fruit glistened formidably, and Poma could smell its heady sweet scent from several feet away. Something stirred within her anew. She yearned for it.

"I don't understand. It's perfect."

"The problem isn't with the fruit."

Poma glanced back at Sitra and instantly realized what it was she meant. The fruit was ready for the picking, but Sitra wasn't. There was no curve to what should have been the shapely parts of her body. There was no swell to her breasts. Nothing about her looked rounded or buoyant.

Nothing about her looked fertile.

"Oh," Poma said quietly, because that's all there really was to say.

"I never managed to find a partner, but I didn't mind, I had lots of company at home. I waited for the changes, so I could add my daughter to the mix, but they never came. Everyone else got tired of waiting along with me. First my sister left. She found a partner and her changes came as they should. They decided to find a new house after they both had their daughters, and our house became far too crowded."

She paused, clearly upset and trying to compose herself before continuing.

"Eventually our mothers got tired as well. They planned on travelling. They told me if the changes came, if I needed their help, I could send a message to bring them back, but it never happened. I decided eventually to come visit my tree again—to see if something had become of it, and this was what I found. There was never anything wrong with my tree. It was me."

"But it's clearly ripe," Poma said, her hunger almost overwhelming. "You could still eat it."

Sitra shook her head.

"I could, but I know it wouldn't do any good. Nothing would grow from it. It would be a waste, like planting a seed in dead earth."

"You can't know that for sure." Poma gave in to the temptation to touch the fruit and walked over to caress it.

It came free in her hands, begging for her to bite into it. Her entire body began to tremble, and a moment's light-headedness forced her to her knees.

"Oh, Sitra. I'm sorry. I didn't mean to dislodge it. It just looked so inviting. I-I wanted to feel it."

Poma's body ached, some of her muscles cramping at being denied what they had come to the orchard to claim. Sitra walked over and knelt down beside her, resting a steadying hand on her shoulder.

"It's okay. It would have fallen soon anyway. You just accelerated the inevitable." Sitra gave Poma a strange look, falling deathly quiet for a few moments. "Do you want it?"

Poma choked and nearly toppled over at the notion. She eyed Sitra with new intensity. She had never heard of anyone doing anything like that before, consuming the fruit from another's tree. It could be worth a try.

"Do you mean it?"

Sitra nodded.

In that moment, Poma finally had the choice that she had yearned for. She could give in to her instincts and her urges and devour the fruit without any promises or guarantees of a particular outcome, or she could politely refuse Sitra's offer, since she really had no claim on the fruit in the first place. She sat there contemplating, ever so grateful to even have the opportunity. Eventually, she decided she did want it after all. This wouldn't just be a way to possibly ensure the continuation of both her and Sitra's family lines, but it would also be a true adventure—a first.

"Then I want it."

Sitra helped her hold the fruit as she ate, Poma's hands

shaking so severely from sheer excitement that she could hardly manage to lift the fruit to her mouth. Eating it was pure bliss. She had never tasted anything so satisfying. Her entire body seemed to celebrate as she swallowed each morsel and Poma responded by trying to take it in even faster, to the point that she could barely breathe. The remainder of the devouring became a blur, an exhilarating, sensory explosion. The only thing that kept her grounded during that time was the sensation of Sitra's hand touching hers.

After she had finished, it took some time for Poma to regain her senses. She rested, murmuring happily in Sitra's arms until she could speak again, just staring up at the blue sky and enjoying the pleasant glow that eating the fruit had provided. Finally, Poma found her voice again.

"I wonder if my own fruit would have tasted so good, had I eaten it before it had fallen," she said.

Sitra shrugged. "I guess you'll never know. Does it matter? Did it work?"

Poma fought through the haze of pleasure to note the gentle stirring already beginning within her. Her mother had described that feeling to her many a time, a tickle and a tingle combined with a mild discomfort. Poma nodded.

"It worked."

Sitra smiled, but with an air of bewilderment.

"I've never heard of anyone doing it this way before."

"That doesn't make it wrong," Poma insisted. She then struggled to get to her feet. Sitra assisted.

"What do we do now?"

"I'm doing exactly what I had planned before I found that rotten fruit. I'm heading home to await the birth and seed expulsion. And I intend on getting there before walking gets too awkward." Poma knew her belly would continue to expand as her daughter and the seed for her daughter's tree grew within her. In a few days, when they were ready, her body would force both out.

Poma would then have to deal with the obligations of parenting she had been avoiding for so long. She also would have to plant the seed and upon her daughter's fifth birthday, after Poma had nurtured both to a certain level of maturity, they would return to the orchard to transfer the seedling, just as she had done with her mother.

Sitra balked at this, her expression falling. Poma could only guess that since Sitra had some claim on her daughter as well, this is not what she had been expecting.

"Look—I understand she's as much your daughter as she is mine," Poma said. "But it's my home, and she's inside of me. This isn't a standard coupling. Neither of us agreed to any of this beforehand, so you and I have to figure this out as we go."

This didn't seem to offer Sitra any consolation.

What Poma did next took even her by surprise. Sitra was still effectively a stranger; she barely knew anything about her, but having eaten her fruit, they were now irrevocably connected. This would not be an ordinary relationship by any means.

"You can come with me...if you like."

Sitra nodded, her face lighting up again.

As Poma began her descent, Sitra moved up beside her and took her hand. She told herself Sitra was only doing this to guide her down the hill safely but, in her heart, she knew there was more to it than that. They were bound by something new, something different. Sitra's offer had been a cure to her loss. In accepting that, Poma had become the cure to Sitra's loneliness. They had found in each other something they needed—something that had been missing.

Now it was just a matter of explaining everything to Poma's mother with the hope that she would understand. And she would. Poma knew it.

Her mother wouldn't care who Sitra was or how her granddaughter had come to be. She had never been one to judge. She would love her granddaughter no matter what, without question, without care.

Even if she had come from the fruit of another's tree.

A Toronto native currently living in Sambro, Nova Scotia, Chantal Boudreau is an avid and prolific author with over sixty credits to her name. She is the author of the Fervor series of novels, as well as the Masters & Renegades series and The Snowy Barrens trilogy.

Boudreau is likely best known for her work in short fiction, and the anthologies she has appeared in have been shortlisted for both the Bram Stoker award and the Aurora award.

Her extensive short-fiction bibliography includes fantasy, dark fantasy, and horror. To date she has over seventy published short story credits.

CONCERNS
LIANA CUSMANO

A cold, gray light bled into the studio apartment that October morning as Dylan stared at the ceiling, wide awake. Emma was snoring softly beside xem, turned towards the floor-to ceiling window that looked out over the sleeping city. Reaching out, Dylan trailed one finger along her right shoulder blade, brushing a lock of dark hair over her skin.

The apartment was small, but with high ceilings and hardwood floors. Dylan's blazer and paisley neckerchief lay draped across one of the two chairs at the small kitchen table and a single succulent sat on the nearby counter.

"I managed to kill a succulent once," Dylan had said when xe had first seen it, weeks earlier. "I overwatered it."

"Sounds just like you," Emma had remarked, checking the soil in the little gray pot. "A keen bean."

Dylan felt her roll over. Xe wrapped an arm around her as she settled her head on xyr chest, folding her legs against xyr long frame.

"What've you got today?" she murmured, her voice

sleepy.

"Debate prep. Then that town hall."

"Just do what you did last night on the panel. Are you nervous?"

"No," xe lied.

"Don't let the Conservative intimidate you."

"I don't know that I've ever been intimidated by anyone who identifies as a Conservative."

Emma laughed and sat up, swinging her legs over the edge of the bed and stifling a yawn. Dylan stared as she stood and crossed the apartment towards the coffee maker.

"You're so beautiful," xe whispered before xe could stop xemself. She turned and smiled at xem, her eyes soft. When Emma left the room and turned on the shower, the sound of running water gently washed away the thick morning stillness, and Dylan felt calmer and more comfortable than xe had in weeks.

"I'm at the campaign office all day today, if you want to come by and prep there," she said later, bringing two coffees into bed. She'd made a cappuccino in the Millicent Fawcett mug for her, black coffee in the Che Guevara mug for xem.

"I'll pass by."

"Simon will be there." Dylan shrugged.

When xe got dressed and leaned over to kiss her, xe could see her phone lighting up with dozens of notifications from the bedside table.

"Some candidate probably said something stupid," Emma said, glancing at it absentmindedly. "I'll be at the office in about a half hour."

"I'll wait at least an hour before I show up." They kissed once more before xe left.

***

"You did great with the question about social housing," Liam said, squinting through the windshield. He and Dylan were in Liam's rusty five-door hatchback, crawling through wet traffic after the town hall that evening.

"You don't think I went too easy on the corporate real estate developers?" Dylan's fingers moved automatically to tug at xyr absent neckerchief, forgotten at Emma's kitchen table.

"The other candidates pretty much exhausted that. It gave you time to expand a little on the platform. But, you messed up by mentioning the toxic waste dump." Dylan winced. "That's in the next neighbourhood over, the one closer to the river."

"I totally forgot."

"You talked about it in that radio interview last week for like, ten minutes."

"The context was totally different," Dylan sulked, staring out the window.

Liam glanced over at xem and sighed, "Don't do that thing you do, where you focus on one mistake and get all hard on yourself. You were excellent; better than in your first debate."

Dylan groaned. "So embarrassing."

"'Hi, I'm Dylan. I'm going to imitate a deer in headlights for fifteen minutes,'" Liam mocked. "And then you did fine, like you always do. You freak out every time for no reason."

"I've always been like that, since high school."

"And those debates didn't even matter. This is different. I really think you're going to win."

"The chances are small."

"The same way they are for lots of candidates in a third party. But anything can happen." Liam turned on his flasher and took the exit. "In any case, I'm only your campaign manager so I can put this on my resume. You know that, right?"

"If anybody calls me and asks for a reference, I'll tell them I would have been better off without you."

Liam laughed.

Leaning xyr forehead against the window, Dylan watched the downtown lights flash by behind the glass. The hatchback trundled into xyr neighbourhood, a gentrifying part of town where crumbling apartments were giving way to pop-up shops.

"Was Emma able to help you at the campaign office today?"

"Yeah, she's been great." Dylan said, xyr voice even.

"What is she, managing director?"

"Executive director."

"And she's had all this time to prep a baby candidate like you? Aren't you over there like, every day?"

"She recruited me. And she promised she'd help."

"It's because she thinks you have a chance." Liam nodded to himself, convinced. "Isn't she also the leader's campaign manager?"

"No, that's Simon," Dylan said. "Who's forgetting things now?"

"I can hold together your ridiculous schedule—interviews, debates, canvassing—and drive you everywhere, and organize your volunteers, and make sure you remember to eat."

Liam slowed to a stop outside Dylan's apartment. "Which you haven't done tonight," he pointed out. "So excuse me if I forget a couple peoples' names."

Out on the sidewalk, Dylan surprised him with a tight hug.

"I wouldn't be able to do this without you," xe said, xyr voice muffled.

"I know," Liam said matter-of-factly, but Dylan knew he was smiling. Pulling away, he opened the driver's door and became serious. "I know you're tired. But we're almost there, just a few more days. I really think you're going to win, Dyl. I'll only take a little bit of credit on election day."

He shook xyr shoulder in mock exasperation. "Now eat something. We're going canvassing tomorrow afternoon, but your morning's free, so sleep in. Make some pancakes."

Dylan's apartment was narrow and spare, a small kitchen and even smaller bathroom sandwiching just enough space for a bed, a table, and a chest of drawers. Xe had only just dropped xyr satchel and peeled off xyr damp blazer when xyr phone buzzed with a message from Emma.

How did it go?

I didn't let anyone intimidate me. How's damage control?

The candidate who posted it apologized. He did it a long time ago, and if the Women's Federation supports us then maybe we won't have to ask him to step down.

Dylan put a pot of water on the stove to boil and rummaged in xyr kitchen cupboard for tea. *People know the abortion debate is closed—I think it'll blow over. How are you doing?*

By the time the water boiled, Emma still hadn't replied. Dylan turned down the heat and grabbed a mug.

Tired, was the eventual response.

Then, *I miss you*. Before Dylan could respond, the message was deleted.

Me too, xe wrote back.

We're hosting a quiz night tomorrow, Emma wrote. *You should come after canvassing.*

How do you know I'm going canvassing?

I check the candidates' events' calendars. Sometimes I plan my schedule around yours.

Dipping the steeper into the hot water, Dylan wrapped xyr hands around the heat of the mug and imagined that Emma was there in the kitchen with xem.

I'll see you tomorrow night.

I can't wait to see you, was the reply. *And hold you in my arms.* Dylan stared hard at the phone screen until the words vanished.

Me too.

***

Dylan had had xyr first event at an elementary school that day. Sitting in a nearby café an hour beforehand, Emma had watched xem fail to swallow more than three bites of granola and offered to buy xem a coffee.

"I read a few of your pieces when I vetted you," she said, handing xem the cup. "The personal essay about black coffee's my favourite. I showed it to Simon and he liked it a lot too."

"It's a bit cliché," Dylan admitted. "The anxious writer who depends on black coffee."

"I think it's sweet." She brushed xyr shoulder as she sat down. They were already looking for any excuse to touch one another.

"I'm really grateful that you come to my events, but I feel like I'm distracting you from your job," Dylan mumbled. "I'm sorry," xe added, even though xe wasn't.

"This is my job. Someone needs to take care of you when Liam remembers that he's a grad student," her eyes were kind. "And you're just starting out. Look at you, your hands are trembling."

When she covered xyr hand with hers, their fingers interlaced as easily and as naturally as if the moment were banal, as if they held hands all the time.

"I'll probably be the first openly non-binary trans person these kids ever see," Dylan fretted, squeezing Emma's fingers.

"You're not a spokesperson for the whole trans community. Just be yourself."

They kissed for the first time beneath a canopy of autumn leaves after the event. Three blocks from the school, Emma had quickly looked to the left and right of the suburban street, grasped Dylan's neckerchief and pulled xem towards her. Later, in the quiet afterwards, she twined her legs against xyrs as they lay close together in xyr bed. A fortnight of orbiting one another, of feeling the same gravitational pull—in meetings, at fundraisers, during protests—had them sliding towards one another in a way that felt almost inevitable.

"You were so gorgeous," she whispered. "You made banning single-use plastic sound like the most interesting thing in the world. Those kids loved you."

"Did you like the way I explained that I look like I'm

a girl but I'm not?"

"It was perfect. You were perfect." Dylan kissed the top of her head. Every strand of her hair seemed to glint in the afternoon light.

"I never had that," xyr voice caught. "I knew something was off when I was a kid, but I didn't know what it was. If there was even one trans kid in that crowd, just one—" Emma threaded her fingers in xyrs and squeezed. She held xyr hands until they stopped trembling.

***

"Why should I vote for you?"

The woman had a bulging shopping bag in one hand and a c   hihuahua in the other, cradled against her chest. It stared beadily at Dylan as the three of them stood outside a grocery store, in one of the more affluent neighbourhoods in the riding. Liam and other party volunteers were approaching unsuspecting shoppers all around them on their last Saturday of canvassing before Election Day.

"You're young, you don't come from an established political family, this is your first election campaign," the woman rattled off. "Politicians are full of shit. Why should I vote for you?"

"For all the reasons you just gave me." Dylan calmly repeated a variation of what xe had been telling similarly jaded people all afternoon, and throughout the entire campaign—if voters believed that the system was broken, and that the people who kept being elected kept failing to resolve the same problems, then it was time for radical change.

"Our party has the youngest and most diverse cohort of candidates in this election," Dylan said. "And almost none of us are career politicians—we didn't study political science and then go to law school, just so we could sit in the House of Commons and collect a paycheck.

"Have the Liberals or the Conservatives been using their money to protect the environment, or to help small businesses, or to implement Pharmacare?" The woman didn't take her eyes off xem. Her chihuahua snuffled. "They've had MPs that were so awful the only time they got up in the House was to close a window."

Over the past several weeks, a few of the people who had approached xem with skepticism had walked away from xem in surprise. Some had stopped for a long while, asking questions or sharing stories—they had a parent who couldn't afford their medication, a friend with a Ph.D. who worked at a diner. "What are your concerns?" Dylan had asked, over and over again, at grocery stores, in front of metro stations, at city halls. "What are your biggest concerns?"

"I'm polling at thirty percent right now," xe said, returning the c   hihuahua's stare and nodding at the nearest election signs. Two dedicated volunteers had managed to tie Dylan's around a telephone pole ten feet above the ground, placing xyr face high above the incumbent's. "Which means; I'm the only one who can beat the Conservative." The woman hefted her chihuahua under her arm, squinted at Dylan, and asked where she could go vote on Monday.

Later that evening, Dylan leaned xyr head back against the headrest of Liam's passenger seat and sighed. The others had disappeared into a nearby coffee shop, leaving Dylan and their youngest volunteer, Jordan, in the parking lot.

Xyr phone buzzed. Emma's message was funny, salacious and tender, all at once. Soon the words were gone, but so was Dylan's tiredness. Smiling, eyes closed, xe thought of the way Emma stroked xyr face when they were alone.

Opening xyr eyes, xe saw Jordan staring at xem intently in the rearview mirror.

"How do you just keep going? How do you keep talking to people, and saying the same things over and over, even when it feels pointless?" Barely out of high school, Jordan was usually the first volunteer to arrive on site and the last to leave. Dylan had developed a soft spot for them.

Xe hesitated. "I don't know," xe admitted. "You just do it. Sometimes you can get through to people, and that's encouraging. Other times you can't. Did I tell you about the guy who didn't believe in climate change? Or the woman who said that I'm sick and I need to see a doctor, and all trans people should be sterilized?"

Jordan shook their head, eyes going wide.

"What was I going to do, argue with her? I told her I disagreed and I moved on. Then I went home and cried about it a bit," xe shrugged. "When I have a bad day, I talk to Liam, or to Emma. It's helpful to have good friends around. People who care, like you," xe smiled.

"You make it look so easy. You just open your mouth and… and people want to hear what you have to say. And you're so kind, and smart." Jordan blushed. "It's so cool to see a non-binary person running. I wish I was eighteen. I won't be able to say I voted for you when you win."

***

Dylan felt jittery, buzzing with anticipation when Liam dropped xem off in front of the bar that night. On xyr way towards the back room, where xe could hear the sounds of what was definitely a quiz night, xe ran into Simon. Tall and dark, his voice always deep and measured; he had a tone and a smile that always put Dylan instantly at ease. It seemed like nothing could faze Simon.

"Emma will introduce you to Jocelyn. She wants to know how you've managed to climb ten percent in the polls. I've told her about your pronouns, but she'll probably mess up." His expression was apologetic.

When Dylan walked into the room, crowded and raucous, xe instantly made eye contact with Emma. Xe saw her face light up from the other end of the room and felt like xyr stomach had bottomed out. Sipping a beer at the bar a few moments later, xyr throat tightened as xe watched her, handling the scoreboard and managing the crowd. She was so beautiful, and she looked so tired. Dylan wanted to gather her up in xyr arms and take her someplace quiet and faraway, where they could be alone together.

When the final points were tallied up and prizes given away, Dylan hopped off xyr stool and made xyr way through the mass of people mingling. Every volunteer or candidate who called xyr name and wanted to talk felt like a bitter obstacle between xem and Emma, including the Party leader.

"This is Dylan," Emma said, with barely concealed pride.

Jocelyn looked xem up and down. She was a small woman, with short dark hair and piercing eyes. "I've heard a lot about you."

"I hope that's a good thing." They shook hands.

"We wouldn't give a winnable riding to just anyone." She motioned to Simon, on the phone in a corner of the room. "Your volunteer application wound up on his desk and he knew right away that we wouldn't want you handing out flyers."

Dylan blinked. Xe looked questioningly at Emma. "I didn't know—"

"I'm the one who called and convinced you to run," she admitted. "But the very first person to consider you was actually Simon."

"He has a knack for recruiting the right people," Jocelyn nodded. "And it's so important to have young women like yourself on the ballot."

Dylan's insides froze. Xe felt Emma take xyr arm. "Xe is great. And all xyr hard work is paying off. It's thanks to xem that this riding is getting so much coverage."

"My apologies," Jocelyn's voice was sincere. "Smart young people like yourself."

Once they were finally in the silence of xyr apartment, Dylan hastily put the chain on the lock and then immediately caught Emma in xyr arms, pressing xyr nose into the side of her neck and breathing in as deeply as xe could. Xe could feel all the tension melting out of xyr body as Emma gripped xem tightly. She held xyr face in both hands and kissed xem.

"I can't stay long," she sighed. "Simon's coming to my place. And I have to be up early tomorrow for that press— god, you're so beautiful." She wrapped her arms around xem and they fell onto the bed, their kiss long and deep. Eventually, Dylan put xyr head on Emma's shoulder and was still. Xe could feel her heart beating against xyrs as she put her hand to the back of xyr neck.

"Does it change anything that Simon wanted you as a candidate?"

"Not really…I guess I just feel even guiltier now."

"He knows I have a crush on you," Emma said, as though that made everything better.

"Is that what this is? A crush?"

"No," she said, her voice low. "You're tired, bean. We can talk about this later." Dylan couldn't find it in xem to protest. They lay in silence, Emma's fingers in Dylan's hair.

"Everything was fine before I met you," she finally murmured. "I could've gone on pretending my whole life. And then you happened." Dylan propped xemself up on one elbow and kissed her forehead. After she left, her absence felt like an ache in xyr bones.

***

Dylan woke up early on Election Day, feeling the coiled anticipation that came with being poorly rested and over excited. Xyr adrenaline took a hit when xe walked into the campaign office and came face-to-face with Simon.

"Good luck today," he said. "Before I forget…" he rummaged through his shoulder bag and handed Dylan xyr paisley neckerchief. "This is yours." Dylan took the neckerchief without saying a word. Simon gave him a wry smile, his dark eyes unreadable.

Are you alright? Dylan sent the message before hitting the third intersection of the day, in the heart of xyr riding. Pins and flyers in hand, xe, Liam, Jordan, and a few others were making their final effort, loudly reminding every passerby to get out and vote.

Yes, was the response.

What are we going to do?

I don't know. Let's just get through today.

Xe could imagine Emma frowning at her phone screen, an island of quiet distress in the whirling energy of the campaign office.

I want you to know how proud I am that I convinced you to run. And no matter what the results are, the best thing that happened to me during this campaign will always be you.

After a few seconds, the words vanished.

That evening, an hour after the polls had closed, Dylan and xyr team were in a downtown conference hall, toasting their hard work as the results from Atlantic Canada came trickling in. Dylan felt jumpy and tired, but xe could feel the weight of xyr own expectations slowly sliding off their shoulders, knowing that there was nothing left to do but wait. The hall began to fill up, but Emma was nowhere in sight. There was a flicker of excitement as a riding in the Maritimes changed colours more than once, from red to blue to yellow, before finally settling on red.

Their first win came in an eastern province. By then, the hall was packed with candidates, volunteers, staff and supporters, talking loudly while their eyes remained glued to the many television screens mounted on the walls. A cheer went up when the margin became decisive. Another cheer rang out when Jocelyn entered the hall, Simon and Emma close behind. The rest of the room fell away and Dylan took a single step forward, but Emma's eyes were wide and unhappy, her face pale. She shook her head almost imperceptibly as Simon steered her into a corner of the room, looking uncharacteristically pained.

"This is good," Liam bobbed his head, already on his

fourth drink. "This is really good. I told you, Dyl, I told you!" Dylan smiled. Xyr lingering doubts began to vanish as, slowly, the party colours crept further west. Ten other ridings in two other provinces, then fourteen more ridings, then twenty. "It's a yellow wave!" someone finally shouted, and the hopeful, almost disbelieving tension in the room broke wide open. There were cheers as candidates congratulated one another, the noise in the hall reaching deafening levels with every new seat.

The screens boasted an onslaught of victories in one electoral district after another.

Dylan's stomach somersaulted when, finally, xyr face appeared on every screen in the room. At that moment, Emma walked back into the hall and took in the already huge margin on the nearest television. Finding xyr gaze instantly and without taking her eyes of xem, she moved through the crowd directly towards Dylan and, heedless, threw her arms around xem.

As the numbers climbed, the voices in the room built and built. The Conservative incumbent's face appeared on the screen for the last time before quickly, decisively, sliding away to make room for Dylan's. The crowd's roar shook the walls.

Liam was shouting. So was Emma. Dylan could barely understand a word they said, xyr head spinning. Emma's arms tight around xyr neck and her body against xyrs were the only things that felt real. Jordan and xyr volunteers were jumping up and down. The crowd surged around Dylan, everyone shouting and embracing. When the last of the results came in, the entire province was one solid colour. Champagne corks popped, sailing over the crowd, and candidates began to spill out into the streets, inflamed by the staggering, unprecedented success of being the Official Opposition.

"I need to prepare for media," Emma's voice was loud in xyr ear. "Don't worry, I'll be back." Giddy and bold, Dylan kissed her cheek before she disappeared into the crowd.

Hours later, after the final toasts and the victory speeches, Dylan, Liam, and dozens of others were still in the hall, jubilant and exhausted. "I'll be your chief of staff," Liam said, flushed and grinning. "But only so I can put it on my resume."

Laughing, Dylan felt a hot, triumphant feeling in xyr whole body, a joy and pride that would last xem weeks. Xe thought of the one trans kid who had surely been in the crowd that day at the elementary school. Xyr phone buzzed.

I'm so proud of you, bean. Hundreds of thousands of queer and trans people all over the country are proud of you. You are so amazing, and so brave. You've already inspired so many people.

Emma sent xem one more message. Dylan kept xyr eyes on the screen, waiting for it to disappear. It didn't.

Liana Cusmano is the President of the Green Party of Canada from Montreal, Quebec. 2022 will see the release of their first novel, Catch & Release, *from Guernica Editions. Previous publications also include "Matters of Great Unimportance" in Influence and Confluence, East and West: A Global Anthology of the Short Story, edited by Maurice A. Lee, and, "Superhero Pill" in The Radiance of the Short Story: Fiction from Around the Globe by editors Maurice A. Lee and Aaron Penn.*

WHEN WIZARDS SING
STEVE CARR

He is old, older than anyone I have ever known. I look at him as he rests; his pale, expressionless face seeming unfamiliar. I wonder if it was only a year ago that his balding head was thick with hair the color of a fiery red sunset? On his lap, the patchwork quilt bordered with a fringe the color of golden reeds, is one that I made for him. My fingers ached as I stitched each square, using exotic cloths from uncharted islands, while I watched him age so rapidly. Beneath the quilt is a frail body that once, in days when he was well, could playfully carry me on his strong back. It is his brow that most looks withered with age, lined and cracked like an oil painting exposed to excessive heat. In the tradition of our years together, I lean and kiss him there.

His eyes suddenly open; two red-rimmed, glassy-jewels, that nonetheless remind me of his ability to hold me with his stare alone. While all else is lost, his gaze is still magnetic and piercing. From the beginning, his eyes have been maps, and I have sought in them the direction to my most perplexing problems. Should I go home? How long will I live? What about the monsters beneath the sea?

He begins with memories, history lessons he taught me long ago. He speaks as if I don't know these things.

"The nests of El-wasr-kat are scattered among the cliffs above the waters of the Great Pearl, or Sin-so-tokar. The nests are finely woven, made of silvery seaweed, intricately woven hairs from albino otters, brightly colored coral glazed and fired in volcanic kiln and spun brass from artifacts from sunken ships."

His voice is not nearly as weak as the blood that pulses through his veins. As his parchment-paper lips move and words are expelled. I hear him clearly, as if from years ago, gently scolding me for being inattentive. Straightening, my back held tense and upright, I wait for just a moment, and then he begins again.

"From the nests of El-wasr-kat we could see the whale graveyards just beneath the curling white foam atop Sin-so-tokar. I have known some of the greatest whales of sea history. Dandor Magnifico, the leader of the sixteenth century undersea rebellion. Bortend Tremor, the largest whale in recorded sea history. Amsar Dolphninia, the great Blue that translated and taught the language of man to the creatures of the sea. Each one, and many more, entombed in shimmering rainbows of coral, guarded by the legions of deadly striped blow fish and ever-so-watchful sea anemone.

"They come there to die, to Sin-so-tokar, those that are not slain by man, or washed ashore on distant lands, and while in their death ritual impart what they know and have seen, and every word-song is passed on for all generations of fish and mammals of the seas."

He leans forward and coughs, wheezing so loudly that it reminds me of the wind that curled about El-Wasr-kat during storm season. He doesn't take his eyes from mine and pushes aside my hand stretched out to catch the quilt sliding from his knees. He lets it fall and each image carefully sewn into the quilt—the mating of eels, the swarming of terns, seahorses and jellyfishes—falls to a heap at his feet. As he rests back against the chair, for an instant I see him as he was, not as he is.

"I am the first of the line of Beto-Dar-tokar and my nest was decorated with gold from the sunken treasures of Atlantis." A smile crosses his face forming and fading as quick as a shark's laugh. "Do you remember when we first met?"

I do. I do remember.

***

During three rainy weeks waiting for better sailing weather, holed up in a run-down hotel in Patagonia, we played cards and caught up on sleep while fending off boredom until it was reported that the storms at sea abated. We set sail on a day when the sun was white and threatening. Sun-browned children on the pier held their hands above their eyes and barely offered a wave. None of the adults, old men with weathered faces and striking women with long hair and dark eyes, wished us luck or bon voyage. Someone had tossed red flowers in the glassy water as we parted, and they drifted quickly out of sight as we were hurriedly carried away by a mysterious wind. We sailed south, then west, and when the storm hit, and the compass broke and the radio no longer worked, we were set adrift in the waters of the Southern Hemisphere.

When we left Patagonia there were four of us, but soon after the storm hit, Leon sickened. Though we quenched his thirst with our precious water, and fed him our best fruit, he died from a terrible fever on a moonlit night, in the arms of Armando who loved him.

They had met six years before while both were in the Brazilian Navy, hiding in whatever places they could find while on board a frigate to satisfy their desires. It was on a white sandy beach in Rio de Janeiro that I met them. We lay on our towels beneath the blistering sun and they regaled me with tales of their previous unsuccessful attempts to navigate yachts in the open ocean. Leon's quick wit and humor and Armando's intelligence and sincerity drew me to them, and we became fast friends.

"It was Leon who knew the stars!" Armando cried as we lowered Leon's body into the sea.

And this was true. He was the one who knew most, though it proved too little, about the stars and how to navigate in the southern part of the world. Of us remaining three, only Armando had sailed south of Patagonia, but he knew nothing of stars or wind directions or currents. He knew how to handle the sails and with those broken, tattered and in pieces, he immediately fell into despair.

"We will live through this," Jacques told us, trying to shake Armando from his lethargy and attempting to dislodge my feelings of impending doom. Jacques would stand on the bow of the small boat with his hands raised and his handsome, tanned face glistening; his voice would carry over the calmness of the sea. "I'll not let you die," he told us, "we will live to remember Leon."

At night Jacques and I would cuddle together beneath the blankets and console one another with kisses and caresses, but our affection felt hollow and sad. With Armando staying apart and silent but to sob in the dark beneath the stars, we couldn't feel happy or hopeful.

Many nights we traveled slowly on the water, carried this way, then that. It was Jacques who awoke in the middle of the night and would keep watch from the bow, while I lay beneath the blankets and tried to recall how it felt to walk on land, to see a tree or feel the dirt. Armando was sinking deeper into his own darkness, forever shaken by the loss of Leon. I too, was without hope; sorry for the life I would never have, immersed in my own self-pity. After Jacques would rise to take watch, I would fall asleep, tortured with nightmares until morning.

On which day or night, what month or date we lost Jacques, I do not recall. It could have been the fourteenth week or the fortieth day. Only Jacques was keeping a record of such things in the ship's log. I had awoken after another terrible night of horrific images flashing in my head and found that I was alone. Armando was huddled on the cot nearby, still sleeping. I arose, dressed, climbed up from the cabin and shielded my eyes against the glaring sunlight.

"Jacques?" I called out.

There was no answer.

There was a slight breeze carrying the smell of distant rain, the sound of water hitting the sides of the boat, but it was quiet in only a way that a sea can be.

"Jacques?" I said, again.

I didn't need to lower my hand from my eyes, to look about the boat. Some intuition, some unfathomable knowledge told me that Jacques was no longer on the boat. How, or why he was no longer on board I would never know, but certainly he was gone. Now, it was just me and Armando.

In the following days and nights I lay beside Armando with my arm around him as he barely moved, seldom spoke, and only ate or drank at my gentle urging. We rarely climbed to the deck and though small storms came and went, we didn't bother being concerned about our safety or worry that something needed to be secured or repaired. Together we drifted in and out of sweat-drenched nightmares, consumed with sea-fever, both unaware of days and nights, and soon too weak to go above and see if land was near or not to be seen at all.

"We're going to die," Armando told me as if it were fact. To hear him say it aloud suddenly frightened me, and I didn't want to die. "No, Armando, we're not going to die." I pulled my friend Armando close to me and cradled him in my arms until he drifted off to sleep. His breathing calm and steady, my heart beating with renewed interested in life, in living. I climbed from the cot and stumbled up the stairs to the deck. The breezes were light, soothing, warm and full of smells: earth smells. The stars were clusters of fireflies blinking in the black sky.

I strained to see out into the dark, feeling, knowing that there was land somewhere close by. I made my way to the bow of the ship and tried to see some sign of land. I watched for a coast illuminated by the thin slice of moon, or a campfire, or a resort with lights and music. Then I heard it, faintly at first, the sound of a chorus. It was as faint as a flock of birds heard from a great distance, but more melodic. I shook my head thinking I was imagining it, but as the boat moved, the sound of the singing became more pronounced. It was a chorus of men, singing from somewhere out in the dark. I leaned over the bow.

***

"It was not our nature to take in humans at El-wasr-kat," the old one tells me as his thin lips quiver and a small gem of spittle collects on his lower lip. "Once, Portuguese whalers happened upon our nests and destroyed many of them and killed many of us. Their ship was crushed and every sailor destroyed by the whales awaiting their final breaths before burial in Sin-so-tokar. Until then, we had only heard of humans, but afterward we vowed to never protect them as we did the sea creatures."

He leans back and raises his thin hands to his face, traces the curves of his dark eye-sockets, the sagging skin of his once strong jaw, and the path from his chin to his neck. Both hands move across his skin like spiders dancing on water.

"I was warned that you would bring great harm," he tells me, once again locking his eyes with mine. "I was encouraged to toss you back into the sea. The council of wizards pleaded with me to abandon you to what should have been your fate, the same fate as your companions."

"Jacques," I whisper, catching myself unaware of his presence in my thoughts.

***

The headlong tumble into the water, even as it occurred, somehow seemed fitting, as if it was the natural course of events that I should drown in such a simple fashion. The boat merely lurched, momentarily jolted by a strong current, and in a rush of seconds the black sea consumed me. I knew that I was leaving behind one world and entering another. It didn't strike me that I should attempt to swim or call out to Armando. My thoughts were of Jacques.

***

In Colón, Panama, I secured my yacht at the pier. Then Leon, Armando and I wandered around town in search of a good bar. In an alleyway we saw a sign hanging above a door with the words "Drifters Inn" on it and heard music coming from inside. It was a small saloon decorated with anchors, ship's steering wheels, and hundreds of conch shells. There were a couple of booths and three stools at a short bar. Through the haze of cigar and cigarette smoke I saw Jacques, sitting alone at the end of the bar. His duffle bag was on the floor next to where he sat.

We needed a fourth sailor for our planned voyage to circle the bottom of the world, and without knowing a thing about him, I was certain he was the one.

"I'm from Marseille," he said in a thick French accent a few minutes after I approached him. "I've been left stranded here almost penniless by the owner of the yacht I was Captain of."

I told him about our plans and while I stared into his ocean-green eyes he told me how he'd been a sailor since the age of sixteen.

We sailed from Colón a few days later, and a week later Jacques joined me in my bed.

***

I awoke from what seemed a very long slumber, feeling as if the world beneath me was a racing boat speeding headlong through darkest waters. I looked up at the night sky and watched the starscape change and wondered how it was that I had landed on the boat. I expected to see Armando lean over me, or hear the creaking of the deck, but

I also knew that without the sails the boat could not move so fast, and that what was beneath my back was alive.

I reached out my fingers and felt the cold, wet body of the thing that carried me. Stretching out, I measured it to be more than the span of my extended arms, and much longer than my height of six feet. I rolled over onto my stomach and faced the direction of the creature's head. I was being carried on the back of a whale and, as it cleaved the water at a dizzying speed, I felt no fear of being tossed from its back or pulled into the depths. I patted its sides in a tentative gesture of thanks and friendship, and let it carry me forward.

Of Armando's fate, I cannot say.

***

"We are taught to sing even before we speak, before we learn the magic of wizardry. We are taught the songs of dolphins, sea birds, and the many varieties of whale," he tells me. He opens his mouth and his gray tongue flutters as he emits a small musical note in the c-range.

"Thank you," I tell him, then answer back, giving two lower-toned notes in the fashion he taught me years before.

"You were a quick learner," he says as he rests his back against the chair and lets me, at last, put the quilt over his legs again.

"I had the best teacher," I reply, wanting to pat his hand as if he were the old man he had become.

"Already, you've forgotten me, forgotten who I was," he tells me as he closes his eyes and his face smooths to nothingness.

"Never, never," I assure him, but I fear that he might

be right. There is so much about him that is different. Only his eyes, how they look at me, are the same. A song becomes stuck in my throat and I warble a sad "I'm sorry."

***

El-wasr-kat was suddenly in front of us, rising out of the dark water like a giant. It eclipsed the glow from some distant phenomena of light. My eyes were stunned by the silhouetted blackness of the large rock out in the middle of the sea. How had I missed the light before? Was it from the south, the southern light? Aurora Australis?

And the music, the chorus of song coming from the rock, seemed to ebb and flow in a pattern that was equally enchanting and terrifying. Never had I heard such a hypnotic sound; a mixture of male voices, whale songs, flutes, and the rich texture of bows across the strings of a hundred violins. The music arose out of the dark side of the rock, almost as if the rock was singing. I sat up on the whale and cleared the spray from my eyes. Maybe, I reasoned, I have died and am entering heaven. Or hell.

In the blackest shadow of El-wasr-kat I became instantly aware that my whale-companion was in the company of a number of other large creatures, also whales. They gurgled and hummed, sang and chattered to one another. My whale, if I could call it mine, slowed considerably. In the dark I could hear its body sliding along the body of another whale, then another, and another. I strained to see into the darkness of El-wasr-kat, to detect what, or who, was making such music, but I couldn't discern any living things.

Then silence fell, and I lay upon the whale's back, and held my breath.

Light from the rising sun struck the water all about me

and I cried out in pain as a dazzling rainbow of light lifted out of the water and momentarily blinded me. My hands over my eyes, I feared opening them, afraid of having my eyes burned from their sockets, but I knew that I would have to look. Beneath me the whale had become very still, and the voices of El-wasr-kat rose even higher, but now were thick with baritone and tenor sounds as if sung by trained opera singers, and these lower notes were held for what seemed an impossible length of time. I removed my hands from my eyes and had my first look at El-wasr-kat and saw it bathed in light. It was a golden half-shell of a volcano covered with hundreds of glittering nests. In each nest stood one or two men, facing the light and draped in gossamer garments of black and gold, decorated with starfish and conch shells.

Beholding the beauty of that, I also looked about me and saw that there were about twenty whales of different species all facing El-wasr-kat, and surrounding the whales were fish and sea mammals of every type and color. The water seemed very shallow because, easily seen beneath the surface, there was sparkling coral, seemingly woven into a tapestry more elegant than I'd ever witnessed and reflecting like a jeweler's window in sunlight that bathed it.

For fear of missing something, I turned from one sight to another, ignoring the last shudder, the final breath, of the whale that had saved my life and carried me to El-wasr-kat.

***

"I don't want you to die so unhappily," I tell him, this time grasping his hand in mine and holding it to my cheek.

"We learn that air is the spirit of all things," he tells me. "My air will be yours and that makes me very happy," he says.

"We should never have left El-wasr-kat," I answer, knowing that for all the years sharing the nest above Sinso-tokar, I had not aged more than a few days, and that I'd heard and seen more wondrous things than can be expected of any mortal on Earth. And now he was paying with his life for the price of being carried to civilization. This done out of love for me.

"You weren't born of the wizards of El-wasr-kat," he says, then falls silent for a moment before taking my hand in his. "And I wasn't born of humans in this place you call home."

"I could take you back," I suggest, knowing that he is too near death to survive even a short journey to a coast where a dying whale would begin its pilgrimage back to El-wasr-kat and carry us along.

"Sing to me," he tells me. "A joyful passing into the realm of air is possible only when wizards sing."

"What shall I sing?" I ask.

"Of the morning when I carried you from a whale's back, up into my nest and we became as one."

I open my mouth and from deep within me arises the song of a wizard.

Steve Carr is an author with over 500 writing credits to his name. He has been nominated for the Pushcart Prize twice. In 2019, he was on the cover of the Inner Circle Writers' Magazine inaugural issue and dubbed "The King of Short Stories."

His first novel, Redbird, *was released in 2019.*

CAUSE AND EFFECT
RHEA ROLLMAN

The year Sarah Fisher turned thirty-five, three things of note happened to her.

In the United States, the state of Arkansas passed the first of several pieces of legislation targeting trans youth. The bill banned trans girls from playing in sports, deprived young people of access to trans-affirming health care, and made it a crime to support trans youth in their inevitable efforts to get around the repressive new laws.

Sarah, who lived in Canada, watched the news from the US with a deep sense of impotent rage. It was rare enough for her to watch the nightly news; rarer still for her to feel so personally affected by it. It was hard to watch the spirited protests and heart-felt speeches from trans kids and their parents, and know that nothing they said would change the hearts of right-wing lawmakers intent on pursuing a hate-filled agenda against queer people. It was even more frustrating to watch events unfold and realize there was nothing that she, a trans woman living in Canada, could do about it. She did make a token donation to one of the local organizations fighting the bills. This wasn't easy, but upon reviewing her precariously balanced bank account she figured that by skipping on the two bottles of wine she normally purchased each bi-weekly pay period, she could afford a $40 donation to the American group. The thought that the extent of her gesture was to sacrifice a couple of bottles of wine—in a protest against right-wing legislators who were willing to sacrifice the lives of trans children—somehow made her feel worse about the entire situation rather than better.

The second thing that happened to her that year was that her long-term partner broke up with her. This happened several weeks before the events in America. Things had been unsteady in their relationship for months, so it didn't exactly come as a surprise. And as a trans woman, she'd always harboured a cynical sort of attitude that true and everlasting love was something that eluded her kind. Objectively she would dismiss such a notion, but deep inside she had to admit the accumulated evidence of a lifetime was quite compelling. She tried to convince herself that the extra space in her life would give her time to work on her own transition, and a greater freedom to get to know the self she had always suppressed. Yet somehow that was cold comfort when set against the realization that someone who'd featured front and centre in her thoughts for the past seven years no longer cared about her in equally centralizing fashion. Transitioning required a great deal of determination and imagined self-assurance, and the break-up was a hit to her confidence right when it was at its most vulnerable.

Both she and her ex-partner, Melanie, were determined to be friends, and reassured each other that the break-up had nothing to do with Sarah's transition. But, deep inside, Sarah knew that nothing happened in her life that was *not* related to her transition. Decades of living in the closet, and then the fraught act of emerging from the closet, underscored this for her. Struggling to transition one's presentation of self in a world that remained confused at best, and deeply transphobic at worst, meant that every single thing that happened to her, or by her, was touched in some way by her gender identity. However supportive her ex-partner might be, she couldn't help but wonder how many of those countless micro-fractures which rendered their relationship vulnerable over the years could be sourced back to her transness.

As a result, when she went out in the world these days, not only were her thoughts filled with a constant narrative of "Is it because I'm trans that that person just acted that way?" but a new narrator whispered a follow-up question: "And is this connected to why we broke up?"

The third thing that happened to Sarah Fisher that year, was that a ghost came to live in her house.

It made its first appearance on a Thursday night some weeks after the break-up and mere days after the events in Arkansas. Its presence at first was appropriately nebulous. Sarah awoke in the middle of the night and had to go to the washroom. She got up, turned on the light in the hallway, and went into the bathroom. She conducted her business there swiftly, sleep still tugging at her consciousness, and stumbled back through the hallway, turning off the lights as she went. She crawled into bed and hastily slipped back into a sleep that happily reclaimed her. When she awoke the next morning, she had a sudden memory of seeing a figure sitting in the armchair at the end of the hall after she left the bathroom that night. A chill spread over her, partially eased by the reassuring possibility that she'd dreamt the whole thing. She sat bolt upright, threw off the covers and hurried out into the hall. The armchair was empty. Just a dream, she told herself. Still, when she went to bed the following night, she decided to leave the hallway light on, if only for her own peace of mind.

Two nights later, as she drifted off to sleep, she heard a faint noise in the hall outside her room. It sounded like footsteps. The distraction of this vague sound competed with the exhaustion of a long day as she debated getting up. It could simply be the pipes, she reasoned—they were always noisy on cold nights. Alternately, it could be mice, she reflected. That thought conjured up its own array of unsettling consequences, although on the whole she thought she would prefer to have mice in the house rather than a ghost. This was the last thing she remembered before exhaustion got the upper hand and she drifted off to a fitful night's sleep.

Final confirmation of the ghost's presence came the following Thursday, a week to the day after its first purported appearance. Sarah got up in the middle of the night to go to the washroom, as was fairly common for someone taking the array of hormones and androgen-blockers that she was. Things might have transpired as uneventfully as they did a week earlier, only on this occasion Sarah was jolted back into full consciousness by the need to replace the toilet paper roll. Even that might have been an automatic maneuver, but she dropped it and it rolled behind the toilet, requiring her to get on her knees and reach back to retrieve it. By the time she was upright and the toilet roll repositioned, she was also fully awake. She later blamed this entire sequence of events on her transness—if she hadn't had to get up in the middle of the night to use the washroom, what happened next might never have happened at all.

What happened was that an awake and frustrated Sarah flushed the toilet, exited the bathroom, turned off the bathroom light, and looked down the hallway to see an elderly woman sitting in the chair at the far end. It was a green armchair that had belonged to Sarah's grandfather, but the figure sitting in it bore no resemblance to any grandparent—or other person—Sarah could recall. The face was not unpleasant, merely distracted and staring down and slightly to the left. The entire figure shimmered in precisely the way Sarah would have imagined a ghost to shimmer, something like a distorted yet clearly discernible holographic projection. The woman had white curly hair—which might have been grey, or even blond, given the shimmery distortions—peeking out in wisps from beneath an old-style bonnet which covered the top of her head. She was wearing a quaint night-gown that had small shapes embroidered over it—little flowers, perhaps—not entirely discernible because, well, she shimmered.

Sarah stood frozen to the spot, a panicked chill rooting her there. Her brain did several things at once. It hoped that maybe she would wake up. It also hoped she would blink and the figure would be gone and she'd realize it was never there to begin with. The panic that surged through her prevented her from considering any sensible course of action, like moving or fleeing. Instead she remained there, staring, until a few moments later the figure stood up and, without once glancing in her direction, walked into the adjoining study.

At this point the panic subsided just enough for Sarah to think a bit more clearly. She considered running out the door—which in any horror film would have been the advisable thing to do—but part of her was affronted that a ghost would invade her house at this already deeply troubled point in her life and ruin a perfectly promising and much-needed night of sleep.

So, Sarah picked up a large broom which was leaning against the bathroom door, turned on every light within reach—the bathroom, her bedroom; the hall light was already on—and advanced toward the study, broom held out menacingly in front of her. She could see no sign of movement or of anything inside the room and hastily flicked on the study light which was located by the doorway. She entered. The room was empty. She did a quick search for good measure—nothing was behind the door, nor crouching beneath the stand-alone mirror. There was no closet. She opened the curtains: the bright lights of the streetlamp just outside the house illuminated the street clearly, and there was no movement there either.

Needless to say, Sarah did not sleep for the remainder of the night. She spent a couple of hours sitting in her living room sipping tea and reflecting incredulously on the evening's events. Later, the adrenalin wearing off, she grew tired and crawled back into bed but was too nervous to turn out the lights and instead lay there playing games on her phone until her alarm went off. She had no excuse not to go to work, so she picked up her routine as usual—

get showered, get dressed, eat breakfast—and walked to work.

The events in Arkansas didn't go away because she now had a ghost in her house, and neither did her break-up. At least she had something new with which to occupy those thoughts and she couldn't decide whether to be fearful or grateful. She could, however, not wait to tell her friend and co-worker Arlene about the events of the previous night.

"So," she began, as they sat on a bench outside their office at lunchtime, digging into their respective meals, "I think I've got a ghost in the house."

"Go ON!" remarked Arlene, picking intensively at her pasta with a chopstick. "Nan had one in the house when we were growing up in Placentia. Nice ghost though. Nan said she was right friendly. I never did see it, but always got a positive feeling when I went over there."

"Well, I actually saw this one!" Sarah responded, irritated with Arlene's typical habit of making a conversation about herself. Having acquired a ghost, thought Sarah, meant that the focus of this conversation ought to remain decidedly, centred on her.

"What did it do?" asked Arlene.

"Just sat there, at the end of the hall, and then got up and went into the study and vanished!"

"It's trying to tell you something," declared Arlene authoritatively. "Ghosts don't appear without a reason."

"That's what I figured," replied Sarah. "But what do you think it's trying to tell me?"

"Hell if I know," said Arlene, closing up her lunch bag. "You could try burning some sage. When I was seeing Don, he told me his sister did that to get rid of a nasty spirit in her house. Do you remember Don? I seen him just last night, actually, and do you know what he said to me? After the scam he pulled last weekend that I told you about? So he says…"

***

Later the same day, Sarah was offered a ride home by Annette, another co-worker she had gotten to know over the past few months. Sarah greatly looked up to Annette, whose opinions seemed to mesh perfectly with hers on most things. Annette was one of those people who only started pursuing a friendship with Sarah after she came out as trans. Annette wasn't the only one like that and this was a strange phenomenon Sarah had been unprepared for. Part of her felt she ought to be offended, but part of her was secretly quite pleased, since she'd always looked up to Annette and her friends, and deep down yearned to be part of their circle. Truth be told, she had a bit of a crush on her, and although she preferred walking to and from work, she wasn't about to turn down the prospect of a ride if Annette offered.

As they pulled out of the parking lot, Sarah shared her exciting news about the ghost. She wasn't sure how Annette would react, but relished being able to share something beyond routine pleasantries with a person she hoped very much to impress.

"A ghost!" exclaimed Annette, cursing at the drivers holding up the lane ahead. "What do you think it means?"

Sarah admitted she didn't know. "What do you think?" she asked Annette. "Is it trying to tell me something?"

"Beats me," said Annette. "Just don't go buying sage to burn. That shit is endangered, do you know that? And it's cultural appropriation as all hell for white settlers to go burning it in their gentrified houses. Speaking of which, did you see the earrings Arlene was wearing today? *Dreamcatchers?* She hasn't got an Indigenous bone in her body. You know, I was reading an article yesterday about cultural appropriation in the craft industry…"

The ride, as always, was over far sooner than Sarah wished. It ended before she had either the opportunity to bring it back around to her ghost, or to figure out a sensible way to ask Annette in for tea.

The nightly visitations continued. The following week, Sarah's ex-partner came by to visit and to gather some items she'd left at the house. This gave Sarah the opportunity to tell her about the ghost. Her ex, Melanie, didn't seem to know what to think.

"A ghost?" she repeated. She looked a bit concerned, in that way people do if they're worried you have depression or something. Sarah did her best to maintain a front that exuded cheeriness and stability and hoped Melanie would take the matter seriously. She still deeply respected her opinion and figured if anyone would have useful insight to offer, it would be her.

"You know," Sarah mused after sharing a few theories about the ghost's presence. "If you wanted to stay over some night this week, you could probably see it too. I was thinking having someone else here might change the situation, maybe provoke a different response or maybe you'd notice something I was missing. We could make dinner too. It would be kind of nice for us to hang out, and it would really mean a lot to me."

"I don't know," replied Melanie, doubtfully. "I'm working the early shift every day this week, so I really can't be up in the middle of the night. You know you should ask Arlene to stay over some night—she lives just down the road and I bet she'd be really into that kind of thing."

Sarah often wondered whether Melanie was intentionally trying to communicate that she had new and different priorities, or whether it was accidental. It hurt just as much either way and so Sarah brushed off the matter as cheerily as she could. Her ex appeared to sense her disappointment.

"You know," Melanie began awkwardly, "they say sage…"

"Yes," interrupted Sarah testily. "I know."

A few weeks later, Sarah had the opportunity to try out her story on a perfect stranger. After an early breakfast meeting downtown she lingered to enjoy the unusually nice spring weather. Soon she found herself shopping in one of those hippie-esque boutiques that always seemed to pop out of nowhere and then disappear again just as one was getting used to its products. It was an early Saturday, and only Sarah and the shop clerk were in the store. While she browsed, an awkward silence descended which she knew ought to be filled with the sort of mindless chatter that she was never any good at. Feeling increasingly awkward about the silence, she banteringly told the shop clerk—a young woman with long blonde dreadlocks and a southern shore accent—about the ghost residing in her house. The young woman gaped and looked quite impressed.

"You should definitely burn some sage," she said. "That shit will clear your house of any unwanted energies like nothing else."

"I most certainly will not," replied Sarah haughtily. "I rather like my ghost, to be honest. I don't see why I would want to chase it away."

The shop clerk nodded knowingly. "Yeah, it can be good to have a friendly ghost around the house. You know my great-aunt had a ghost in the house, I used to feel her presence when I went over to visit and it was just the warmest, most pleasant feeling I'd ever get anywhere. Now my great-aunt, let me tell you, she had some stories. I've got to tell you this one, it was about her dad who went out fishing one Christmas Eve…"

Sarah had to gradually accept that the vast majority of people appeared more interested in their own lives than they were in her ghost. Conversations never seemed to go quite the way she hoped. She couldn't figure out why what, to her mind, was an absorbing topic of conversation never seemed to hold the attention of the people she shared it with. At times it made her feel quite lonely.

Sarah often struggled with loneliness. This was also something she attributed to her transness. When you hold on to a secret for so long, it can make you feel really lonely inside, knowing that you're the only person aware of it. Sarah had been popular and always had a number of strong and positive relationships—family, friends, lovers—but the most important aspect of herself was something she'd kept hidden from all of them.

Once she came out it was a tremendous relief, but the

loneliness she'd always felt didn't go away. It shifted, and settled around her in the form of a resigned awareness that the transition she was going through was not something she could ever really share with people around her. She could tell them about it, but there were limits to empathic listening. Other people expressed sympathy when she was misgendered or faced bureaucratic hassles during transition, but ultimately they couldn't understand the isolation that comes from constantly worrying about how you're perceived by the people around you. Misgendering and awkwardness fuels the unstable awareness of how you are mirrored back by others, and while she was glad to be out and no longer harbour that deep secret, it didn't eliminate the loneliness, only changed it.

Perhaps that was why she wasn't more afraid of the ghost than she was. Having a ghost in her house—one that clearly harboured an inscrutable secret of its own—became oddly comforting after a time. Routine was always comforting to Sarah, and knowing there was another entity around—one that would be predictably sitting in her grandfather's green armchair whenever she awoke in the middle of the night—was somehow reassuring. It reminded her of a spider she once found in her bathroom.

Sarah abhorred spiders, they terrified her and her partner was always the one that had to deal with them when summoned by Sarah's blood-curdling screams. But one night about a year earlier, when her partner was out of town for a couple of weeks on a trip, Sarah was sitting in the bath and noticed a long-legged spider nestled into the corner of the bathroom farthest away from her. Instead of terrifying her as it normally would, she felt oddly comforted. It made the house seem less empty. Here was something familiar—another living entity sharing the space and absorbed in its own matters. She came to feel a sense of pleasant familiarity when she saw it sitting there every night as she soaked in the bath. It disappeared shortly before Melanie returned, which was just as well. Sarah did not consider long-term residency in her house a viable option for an arachnid, no matter how comforting its presence might have been for a time.

Nevertheless, she struggled to try and determine what the ghost's presence signified. What was it trying to tell her? Was it related to her transition?

Was it a future self she was seeing, trying to communicate from the future and tell her that everything would turn out all right?

Or was it a spirit trying to warn her against pursuing surgery? The thought of surgery made her nervous, of course, so it wasn't like she had no doubts or uncertainties. But overall she was committed to the decision and looking forward to life after it was all over. But what if the ghost was trying to warn her off the idea?

What if it was one of her ancestors, trying to bring her a warning? Sarah once had her aura read in a new age store, and the proprietress told her she was closely protected by spirits from her mother's side. Was this one of them? Was it some unknown foremother trying to warn her about a looming danger? Or trying to reassure her that things would be okay?

Or did it have some entirely unrelated source? Was it connected in some way to the house? Yet Sarah had lived there for over five years before the ghost revealed any sign of its presence.

Some years earlier, Sarah had a friend who was convinced her apartment was haunted by the spirit of a cat. This cat spirit was apparently quite pleasant and loving around women, but it got its back up in the most terrible and fearsome way when men came to visit the apartment. Or so the friend told her, as no one else could actually see it. Her theory was it had most likely been abused by some man during its lifetime and so had a natural and perfectly understandable aversion to all men.

Sarah considered the possibility that maybe a spirit had been invisibly present in her house ever since she'd moved in five years earlier, and that they'd co-existed perfectly amicably and oblivious to each other until Sarah's hormones had disrupted the astral gender balance of the residence. Maybe ghosts were sensitive to the hormonal composition of the physical bodies around them? Sarah briefly reflected on whether this was a brilliant theory that would help her become famous someday. Probably not, she concluded. No one else even seemed very interested in her ghost.

Maybe the ghost had issues living with women? Or maybe it was more at home around them? And what were its feelings toward trans people? The ambivalence of the ghost's reaction to her—it mostly seemed to ignore her—made it hard to determine whether the spirit was benevolent or malicious. That it was one or the other, she had no doubt—ghosts simply weren't ambivalent by nature, everyone knew that.

Such were the thoughts that distracted Sarah on more occasions than not, as she mulled over the presence of the ghost in her house and tidied things up at her job in preparation for her looming surgery.

She figured that maybe the ghost would eventually tire of its routine and send some hint as to its purpose and presence. Maybe it would lead her to some hidden trove of letters in the house? A love locket buried behind the fireplace? Maybe it would decide to communicate—perhaps point to a relevant book in the study, or etch a message into the steam in the shower—so as to convey even a hint regarding its purpose in the house?

No message ever came, and only once did the ghost vary its routine. One night, rather than sitting in the armchair when Sarah got up to use the washroom, it was standing beside the armchair. Its back was turned to Sarah—normally she could see its face—and it fled into the study the very moment Sarah appeared, rather than lingering as it usually did. Sarah didn't even initially register the difference—it was only as she was crawling into bed that she realized something unusual had happened, but by then the ghost was gone for the night.

What did it mean? She reflected furiously the next morning on what she had done differently the previous day that might have caused the ghost to react in that fashion. Several possibilities occurred to her. She had replaced the door to the study earlier in the day, since there was a growing crack in the original. Was the haunting related to the door? Was pressed wood somehow a trigger for ghosts, or did it miss the original one? She'd also left the study light on by accident that night. And earlier in the day she'd finally asked Annette out—she agreed, and the whole thing was terrifying and delicious. Was the ghost upset? Or approving?

Then again, she'd also booked the flights for her surgery earlier that same day. Furthermore she had received an email from her mother that evening—the first time her family had contacted her in quite a while. For that matter, she had also stopped taking estrogen, as was required six weeks before surgery. All of these actions circled relentlessly in her thoughts, as she mused on which of them might have caused some shift in the astral plane. Part of her wondered if she had driven the ghost off for good. But sure enough, when she got up the next night it was sitting in the green armchair as usual, and returned to its regular routine.

The reader might get the impression the ghost was all Sarah thought about those days, but that's far from the case. Sarah's relationship with her ex continued to stumble forward, and although it continued to occupy a significant space in her thoughts, the pain she felt so acutely at first started to subside, as she had grudgingly known it would. Her relationship with Annette also continued to lurch forward in deliciously stomach-churning fits and starts. The ghost seemed a big thing when it first appeared, but it gradually faded into a supportive background role as part of an increasingly stable daily routine.

When it first appeared Sarah had considered photographing or video-taping it on her phone, and decided against it. She'd watched too many creepy horror movies involving cursed videos and the like. Plus, as much as she hoped the ghost would do something to reveal its backstory, the less courageous side of her appreciated its amicable standoffishness.

The ghost vanished for good when Sarah finally had her gender confirmation surgery. The perceptive reader might at this stage accuse the author of leaving a hole in the narrative, and point out this means *four* things of note happened to Sarah that year, not three like the beginning of this account claimed.

That's not how Sarah would see it. As she saw it, the other three happenings—discriminatory laws passed by legislators; the break-up; the appearance of a ghost in her house—were things that happened *to* her, without so much as a by-your-leave. Her surgery, however, was something she *chose* to do. It was something she had fought for, scrimped and saved for, been required to formally beg for, and overcome a range of fears and doubts in order to commit to. If there was anything she'd done in her life that had any agency, this was it. Of course, it was in response to circumstances beyond her control— her gender identity—but it was how she had, following a great deal of trial and error in life, decided to respond to those circumstances. It was the closest thing to an authentic decision that she, or anyone, could ever make, she reasoned.

The disappearance of the ghost after her surgery was apparently something else that was out of her control. It was there the night before Sarah left to fly to Montreal. She was up the better part of the night packing and being nervous, and confessed later that she had perhaps not paid the ghost as much attention as she usually did. When she returned, it took her a couple of nights to realize the ghost was gone. She'd been excited to see whether her post-surgery status would spark any difference in the ghost's routine, but when she got home from the airport she was so exhausted that she crawled into bed and passed out.

The next night, she was still so busy getting used to the routine of dilations, and still exhausted from the surgery, that she completely forgot to get up to check on the ghost. It was only on the third night that she awoke sometime after midnight, and although she sat in the hallway for at least an hour, the ghost made no appearance the entire time.

Not then, nor any night thereafter. The ghost, it seemed, was gone for good.

Was it the surgery that had driven it away? Was its mission accomplished? Or had Sarah ignored its warning, and now there was no further point in sticking around and wasting both their time? Sarah harboured a range of theories over the ensuing years. But, she eventually admitted, she would probably never know.

Had it even been related to her transness in the first place? She weighed the evidence against her instincts. There are times, she knew, that you can be certain a message is being conveyed, even if you don't know precisely what that message is.

Whenever she told people about these happenings, especially in her later years, they scoffed at the idea that the appearance and subsequent disappearance of a ghost would have anything to do with her gender identity.

They were wrong, of course. Of that Sarah had no doubt whatsoever.

Rhea Rollmann is a multiple award-winning journalist currently living in St. John's, Newfoundland. She has won the 2017 Atlantic Journalism Gold Award for Best Commentary; the 2021 Atlantic Journalism Silver Award for Best Community Newspaper News Story; was a finalist in the 2018 Canadian Association of Journalists Award; as well as a variety of academic awards.

STAR-CROSS'D
ALI HOUSE

"I can't believe I let you talk me into this," Rayne declared as she looked at the five-star hotel before her. She nervously adjusted the Colombina mask, hoping it would cover enough of her face to properly disguise her identity.

Mylie burst out laughing, her melodic voice carrying across the cool night air. Her smile was wide beneath her own mask. "You've let me talk you into much worse, and you know it," she said, nudging Rayne with her elbow.

Rayne didn't reply because it was true. It wasn't her first time showing up to an event without an invitation, nor was it the most dangerous thing Mylie had ever talked her into doing. There were no narrow rooftop paths to follow or high-stakes betting going on. If she wasn't allowed through the door, then she'd simply have to go home. And that couldn't even be considered a terrible outcome, since she could stop by Paulie's and get a slice of pizza on the way.

Then again, Mylie's plans were almost always successful. Although Mylie was still in high school, there was a magic about her that most people became enamoured with, allowing her to pretty much get away with anything. It was one of the many, many reasons Rayne enjoyed being friends with her. She was too nervous to come up with inventive plans of her own, so she was honoured whenever Mylie included her in such outings. Even if it meant wearing a weird silver mask that didn't fit her face quite right and dressing up in one of Mylie's old ball gowns. Rayne almost burst out laughing at the thought. She couldn't imagine owning a single ball gown, let alone having enough of them to share out for last minute costume parties, complete with complimentary masks, purses, and shoes.

Mylie started walking towards the hotel, the full skirt of her emerald gown swishing as she headed towards the private entrance to the ballroom. There was a short line-up of people at the door, all wearing elaborate outfits, waiting to be allowed in.

Rayne took in a deep breath as she hurried to catch up with Mylie. Her heartbeat began to accelerate as they neared the line, but it wasn't for fear of being denied entry. If her parents found out that she was going to a party thrown by the Caldwells they'd kill her. Or, at least, ground her for a century—if not longer. Her parents had hated that family for over a decade, ever since her father was unceremoniously fired by Reg Caldwell in an underhanded attempt to gain more money and power, and they'd forbid her from ever interacting with a Caldwell or purchasing any of their electronics. Neither task was difficult to achieve—the Caldwell children went to a private school and lived in the 'rich' part of town, and the electronics produced by CE Ltd. were so over-priced that Rayne felt no desire to ever own such a thing. In fact, at her high school it was considered lame to own any CE products. The only person who could get away with it was Mylie, and that was because she'd been kicked out of the private school, thus achieving the highest level of cool attainable.

"Your invitations," the man standing at the entrance said as they stepped up to him. He was dressed in a tuxedo with tails, and was the only person around without a mask on. It was probably because he didn't want to hide the pinched look on his face, which clearly read: 'If you mess with me, you'll very quickly regret it.' There was no doubt in Rayne's mind that he'd already branded the two young women as gate-crashers and was itching for an excuse to bar them from entry.

Mylie opened her purse and handed over her invitation with a grand flourish. It was on thick, cream-coloured paper, with gold accents. Rayne wondered why the Caldwells didn't bother with electronic invitations, since they were so big into technology, but figured that they couldn't program anything as pretentious as a physical invitation embossed in actual gold.

"And yours?" The man stared at Rayne, almost glaring at her.

"She's with me," Mylie interjected, her voice strong and self-assured. Rayne tried her best to emulate that feeling, standing tall and confident in her dark blue borrowed ball gown.

"This invitation does not have a plus one," the man replied, his voice flat and unimpressed.

"I know," Mylie said as if it was the most obvious thing in the world. "I phoned Auntie Bess days ago to tell her that my cousin was in town from Portugal and that she totally had to go to this ball because she simply loves these kinds of events, and Auntie Bess told me that of course my cousin could come and that she'd make sure that it was okay, and I thought it was strange that she didn't send me another invitation, but I assumed that there'd be something waiting for me at the door, since that's what happened last time. But if that isn't the case, then I can go inside and find her, and she can sort all this out herself."

Mylie batted her eyelashes innocently at the man. If the overly-long diatribe didn't knock him down a peg, then the mention of 'Auntie Bess' Caldwell certainly had. After a quick glance at the name on Mylie's invitation, he cleared his throat and tried to pull himself back up to his former stature.

"That won't be necessary," he said, waving the two of them along.

Rayne wanted to laugh in his face and skip past, but she maintained her stature and followed Mylie's lead, walking through the doorway as if there was no doubt they belonged. Of course, that didn't stop them from breaking out in a fit of giggles once they were far enough away.

"You're amazing," Rayne said, smiling and shaking her head.

"I hope you're taking notes," Mylie smiled back. "Now, let's see what they have to eat."

As they entered the ballroom proper, Rayne couldn't help being amazed by the spectacle. Large crystal chandeliers hung above the crowd, reflecting light off the gold and marble accents, while a string quartet played classical versions of popular music. Everyone was wearing elaborate masks—some covering half of their faces, some covering their full faces—along with stylish gowns and elegant suits. For a second, Rayne felt as if she'd walked into a movie scene. It was the most glamorous event she'd ever snuck into.

Mylie smirked at her awe but said nothing and grabbed her by the wrist, tugging her towards the buffet table. There were numerous waiters in black pants, white shirts, and black ties holding trays of food and drink, milling about the room, but Mylie slipped past them all. She firmly believed that the waiters at these types of events secretly hated all the attendees, so they made every effort to ignore certain people or only come near when they were already eating or busy talking. She didn't begrudge them any hostility—in fact, she delighted in it, as did Rayne. Nothing was funnier than watching a Very Important Person get flustered as a waiter with mini Beef Wellingtons completely ignored them while moving further and further away.

The buffet table was on the left side of the room, near the wall. Only a few people milled around it, picking up samples of the delicacies it was laden with. That was another reason Mylie loved the buffet table—most of the people at these events liked to pretend that they were too good to fetch their own food, so never went near it, leaving all the tasty snacks unclaimed. The two of them descended on the buffet with youthful exuberance, sampling every item and gossiping about the other guests in hushed voices. It wasn't long, however, before Mylie finally had to bite the bullet and go talk to the hosts.

"Will you be okay on your own?" she asked, while checking her appearance in a small hand mirror.

Rayne nodded. "I promise to stay as inconspicuous as possible and keep out of trouble until you get back."

Mylie smiled and dropped the mirror back into her purse. Then she smoothed the front of her dress, squared her shoulders, and headed into the crowd.

Rayne ate one last piece of pear and prosciutto with goat cheese on crostini as she watched Mylie make her way to the other side of the ballroom where Mr. And Mrs. Caldwell stood, entertaining the group of people clustered around them. Even though she couldn't make out their faces, she knew it was them simply by the energy coming from that area. The hosts of these events were always more animated and electric than any of the other guests.

There were a few chairs back near the entrance but most were occupied and Rayne didn't want to risk anyone striking up a conversation. Instead, she moved a few feet away from the table and found an empty spot near the wall to stand. Staring out at the crowd, she recognized a few attendees—prominent business people; the wealthy and famous; the 'old money' who'd basically run the town forever. Some she recognized by voice or body language, but mostly because the people would keep raising their masks, as if they couldn't bear an entire evening of not showing their face.

"So, come here often?" a voice to her right asked.

Rayne turned, startled, and gazed upon a young woman about her age, wearing a dark grey dress and a black lace Colombina mask. There was a smile on her face, as if what she'd said was greatly amusing.

"Does that usually work?" Rayne replied.

"Is it working now?"

She shook her head.

"Then the answer is a definite 'no'. Ten out of ten rejections."

She couldn't help laughing. "Well, I commend your tenacity."

The other girl gave a slight bow. "I usually take it upon myself to find those who look as bored as I feel and greet them."

"A commendable effort," she smiled.

The young woman in the grey dress held out her hand. "I'm Jules."

Rayne took her hand. "Rayne," she said before mentally kicking herself for giving her real name. Hopefully she wouldn't be prompted to give a last name.

"So, Rayne, what brings you to this section of the wall? Not much of a dancer?" Jules asked, motioning to the dance floor.

Rayne looked out at the numerous bodies waltzing to the music. Some were doing perfectly choreographed dances as if showing off numerous dance lessons, while others were merely showing off their alcohol intake. "Well, I like to dance, but something about doing it in front of all these people makes me hesitate. Besides, I'm mostly here for the food."

Jules held back a laugh. "Nice. Have you tried the honeyed figs? They're delicious."

She nodded emphatically. "Oh, I've tried everything

on the buffet table—even the stuff I couldn't recognize."

"Wow…" Jules gave a low whistle. "You're much braver than I am. Some of that stuff looks so odd that I can't help but be wary."

"Yeah, some of it can be pretty weird, but I've realized that the people who host these kinds of things would rather die than serve anything subpar."

A look of admiration filled her eyes. "Smart. I see this isn't your first time at one of these things."

Rayne gave a small bow.

"Well, now that you've imparted your wisdom on me, I feel like I owe you something." She paused, putting a hand on her chin in an exaggerated expression of thinking. "Wanna know the best place to sneak away from all of this? It's much more relaxing than hanging around a wall, watching other people schmooze."

Rayne paused. She was pretty confident that this person wasn't going to lure her away and murder her, and—other than Mylie—she was the most interesting person at the party. And who knew how much longer Mylie would be away, chatting with the Caldwells? It sure sounded better than standing next to a wall, trying to avoid everyone. Finally she nodded.

Jules smiled wider. "Grab some stuff from the buffet and meet me by those stairs in thirty seconds!" Then she took off in the opposite direction she'd just pointed in.

Rayne smiled, shook her head, and made her way over to the buffet table, picking up one of the small plates stacked on the side and discreetly piling canapes onto it. When the plate was full, she took another and placed it on top, hiding the amount of food she was making off with.

The staircase Jules had pointed at was on the other side of the room from where she'd entered. There were actually two staircases, one on either side of the room, framing the stage where the string quartet was set up. Nobody used them, except for the hotel staff, and Rayne had no idea where they went, but she was suddenly curious to find out.

Jules was standing next to the stairs, and as Rayne approached, she held up a bottle of wine and smiled wickedly before dropping it to her side and hurrying up the staircase. Rayne smiled again as she followed. At the top of the stairs was a short hallway lined with plush carpet, which eventually turned right into a hallway with an elevator, but that wasn't where Jules was taking her. They turned left instead, into a small square room that was lined with empty racks and clothes hangers.

"Ta-dah!" Jules said, holding out her arms. One hand held the bottle of wine, and the other had two wine-glasses. "I found this a while ago, at another one of these things. Since everyone attending comes in from outside they don't use this section, so it's a great place to go when you tire of all the pomp and circus."

Pausing, Rayne noticed that she could still hear the music playing, but it was further away and she couldn't make out any voices. For the first time since entering the hotel, she felt herself relax. "It's amazing. Your tip is much better than your intro line."

Jules smiled widely and began to pour each of them a glass of wine. They settled on the floor of the empty cloak room, their skirts tucked around them. Jules raised her glass and Rayne followed suit, toasting to having escaped the party.

"Guess we don't need these," Jules said, pulling off her mask and tossing it on the floor. Rayne wasn't sure what she was expecting, but the face under the mask was entirely unknown to her. It was, however, a very nice-looking face.

"So, what brings you to this shindig?" Rayne asked, hesitantly removing her own mask. Even though she didn't recognize Jules, she was worried that Jules might recognize her and realize that she wasn't on the guest list. She watched as Jules' eyes scanned her face for a few seconds before relaxing.

"The parents, of course," Jules replied, sipping her wine. "Sometimes I can get out of it, but usually it's all, 'You'll embarrass us if you don't show up,' 'You'll embarrass us if you don't smile,' 'You'll embarrass us if you wear grey'." She rolled her eyes and took another drink.

Rayne nodded at her dress. "I see they caved on that one," she said, taking a sip of wine.

Jules smiled widely, the expression lighting up her whole face. "I made sure to stay away until just before it was time to leave. That way they either had to wait for me to change and arrive late, or let me go in this. Sometimes you've gotta let the parentals know that they aren't the boss."

"I like your style, Jules."

"I guess that your parentals didn't have a problem with your choice of dress. That colour really suits you."

Rayne took another drink. "Oh, I… uh, I'm a plus-one." She'd thought that her excuse was a good one, but then she noticed Jules' eyes narrowing slightly.

"Hmm… I thought that there weren't any plus-ones tonight," Jules said slowly, regarding her carefully. "So if that's the case, you must be a gate-crasher."

Jules smiled dramatically, and Rayne felt her blood run cold. Should she confess everything? Should she run? Could she get out of here before the guards were alerted? Why had she let herself follow this stranger away from the party? Why hadn't she just stayed in one spot and waited for Mylie like she was supposed to do?

"Brilliant!"

Rayne was equal parts startled and confused. "What?"

"That's brilliant," Jules smiled. "These parties are so stuffy. I love a good bit of intrigue. Now, let me guess…" she paused, leaving Rayne confused and unsure what to do. "Mylie, right? She's the only one I can see pulling off this kind of thing."

She shrugged, figuring that it was best not to implicate her friend.

Jules laughed. "I get it. Innocent until proven guilty." She waved her hand in the air, as if brushing away her past thought. "Okay, now that I know you're definitely interesting, you have to tell me everything about yourself."

And for some reason Rayne did. She never gave her full name or the names of any of her family or friends, but she spoke about her school and the neighbourhood where she grew up, and some of the adventures Mylie had taken her on. She wasn't sure what it was that made her want to spill everything, but perhaps it was the fact that while she was speaking, Jules looked at her with rapt attention.

When she finally stopped, Jules shared some anecdotes of her own, and soon the two were chatting like old friends. Rayne had never felt like this with anyone else. She loved seeing Jules laugh and smile. If the world was going to end in the next five minutes, she wanted to spend those minutes right here.

At one point, after a particularly good laugh, Jules reached out and laid her hand on Rayne's. Rayne blushed as she looked down at the intimate gesture and Jules quickly withdrew her hand.

"I'm sorry," Jules said. "I shouldn't have…"

"No," Rayne replied, feeling her cheeks blush redder, "it's okay." She thought she saw a bit of a blush creep into Jules' cheeks as she put her hand back over Rayne's.

"This is okay?" Jules asked, her voice soft and low.

The energy of the room suddenly changed to something quieter and more intimate. The music faded into the background, creating a universe where only the two of them existed.

Rayne nodded. "Definitely okay." She felt herself lean forward slightly, almost as if she was being pulled by a magnet. "It'd also be okay if you…"

The ends of Jules' lips quirked up in a smile. "If I were to get closer?"

"Perhaps even…"

She leaned in. "Kiss you?"

Rayne gave a slight nod. "That would definitely be okay."

Their lips met, but the moment was soon interrupted by a buzzing sound from Rayne's purse. The two broke apart, startled by the intrusion.

"Sorry," Rayne said as she reached for her purse, mortified that it was her item which had ruined the moment. Taking out her cellphone, she silently cursed her luck. On the screen was a message from Mylie: 'Where R U?'

"Sorry," she apologized again. "My friend's wondering where I am."

"I guess we've been away for a while..." Jules trailed off. "Um, could I get your number? I had fun, and maybe, you know, if you'd like to hang out or something sometime..."

"Do you have your phone handy?" Rayne asked. Jules reached into a hidden pocket within her dress and pulled out an expensive CE Ltd cellphone, and Rayne instantly felt jealous—of the pockets, not the phone. They exchanged numbers, texting each other to make sure they'd remember who was behind the new name.

Suddenly Jules' phone buzzed, and as she read the message, Rayne watched her roll her eyes. "Looks like I have to rejoin the party ASAP," she said, taking one last sip of wine. She placed her glass on the carpet, next to the half-full bottle and empty plates. "Just leave this here— someone will find it and clean it up later." She placed her mask back on and stood up. "See you around, Rayne," she said, smiling brightly before disappearing into the hallway.

After she was gone, Rayne quickly messaged Mylie, letting her know where she was. She didn't want to rejoin the party just yet. A couple minutes later, Mylie showed up, a knowing look in her eyes.

"So...?" she prompted, stepping into the coat room.

Rayne smiled. "I think I'm slightly in love."

A smiled broke out on Mylie's face and she quickly sat down next to Rayne. "Tell me everything."

She spilled all the details, unable to stop herself from gushing.

"So, Jules, eh?" Mylie said, when she was finished, letting her voice trail off.

"Yeah," Rayne replied. "Why did you say it like that?"

"Oh, it's just that her family prefers to shorten her name to Anna." Mylie's smile widened as she watched the penny drop in Rayne's mind.

"No…" Rayne said. "She's not…"

Mylie nodded. "Julianna Caldwell herself."

Time seemed to stop as Rayne realized that not only had she met a Caldwell, but she'd spent the past however many minutes flirting with her and had made plans to flirt some more. If her parents found out, they'd lock her in the house and forbid her from ever leaving. She turned to Mylie, eyes wide with panic. "What am I going to do?"

Mylie couldn't help laughing. "I don't know, but I can't wait to find out."

Ali House is an award-winning, bestselling author, originally from Newfoundland. To date, House's short fiction has appeared in every volume of the From the Rock anthology series, as well as Bluenose Paradox, Kit Sora Artobiography, and Terror Nova. Her short fiction was collected in 2020 in The Lightbulb Forest. Previous novels include The Six Elemental and The Fifth Queen, both a part of her creator-owned Segment Delta Archives series. Other works include the fantasy series Choose Your Own Adventurer, The Santa Claus Protection Program, The Island Adventure as a part of the Slipstreamers series of novellas, and Variety Show as a part of the Engen Universe.

FELICITY
HANNAH JENKINS

She awakes exactly as I do.

We quietly roll and entwine our fingers between each other, like ivy, wrapping its way across an old Victorian terrace. I am now unable to distinguish my thigh from the blue-black pajama bottoms that encases them, or her hand from my stomach where it gently roves amid the blankets.

We lie here, in this room that smells entirely like her. I briefly register the dim, blurred glow of a desk light upon her abandoned copy of *The Importance of Being Earnest*, the gentle hum of our refrigerator drifting through the crevices of the bedroom door. In this moment, I am every bit as in love with myself as I am with her.

I want to remember everything about us. I want to taste every shared breakfast, and every overpriced piece of cinema popcorn. I want to feel the tingles she sends down my spine as she runs her nails through my hair, or presses her fingertips against my wrist in the empty supermarket. I try to hone in on the fuzzy soundtrack of her voice that reverberates in my mind as she reads Voltaire and tells me I look beautiful in white.

But right now, her even breathing is a sound I am prepared to forfeit the English language for. My mind softly sways in the gusts of her exhales, like loose dandelion seeds in the wind, wondering if it may call this summer breeze a home.

As I accidentally brush my lips across the warm skin behind her left ear, I realize that one of us ought to feel embarrassed soon, worry what this means, think that perhaps this isn't quite what roommates do. But we don't. This throw blanket is so warm it would be a disservice to cast it off for something as trivial as shame, anyway.

Tomorrow, I muse. *Tomorrow sounds like a lovely day to think.*

Hannah Jenkins is an author and poet. In 2020 she was awarded the Moynes-Keshen John McCrae Poetry Award. Im 2022 Engen Books will release her first poetry chapbook, The Birds Come Back in the Spring.

OTHER LIVES
WILL J FAWLEY

I'm in the library trying to finish writing a spell for the critique that begins in less than an hour. My best friend Monica and I are camped out in the Arcane Section, at our favorite table in the corner. It was where we met freshman year when we were both trying to escape the roar of the casting parties that pulsed through the school all night.

Even though the library's open-air enchantment acts as a magical skylight, making you feel like you're outside, Monica gets up and stands next to the window. She pulls back a heavy velvet curtain and looks out at the town below. The Campos do Jordão Escola de Artes Mágicas (CEAM), or "cyan," as the school is affectionately called, is in an old timber-framed building that looks like a hotel to any nulls passing by. CEAM sits on a mountain over-looking the European-style town below, where flocks of parrots flying between Candelabra Trees give away the fact that it's actually located in Brazil.

"You know, if you didn't write your spell over the summer, the next hour isn't going to make much of a difference, right?" Monica says, stepping back from the window and leaning over my notebook to see what I'm writing.

"I have to bring something to class." I say as I flip through a stack of books with a speed-reading charm. My pen floats through the air taking notes for the energy transfer spell I dreamed up years ago when I still thought I might follow the practical route and go to MagiTech, the technical school for magic where graduates actually find jobs.

I remove my glasses and massage the bridge of my nose, taking a power break to regain my focus. A blurry Monica shrugs and conjures a tiny serpentine dragon, which makes figure-eights between her fingers. "You must have had a lot of fun if you didn't get *anything* done over the summer." Her hair is long and curly and she releases it from a hair-tie to transform it from ponytail to kraken. The dragon nests in her curls.

I put my glasses on and get back to work. "I did. I'll fill you in on the details after class."

"This Teo must have been something." The dragon peeks out of Monica's hair and snorts a puff of smoke near her cheek so it looks like she's chainsmoking.

"He was. He is," I say. "Now let me focus on my spell."

"Touchy." The dragon crawls up Monica's arm. "If he had magic he could have helped you with the spell."

"Yeah, but he doesn't, does he?" I snap. "That's why I'll never see him again." Teo can't know about magic, or me, so I had to erase his memory the night before I came back to school. I scratch at the stubble on my chin and look out the window, letting my eyes focus on a hillside in the distance. "How am I doing for time?" I ask.

"You know I love and support you, Paulo, but this is serious. You can't date a null."

"Just tell me what time it is."

Monica gives me a dirty look. "I'm just looking out for you," she says as she conjures a moondial in the air in front of her. "Class started five minutes ago."

"Shit!" Gathering the potential energy in the library is easy because the afterburn of old spells stick to the ancient tomes like cobwebs. They actually put a lockdown spell on the room to limit spell usage in the library, but there's still enough power available for me to dualcast—first a follower spell on the stack of research books beside me so I don't have to carry them, then an autocomplete on the rest of the spell I'm working on since I don't have time to finish it.

The autocomplete is the equivalent of spell-checking an essay in the null world. It ties most things up nicely, but it also randomly crosses its wires and misspells a few crucial components here and there. It would be quite dangerous if we were actually casting these spells, but it's just an exercise anyway, so it should be fine.

***

The desks are already arranged in a circle when Monica and I arrive for the critique.

"Paulo, Monica, have a seat," Professor Everhart says. She's young and German, and has this way of speaking in a monotone so you can never tell if she's angry or happy. I always assume the worst. She conjures two desks for us and we sit. "We were just catching up on the summer and discussing who will present the first spell."

I avoid eye-contact and pretend to focus on the stack of books hovering beside my desk. There are fourteen students in the workshop and only time for about four or five spells each class, so if I play this right I could have an extra week or two to finish my spell the right way.

"Paulo, why don't you start us off," Everhart says.

My forehead stings with sweat and I try to casually wipe it off with my sleeve. "Yes, why don't I?" I say.

I conjure my notebook from the stack of books beside me and it floats in the air in front of my desk, turning to the page of the spell.

I assemble the energy around me and push it into the notebook. A bead of sweat trickles down my temple as the words begin to glow and then crawl off the page, duplicating themselves over and over with my copy/paste spell. The words find their place in the air in front of each student so they can review and critique my work.

The room is quiet as everyone reads. I look around the circle at the faces of people who are too busy thinking about presenting their own spells to care. Then there are the three witches—Marcella, Gabrielle, and Flávio. They think every spell they cast is gold just because they're descendants of the wizards who founded CEAM. Marcella and Gabrielle get some kind of sick joy from tearing apart other people's spells, and Flávio just likes to throw around theory vocab to compensate for the fact that his own spells suck.

"Have you tried it, like, from a different point of view?" Marcella says. "Like, what if the caster was actually the target?"

"Yeah, what if," Monica mumbles from beside me, rolling her eyes at the witches.

"That's an interesting perspective," Professor Everhart says.

"I just don't really get what the point of it all is," Gabrielle says. Marcella nods because the witches always back up each other's stupid ideas, and there seems to be a consensus around the room from all the students who aren't really paying attention, but want an easy way to look like they're engaged in the discussion.

"I think it falls a little flat," someone else says.

"It just doesn't really grab me," another echoes.

And then I'm really in for it when Flávio pipes up. "The combination of spiral whorls in the casting is likely to implode time and space, or even create a black hole."

I look over the text and he's right. Stupid autocorrect.

I know I should have taken the time to write a better spell, but the criticism still stings.

My mind wanders as I shut out all the negative feedback. I nod as the class continues to tear my spell apart, but I'm really thinking about what it would be like to live in the null world—how much simpler it would be. I could drop out of school and move to the suburbs of São Paulo to attend MagiTech and learn a job skill like healing arts or energy production. Or maybe I could be a normal writer of books or blogs or tweets or whatever it is that nulls write these days.

I loved hearing Teo talk about the latest philosophy and science coming out of the null world, like quantum theory and the idea that consciousness has an impact on the Universe. It fascinated me that nulls were arriving at the same conclusions about the Universe that wizards have been using to shape reality for millennia. It gives me hope that one day everyone will know about magic and we won't have to wipe people's minds to keep it a secret anymore. Teo and I stayed up late into the hot summer nights talking about books and big ideas, and now those conversations are all gone from his mind, as if they never happened. But I remember.

***

I met Teo playing Wizard Crown, of all things. It was the beginning of summer break and I was sick of hanging around in my hometown in rural São Paulo estado. I spent those first days of break by the pool drinking coconut water and maracujá juice while my parents were at work. After a couple weeks I started to feel restless. The null world used to be home, but now it felt fake somehow, like shadows on the wall—shadows cast by my real life at CEAM. Growing up, I was an outsider who didn't have any close friends, but when I got to CEAM I met Monica and finally felt like I was somewhere I belonged.

I found my old Wizard Crown decks tucked away in my bedroom closet, and I guess I was going through magic withdrawal. I figured since I wasn't allowed to cast spells in the null world, I would do the next best thing, play a card game that let me pretend to cast spells. A couple of days later I went to the local game store for a tournament, and Teo and I were paired up in the first round. He barely said a word, but I admired his skill at the game. He made some genius plays using the difficult mindshape strategy, which only the best players even understand. It was exciting, each turn a riddle to be solved, and it reminded me why I had loved the game as a kid. When the tournament ended and everyone left, we exchanged phone numbers and Teo invited me over to his apartment for a match.

We hung out almost every day for the rest of the summer. There was something irresistible about Teo that made me want to consume him and make him a part of myself, something that made me want to turn myself inside out for him. So, against my better judgement, I spent the summer telling him all about the school I really went to, and even showed him a few simple spells.

And then, when it came time for me to go back to CEAM, I had to erase his memory of the entire summer, of ever meeting me.

"I promise I won't tell anyone," Teo said, leaning against me to rest his head on my chest.

It was the night before I had to leave for CEAM and we sat on the sofa in his living room.

"I know, but I have to do this." I closed my eyes and twirled my fingers over his face, letting sparks leap between them like lightning bugs. He caught one and it danced in his closed fist for a few seconds, glowing between his fingers before fading into the air.

"I wish I could do that," Teo said. "If I had magic I could leave this shithole and be with you for real." He gestured to the messy apartment, empty Skol cans and overflowing ashtrays like mini Pompeiis on the coffee table. He cleaned the place every couple days, but his mom just trashed it again when she got high.

I started to feel guilty about going back to CEAM and leaving Teo behind to take care of his mom. "Maybe I'll just drop out and go to MagiTech. Then we can be together for real."

"What's MagiTech?"

"The Magical Technical Institute. It's a technical school for magic. You know, where you learn practical skills and get a job. Of course you still can't tell nulls about magic, but you get to live in the normal world and interact with real people."

"I don't want to hold you back," Teo said. "Spellcrafting is your dream, and CEAM is your life. You have to go back."

"I know." I closed my eyes and kissed him on the forehead. "And I have to do this," I said.

"No, wait! Paulo, I…"

I waved my hands over his head, letting my fingers weave through his curls as the sparks of the memory wipe spell slipped into his mind and altered the shape of his memories.

***

I needed a break from the library, so I came back to my room to do some good old-fashioned internet research. There's not much real magic to be found online because it's all kept in libraries like the one here at CEAM, so I'm mostly just surfing the web, looking up new Wizard Crown strategies. I check my favorite site, SpellSeige, and read an article about an upcoming tournament and the strategies players plan on using, which mostly revolve around casting as many spells as quickly as possible to win. I don't really care about winning, for me the game is more about creative thinking, so I'm drawn to a thread about the mindshape strategy. Something about the way the poster constructs sentences feels familiar, and I look up at the screen name—MindMageT. With so few people brave enough to try the strategy, let alone advocate for it on SpellSeige, I don't have to ask what the "T" stands for.

My heart races as I click on Teo's profile. There are links to several of his social network pages and I scan the pictures, looking at the round face outlined by wiry side-burns. I also learn that he's spent the summer working at the store where we met playing Wizard Crown.

With Monica's voice echoing in my mind, pleading me not to take this any further than I already have, I create a fake account and message MindMageT through the SpellSeige site.

-Sweet mindshape strategy, I type.

-Thanks. I've actually had some luck with it, he responds a minute later.

-That's awesome. It's so hard to pull off.

-I know, right? Have you tried it?

-No, but I played against someone who beat me with a similar strategy over the summer.

-Ha. Not many people try it. Could have been me. Do I know you?

-I don't think so.

I download the SpellSeige app, and we chat like this for a couple weeks, the constant buzzes of the phone in my pocket making his presence in my life almost real. Then one day I get the message:

-Can I ask you something?

-Yeah.

-Do you ever get these weird feelings that things are

connected?

-What do you mean?

-Do you ever think that maybe without me or you, or us chatting right now, the Universe would be different somehow?

-Everything would be different.

-Are you sure I don't know you?

I can't lie to him a second time, so I tell him the truth about the summer, all of it. Then, I go home for the week-end and sneak into his apartment to erase it all from his memory again.

***

A couple days later I'm working in the library and Monica comes in to invite me out on the town. We enchant our winter robes to look like a smart Armani jacket for me and a sleek slate grey dress for her, and take the bus down into the town. We buy hot wine from a street vendor and sip it as we walk down the European-style streets until we get tired and find a patio outside a German brewery.

We sit at a table by a heater and sip hot chocolate. Our breath is visible in the air and we take turns twisting it into different forms in the air. Monica's becomes elaborate dragons, and mine are all images of Teo's face. It's almost like he's sitting across from us.

"Meu Deus, Paulo," Monica says. "You really need to let that boy go. You know you can't be together."

"I know."

She takes a sip of hot chocolate and licks the foam from her upper lip.

"Can I tell you something?" I ask.

"Is it about the boy? I wish you wouldn't. It's not

healthy. For either of you."

"I've been chatting with him online," I say, not looking up from my cup.

"Meu Deus."

"I'm not doing it anymore."

"That doesn't make it any better," Monica says.

"I know, it's just that I've tried moving on, focusing on school, anything to distract myself, but I can't."

"You also can't date a null."

"I wiped his memory."

"How many times?"

"Four."

"That's not kid stuff, Paulo. Memory magic is dangerous. It leaves a scar each time."

"I know, I know." My breathing quickens and my heart skips a beat.

"Maybe you should use the spell on yourself," she says.

Maybe she's right. The first time I cast the memory spell on Teo, I thought it would be fine as long as no one knew about it. But now I carry the weight of that knowledge alone, and it's breaking me.

Neither of us says anything after that. It's one of those quiet moments when you suddenly feel a shift in a friendship, like one of you has pulled out of it. It's imperceptible on the surface, but the connection is suddenly cut, and the next thing you know you're just two strangers sharing a table at a crowded café.

***

As the semester passes, I try to take Monica's advice and move on, but without Teo to occupy my thoughts, each task becomes a chore. I stop doing my homework and spend my time in the library reading books about the null world and dreaming of a simpler life. I don't care about spellcrafting, or school, or Wizard Crown, or anything, until one day late in the semester. I get to class early because I don't have anywhere else to be and I don't want to have to be the one to decide whether to sit next to Monica or not. There's still an empty desk beside me when she comes in, but she sits on the other side of the room. The witches stagger in late, looking hungover. Apparently it's been a rough semester on everyone. Once everyone is settled in, Professor Everhart explains the final exam. "You will each write a new original spell." No big deal. "And on the final day of class you will cast it before a panel of judges." The class buzzes as everyone reacts at once, chatting with their neighbors.

"Now," Everhart says, raising her voice to be heard over the chatter, "The exam will be held in the library, and the school's protective barrier will be lowered for the duration of the exam so you are able to unleash your full creative potential."

This changes everything. I tune out the rest of the professor's lecture because I'm suddenly struck with inspiration to write a new spell.

***

Back in the library, I conjure a hot cocoa and sip it as I page through ancient volumes looking for the elements I need for my spell. The smell of the chocolate is sweet in contrast to the musty room and the open air enchantment reveals dark clouds rolling in overhead. Monica's usual seat beside me is empty, but I don't have time to think about my former best friend right now. I'm too busy working on my spell.

I start by cracking the spine of a blank spellbook and making an outline of the components of the spell. A strong magic source. I can get that from the huge amount of potential energy that's built up in the library for centuries like a thick dust that coats the shelves. A way to channel that force. I'll need to work on that part. And a subject to receive the magic. Teo. The final exam, while the barriers are down, will give me a chance to gather a huge amount of energy from the library to cast a spell more powerful than I could any other time. I can use this opportunity to cast a spell that will give Teo magic, and with it, all of his memories of the magical world—and me—will return.

The next months are a blur of research and writing. I find examples of people who have crafted similar spells. They don't usually end well. Jefferson Kotchman tried to cast a spell to give his daughter magic and he and his daughter both mysteriously disappeared during the casting, never to be seen again. An unnamed Tibetan wizard tried to absorb the energy of some wild goats and managed to turn the population of a small village into a herd of goats instead. Muti Saliba's attempt opened a portal that acted as a magical black hole which sucked him and his royal academy of magicians through to god-knows-what on the other side.

A million things could go horribly wrong with this spell, but if there is even the slightest chance that I can do something to be with Teo for real, it's worth the risk

***

The week before the final exam I spend 18 hours a

day in the library, so I'm half asleep at the table when my phone buzzes at 4 a.m. It's a notification from the Spell-Seige site. I haven't talked to Teo online in nearly a month because I've been so focused on the spell, but I can't resist reading his message. Maybe he's finding his way back to me on his own.

MindMageT said: I found you in my buddies list on SpellSeige but I don't remember playing against you. I don't know why, but I got this feeling and I looked you up online. I know this sounds creepy, but I think I know you, or pieces of you. Fragments that don't fit together to form a cohesive whole. But they're there in my mind and it's driving me crazy. Something about a school. You're a teacher? Some place called MagiTech? I know it sounds stupid, but I just have to know if any of this is real, if you're someone. Someone I should know. I feel like I dreamed this other life and you were a big part of it. Like, maybe you held that life together somehow. Anyway, please just write me back and tell me I'm crazy so I can go on with my life. -Teo

I squeeze the phone until sweat builds up in my palms and it starts to slip from my grasp. I've used the memory spell too many times, and it kills me that Teo is in pain and doesn't even know why. His mind is all twisted into remembering pieces of me that don't add up. A teacher at MagiTech? At least he remembers pieces of things I told him. I have to hold onto that for now. The best thing I can do is focus on my spell. Once I give Teo magic, his memories will return and repair his mind. I put the phone down and get back to writing.

***

The open-air enchantment reveals dark clouds above the library, but a few faint rays of sunlight still filter through. Everhart and two other professors sit at a long wooden table in the center of the room and call students up one at a time to cast their final spells. Several students shuffle through their routines. One turns off the open sky enchantment to reveal what is truly above us. Some rafters. Another pulls all the books from their shelves and builds a spiral staircase out of them. When it's Monica's turn, she also removes the books, but turns them into shelves, and then turns the shelves into books that stack on them. It's a brilliant twist on a classic cloaking spell. And the knowledge in these books is by far the most valuable thing in the school, so it's extremely useful too.

"Very well thought out," Everhart says.

"And superbly crafted," says another professor as he casts a spell to analyze the quality of the transformation. "We may even be able to get this approved by the council for school security."

I lock eyes with Monica for a moment and give her a weak smile. Getting your spell approved is the dream of all the students in the creative spellcrafting program. I wish I could be happier for her, but I haven't spoken to her since the last time we went out, and I'm spending all my mental energy thinking about the spell I'm about to cast. I wipe my palms on my jeans and take a deep breath. I'm putting Teo and myself in danger. I could make us disappear or turn us into goats, get kicked out of CEAM, or maybe even be prosecuted by the council.

"Paulo, you're up."

***

The first time Teo invited me over to his apartment to play Wizard Crown I forgot my deck, but neither of us minded because our connection was never about the game. I sat at the kitchen table that was piled with his mom's unopened bills. The kitchen was tight and dishes were stacked up on the counters and in the sink. There was a towel rack on the wall that was painted to look like a guava wearing dark eye-shadow, heavy rouge, and lush ripe lipstick. Teo put a filter in a pour-over coffee maker and lit a gas burner to heat a kettle of water. While the water boiled, he began washing the dishes. We were the same age, but I admired the way he seemed much older and more responsible because he'd been taking care of his mom for so long.

"Do you want help with those?" I asked.

"You can dry them." He pulled a towel down from the guava rack and tossed it to me.

I got up and stood beside him at the sink. Our shoulders touched as he handed me a plate.

"Thanks," he said. "Usually I just do this alone."

"Wash dishes?"

"Everything."

I nodded, not sure what to say. I had to sneak away from my parents to get five minutes of privacy.

"So what do you do when you're not doing, 'everything?'" I asked, gesturing to encapsulate the apartment.

"Like besides Wizard Crown?"

"Yeah."

"I don't have time for much else."

"Oh." I dried another plate and set it on the counter.

"But what do you think about in the moments between."

"I don't know," he said. "Things like space and the Universe, what's beyond Earth, and what we're doing here."

"More everything."

He laughed. "Yeah, I guess you're right. More everything. But what else is there?"

"Nothing."

We both laughed. It was amazing to share this weird intimate moment somewhere on the edge between profundity and nonsense. It was like those big ideas I could never quite put into words were immediately understood between us without speaking them. It was a magic of its own.

"So why do you think we *are* here?" I asked.

"Who knows. I like to think it's all a cycle, you know? Like the Universe is this big, infinite thing but it lives and dies and is reborn again. So we're all just tiny pieces of this infinite life, and our minds are a piece of a bigger consciousness."

He's describing the fundamental nature of magic, the cosmi-consciousness wizards connect to in order to create. It's like he intrinsically understands a concept I'm not sure I even grasp, what some wizards spend a lifetime trying to comprehend. "Doesn't that make us meaningless in the big picture?" I said, trying to avoid the topic of magic and anything I would have to delete from his mind.

The water came to a boil and he drained the sink and dried his hands. "No, it means we're a part of it. Without you or me, the Universe would be different." When he handed the towel to me, our hands touched, and I felt this

intense connection, like maybe we *were* pieces of something greater, and those pieces fit together with each other
as much as with the Universe.

We spent the rest of the afternoon talking over coffee
about our favorite books and our views on God and quantum theory, and what kept us alive despite the crushing
weight of inevitability.

***

I take a deep breath and push my fears aside as I remember that first conversation I had with Teo at his house,
how he understood magic already, was destined for it.

I take my position in front of the professors. First, I
close my eyes and feel my way through all the potential
magic energy in the library. It radiates from everything,
the students, the professors, the residue of the thousands
of spells cast in this room before me, the books on the
shelves and the open air enchantment above us. I draw it
all together, feel it boiling inside me. Then I conjure a like-
ness of Teo in front of me that will act as his proxy for the
spell, something for me to focus on as I weave magic into
the real Teo. I begin pushing the energy toward the Teo in
front of me and as I do, the energy I have gathered begins
to take form and pulse with its own gravity.

I resist its pull at first, but soon I have to strain against
it as it compresses me, making me feel like my head is
caught in a vice and my heart is going to rupture. The tug
grows stronger, until I lose my power over the spell and
my mind is pulled into the mass of energy.

Inside is a universe full of Earths, solar systems of the
familiar planets rotating around their suns, galaxies of
Earth systems, galaxy clusters, on and on throughout the

cosmi-consciousness. I travel to thousands of these worlds in an instant. On one of them I'm a famous spellcrafter. In another I'm a professor at MagiTech. In infinite permutations Teo is with me. In many of the scenarios his mind is consumed by my spell in various horrible ways that leave him a husk of the person I love. A chill crawls up my spine, and my extremities tingle with cold. I'm suddenly aware that these aren't potential realities, but worlds that actually coexist somewhere in the ramifications of the moments that make up my life.

I finally understand the essence of magic which Teo always seemed to instinctively comprehend. I continue to travel from Earth to Earth, reliving every mistake I've ever made, until the weight of the worlds is too heavy for my mind to withstand, and I slip back to my place in the cosmi-consciousness.

***

When I wake up, I have to blink a few times to adjust to the harsh lights of the infirmary. I think I'm dreaming at first when I see Teo's face above me. I blink again and open my eyes slowly. Teo is still there. His face is slimmer, his sideburns have filled in, and his hair has grown and is now tucked behind his ears. He looks older, changed.

"Are you okay?" he asks.

"Yeah, I'm fine. You're here. Did it work?"

He nods solemnly. "They told me all about it, how you transferred your magic to me." He begins to radiate with a bright energy. When he squeezes my hand, the light pulses through me, making me feel warm and whole. I try to push the light back to him, but it fades as soon as it touches me.

"Magic cannot be created or destroyed," Professor Everhart quotes as she steps into my field of vision. "That was quite a stunt you pulled, Paulo. You're lucky to be alive."

I realize that. Monica comes into the room and stands behind Teo. She smiles sheepishly toward me and gives a small wave. I try to smile back but my body feels distant and I can't be sure if it's obeying my commands. The world hums with a different intensity now, as if I can sense the afterburn of every spell that has ever been cast, but can't touch it.

"You broke the laws of society, magic, and the school—there will be major consequences." As Everhart lectures me, Monica makes a yap-yap gesture with her hand behind the professor's back. She always knows how to diffuse a tense situation. I smile at her for real this time, and she smiles back.

"You can't be a student here anymore since you no longer have magic, and there may be legal ramifications," Everhart says. She looks at the floor, probably afraid I've become some kind of magic black hole that will steal her powers as well.

"I understand." I know this is bad, but all I can think about is the experience on the other Earths, and how lucky I am that my stupid spell worked, despite the side-effects. At least I didn't turn us into goats.

"I'll leave you to recover now," Everhart says.

After she leaves, Teo comes closer to the bed again and I realize the aged look in his face isn't due to the physical changes or the time we spent apart, it's caused by a weight that he now carries. As I look at Teo, I see reflections of the shells of him I left on other Earths. I begin to cry, and he wipes away the tears with his hands.

"Can you ever forgive me?" I ask.

He gathers energy in his palm and stares at the glow cradled between his fingers. "I don't know if this is what I wanted."

I nod and more tears leak out as I imagine losing Teo all over again, for good this time.

"But I'm here," he says. "And I remember everything."

Will J Fawley was born in the United States and currently living in Winnipeg, Manitoba, Fawley is the author of multiple short-form stories including "We Draw the Lines," Parallel Prairies, Great Plains Publications "The Suns of Terre," Unburied Fables, Creative Aces Publishing "Uprooted," Expanded Horizons; First published in The Northern Virginia Review, Volume 30 "The Gravity of Desire," Another Place: Brief Disruptions, and Bushmead Books "The Black Sp.t," Sassafras Literary Magazine.

THE COLLECTION
ISOBEL GRANBY

Included in the Last Will and Testament of Alexander Young McLachlan, signed at Edinburgh, 18 — , sealed separately.

My dear George —

It is not wise to write from the Botanical Garden. First, there are so many distractions, between the people coming through every now and again, and the plants themselves, and second, it is damp, and my paper will tear before long if I am not brief. Still, when I write to you, I cannot help but gravitate to the Palm Room, where I am now. There is so much of you in these glasshouses, so much that I have crafted with the express intent that it should please you, and in the meantime, it entertains the public as they trickle through, learning something, I hope, and often remarking on the exotic specimens, as you might expect. There is so much here that is exactly as you would expect, my dear George, and a few surprises perhaps, all of which would rouse your laughter. I hope, when you see it, that you will find it pleasing.

Each specimen that you have sent has become part of this tale, the story that visitors read between the lines of spare fact depicted on the labels; name, country of origin, and collector, all presented without detail or comment, as you instructed. The visitors will know you almost as I do, intimately and remotely, lovingly and frustratingly, without finding satisfaction—but beyond the garden itself, I have written all that I could of you and your voyages of collection. If I could speak in your voice, if I could capture your exquisite sense of adventure, I would—but the only words I have are my own. You knew this, when you left your specimens in my possession, and you trusted me to find the right words to tell your story. I wish you had not, sometimes, when I find myself at a loss for how to speak of you. Yet, those who come to the garden will speak of you, even if they have not read the published accounts, and they will know of you.

It was your ghost orchid, the rare and strange flower that you sent me, wrapped in taffeta as though it should be the jewel in an exotic crown that I considered the beginning of the story, though it was not the first specimen that you sent. It was the one that ensured my devotion, despite my other preoccupations and misgivings, despite my slight and continuing envy of your seeming freedom. I saw then, as I have seen since, that you play your part in this high melodrama that we call life, and that mine would be to tell of your exploits, as you will never do, for distraction and lack of inclination to boast of them. All this from a flower, sent long ago! It was a simple act and a small gift, but one that I have always remembered with love. You were just a year too late to be its discoverer, but I have preserved, in the herbarium, our specimen.

You will be part of such a story forever, I hope, and I

hope that I have done well in recounting the part that we have shared. From the moment that I decided to make a career of curating your specimens, rather than joining in their collection, I have considered myself a storyteller, in the old and sacred sense that perhaps once was used to mean something just and true. You have, on certain occasions, expressed regret at my absence from your expeditions. Do not regret it any longer. If I have given your name greater prominence in the scientific community, I can rest at the end of my days with some satisfaction.

You lately sent me a flower yet to be named, pressed on the banks of the Orinoco between the pages of Tristram Shandy, and I wrote every detail on it—the specimen, not the book—down to the page number. Of course I have yet to read the book. You always did come up with unusual ways to recommend a novel. It is odd—I write as though you were not there, when in fact I am writing in case of my own death. I suppose a ghost writing to a living man is much the same as the other way round. But do not think of me as a mere phantom—I would have you think of me as I was, as I am writing this, alive and well, a plain, scholarly man writing from the place he has been fortunate enough to curate for a while.

Some day you will not return. This will be whether I am here or not, for I have no apprehensions of your seeking a quiet retirement. Should I still live when that day comes, I have promised you, though unspoken, a period of mourning, as I would be left to imagine what your end might have been. Perhaps it is wrong that I can look upon that day without flinching, for the sake of my pen and your story—trust that although I can imagine what may come when you are lost to me, to the world, it is no easy task to me. But you know, my dear, I must do it.

My dear George, I am no great optimist and I do not trust to fate. This letter is a second, private will. It is a confession that I leave to you alone, for there are words in it that must not be read by others. We had to make choices once—as everyone does—and I often wonder what would have become of us had we been travelers together, and yet if that had been, who would have told stories of us? I do not regret my marriage to Violet; do not let her think that I ever did, nor that I was ever doubtful, especially once our union was blessed with our sweet Alexandra.

It is of your goddaughter that I would speak next, in fact, and I would leave instructions beyond those I have left in the will itself. I mean for her to carry on my work, but if her temperament is not so patient as my own, I entreat you to train her as best you can in the techniques of preservation and cataloguing of plants, as I have practiced them over the years. She is already showing promise— she presses flowers and keeps them—but she lacks the patience that I have long cultivated and in truth, she resembles you more than myself in her temperament. Certainly it is wrong to smile at such willfulness as she has shown, but she is so like you that I know she will do as she likes, in spite of my fears for her; if she is as clever as you, she will ease these fears on her own merit, as you did. I entrust her training to you, once I am gone.

I promised you, many years ago, that whatever you sent me would find a home in this garden, and would be your legacy, but you must know that it is not only the plants that matter to me. They are vital, yes, and they are the greatest step forward in the knowledge of science that we will contribute, but the work is not all, and if you could see me as I write this you would laugh, for I am sitting amid our plants, even as I claim they are not all that matter to me. But we come to the heart of this letter at last, and to write unflinchingly requires the presence of old friends around me, particularly those that remind me of you.

There was, perhaps, a time at which my love for you would have frightened me into decorous silence, but I intend no more to be ruled by my own weaknesses. I am determined that I will be courageous—in these pages at least. It is easier to be courageous in death; it is much harder to live with one's own courage, and the consequences of it. Again I think of Violet—who, perhaps, would not understand that I can love both her and you—who would see only what she would believe to be a betrayal. Perhaps one day, should we see one another in person again, I will find the courage to say this to you, in the rash and heedless way that love allows. If that happy occasion should be, I will burn this letter and its evidence of cowardly hesitation.

Show this letter to none—it is not for my sake that I ask such concealment of you—it is for yours. If you someday speak of it, do so with the knowledge that you hold my very soul within these lines, and that I would not hurt you for the world, but that the world may hurt, nonetheless, and in spite of our intentions. Such a love does not belong to this modern world and its gentlemanly inhabitants—rather it is that of adventurers in the great days of exploration, perhaps; a love such as the world-rovers of old might have shared.

All this time I have been telling your life through a specimen, a seed, a flower, with your adventures inextricably attached to it. Now, I must look forward and tell the life that will be after I am no longer there to record it. I have spoken of love in these pages. Should another than yourself read it, you may never be given the letter at all, for fear of the risk to your life and reputation, but given the choice between cowardice and courage, I had to choose the latter. May your days be many and merry, if you do live to read this. Do not mourn me overlong, but do remember me—sit in our garden, dear George, and know that our work was not for nothing.

Perhaps I will see it, as only the dead can, as tiny and insignificant as it is. Perhaps, also, I will not care that it is so small, only that it is still cared for by the one for whom it was meant.

Treasure it, George —
With love —
Alexander Young McLachlan

Isobel is an author and poet currently living in St. John's. Their previous work includes "The Date-Book," for Queer Sci-Fi "Ink" anthology, "The Second," from the Metapsychosis online journal, "Portrait of a Lady," from the Queer Sci-Fi "Migration" anthology and "The Mark," from Lighthouse Digest. They have been shortlisted or won multiple awards for their work, including the Chatterton 250 Poetry Contest, the 2020 Gregory J. Power Poetry Prize, the 2020 Íslendingadagurinn Open Prose Prize, the 2019 Helen M. Schaible Sonnet Contest, and the 2019 Íslendingadagurinn Open Poetry Prize.

1984
DC DIAMONDOPOLOUS

James, as the doctors and staff at St. Mark's Regional Hospital in San Diego insisted on calling him, applied pancake make-up over the band-aid camouflaging the skin lesion on his chin. He was glad to be home, surrounded by his Nippon figurines, the ornate lampshades with exotic scarves draped over the top, and his trunk of overflowing satin and silk costumes, boas, several strands of pearls, and oodles of costume jewelry. His move to San Diego had been a windfall—the most money he'd ever made doing drag. He lived to entertain. On stage, he was Jasmine and loved. Standing-room only. Now he was sick. How long would he be able to afford his apartment in Hillcrest?

The obituaries from three newspapers spread across the coffee table. Circled in black were the names of seven young men.

Jasmine wanted to live, to work again at Glitter Glam Drag. But James didn't.

No can do, James. You're not going to pull me down today.

It's Pride. I'm going to party.

Donna was coming.

At St. Mark's, the only person who bathed and dressed him, changed his sheets and consoled him was Donna, the pretty dyke nurse who was now his source for food, medication, and shots—his entire life.

It was Sunday, her day off, and she promised to take him to Pride. Jasmine had never missed a parade, but James's taunts of looking butt-ugly opened more scabs than he had on his body.

Jasmine dressed in black sweatpants and a gold lámay blouse, brushed her long stringy hair, pulled it into a ponytail, and clipped it with a rhinestone barrette. She applied red lip gloss and blue eyeshadow.

When James fell ill and admitted himself to St. Mark's Regional, the doctor asked how many men he had slept with. *Was he kidding?* "Honey, how many stars are there in the heavens?" Hundreds, thousands, in parks, bath houses, clubs, from San Francisco to LA and San Diego. The doctor had kept a straight face when James answered. The nurse turned her back on him.

Gay liberation tore the hinges off closet doors. Men like him left the Midwest for the coasts and found a bacchanal of men, a confectionery of sex and drugs, a feast for the starving who thought they were alone in the world.

James's life had been about dick and where to get the next fuck. Jasmine's life was drag, antique stores, and *Vogue Magazine*.

When his conservative, homophobic, fundamental Christian parents caught him in his mother's dress and high heels, they demanded, "Get out now and don't you ever come back." He promised them, "I'll live up to your expectations. I'll make the most of a trashy life."

Jasmine grabbed a green boa from the trunk and wrapped it around her neck. *You think that'll hide your Kaposi's Sarcoma,* James baited. Jasmine tugged at the feathers that made her neck feel on fire.

Grace Jones's, "Pull up to the Bumper" boomed from the ghetto blaster. Jasmine wanted to dance, but her legs ached. *You can't even walk, sucker.*

"Shut-up, James." Jasmine said, pulling herself up and moving to the window.

When he heard a car, he backed out of view. James never wanted Donna to know what she meant to Jasmine.

He held onto furniture as he made his way to the red velvet couch and sat, poised, waiting.

Donna knocked and opened the door.

"Well, don't you look jazzy," she said, pushing a wheelchair inside with a rainbow flag attached.

You'll look like a sick bastard in that baby buggy, James bullied. Everyone will know you have AIDS.

"I can't go."

"It's up to you."

"Are we so pathetic we need a parade?"

"Yes." Donna pinned a button that read, *Gay by birth, fabulous by choice,* on his blouse. "We need to pump ourselves up. If we don't, who will?"

"They want all queers dead. Looks like they'll get their way."

"Not everyone. 'The Blood Sisters' keep donating blood, and they're delivering food and medicine."

"Thank God for lesbians," he said and wondered if gay men would do the same if lesbians were dying.

Donna released the footrests on the wheelchair.

"I'm not going. Everyone will know I have AIDS."

"You do, James."

He looked away, not wanting to disappoint the woman who showed him so much compassion and strength.

"What if I run into someone I know?"

"You'll know what to say."

"Like I'm dying of pneumonia. Like all those fake obituaries," he said, kicking the coffee table. "Fucking closet cases. Even in death." Jasmine felt the weepies coming on. James scolded, *Be a man. Only sissies cry.* But Jasmine was female, too. "In my obit, I want you to put that I died of AIDS. I want everyone to know."

He held onto the seat of the wheelchair and winced as he pulled himself up. The smell of barbecue wafting in from the open door reminded him of summers back in Kansas City, his mom cooking the catfish that he and his dad caught in the Missouri River, his dog Corky—was she still alive?—joyful memories that always left a wake of loneliness.

Today was supposed to be happy, floats with dancing bare-chested boys, banners, dykes on bikes.

Donna shoved the wheelchair forward. "I've brought water and trail mix."

"Poor substitute for poppers and quaaludes."

Donna laughed, pushed him outside, and shut the door.

The ocean air breathed vitality into his frail body. He raised his face to the sun and began to gather life like flowers. A bouquet of drifting purple and orange balloons floated high toward the swirling white splashes in a blue background. He heard applause and whistles as he watched a float pass by on Park Boulevard. "Go faster, Donna. I don't want to miss anything." For just one afternoon he wanted to wave the rainbow flag and cheer the parade on and forget about himself and all the dying young men.

DC Diamondopolous is an award-winning short story, and flash fiction writer with over 300 stories published internationally in print and online magazines, literary journals, and anthologies. DC's stories have appeared in: Penmen Review, Progenitor, 34th Parallel, So It Goes: The Literary Journal of the Kurt Vonnegut Museum and Library, Lunch Ticket, and others. DC was nominated for the Pushcart Prize twice in 2020 and also for Best of the Net Anthology in 2020 and 2017. DC's short story collection Stepping Up is published by Impspired. She lives on the California central coast with her wife and animals. DC brings with them the short story 1984, a daring piece about one of the major struggles facing the community. Find more at the website dcdiamondopolous.com.

INHERITANCE
V.F. MARINER

"At least he died peacefully. There has to be some comfort in that."

Jaime nodded while taking a swig from her coffee, decidedly noncommittal. It was a narrative she was getting sick of hearing as she thanked the local townspeople for attending her father's funeral. She had cut contact with Jared Kendall twenty years ago over irreconcilable differences. From what she had heard through the grapevine her father hadn't changed any of his cantankerous habits. If anything, he had gotten worse in his old age. Still, family was family and when she received the news of his passing, she drove the three hours from the city without hesitation. Her black business casual blazer, her usual attire at her private practice, seemed oppressive amidst the heat of gawkers mingling as mourners. So far everyone had been kind enough to her face but she could still hear the whispers at the edge of the reception.

"Is that really Jaime? What's it been, twenty years?"

"I hear she's some kind of butch now?"

"That's what they say. Have you *seen* that haircut?"

"The crab apple sure doesn't fall far from the tree, eh

Steve?"

There was a strange comfort knowing that the town nestled amongst the salt marshes had remained as predictable as the tides it relied on. Her father, always the eccentric, had often been the source of local gossip even before Jaime left to pursue her career as a psychiatrist. Her choice of a career had bothered her father more than even the most insidious of tall tales being spread by their neighbours.

"I didn't raise a child on my own only to have her grow up and push pills! Where's your sense of decency, your love of creativity?!" Their already strained relationship had snapped on that day and for the most part Jaime hadn't looked back since. Still, she had to admit the pang in her chest at her father's passing. She had told herself long ago to give up any hope of reconciliation, but the finality of death is not something that can be eased by mindfulness exercises and worksheets. No matter what she told her clients.

After the funeral reception had finally drawn to a close, Jaime drove to the local convenience store; the one licensed shop in town. The cashier gave her a sympathetic look as she rang in her single malt Scotch.

"He's in a better place now, the poor dear." Jaime nodded as she was handed the receipt and quickly drove back to her father's now empty home.

Even as her father's health had steadily declined at the hospital, his wishes had been very clear — the house was to be sold and the proceeds to go to the local library. Given the view of the marshes the house hadn't been on the market two weeks before it was snatched up by a summer resident. Jared's only stipulation in his will had been that Jaime get to spend one last night in the family home and for his collection of journals to return with her to the city. She hadn't even known he was sick, let alone about the weird clause in his will. There had been no material incentive in the will for her to follow her father's last wishes. There was only a deeply ingrained need to honour the dead, something she was quickly regretting as she settled into the sagging couch in her father's living room. She couldn't be certain it was the same one where they had fought twenty years ago but it would not surprise her if it was. It was certainly battle worn. She poured herself a drink and began to flip through the journals her father had deemed important enough to leave as the sole inheritance to his only child.

August 3, 1986

Had the Petersons over for a bonfire tonight. I saw the lights dancing out on the marsh again. Amelia insists it's just the fisherman's boats catching the fog in the bay, but I know there is something else out there. They move too erratically to be any kind of boat light, and the weather was clear for the fire. Jaime figured out how to roast marshmallows without burning them black. I can't get over how fast she is growing up.

A deep ache settled in Jaime's chest. She took another sip from her drink and flipped to another random entry.

April 17, 1992

The ice broke on the marshes today. No more skating after school for Jaime and I 'til next year, I guess. I tried to work on the budget while the winter tires were taken off at the shop. I wish Amelia was still here. She was so much better at this than I.

As much of a flake as her father was, at least he hadn't run off while she was away at camp one year. As Jaime had grown older and spent more alone time with her father, she couldn't blame her mother's disappearing act but it still burned all these years later. Some wounds remember more than others, even underneath all the scar tissue. She refilled her glass and reached for another journal. She wasn't sure which decision she would come to regret more.

October 15, 1993

The apparitions are getting worse. Jaime insists she can't see them but she's been spending the night at her grandmother's more and more. People weren't kidding when they said the teenage years would be difficult. These white shrouded figures don't even seem to be walking anymore, more like floating across the marshes. It's getting colder out but the ground hasn't frozen through enough yet for that trek to be made by any mortal without leaving some kind of evidence. I will put on some hip waders (again) tomorrow and try to find the footprints. How do you trace the footsteps of a ghost?

February 26, 1996

The lights are so bright I couldn't sleep again last night. They haven't entered the house since I woke Jaime up screaming last week. The neighbour's lights flicked on, dousing the marsh in amber light but they were there. I know they were. Are. They're waiting. I can feel them.

August 21, 1998

The shrouded figures come later in the midnight sun but they are still there, just on the horizon. Jaime has grown sick of me talking about them, and the neighbours can't seem to stop talking about them. Not that anyone seems to believe me at this point. I wonder what they want, why they keep coming back?

At this point Jaime wasn't sure if her deranged father had been talking about the neighbours or the supposed apparitions he insisted inhabited the marsh. Hungry for something to occupy their time, some of the other locals had gone as far as to camp on the edge of the marshes, but no one else had yet to see anything close to resembling her father's imaginations. Pouring her (third?) glass of Scotch she braced herself to find the entry for the day she left. There wasn't one. Her father mostly kept track of his sightings after that. She slowly sipped at her Scotch as her father's entries became more frequent while his handwriting grew increasingly erratic.

October 3, 2014

They are coming. They are here. We are not alone. I see them in the day sometimes, peering from the shadows. They are watching. They are coming.

May 16, 2016

I can feel them even when I close my eyes. I will not let them win.

Jaime nearly jumped out of her skin as she heard her phone going off in her back pocket. She saw her wife's reassuring face staring back from the caller ID.

"Hi, Elsie."

"Hey, dear. I know it's late but I just wanted to check in and see how you're doing. How was the funeral?"

"Long. But okay. It's weird being back here. I miss you."

"I miss you too. I know you and your dad weren't close, but I'm sorry all the same. I love you."

"I love you too. I can't wait to be back home with you. Trust my dad to put some inane clause in his will asking me to spend one last night at the house. I think he was still seeing his stupid ghosts. It looks like the hospital had him pretty drugged up at the end. I wonder if they ever came to visit him."

"The ghosts?"

"Who else? It's not like he kept ties with anyone in

town."

"Let the dead keep the dead, Jaime. I get wanting to honour your dad's wishes but let his ghosts die with him. You don't owe him anything anymore."

"I know, love. I'm still planning to head back tomorrow morning."

"You should probably put that Scotch down then."

"You know it's creepy when you do that, right?" Jamie replied.

"Ten years of marriage can do that to a person."

"I know, I know. I'm going to hit the hay and try to get this over with. I love you and I'll see you tomorrow. Goodnight, love."

"'Night, love. See you tomorrow afternoon." Elsie answered.

With everything else packed in boxes, Jaime opted to use her coat as a blanket. Kicking off her shoes she settled into the couch, thankful for the sleep incentive brought on by the half empty bottle nestled next to the boxes. Sleep came hard and fast. If the ghosts her father swore by did exist, they were as silent as the grave.

She awoke to the sound of her phone alarm at 7am sharp. Her mouth seemed stuffed with cotton balls but she was eager to get on the road. She dropped the keys to her father's house off at the church on her way out of town. The local librarian had arranged to have them picked up there once she was gone. Jaime couldn't wait to put this whole town behind her once and for all.

As the fog cleared from her windshield she could have sworn she saw lights dancing on the marshes. She shook her head and gave a closer look. It was just a couple duck hunters heading out across the marsh and waiting for first light. Catching herself giving a nervous chuckle under her breath she increased her speed and didn't look through her rear-view mirror until the marshes had been replaced by the more familiar scenery of skyscrapers and traffic lights.

Elsie was just starting up the barbeque when she pulled in. She finished rolling up the deep blue barbeque cover and placed it on one of the patio chairs. Jaime gratefully fell into her hug, taking in her familiar scent and warm embrace.

"I missed you so much. That was the longest three days of my life."

"You're home now, dear. You're safe again."

Some of their friends came over after supper to sit around the bonfire and swap stories over beer and smores. It was one of the last clear nights of the fall and just brisk enough to still warrant a sweater next to the dancing flames. Jaime gave a start as she saw what appeared to be a white cloaked figure standing behind Elsie.

"Jaime, what's wrong?"

She shook her head and looked closer. "Sorry, love. The barbeque cover spooked me that's all."

"Okay, that's enough beer for you. Time for some water." Elsie snuggled in closer to her wife who gave her a playful jab in the ribs.

"Whatever you say, boss."

The shadows could wait.

V. F. Mariner is a fresh talent from Grand Manan, New Brunswick celebrating their first published work in Acceptance. *Mariner sits on the Spoken Word committee in Fredericton.*

THE VILLAIN IN YOUR LOVE STORY
LOREN GREENE

"I don't want to offend anybody here, but what if you just came out and told Nessa that Grace is asexual?"

The remark hung in the air for ages. Grace stared down at the table, her lips a fine line.

She'd brought up that word, and the *implications* of that word, twice. Once, with Simon, and once with her best friend, Jean. And then it was shelved, never to speak of again. Grace didn't even want to *explain* it to anyone again; that was why she'd told Simon to tell those he thought he needed to inform. It was a relief to discover there were words for what she felt—or, more accurately, didn't feel—but she wasn't ready to embrace them; not *a*sexual, not *a*romantic, or any other label for that matter, *a*-or otherwise. As far as Grace was concerned, her love life was her business and no one else's. She didn't need to join clubs, march in parades, or wear badges.

Someday she might want to, but not today. Not right now and certainly not as a justification for why she wasn't a threat toward Simon Summers' new girlfriend.

Grace tried to welcome her inevitable third wheel status, even embrace it for Simon's sake. Any girl interested in Grace's now-ex-boyfriend would undoubtedly be impressed *by* how well he understood women. Since she'd known him, Simon had as many female friends as male ones, and he'd been the easygoing guy everybody liked in his enormous group of friends. His inner circle of trusted confidants, though, that was small. Grace and Kirk were two he could talk about anything with.

Simon's best friend was a jock, the ace of their small-town high school basketball team. Kirk made Grace nervous, at first. If you went by fiction stereotypes—and she'd had little other exposure—the jocks were the ones making fun of people like Grace. For a long time, she'd felt like a background character in her own life. But Kirk turned out to be a softy, like Simon. Despite good looks, overenthusiastic devotion to the NBA and a constant stream of house party invites, Simon and Kirk were two of a kind in tearing up over romantic drama movies and watching magical girl anime. A marathon-running, bespectacled nerd prince and a goofy six-foot-five varsity basketball star might sound like a strange combination, but Simon and Kirk had been each other's wingmen since they were kids.

Now, almost without warning, there was a new player in the game. Grace wanted to like Simon's new girlfriend as much as she liked Kirk and all the rest of Simon's friends. Unfortunately for Grace, who didn't have any experience dating anyone *but* Simon, she didn't realize just how much of an ask that was.

"I want to tell you something," Simon had opened the conversation with a deadly serious expression on his face.

"And I understand if you're mad, but I need to ask you first."

They'd been at the same cafe he used to take her on dates back in high school. Now that they were attending university in town, it wasn't nearly as far away anymore. The cafe had transitioned from affordable date location to their regular hangout spot.

Grace set her hot chocolate back down warily. She'd noticed Simon wore nice clothes rather than his usual collection of graphic tees, not only today, but over the last few weeks. His untidy blond hair even had a bit of mousse in it. Something was up, though she hadn't been able to put her finger on what. "Okay. Hit me."

"There's this girl." He bit his lip. "In my chem class. Nessa is her name. We've been paired up for a project already, and she's really sweet."

"Okay," Grace repeated.

"I'd like to ask her out." He exhaled in one quick puff, as if laying down a heavy weight.

Grace blinked. "Okay," she said a third time. She ought to have guessed from his appearance, she supposed, but this was unfamiliar territory for them both. "Is that it? That's the thing?"

"That's the thing." Simon's cheeks were pinker than hers, and Grace had worn more than a hint of blush that day. Current trends in her favourite Tokyo street fashion magazines had recently shifted Grace's personal palette toward super-pale bases with a generous blush. She liked the contrast of the pink against her pale skin, especially in winter. "So. Yeah."

She laughed, because she wasn't certain what to say,

or how she was supposed to feel about it, for that matter. "That's not something you need *my* permission for."

"But I want it." Simon's face was so earnest. He was too cute; as endearing as ever. "It's important to me. I don't want you to think I'm leaving you behind, or something like that. After all, you were my first girlfriend. And one of the people I can talk to about anything."

"That's...wow. That's sweet." It was the most Grace could say without her face betraying her thoughts. Simon had been her first boyfriend, too, but the difference between them was that she didn't expect to have another.

There was a level of expectation that came with being in a *relationship*. Simon had been understanding of her feelings for a long time—he had a unique way of looking at things; that was probably what drew them together in the first place. People said he was *too* nice for his own good.

No matter how nice, though, there was only so much she could ask from her boyfriend, when she'd recognized he must be struggling. Aesthetic attraction and companionship weren't enough. Simon wanted a romantic relationship, and everything that came with it, and after a year of dating, Grace did not. She felt certain she never would; not with him, or anyone else.

Their peculiar status quo had been fine for her, but she'd let it go on long enough to see that he needed more, and if she left it up to *this* guy, he probably wouldn't say anything until it was too late to turn back.

Grace couldn't risk that. Not with the person she told everything to; the secrets she didn't dare divulge to Jean and Kana, her best girl friends. Simon was irreplaceable, even if that meant letting go of the physical affection she'd become accustomed to. Even if that meant another girl would eventually come after him.

She'd asked if he wanted to start seeing other people. There were clumsy days after that, where neither of them could be sure what was appropriate anymore. Then, very quickly, they fell into a new normal that closely resembled the old. Until he was *seeing* other people, Grace could almost—*almost*—pretend nothing had changed between them.

And now, here it was. Grace herself invited him to start seeing other people, and now he'd found someone. This had to happen eventually; she'd known it would, but for some reason, her stomach still clenched itself into a tight ball.

Grace tried to show enthusiasm, certain the look on her face must have already given her away. "That's great, really great. Tell me all about her!"

"You mean it? You're not upset or anything?"

Not upset. I'm not allowed to be upset. "Why should I?" she said brightly. "We broke up ages ago."

Simon studied her eyes so intently Grace drew back a fraction.

"It's stupid, right?" He laughed, a hollow sound. "I kind of need your approval before I do anything else here, even though, yeah, I guess it's been a while. I told Kirk that I was holding back on making a move until I asked you. Told him not to tell the other guys, 'cause they'd definitely give me a hard time. They don't really understand us like he does. But it didn't seem right to ask her out until I talked to you about it."

Grace smiled, reached over to take his cool hands in hers. She'd never been all that comfortable with PDAs when they were dating, but now that it was over, they were more physical than before. The *expectations* were off the table. "I don't think it's stupid. In fact, I'm happy that I heard it from you beforehand. If I date again someday, you'd be the first one I told."

She doubted she ever would, but that wasn't the point.

Grace recognized, after *the end*, that things would change for her and Simon. They couldn't go back to the same friendship they'd had before, but they couldn't stay in the relationship, either.

For over a year, it was as though the two of them had been out on the stormy, merciless sea, in tiny lifeboats with no paddles. They'd always been tethered together, but never in the same boat, not even once. Grace could see Simon, see the waves breaking over the side of his lifeboat and the water coming in, but no matter how hard she tried, she couldn't move her boat any closer to where he was. The rope that tied them was constantly strained to its limit. It might break at any moment, and she'd never see him again. She couldn't blame Simon if he looked for someone to toss him a life preserver.

A week after that, Grace met *her*. A first-year student, like them, and Grace noticed a brief sense of relief when she set eyes on Nessa for the first time. She wasn't strikingly beautiful or exotic. Her clothes and mannerisms suggested one of those down-to-earth nerdy-girl types.

Thank God. We're on the same level, I think. Grace hadn't been sure what she'd do if Nessa turned out to be some glamorous model. She already had the kind of name you'd read in a book, maybe about mermaids, or sword-toting heroines. Like a Dungeons & Dragons character. She was just Simon's type.

"You guys are gonna love each other," he'd promised. It was clear he was eager for them to get along. His eyes were shining. "You have tons of stuff in common."

Grace smiled and nodded and hoped so. Nessa carried herself with confidence and wore her hair in an elaborate style. She sported two high pigtails with straight bangs, and a braid threaded from the side part in her hair to the ponytail holder.

Cute, was Grace's first thought.

Her clothes were also charming, ticking many of Grace's boxes for style and taste. Nessa wore a skirt that fell halfway between her knees and her waist, with electric blue tights and black wool leg warmers layered on top. A hand-knitted rainbow scarf wound around her neck, even though they were indoors.

She looks like my kind of person. That was promising, so Grace took a deep breath; introduced herself with the most charming smile she could muster. "It's so nice to meet you. Where are you from?"

"From here," Nessa replied. "I grew up in St. John's."

"That's great! I guess you don't have to drive back and forth every day to get to school. I used to wish I lived in town, haha." She laughed weakly, then groaned internally, realizing how lame that sounded.

Nessa quirked one eyebrow in response. "Yeah, I guess so."

"How did you guys meet?" she rushed on, though

she'd already asked Simon the same question.

Nessa eyed her. Grace tried not to jump to any conclusions. "We're in Chemistry class together," she said in an even voice, "but then I recognized him when I saw him again at the D&D meetup on campus."

Grace couldn't help but think something was missing from that answer, but almost as soon as she thought it, she doubted herself. Nessa didn't sound all that *interested*, for some reason, not in the way she might have expected for a girl in the exciting first week of dating someone. Then again, Grace's own metrics were a bit broken. They were in university now, after all. It could be completely normal to act aloof in the early days. "Of course," she said, nodding. Tabletop games were an interest she and Simon didn't share. "That's great that you play D&D. He's always trying to convince me to join."

"Grace is super into alternative fashion, like you," Simon put in, as if reading her thoughts. "And crafting. She's good at making jewellery, sewing outfits. Designing stuff. And she's studying design too, of course. And Japanese."

"Of course," Nessa echoed. "Simon told me you were into Tokyo street fashion. That's…unique."

She was a bit cool, and something about the way Nessa looked at her made Grace's hair stand on end. She fumbled for another topic of conversation. "Have you met any of his other friends yet?"

Grace would have liked to hear what Kirk thought about this manic pixie dream girl of Simon's. Did *he* approve?

"Not yet," Nessa said thoughtfully. "For some reason,

he wanted me to meet you first."

That was the first and last time they met.

Nessa wasn't interested in getting to know Grace better, did not want to hang out with her, and moreover, didn't hesitate to say it. And that was *that*. Simon had no choice but to keep the two women in his life apart, and hope they'd eventually warm up to each other. Grace tried to stay open-minded; the ball was in Nessa's court, she thought. They didn't need to be BFFs, after all. They just needed to get along enough that Simon wasn't pulled in two directions at once.

After a tense month of watching his best friend fall apart, Kirk invited Grace to a mini-conference at the local pizza parlour. Invitees were on a need-to-know basis; the two boys, Grace, plus her best friend Jean, for emotional support. That was when Kirk brought up *that* word, asexual, in the company of the only four people in town who were privy to the information. "You don't *have* to tell her. I'm just saying, if Nessa knows about the asexual, um, thing, she might be a little friendlier to Grace. I'm sure she's uncomfortable with another girl being so close to her boyfriend. You guys even live near each other, and Nessa's out in town, far away from you both. Of course she's going to be anxious. I'm sure that's why she doesn't want you and Grace hanging out."

"You shouldn't have to tell her that!" Jean poised for attack as she laid both palms down flat, her glasses tipping so far down her nose they almost clattered to the table. She'd liked Nessa, at first, but nobody messed with Jean's friends, and Grace was her nearest and dearest. They'd known each other since grade school. "This *anxiety* is all in Nessa's head. It isn't her business who Simon hangs out with, or why. Grace's sexuality has nothing to do with it, and she's been perfectly nice to this girl so far."

"Of course she has." Simon shot a pained glance their way. "You've done your best. I've seen it. I, I really don't get it."

"*I* get it," said Kirk. "I get it, but you're not gonna like it."

"Yeah, I don't suppose I will." Simon scowled, an uncommon expression for him. He ran a hand through his unruly mop of curls. "It's because Grace is single, right? But that doesn't make sense, because we already went out, so that means she isn't a threat. We were going out for over a *year*."

Grace didn't say anything. Even in the company of people she trusted, she didn't enjoy discussing this topic. The sense of failure at the end of their relationship, and the sense of relief that accompanied it, were still fresh. Even her own anxieties from the early days, before she'd discovered the *a*-word, had been on her mind since all of this began. This time, though, it was out of her control, because it wasn't about "Simon and Grace" anymore, it was "Simon and Nessa, plus the third wheel, Grace."

And even if Grace didn't *mind* being the third wheel, even if she wanted to *embrace* it, Nessa's opinion was worth more weight than hers now. To any outsider, Grace would be painted as the villain in the story of Simon and Nessa; the ex-girlfriend who couldn't take a hint. She wasn't the helpless maiden in the other lifeboat anymore; she was an anchor, dead weight keeping him from reaching refuge.

Jean shifted half an inch closer to Grace, as though

protecting her best friend through aura alone.

"Nessa said she was going to be totally fine with this," Simon continued. "She said it was great that I have lots of female friends. They have so much in common. I thought they were going to hit it off even better than she and I did."

"Actually," said Kirk, "that's probably it, right there."

Three of the four of them suspected it. Only Simon shook his head in confusion. "But *why*? Grace has been super nice to her, and I've told Nessa how supportive she is of us getting together. And she's always, always been there for me. Lots of guys have best friends who are girls."

"Yeah," said Kirk, "but very few of those girl best friends are ex-girlfriends."

Jean nailed Simon with her patented Stare of Truth™. "They're similar," she pointed out. "Grace and Nessa both dress a little off-the-wall, are into nerdy hobbies—sorry, Grace—and are pretty close in the looks department. I think she's noticed that Simon has a *type*. It's probably making her feel a little, you know, insecure."

Kirk took a deep breath then let it out, drumming his long fingers on the red-plaid Formica tabletop. "Listen, none of you guys are exactly serial daters, so I hate to have to say this, but even without the *type* part, an ex-girlfriend is a threat. That's why I'm wondering if telling Nessa that Grace isn't, uh, interested in stuff, will help." He looked up and met Grace's eyes, as though seeking permission: they were friends, but they weren't that close. She hadn't even been certain that Kirk had known the *a-words* until that day.

"He's right, you should tell her," Grace said slowly. "I

don't like it, but if she knows, it'll be easier for her not to see me as a threat. It'll take some pressure off."

The relief on Simon's face was palpable. Kirk's, too. Only Jean looked irritated, sitting back in the booth, her long brown hair falling over her face. *Easier*, that was for certain, not to have to hide it. But there was something about the label, something about a stranger *knowing* Grace didn't feel the way she was supposed to feel, that made her shrink in Nessa's shadow.

After Simon drove her home, Grace flopped down on her bed and covered her eyes with her hands, desperately close to angry-crying. She felt sick. It wasn't fair that she had gotten caught up in all of this; she hadn't asked to be *different* from anyone else. She'd *wanted* to feel the way other people did. She'd wanted to fall in love with Simon. Wasn't that inability punishment enough?

Her phone buzzed almost the moment she shut her eyes. Grace turned it over, blinking to clear her vision. The letters of Simon's name wobbled in unshed tears. *"Looks like we're fighting she isnt happy I went out tonight without telling her."*

Grace's stomach somersaulted. "Oh no," she texted back, swiping her sleeve across her eyes. "I'm so sorry. Are you OK? Is there anything I can do?"

"No its ok but she tracked me on gps. Asked who I was with at Pizza E."

Anger rose in her chest, but she tried to stomp it down. What gave this girl the audacity to stalk Simon and harass him about who he spent his time with? They'd only been dating for a month, for God's sake. "Well, tell her the truth. You were with a group of people, not just me."

And even if it *was* just her, Nessa still didn't have the right. But Grace had given her blessing for Simon to move on, and she didn't have a way to take it back.

"Yea I told her but it didnt help. Gonna talk to her about ace thing. Sry do you think you can get your own lift to school this week?? Because she knows where you live and all."

"Okay," she replied, grateful Simon couldn't see her face right now. She had to support him, even if she thought it was ridiculous. "I'll borrow Mom's car. Tell me when we're in the clear."

"I'll eat lunch with her alone this week too maybe time alone will help?? Sry pls dont think I'm abandoning you I wanna fix this."

The gut punches came one after another. Then the last message came in, before Grace could reply to the ones before it.

"Give it a week or two to settle down. Promise you I wont be going anywhere."

When he didn't text her again that night, Grace steeled herself and prepared for a week of watching her back, of going out of her way to avoid one of her dearest friends. Somewhere inside, she still held out hope that this would all magically resolve itself. Maybe the *a-words* would be enough. Maybe Nessa would go home, Google them, and feel satisfied. And realize that Grace would never be, had never been, *a*-threat.

Grace was walking to the car, parked in the visitors' lot, when she spotted Simon huddled on the curb by the front tire of Mrs. Ryan's Honda Civic. She hadn't seen him in almost three weeks.

"Were you waiting for me?" Grace checked her phone reflexively, but there were no new messages. There hadn't been any since that night at the pizza parlour because Simon was afraid Nessa would ask to see them. "Sorry. If I'd known you wanted to meet up, I would have come straight here after class. How long have you been waiting?"

"We broke up," he said.

The first emotion that coursed through her was relief, followed quickly by guilt. Grace pasted a shocked frown on her face, hoping he hadn't sensed her gut reaction. "Oh, no. I'm so sorry."

"Are you?" Simon's voice had a note of bitterness to it.

Grace didn't reply.

"I wouldn't blame you if you were happy," he said at last, hanging his head. "Grateful you don't have to deal with her anymore."

"No," Grace said, sitting down beside him. "I'm not happy. A little relieved, though, and I hope you don't mind me saying so. It might be better that it was over sooner than later. There was so….much." *So much discomfort for everyone involved*, she wanted to say. *Not only for me.*

"I guess," he said hollowly.

She wasn't sure how to comfort him; no experience of her own to draw on, but suddenly she was the first responder. None of Jean's brief flings in high school had required more than a tub of ice cream and a funny movie. They were in uncharted waters. "If it has to end, it's better that it ends before you get too involved. Right?"

"Yeah."

She sat next to him on the curb, taking his stark white hand in her fluffy mittens. The icy concrete bit into her thighs through her fleece tights. "This relationship hasn't been as good for you as you wanted it to be," she said. "I'm sorry, but that's how it looks from where I stand. I know you wanted it to work."

"Yeah," he said again.

Grace put his arm around his shoulder and wished Jean was there. She and Simon had never been that close, but Jean would know what to say to make it better. "I know you really liked her."

"It took a long time to…to get to a point where I liked somebody. Else."

They'd forgotten to give Grace the handbook for what to do in this situation. "God, I'm sorry. This was all my fault. She wouldn't have been so paranoid if I wasn't around."

"It's not about you, no. It never was. That's the problem. It's about me."

She'd come a long way from the shy, quiet girl she'd been in high school; worked hard to be someone who spoke for herself, but Grace was at a loss for words now. All this time, hadn't Nessa been insecure about Grace being too involved? Jealous of their closeness?

"I didn't see it before, but I should have," Simon continued. "Of *course* it's about me. She doesn't care that you're not interested. She doesn't care that you're ace, or how long ago we broke up, or under what circumstances. What she cares about is whether I still love you. And she wouldn't take my word for it."

Grace swallowed hard, afraid to ask if there was any chance that could be true. She didn't actually want to know. "Oh."

"She said I had a choice. No more half-ways. I had to end things with her, or end things with you."

All the air seemed to go out of Grace with that one sentence. Her pulse thundered in her ears, as Simon's voice and face seemed to fade away. *End things with you*, as though they hadn't already ended it. As though they hadn't been through the first motions of a breakup each time Grace thought too hard about what it meant not to feel the spark. She'd had to experience it ending over and over and over again, bailing out her own lifeboat in the storm each time, watching him bail his from afar.

And he'd been inching a little closer to shore, bit by bit, in the months since they were no longer an *us*. The storm was over, but they continued to drift, connected by choice. Grace wouldn't have blamed him for cutting the rope and kicking his way to safety without her.

"She thought it would be better to end it now," he was saying, still woodenly narrating the end of the entanglement. "Better than always wondering what we were up to. She said she hated feeling jealous all the time. It was hard on her."

Grace smothered a sudden burst of anger. "Hey, it's been hard on me, too. I don't like being the villain."

"Yeah," he mumbled, and then she felt his shoulders quake. "I just, I thought…"

She wasn't sure what she'd do if he cried. He *never* cried. "Simon…"

"Sorry." He swiped the sleeve of his jacket across his face. "I shouldn't even be telling you this. It won't do either of us any good."

Grace wasn't sure that was true. "It's okay, I think we should talk about it." There'd be someone else, someday, for Simon, she was sure. She had to recognize the signs. He'd have to make sure they understood. She couldn't expect him to go through this over and over.

"I thought there was gonna be some way it would all work out. I thought she'd come to her senses, and geez, Grace, I don't know what to think. I can't believe she made me choose." He leaned his head on her shoulder, and then tears slid from his squeezed-shut eyes. "And I really liked her, and it's been a long time since I liked someone like that. I didn't know if I ever would again."

"I know. But you did, and you will." She wrapped her arms around Simon's broad shoulders, conscious of her own shame and sadness and anger struggling to erupt. Grace buried her nose in his thick mop of hair; willed herself not to let even one sob escape. With one hand, she plucked away the glasses that were fogging up on his nose. "I know," she repeated. "You're going to be fine."

She let him cry, his shoulders shaking with the effort to keep it in. How awful it was to be so devastated over a bond that ended before it had even been fully formed! She didn't envy this part, not at all.

Grace closed her eyes and pulled him nearer, pushing away the flood of her own emotions. Being the villain in Simon's love story was worse than being the heroine had been, but she had to be strong. After all, he'd chosen her. Grace was the one who was still here, not Nessa.

She just wished she felt better about it.

Loren Greene is the award-winning author behind the serialized fantasy epic, "Nobody's Way" on Royal Road, as well as Meet You By Hachiko *and* Edokko, *both HachiPress. She won the January 2021 Kit Sora flash fiction contest with her tale* After Supper Cup.

THE MISMATCH
LISA TIMPF

When the door-chime alerted me to the arrival of a customer, I shot a quick glance at the clock. If I didn't leave soon, I'd miss the start of the game. Then again, without fans there'd *be* no demand for the games...

I coaxed my features into a pleasant expression and turned to face the man who'd just walked through the door. As he traversed the short distance to the service counter, I appraised him, hearing Jaiden's voice in my head. *If there's a doubt, turn them away. We can't afford to sell tickets to cops.*

Seeing nothing alarming in the man's demeanor, I leaned forward. "How may I help you?" I asked.

"This is Ninth Street Books, right?" He glanced up, his eyebrows raised.

Eighth Street, actually. But giving the wrong name was part of the code. "It is. If there's something particular you're interested in, I'd be happy to help you find it."

There. I'd made ritual response.

My customer peered down the aisle to my left, then looked up at the mirror behind my desk.

"There's no one else here," I said.

"No recording devices?"

Late. You'll be late now, for sure. "I assure you," I said, unable to keep a wry smile from my face, "the NAF have not yet cracked our security systems. We're clean."

"I'd like a prime ticket for tonight's game, then. Best you've got."

I consulted the comp-screen. "Front row, blue line. Fifty credits."

He nodded. "Cash," he said, forestalling my next question. He placed a large silver coin on the counter and slid it over to me.

I stabbed the 'process transaction' button, collected the ticket from the printer, and handed it to him with what I hoped would pass for a gracious bow. "Door's at the back," I said. "The one that says 'Staff Only.' Follow the tunnel."

Before I finished my spiel, he'd sped off.

***

Half-way there, I told myself, grimacing as a stab of pain shot through my left knee. The underground passageway's concrete floor wasn't the most accommodating surface to walk on, but it presented the quickest and the safest route, especially for someone like me.

I consulted my wrist chrono. Even though I'd closed up shop promptly after my final customer's departure, I knew the first period would already be well underway by the time I arrived at the arena. If it hadn't been for my knee injury, I'd be on the ice too. For a moment, I imagined gliding down the smooth surface with cool air against my cheeks, just as I'd done so many times before the brutal check that had temporarily derailed my professional hockey career.

I skirted around a puddle of water, wondering how long the Bartol Syndicate would be able to maintain the subterranean labyrinth of passageways that shielded their activities from the prying eyes of the North America First governing party, and from Law Enforcement. Though I heard and saw nothing that would indicate the presence of other travellers, I reached up a hand and loosened my scarf far enough to reveal the neon green unicorn tattoo on my neck. *Best to be safe.* The tattoo marked me as a member of Jaiden's crew, and no other Syndicates would mess with a Bartol employee on their own turf.

As I'd assured the customer, our territory was safe from the police, who, for whatever reason, had chosen not to crack down on sporting activities despite the current government's categorization of such activities as illegal. Not that past practice was a guarantee of future behavior.

The passageway seemed endless. Though having walked it many times before, I knew that not to be the case. Today, I had the sensation that I'd spent the bulk of my life trudging through this dimly-lit concrete tunnel, shielded from the sun, alone—

Not alone, I reminded myself. *I have Zoey.* Funny how a younger sibling who I'd scrapped with on a regular basis in my early years had become such a close confidant, now. How proud Mom and Dad—

I sped up the pace, chewing on the bitterness of my own thoughts.

My parents, who'd succumbed to a virus that swept

through the population during the Second Great Pandemic of 2030, weren't the only thing that had been stripped away by the uncaring tides of world events. The Pandemic and its aftermath had changed everything. When countries outbid each other for goods instead of working together to figure out how to optimize the limited supplies that remained, thousands of needless deaths occurred. It left a bad taste in peoples' mouths, particularly when the United States—which, since 2025, included the swallowed-up provinces and territories that once formed the country of Canada—ended up on the short end of the stick more than once.

And when it seemed like we'd lost enough, lost almost everything, the Fundamentalist North America First party swept into power, telling us we'd lost sight of what was important. They'd boasted about the many improvements they would make and tried their best to convince us that we'd never be taken advantage of again, if we'd only vote for them.

I grunted and shook my head as I rounded the final corner. It's easy to spin a story people want to hear. In retrospect, I wondered whether the NAF party, led by Anton Watson, ever had any intention on delivering on their pledges.

Never be taken advantage of again. That was rich. Maybe the NAF thought being screwed over by your own country didn't count.

No more leisure pursuits, the NAF had decreed, although they conveniently hadn't articulated that as part of their pre-election platform. Citizens were to spend their waking hours working, studying for self-improvement, or training for military service. And there were rumblings that, to appease their vocal far-right base, they were planning to unravel some of the human rights advances so many groups and individuals had fought so hard to achieve over the years.

The NAF had promised productive lives and a revitalized economy, but didn't highlight the fact that the benefits would be accessible only to the privileged few, the families and friends of the elite. The rest of us would be lost in the shadows.

Until the Syndicates stepped up to fill the void.

Here, at last. I tugged my scarf again, concealing the tattoo. Then I pulled the door open and nodded to Gustav, the security guard on duty. The corners of his eyes crinkled in a grin as he recognized me.

"Not playing yet, Kate?" he asked.

"Soon, I hope." I paused to drink in the ammonia-and-sweat arena smell. To listen to the rasp of skates, and the *clunk* of a puck hitting the boards. Then I made my way to my seat, ticket in hand.

***

The anticipation of watching the game wasn't the only thing that had caused me to press the pace through the underground corridors. I'd arranged to meet Ardene Jolinski here, had sent her a ticket in my favorite seating area. I'd met her through the MatchIt app, which I'd signed up for as much to get Zoey off my back as out of a desire to meet a new main squeeze.

Now that I was about to meet Ardene, I regretted making the arrangements. The thoughts of loss that had dogged me on my trek through the corridor still hung over me, and I wasn't sure what kind of company I'd be.

Half-tempted to back out on my evening plans, I looked up to the seating section that held my favourite perch from which to watch the game. I recognized Ardene instantly from her MatchIt photo.

All thoughts of abandoning my evening plans fled. I felt a connection, even though Ardene didn't meet my eye, being intent on the action. A sense that something significant, something weighty, awaited, if I had the courage to pursue it.

I skipped up the steps and slipped into my seat.

After we'd dispensed with introductions, I figured I'd best apologize for my late arrival, explaining that a customer had come in at the last minute.

"Christmas shopping, maybe," Ardene said.

"Could be." Sweat greased my palms. I hadn't advertised my Syndicate connection on my MatchIt profile. I'd simply said that I worked at a bookstore, and left it at that.

"Is it hard for you?"

"Is what hard?" Suddenly cautious, I turned to look at Ardene.

She gestured toward the ice surface with her chin. "Not being able to play."

I turned the question over in my mind for a moment. "Yes and no." I scowled at the ice surface. "My knee's getting stronger. Coach says I can re-start on-ice workouts in a couple of weeks."

"And you really want that, don't you?" Her eyes radiated concern.

I shrugged. "Playing will make it feel like—" I paused.

Why *was* it so important to me to get back out onto the ice? "It's silly, I guess, but I feel as though it's a connection to how things were before. Almost like we're getting back to normal."

Hockey had been an integral part of my life as far back as I could remember; watching the Leafs games on Saturday nights, stumbling out onto the ice, bleary-eyed, for practices on early winter mornings, and spending hours on the artificial ice in the back yard, practicing edge-work and stickhandling. A stubborn part of me clung to the notion that playing hockey would make things feel right again. Or closer to right, anyway.

Even if it *was* illegal, by the current government's standards.

***

I accepted Ardene's invitation to go for coffee after the game, regarding her from under lowered eyelids as she stared out the window at the driving rain. I glanced at her right hand as it rested on the table between us, experiencing an almost irresistible temptation to reach out and touch it.

As soon as I recognized the impulse, I wrapped my fingers more tightly around the handle of my coffee mug. *There's so much you haven't told her. What will she do when she finds out you don't just work at a bookstore?*

My eyes narrowed. Ardene hadn't shared much about her own line of work. All I knew was, given the lack of a neck tattoo, she didn't work for one of the Syndicates.

It wasn't exactly as if my love life, to date, had been a series of triumphs. Maybe that wasn't surprising, given all the upheaval in the past few years. It left me longing for stability, but fearful of being hurt again. Burying two parents was enough trauma to last me awhile. *Do I really need this, now?*

Ardene returned her gaze to the coffee shop, seeming to come back from a million miles away. "Sorry," she said. "Just thinking."

Maybe she's having similar thoughts. A sudden disappointment struck me. "We should all do that once in awhile," I said, trying to keep it light.

"I—" Ardene's persa-comm device buzzed. Her face paled as she read the message. "I'm sorry. I've got to go," she said. "Look, is there a game again next week?"

"Tuesday," I said, feeling relief surge through me. "I'll set you up with a ticket?"

"You bet. See you." She rose from her seat in one fluid motion. I watched her graceful progress to the door, and out into the rain. Then I finished my coffee and headed home.

***

The next Tuesday night after Zoey's game, Ardene and I went for coffee again. After, I bicycled along the familiar streets until I felt tired enough to turn for home. I swung onto our quiet avenue and continued my progress until I reached the large corner house where Zoey and I shared an upstairs apartment. In deference to my knee, whose dull ache articulately expressed its viewpoint about the number of kilometers I'd logged that day, I negotiated the stairs slowly, bike slung over my shoulder. I gripped the bannister so hard my knuckles whitened. Then I opened the door and made my way into the cramped upstairs apartment.

I spotted Zoey sitting on the couch with a lugubrious expression plastered across her face and stopped abruptly, my planned greeting stuck in my throat. *She's holding a bag of frozen peas against her forehead. That can't be good.*

"Headache?" I asked.

"Took a shot in the melon tonight," she said, raising her right shoulder and dropping it. "But that's not why I'm home. The girls didn't feel like going for a drink tonight. Not after what Coach said."

"Shouldn't have chewed you out for your play." I sank down into the couch facing Zoey's beat-up armchair. "You did alright, considering you're missing a few players."

"Not that." Zoey shook her head. "Gate receipts are down. Coach said there's rumblings we might not play next season. The Syndicate is considering a focus on other ventures. That's how he put it."

I leaned back, pondering Zoey's revelation. Though I'd never visited other Syndicates' venues, I'd heard enough that I could guess. Dog fighting. Bare-knuckle boxing. Other, darker, pastimes. In for a penny, in for a pound, that seemed to be the prevailing philosophy. If you were going to break the law, might as well break it in a big way. "But normally, people stay in their own neighbourhoods. It's dangerous to travel too far, especially at night."

Zoey stared at me, expressionless. I read the answer in her gaze.

I shook my head, vehemently. "Jaiden wouldn't swing over to those types of things. That's not what he's about." Jaiden Allvar founded the Bartol Syndicate to keep people like Zoey and I off the streets, not to exploit them. In normal times, he'd have been a teacher, or a coach, or maybe managed a youth club. He'd simply made the best of his aptitudes under difficult times, carrying us along with him.

"Jaiden's not in control anymore." Even though the Wegners, the elderly couple we rented the apartment from, couldn't possibly hear what she said even in the unlikely event that one of them had an ear against the door, Zoey dropped her voice to a whisper. "Jaiden's—gone. Murph Kilpatrick took over."

Kilpatrick. I rubbed my forehead as I tried to recall those few Syndicate under-lieutenants I'd run into during the past year. "The big red-head, with the ponytail?" Not waiting for Zoey's nod, I rose to my feet and started to pace. "So, what's that mean for us?" I asked.

"Our hockey careers might be over after this season." Zoey said the words softly, but I heard the underlying pain. "I don't know what else I can do, for money."

"Good time to start school then," I said, keeping my tone light. As executor of our parents' estate, I'd carefully managed our inheritance, managing so far to keep intact a nest egg that would cover four years of post-secondary for Zoey with a little bit left over for contingencies. Part of the reason I'd sought employment at the bookstore was to avoid dipping into that.

My sister shook her head. "Situation's not stable enough. Plus, they're not offering anything I'd want to learn."

I nodded in reluctant acknowledgement. The NAF-influenced course offerings didn't cater to Zoey's interest in the environment. Quite the contrary. Unless she wanted to attend university for careful instruction in the climate-change-as-mythology theory that the NAF espoused.

I ran my right hand through my hair in a nervous gesture. I promised Mom I'd look after my kid sister. Times like this brought home the magnitude of that challenge. "It'll be okay," I told Zoey. "You'll see."

I froze in place as a thought struck me. *How many times did Mom tell me that? And how many times did she say it when she really didn't believe it herself?*

***

Surely Murph won't change everything overnight, I told myself as I pedalled to work the next day. I opened the bookstore at the usual time and puttered around a bit, tidying up. We did get a bit of legitimate business other than ticket sales. The inventory hadn't cost the Syndicate anything—in the chaos after the pandemic, Jaiden commandeered an abandoned bookstore whose owner had perished without having relatives to leave the business to—so we managed to generate some revenue from book sales. Mornings, though, were customarily slow. Consequently, there was no one else in the store when a broad-shouldered, red-haired man, trailed by two black-clad individuals that I identified as bodyguards, shouldered through the door.

Murph Kilpatrick and friends.

Murph began pacing around the store, pulling out a volume here and there, sometimes grunting in approval and other times scowling.

"Can I help you?"

"Yeah." He looked me up and down. "You can get lost."

"But the store—"

"Doesn't do much business, as you know. Besides, the police sniffed out our headquarters on McKay Street, somehow. Got out just in time. This place, on the other hand, would be a good front. But I have my own people to run it."

I shrugged and bent down to reach for my backpack.

"You're one of the hockey players, right?"

I straightened. "I am."

"I assume you'll still be looking for extra cash?" He tilted his head.

That depends. Doing what? Before I could blurt out that response, I remembered Zoey and the need to keep our nest egg in one piece, if we could. I swallowed, hard. "I would."

He studied me for a moment, then grunted. "Report's about right. Not a fit for our escort service. Can you ride?"

"A bike?"

He nodded, curtly. I tilted my head, considering my options. If I declined this opportunity, maybe I'd be cleaning out the kennels for fight dogs. Or standing on a corner somewhere . . .

It didn't take long to calculate the odds of a person like me, without political connections, finding employment elsewhere given the current economic climate. *Pretty slim.*

I shrugged. When surrounded by choices you don't like, hold your nose and pick the one that stinks the least. That's what I'd always told myself. I'd signed up with the Bartol Syndicate because I saw it as the best option at the time. I'd always acknowledged it wasn't my dream job.

That still held true—now more than ever.

Besides, a stubborn part of me insisted that loyalty had to count for something. Jaiden had helped Zoey and I out of a tight spot. And even if he was gone, the Bartol Syndicate remained as his legacy.

"Courier service?" I asked.

Murph nodded. "Report back here at 1 p.m. I may have something for you to deliver."

He jerked his head toward the door.

I went.

***

I quickly learned it was best not to be overly inquisitive about the contents of the parcels being delivered, although sometimes, smell alone told me that I carried contraband which, if detected by the authorities, would land me in jail. Even if I had been tempted to skim off the top—and I wasn't—the Syndicate had implemented a strong deterrent, in the form of the geo-trackers each courier clipped on at the start of their shift. Every minute had to be accounted for, and on top of that, there were the body-cams, though those were meant to be backup more in the case of someone accosting us and trying to hijack our cargo.

Zoey's eyes betrayed a flash of concern when I told her I'd changed jobs, but she shrugged philosophically. "At least, you won't have to do extra workouts to stay in shape," she pointed out.

Well. There was that. By the end of the day, it was all I could do to haul myself home to eat, catch a TV show, then fall into bed, exhausted. But there was a bright spot. I'd been able to return to the ice, taking a few shifts a game at first, then gradually increasing my ice time. It was the only thing that gave me the confidence that things were getting better.

Well, that and Ardene. We continued to see each other when our schedules allowed it. I looked forward to our get-togethers more than I'd expected.

This was one such night. I'd gone to practice with Zoey early, then reported for courier duty. It'd been one of those days when the sky gloomed overhead, threatening to rain but never quite fulfilling the promise.

As I pedalled toward Ardene's apartment, the few vehicle drivers who could afford to keep their personal cars on the road seemed extra impatient, hogging the road more than usual. I had to put on the brakes, hard, when an SUV cut in front of me at an intersection. My nerves were about shot by the time I reached my destination. Between that and the exhaustion engendered by a busy day, I was less careful than usual about the amount of red wine I drank.

Ever cautious, I'd made it a rule to never stay over, for fear Ardene might see my tattoo. Hockey players like Zoey hadn't been forced to declare an affiliation. Not being tattooed made them easier to trade.

But me, I'd become a Bartol employee after my injury. The Syndicate liked to slap their brand on anyone who handled money for them. It proved an effective deterrent against raiding by other Syndicates. It also provided a visible reminder where one's loyalties lay. Given the stigma against the Syndicates, I wasn't ready to reveal my affiliation to my new girlfriend. Hence, the no-overnight rule.

Despite my resolution, within seconds of opening my

eyes the next morning, I realized I was not, as I'd expected, in the comfortable confines of my own room at home. I'd also developed a pounding headache. Instinctively, my hand went up to my neck. *No scarf.* In fact, I was in my underwear and T-shirt under a comforter on Ardene's couch. *Did I get undressed before bed, or did—*

Groaning, I levered myself up so I could see over the back of the plas-leather couch. Ardene, clad in a loose T-shirt that hung down to mid-thigh, held up a caf-pod between thumb and forefinger. "Coffee?"

"Please." My voice emerged as a croak. As the caf brewed, I dressed quickly and stumbled to the washroom.

What happened, last night?

By the time I returned to the main living area, the steaming beverage, laced with milk the way I liked it, sat on the round dining table. Ardene slid into place in the seat opposite me, eyes glinting, mug in hand. "Some night last night."

"Um," I said. "I'm a little, uh—"

"We just drank a lot, that's all. Or rather, you did." She grinned slyly. "Look, I have to get ready for work," she said, rising to her feet in one smooth gesture. "Mind if I hop in the shower?"

"Go ahead." I managed a feeble wave and settled in to enjoy my drink. But after the first few swallows, restlessness drove me to my feet. Angry at myself for having over-indulged the previous night, and concerned that Ardene might have deduced my Syndicate status as a result of my carelessness, I began to pace.

The door to the study, unusually, was open. Thinking

I might find solace in a book while I waited for Ardene, I headed over to the tall bookshelf beside the wooden desk that commanded a prime viewing spot at the window. As I crossed the room, I found my attention drawn by a photo-plaque on the wall. The image showed Ardene surrounded by a group of what looked like teenage girls wearing peacock blue T-shirts. *Careers in Law Enforcement Seminar*, read the plaque under the photo. *Thanks for your participation.*

I took a step back. Ardene's attire was, unmistakeably, a police uniform. For the second time that morning, my hand strayed to my tattoo.

System and Syndicate were enemies by nature. Our relationship seemed like a classic mismatch.

Why would the App hook us up, then?

One answer came quickly to mind. *Ardene might have known you're Syndicate all along. She rigged the system, to get information . . .*

Tempting as it was to indulge in that particular thought, I couldn't make it fit. Ardene hadn't pumped me for info, not even subtly. If she knew, she didn't seem to care.

But the Syndicate *would* care, if they found out.

I looked at the bathroom door. The sound of running water had ceased, which meant Ardene might emerge any minute. After retreating to the living room, I glanced around, remembering the companionable times we'd shared. I bit my lower lip. Much as I enjoyed Ardene's company, I couldn't let her assume the risk of continuing our get-togethers, even if she wanted to. As long as nothing untoward resulted, Jaiden would have just thought it a good joke on the part of the universe. Others in the Syndicate—including Murph—were less likely to treat a relationship between one of their employees and a cop so lightly. It could put both our lives in peril.

Like ripping off a bandage, this had to be done quickly, or I wouldn't have the courage to do it at all. I scribbled a note, left it on the table for Ardene to find, and scurried out the door and down the hall, my cheeks blazing. When I unlocked my bike and swung up onto the seat, I blamed the mist for the moisture on my cheeks.

***

Hours spun into days, and the pain of parting ways with Ardene gradually subsided to a dull ache whenever I thought of her, which turned out to be more often than I'd have liked. I soothed my jangled emotions by going for long bike rides whenever I got to the point where I couldn't stand it any more.

Four weeks after I'd been assigned to courier duty, I delivered a light but large parcel—likely cash, I figured, although I didn't dare peek—to the bookstore, now the Syndicate's headquarters. The rain drilled down, dripping off the brim of my baseball cap. *Where's the door-guard?*

I knocked. No response. I knocked again. *Drip, drip.* Getting wetter, and madder, by the minute, I finally decided to let myself in, and made my way to the office at the back.

Voices. So, there was someone here. *Wait. That sounds like—*

I couldn't resist stepping past the door-way and looking in. What I saw made me step back quickly, heart pounding. Luckily, the two men conversing were too engrossed in their discussion to notice me. I beat a hasty retreat back to the door, hoping the black carpet-runner would hide my wet shoe-prints.

Just in time. Seconds after I reached the entry-way, Gustav, who after Murph's rise to power had earned a spot in Headquarters security staff, emerged from the washroom, rubbing his hands together. "You just get here?"

If he guesses what you heard and saw— I forced myself to display a nonchalance I didn't feel. "Just stepped in the door. It's wet out there, you know." I shook my arm, sending water droplets flying. Gustav watched, his lip curled in distaste, and took a step back. "I came to deliver this."

I withdrew a parcel from my water-proof pack. When I extended it toward him, Gustav glared at me for a few more seconds. Then he grabbed the parcel, hefted it in his left hand, and grunted. "About time. Someone's waiting for it."

"Anything to go?" I asked.

"No. Maybe later. But don't stick around."

No need to tell me twice. I peeled out of there, swung up on my bike, and raced away. Only when I'd turned right on the next street and passed well out of view of the headquarters did I stop, hoping that a brief rest might persuade my heart to stop hammering.

I remembered Ardene's question, one evening before our breakup. She'd been on a full-out rant about something political, and I'd allowed a look of glazed incomprehension to creep onto my face. "Don't you watch the news?" she'd asked.

I hadn't been, at the time. But I'd started, after that.

And even without doing so, I might still have recognized the person I'd glimpsed at Bartol Syndicate headquarters. The talking billboards on the buses and bus shelters and the storefront displays had given the man's visage a high profile.

Anton Watson. Leader of the NAF.

But what was he doing consorting with the leader of the Bartol Syndicate?

***

I checked my wrist-comm. *Pickup at First and King.* As I rode, I let my mind chew away on what I'd seen.

Only one explanation made sense. It seemed so outrageous that my mind, dismissing it, only to keep circling back. It seemed that far from being enemies, the Syndicates and the government were collaborating behind the scenes. Making sports and entertainment illegal drove a lucrative black market. And if the politicians were skimming off some of the profits to line their own pockets, that would explain a lot.

Dangerous knowledge, if I were right. I paused at a red light, contemplating the significance of what I'd seen. And perhaps more importantly, what it meant for me.

I need to play dumb. Because if the Syndicate suspects what I saw—what I'd likely captured on the body-cam I carried on this shift, like every other . . .

I gritted my teeth and pushed as the light changed. Clearly, I had to make the footage from my body-cam disappear. But should I just dispose of it, pretend I'd lost it somehow, or hand it over to someone who could make use of it?

What about loyalty? Doesn't that mean anything?

I pondered that, as I completed my remaining pick-ups and deliveries. And came to one conclusion. I'd fallen in with the Bartol Syndicate because it was the only avenue for me to make a career of playing hockey. I'd morphed into a different role through necessity. But helping the Syndicates and the NAF perpetrate a massive deception was *not* what I'd signed up for.

I needed to tell someone what I'd seen. In the hopes it would make a difference. The question was, who could I confide in? If the government was corrupt, there was no point going to them. And if they had the police under their thumb . . .

I drew in a sharp breath as the answer hit me. There was one person I trusted, more than any. I may have broken up with Ardene, but she still struck me as the most honest person I knew.

The question was, would she give me a chance to state my case?

***

Half-way to Ardene's place, my legs ached from the pedalling and my hands shook from anxiety. I'd extracted the jump stick from the camera at the end of shift, replacing it with a blank. If this bit of subterfuge was detected, I'd blame it on a malfunctioning camera.

Meanwhile, the drive with the incriminating evidence on it didn't stray far from my mind. I found my hand moving of its own accord to my right jacket pocket every few moments, just to check I hadn't somehow lost it.

When I made the turn onto Q Street, four blocks away from Ardene's apartment, I spotted the two men who had accompanied Murph to the bookstore. They were standing outside a boarded-up building, bikes beside them, having a smoke and shuffling their feet in the way people do when they are waiting for something. Or someone.

I put my head down, hoping to avoid notice. As I rode, I felt a crawling sensation between my shoulder blades. I darted a quick glance behind me, hoping to see them still standing where I'd seen them.

No such luck.

The taller of the two had already climbed onto his bike.

Time to ride.

A quick glance over my shoulder a block later confirmed that I wasn't in imminent peril of being caught. The two men lacked the fluid grace, the sense of oneness with their ride that those of us in courier duty had developed. As I dipped smoothly around the traffic, guiding my bike with the deftness of a jockey piloting a steed in a hotly-contested race, I sensed that I was widening the gap. Still, honking horns and shouted curses behind me confirmed that my pursuers remained in the hunt.

Better that than waiting for me at my destination.

For just a moment, my bike wobbled, mirroring my indecision. Maybe I should come up with another plan, so I wouldn't put Ardene at risk—

But I had no backup plan, and that alone kept me going, my feet pumping rhythmically, my eyes darting around as my subconscious instinctively chose the path of least resistance.

Meanwhile, my over-active imagination continued to torment me with alternate possibilities for disaster, each bleaker than the last. Ardene had normally been off on Wednesdays, but what if the pattern no longer held? Sweat beaded on my forehead as I contemplated the unpleasant prospect of being trapped at the locked door to her apartment.

I skidded to a stop at the back entrance of my ex-girlfriend's building and slipped through the side door, carrying my bike on my shoulder as I had so often done at my own apartment. With the extra burden, I took the stairs more slowly than I would have liked, but I couldn't afford to risk my pursuers spotting my bike outside Ardene's building.

When I arrived at Ardene's floor, I opened the door from the stairwell slowly, holding my breath as I took a look. *Nobody.*

I set the bike down and rolled it beside me as I walked down the hallway, past the first door, the second, and to the third. Finally, I'd reached Ardene's apartment. I knocked on the door, softly, then more urgently.

No answer.

A fire-door leading to the stairwell crashed open on one of the lower floors. *I'm running out of time.* I bit my lower lip.

Only one thing to try. One last gambit.

Ardene must have changed the persona-lock by now, I told myself. I glanced back over my shoulder, expecting to see someone burst through the door from the stairwell at any moment. Then I put my thumb over the reader-plate, and half-sobbed in relief as I fell through the door, the bike beside me. I spun around to lock the door behind me.

"That was quite the entrance."

When I turned back, I saw Ardene standing, hands on

her hips and a quizzical—though not, I was relieved to note, angry—expression on her face. The blue bathrobe she wore set off her eyes and that, plus the white towel wrapped around her head, provided an explanation for her failure to open the door. She'd been in the shower.

"You didn't change the lock." Not what I meant to say, but it was the first thing that tumbled out.

A smile quirked at the corners of Ardene's mouth. "You didn't change your status on your MatchIt profile."

I felt a fierce shiver of joy, then reminded myself why I was here. "I need to tell you something important. But I think I was followed."

To Ardene's credit, it took her only seconds to process this information. Then she was all business. "You hide in the bedroom," she said. "In case they come to the door."

"But—"

"Believe me, I'm better equipped to deal with them than you are."

Sensing that protests would prove futile, I followed direction. I waited, feeling like my whole body was one big ear, listening. But the dreaded assault on the door did not happen. Finally, Ardene, who'd been skulking at the window, signalled that it was okay to come out. "Two men are just leaving. Come have a look."

I slipped over to the living room window and glanced out. "Yeah. Those are the guys who followed me."

"Good. Now, what is it you needed to tell me?"

***

I sat in the stands, waiting for the opening puck-drop of the second period. The championship series for the local men's hockey team had drawn a sizeable crowd tonight. It felt good to be sitting among them, as though we'd turned the calendar back.

Or forward.

The game had been a long time in coming, delayed by the events of the past two tumultuous months. But the new government in power had expressed a desire to restore a sense of normalcy as soon as possible, and that included the resumption of sports activities.

Hockey-mad as I was, it wasn't enough to play. I also liked to watch games, finding that sometimes I could pick up tips by observing my counterparts on the ice. After all, sometimes one small nuance could make the difference between winning a faceoff, or losing one. Scoring, or having the goalie block your shot.

I glanced around at the occupants of the other seats, reflecting that a lot had changed in a few short weeks. I recognized some of my customers from the old days, and adjusted my scarf instinctively, hiding the tattoo I hadn't yet gotten around to having removed. But there were laughing families as well, and older people who a mere two months ago would have holed up in their residences, this time of night, fearful of the perils out on the chaotic streets.

What role Ardene had in the transition, I had no idea. I'd handed over the jump drive, and followed her advice to hunker in place at the apartment Zoey and I shared until I got the signal. And the signal, when it arrived, came in the form of two terse, texted words: "All clear." We hadn't seen each other since the day I'd dropped in on her unexpectedly.

Well, what did you think would happen? She's probably

moved on. It's time you did, too.

I returned my attention to the game in time to watch the home team score a goal, a single-handed effort on the part of the star centre that involved splitting the defense and deking the goalie. In the brief celebration that followed, I didn't notice the newcomer making her way down the row in which I was seated until she stood beside me.

"That's my seat," she said, gesturing to the empty chair to my left.

Out of reflex, I stood to let her pass.

Then I noticed who it was. *Ardene.*

The expression on my face must have startled her. "You don't mind, do you?" she asked.

"Mind? No, of course not. But how did you know which—"

"Which seat to request? You're a creature of habit, when it comes to your choice of vantage point."

"Best place in the house to see the action," I said.

"No argument here. I kept some of the old ticket stubs, from when we went to games together. Call me sentimental." Her expression grew serious. "Look, I would have contacted you sooner, but we've been slammed trying to get things cleared up."

What *things* she meant, I could guess. I'd read in the news that when the NAF first took power, they'd contrived to place some of their sympathizers in the police forces. As a result, the forces had plenty of work to do internally as well as externally to sort through the fallout once the NAF's perfidy had been revealed. I nodded, encouraging Ardene to continue.

"Honestly, I haven't had time to do much besides work, eat, and sleep. But now things have finally let up a bit. I was hoping—" Ardene kept her eyes focussed on the unfolding drama of the game, as though she was afraid to meet my eye. The home team's goalie snagged a dangerous shot from close in, inspiring a round of applause. When Ardene joined in, I noticed the puckered, still-healing scar on the back of her left hand

"How'd you get that?"

"Takedown at the Syndicate headquarters." She turned her head, her ice-blue eyes conveying indecision. "I—wasn't sure how you'd feel about that."

Someone had scored a goal, down on the ice. I could hear celebratory cheering from the fans, but it sounded as though it came from miles away. "Tell me something," I said, knowing I couldn't carry on without having the answer. "Did you date me because of this?" Sneering, I pulled aside my scarf to show her the unicorn tattoo.

"Don't flash that around in here," she whispered, glancing around at the nearest seats to make sure no-one had noticed.

"Why not?"

"Law enforcement isn't going to go looking for lower-level players, but that doesn't mean they'll look the other way if someone gets stupid."

I took the hint and covered up. "You didn't answer my question."

"No. I did *not* date you because of that." The gaze she leveled on me seemed steady enough.

"But now you know."

"I already knew." Ardene shrugged. "That night, at

the apartment—"

I turned away, then, trying to figure out how I felt about things. "We're from opposite sides of the tracks, and you know it. What kind of a lousy algorithm would hook us up in the first place?"

Ardene shook her head. "The NAF—they screwed things up. They made right wrong, and vice versa. I mean, outlawing leisure activities, and then secretly profiting on the black market that arose. Among other things."

"So? A syndicate's still a syndicate. And a cop is still a cop."

Ardene arched her right eyebrow. "Would you go back to working for the Syndicate, now that things have changed?"

"No." I didn't even have to think about that one. "All I wanted to do was play hockey. When he first formed the Bartol Syndicate, Jaiden offered the chance to do that. It was never about being a Syndicate member. It just—I fell into it."

It sounded lame, now that I listened to myself. But Ardene just nodded. "The important thing is, where you go from here?"

"I'm still on contract for another season, with the team. Now that the games are legally sanctioned. I'm going to continue with that, for as long as I can. And after—" I shrugged.

"That's what I figured," Ardene said, leaning back.

"Why *did* the App hook us up, do you think?" I asked.

"Even though our lines of work were somewhat divergent—"

"You could say that."

"We have a lot in common." Ardene raised her right hand and started to tick off the points on her fingers. "We both like sports. Hiking. We like to stay fit. We believe in doing the right thing."

I closed my eyes, considering her words. I'd been right. There *had* been a mismatch. But it was between me and the Syndicate, once Murph took over, not between Ardene and I.

I frowned. Why should it come as a surprise that love crosses the arbitrary lines we draw in society's shifting sands? My own parents—at the thought of them, my throat constricted.

"What's wrong?" Ardene rested her hand on my arm, gently, as though afraid I would shake her off.

"We've lost so much," I said, hearing the pain in my voice. "Lives cut short. Years gone by that we'll never get back."

"All the more reason to seize the opportunities placed before us. To appreciate what we have." Ardene squeezed my arm to emphasize her point. "We can't change the past. You know that. But we have the future ahead of us. All of it."

"You said *we*. Did you mean it?"

"Yes," she replied, her voice soft. "If you want to."

I narrowed my eyes, thinking. Ardene was right. Yesterday's world had disappeared and wouldn't come back. But we still had our lives to live. And living it with someone at my side sure had a lot more appeal than facing it alone. Especially if that somebody was Ardene.

"Yes. I do."

"Good," she said. "Now let's watch the game. This ticket cost me a bundle."

"I can fix that for next time," I said. "Player discount, for both the men's and women's games."

"I knew there was a reason I wanted to keep you around."

Lisa Timpf is a storied author and poet from Simcoe Ontario with over thirty speculative fiction stories published to her credit in a variety of venues, including "Roxy," "Roxy's Rule," and "Gone" in New Myths; "The Disconnect" in Third Flatiron's Brain Games anthology; "The Caller" in the anthology Future Days, and "It's All Good," published in the anthology Enter the Rebirth. She has two novelettes coming in 2021 from JMS Books.

Her speculative poem "No Fairy Tale World" was included in the 2020 Rhysling Anthology, which included all nominees for the Rhysling Award. She was also one of ten finalists in the 2015 Rhyme Zone contest, with the poem "His Hands, and a Question."

Her story, 'The Messenger's Mission,' was featured in Mythology from the Rock.

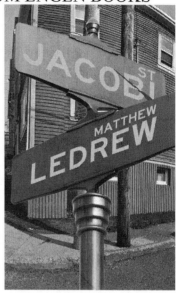
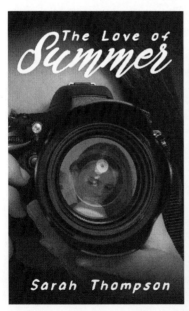
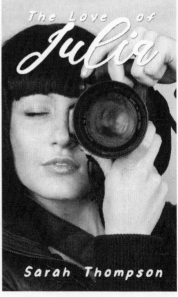

Manufactured by Amazon.ca
Bolton, ON